# *Sinful Secrets*

Other books by Thea Devine:

From Zebra:

*All I Desire*
*By Desire Bound*
*Desire Me Only*
*Sinful Secrets*
*Secret Pleasures*
*Desired*
*Beyond Desire*
*Tempted By Fire*
*Angel Eyes*
*Southern Seduction*
*Montana Mistress*
*Relentless Passion*
*Shameless Ecstasy*
*Ecstasy's Hostage*
*Reckless Desire*
*Shameless Desire*

Anthologies:
*Assassinated*
*Captivated*

From Leisure:

Anthologies:
*Seduction by Chocolate*
*Swept Away*
*Indulgence*

And from Harlequin:

*Night Moves*

# *Sinful Secrets*

THEA DEVINE

KENSINGTON BOOKS
http://www.kensingtonbooks.com

KENSINGTON BOOKS are published by

Kensington Publishing Corp.
850 Third Avenue
New York, NY 10022



All Kensington titles, imprints and distributed lines are available at special quantity discounts for bulk purchases for sales promotion, premiums, fund raising, educational or institutional use.

Special book excerpts or customized printings can also be created to fit specific needs. For details, write or phone the office of the Kensington Special Sales Manager: Kensington Publishing Corp., 850 Third Avenue, New York, NY, 10022. Attn. Special Sales Department. Phone: 1-800-221-2647.



ISBN 1-57566-824-6

First Zebra Books Paperback Printing: August, 1996
First Kensington Trade Paperback Printing: January, 2001
10 9 8 7 6 5 4 3 2 1

Printed in the United States of America

*As always, to my guys: John, ever patient; Thomas, who consoled me when things went wrong, and Michael, who made the Crimean connection.*

# Prologue

## *The Crimea—1856*

*He awoke from a deep dark dream to the distant sounds of the battlefield and the ominous sense that he was not alone.*

*He didn't know where he was, only that it was sheltered and far from the booming guns, and utterly black.*

*And he didn't have the strength to move—he felt weak, disoriented, dizzy, and sapped. He felt as if his bones had melted and there was no skeletal structure to support him.*

*He felt as if he had died and come back to life.*

*And that he could have been unconscious for an hour or a year and even now, he had no sense of time, no sense of space.*

*His throat felt parched and dry as dust.*

*He felt dry as dust.*

*He moved, a tentative flexing of his fingers to see if he was still whole, still alive.*

*He could barely move, and he was paralyzed by the sense of a sentient presence, hovering, watching, waiting.*

*He tried to push himself onto his elbow. "Wa—water . . ."*

*He heard a sound and then he felt something nudging his fingers, and wetness splashing onto his hand.*

*He could hardly hold the tin cup; he drank greedily, barely aware of the warmth and the thick metallic taste of the liquid; and then he dropped the cup and fell back onto the ground.*

*He heard a faint step, a scrape, as the presence came closer and picked up the cup.*

*"Who—are you?" His voice quavered in fear and helplessness.*

*"I am the one who saved you from the bloodletting." The*

*voice was deep, flat, emotionless. "The battle was fierce. Many died. I chose to save you."*

*The words resonated; he had a savior. "Where are we?"*

*"You are safe and you will heal, and in time you will understand. Everything has been set in motion. It is done."*

*"I understand," he murmured. He had been chosen from those dying in a swath of blood; he had a savior. He was alive.*

*He felt a dry, hot hand touch his forehead, and he closed his eyes to the stygian darkness and surrendered to the night.*

# Chapter 1

*The Pig and Poke Pub*
*Wixoe-on-Lyme, England*
*Spring 1880*

They called her the *Position Girl.*

She sat on a platform in the center of the cavernous room, surrounded by a crowd of men who had started drinking hours before she appeared from behind the curtain.

They knew what they wanted: they wanted *her,* and they had their money at the ready to entice her in this nightly mating dance for which everyone played by certain rules.

She wore a different dress and different undergarments the nights she performed and that too was one of the rituals—to all intents and purposes, she *was* a different woman every night.

Only her smile was the same—the mocking, goading *make-me-do-it* smile, at once knowing and elusive.

They wanted to possess that smile, and possess as much of her as their money could buy, and her goal was to make them spend as much for her as any trollop they could take to one of the upstairs bedrooms.

This night, she wore a daring two-piece red satin gown, cut low and decorated with swooping ribbons of velvet trim across the bodice and down the skirt.

The atmosphere became electric as she finally undulated her way across the tap room and onto her platform.

There, she wriggled into a sitting position and surveyed the crowd. A big crowd. A noisy crowd of lusty men who wanted a moment's thrill, paying a woman to take off her clothes.

They didn't even want to touch; they just wanted to look, and to see who would be the one to make the most masculine of demands—and how many hundreds he would offer to tempt her to strip naked.

But, at the moment, all they were interested in was watching her first move.

She smiled—*that* smile—and daintily began removing one of her long black gloves, slowly, tantalizingly, inch by satiny inch, until she held it in her hand.

"Gentlemen . . ." Her voice was soft and throaty, husky from hours of honing this act to arouse the most tension.

She rubbed the soft satin glove across her face, her neck, her breasts, and then pitched it out over the crowd and watched it disappear into the smoke.

She heard scattered applause and hoots of appreciation as she slowly lowered herself onto the platform.

The performance had begun.

The simplicity of it was alluring, and the very thing that had seduced her: it was an auction—the customer bid on what he wanted her to remove, and the more he wanted her to undress, the more money he paid.

And when there was nothing more to take off, the customer willingly paid for her to pose for him.

*Wonderful lovely money, and all they wanted to do was* look . . .

*Pots of money, easy money . . . she still couldn't believe it . . . money to support her indigent and ailing father, for doing some of the things she used to do when his drunken, lecherous friends used to come to their house . . .*

*"Lift your skirts," he might command, showing her off. "Did you ever see such neat ankles?"*

*Or: "Show off that waist, me darling. Now tell me a man can't get a good hold of a girl like that."*

*Or: "Look at 'er bosom. Ohhhh, a man could bury himself in heaven."*

*She had never paid any attention to it; he was and always had been an impotent old man whose first love was the bottle and who was now bedded down with his memories and his bile.*

*And she, ironically, had found employment in the very place she despised for taking her father away from her—the local pub, which catered to men who wanted anonymity, unlimited drink, and women who didn't mind a tickle, a kiss, or showing themselves off.*

*So how different was her discarding her corset and drawers from her lifting her skirts to show off her ankles or bending over a customer to reveal the cleft between her breasts so he would add a groat to his bill in appreciation?*

*It was merely one step farther, and so much better than her previous lot as a waitress, having to put up with groping and sloppy kisses; she was now worshipped as a goddess and her supplicants put hundreds of pounds in her pockets and never even tried to touch her.*

*And she was utterly, completely in control.*

*And she liked* that *part the best.*

She was now propped up on one elbow, sweeping the crowd with her glimmering, goading gaze.

She knew just how to do it; she had perfected it after watching her predecessor, who had had a lot more contempt and a great deal less success.

That part was easy too, and the waiting—that was part of the strategy too—the waiting increased the tension to an almost unbearable pitch, and she knew how to work that tension with sinuous little movements calculated to incite the customers to the prime moment when they were willing to part with their money.

It was coming—it was coming . . . she felt the restiveness in the crowd, she inhaled the unmistakable scent of ale and smoke and sweat . . . and sin.

"The other glove—one shilling . . ."

*Finally . . .*

"Gentlemen," she chided them.

"Ten . . ."

"Twenty—"

Silence . . . no one else competing. She waited until the money was tossed up on the platform, and then she pulled at the glove in the same slow, insinuating manner as she had removed the first, and again, she tossed it to the crowd.

"Shoes—" someone shouted. "A pound for the pair of shoes . . ."

"Two—"

"Five . . ."

She removed her shoes, again with the same slow, exaggerated surety that made them salivate for more.

Her stockings next, which commanded another five pounds, since she was revealing that much more of herself—her garters, her undergarments, her legs, her feet.

And it went on from there, escalating into a brawling, mauling competition to provoke her into removing all of her clothes.

This was the most important part, where she teased them and pretended to torment them with shocking little glimpses of her bare legs and of her breasts, as she lay facedown on the platform with her shoulders over the edge.

The money came thick and fast then.

They wanted her dress—the bodice first and her breasts tucked behind the rigid, lace-encrusted corset and camisole . . . ten pounds for that and for the skirt, which she discarded in a simple unhooking motion, so it pooled at her bare feet; fifteen for her drawers, which she removed in slow, tantalizing movements, wriggling and writhing to slide them down her silky legs until they covered the brilliant red skirt of her gown and she was naked from the waist down.

And then—the posing, before she had even bared her breasts—it amused her sometimes what the men wanted on any given night. Sometimes they wouldn't pay for posing until she was naked. Sometimes they wanted her spread before them, as if the only thing they had come to see was the mystery of her sex.

Sometimes they were coarse and crude; they called her a bitch and a whore, and made demands she pointedly ignored, knowing it would arouse them even more.

And sometimes she wanted to be exactly what they wanted of her and she gave them all they demanded and more.

Tonight, however, was not one of those nights.

"Fifteen for the corset—"

"Gentlemen . . ." she cooed at them reprovingly, as she cupped her breasts. "You can do better than that. You know what *I* have to offer. What will *you* offer?"

"Twenty . . ."

"Twenty-five—"

She stroked her breasts over the corset cover to incite them to bid even higher. She could see the look in their eyes—lustful, rapacious, with a uniquely male desire to make her submit; every time, no matter how often she disrobed for them, she saw that look, and she exploited it to its fullest.

"Ahhh," she sighed, raising herself to her knees and bending forward so that she supported her upper torso on her hands.

Her breasts spilled almost all the way out of the corset, so full and creamy, with just the shadow of their dusky aureola visible to entice those sitting right in front of the platform.

She saw them licking their lips, almost as if they could taste the erotic anomaly of her soft bosom and her hard, pointed nipples.

She looked them over, to invite the rest of them to enjoy her—for a price.

She heard their salacious comments as she moved around the platform to let them all get a look at what their money would buy.

And then she sat back on her haunches and arched her back—and waited.

There was a rustle of anticipation throughout the room, and a buzz of speculation—who would be first, who would be the *man . . . ?*

She could see all over the room, to the bar where the patrons were three deep, to all the men crowding around the platform, closer now, whispering, money changing hands . . . they were going to offer—oh yes, a lot of money to buy her naked nipples.

She looked beyond them for a moment, to the archways in the shadows behind the bar, one leading off into the entryway and another to the staircase to the rooms above, and a third to a hallway near the back door, where there were two men pushing against each other.

She smiled her little cat smile. Eager to come closer they were, and she wanted them closer, she wanted them right up next to the platform where she could see the voracious lust in their eyes. . . .

"Twenty-five!" someone shouted. "Twenty-five for the corset!"

She looked over their heads in the direction from which the voice had come. "Anyone else?" she asked, shrugging off the offer and searching for one better.

They hated that—and they loved it.

The two men in the farthest archway were fighting to get to her, to see her, to see everything, because when one paid they all reaped the reward of her enticing nakedness spread out for their delectation.

Desperate men who could only hide in the shadows and pummel their way inches forward to see her glorious naked body—whenever someone made the offer that would seduce her into revealing the rest of it.

"Gentlemen, gentlemen—" she murmured, running her fingers over the enticing cleft between her breasts.

No one was paying attention to the two in the archway; every eye was on her, and only she could see the two men desperately struggling in the shadows.

"I'm willing to go home if no one among you wants me tonight."

Her tone was insinuating, suggestive, a little playful, a little insolent, as if she didn't care what they did.

She knew the perfect pitch and the right chord. Immediately there was a rustling sound and whispers.

And she sat there like a high priestess, waiting for them to offer their homage in gold.

"Thirty-five," someone called out.

She hardly heard them. Her eyes were fixed on the two in the shadows pushing and pulling at each other—and as one shoved the other into the light, she caught her breath in horror and in recognition of one whose name was always in the news, side by side with that of the queen.

Or was it?

He dove into the shadows again.

"Forty . . ."

*Him* bolting upright suddenly and grabbing the other around the neck—

"Fifty . . ."

A knife . . .

Oh God, that one had a knife—

"A hundred—"

Lifting it, slashing it . . .

Blood spurting everywhere—

"Oh my God . . ." She made a futile movement, her voice, the expression on her face suffused with horror.

The men had disappeared—and no one had noticed.

"Oh my God—" Could only she see the blood dripping from the walls?

"A hundred, mistress—"

"Oh my God . . ." She swung her legs off the platform and reached for her blood red skirt to wrap it around her nakedness.

*"A hundred—"*

She stopped suddenly and looked around. They had said it—someone had said it: a hundred pounds—the most they had ever offered her, the absolute most.

*. . . dear Lord . . .*

She looked around her frantically. All those expectant faces, those glittering, gloating eyes.

She bit her lip, torn between taking the money and investigating what she had seen in the archway.

*The money, the money—who cares about a pair of murderous men?*

She shifted back up onto the platform. "Gentlemen? *What* did I hear you say?"

"A hundred pounds, mistress—"

The bold man who pushed forward held a fistful of notes, and he was not in a mood to hear her say no.

She looked uncertainly at the archway in the shadows and she could see nothing—*nothing*.

And the wall—the wall was clean.

Her heart jumped wildly.

*Maybe I imagined it—*

"Now, mistress—"

Her customers—her men, her supplicants . . .

*She wasn't in the mood to prance around the stage for them . . .*

He laid the money at her feet and she felt like kicking it in his face.

*Didn't you see—didn't you see?*

She picked up the notes instead. A hundred pounds to ignore the fact that someone might be dying in the shadows beyond the arch.

*Her father was dying. And no one had seen what she had seen. What she thought she had seen . . .*

She began unhooking the corset, slowly, to give herself time to regain her composure and the feeling of being in control.

*She had imagined it.*

She kept looking beyond the archway and she could see nothing.

*Nothing had happened; it was just a lapse—a momentary lapse. The money had gone to her head.*

*Except for that well-known face she thought she had seen . . .*

*Really, in this seedy little town—?*

*She had had but a moment's glimpse and then they were gone . . .*

*And there was no blood, none . . .*

She slipped her arms out of the corset and let it fall to the platform.

And then, slowly, she rose up before them naked.

She didn't hear the hoots of appreciation as she turned and posed and postured before them.

She saw none of them, only the scene she thought she had witnessed playing over and over in her mind.

*She had seen it, she had—and that one, she hadn't imagined him either.*

*And the blood . . .*

She felt faint; she felt as if she couldn't bear it a moment longer—the lights, the noise, the heaviness of her naked body as she turned one more time and then again and stretched out on the platform to give herself to the next customer's demand.

*Soon—it would be over soon, the lights would come down and cover her and the shock of what she thought she had seen, and then—and then—she could find out the truth.*

*One more turn—one more pose—one more slithering slide into the last position—*

*. . . there, now—the lights following the line of her body from her feet up her legs, clothing her body slowly and sinuously in darkness until she completely disappeared.*

Blessed darkness—she swiped her clothes and the money from the end of the platform, crawled to the opposite side, and slipped off the edge just as the lights flared up again.

*Over . . .*

She hurriedly pulled on her clothes behind the door of the alcove directly behind the platform, and then she slipped out behind the bar, where the owner awaited his share of the proceeds.

She dealt out the notes quickly, carelessly.

"Harry—the man who was attacked tonight . . ."

"What man?" Harry was barely listening as he meticulously counted the money.

"In the archway—across from the platform . . ."

"Whatcha talkin' about?"

"*Harry*—they were fighting; I saw it clearly. And the one who had a knife was the s—"

"Nah, mistress. Was your imagination. Nuthin' goin' on tonight except they was spendin' like they struck gold, and you gave 'im just what they wanted."

"Harry . . ."

"You're mistaken, mistress. Wasn't nuthin' else goin' on and no one you thought. I would've known."

She looked at him skeptically.

"Get rested for the weekend, mistress. They really want to spend it. They took five girls upstairs after, they was so worked up."

She folded away the thick wad of bills that was her share of the proceeds and tucked it into her corset.

"Thanks, Harry." She turned away uncertainly and walked slowly down the corridor past the stairs to the archway.

There was no one there, the walls were clean, and there was no trace of what she thought she had seen.

She whirled to face the barroom. The platform had been moved, and the patrons had crowded up to the bar and around the tables, and everything was as it usually was after a performance.

She bit her lip. *She had imagined the whole thing.*

She felt disoriented suddenly, as if she had existed in some other dimension when the incident happened . . .

*If it even happened.*

*If she wasn't going crazy and if her mind wasn't playing tricks.*

*Or else it was guilt about what she was doing to earn that kind of money—*

*No, what she was doing was smart—she got to show off her natural assets, she got lots of money for doing it, and the other girls got the benefit of all that suppressed male lust.*

She continued slowly down the corridor toward the back entrance to the bar.

It had been no more than three hours since she had arrived for this evening's show.

It seemed like a lifetime.

She pulled open the door and stepped into the cool black night—and someone grabbed her from behind, immobilizing her body by containing her arms, and clamping a huge, hot hand over her mouth.

She fought—she kicked, she bit, she tried to pinch and gouge—to no avail. He lifted her effortlessly and carried her, her legs flailing, into the horrible blackness of the night—and she was certain in her mind-bending terror that her kidnapper meant business, and she was going to die.

# Chapter 2

*Wrentham House*
*London*

"Luddington's gone again."

Declan Sinclair heard the words just as he turned the doorknob to enter his father's study.

He knew that voice; he pushed open the door to find Ismail seated across from his father by the fireplace.

"Ah, Declan, my boy." Ismail, always the mediator and peacemaker. The last person he would have expected to see at Wrentham in cozy conversation with his father.

"Mr. Prime Minister."

"Declan." His father's dry, papery voice rustled against him like cat's hair standing on end.

"Sir. You sent for me."

"No, Ismail requested you."

"I see."

"Have a seat, my boy." Ismail's mellifluous voice intervening, soothing and smoothing things over. It was too easy to imagine him at work in other quarters with that voice holding sway, convincing and coercing others to gladly do his bidding.

Even he could not resist it; he pulled over a chair and sat, and saw immediately that he had placed himself closer to Ismail than his father and that his father had noticed.

He met his father's sardonic gaze and then turned to Ismail. "Exactly why did you summon me?"

"I want you to find Luddington," Ismail said bluntly. "Her Majesty is beside herself that one of her most trusted secretaries has gone missing and has empowered me to instigate an investigation that is not to be public, official, or involve the Yard. Naturally I thought of you, my boy."

"Naturally," Declan murmured.

"Very diplomatic of you, my boy," Ismail said. "Just the skills I need at this moment. You know, of course, that this is not the first time Luddington's disappeared. I want to be sure it never happens again and without the attendant publicity. That means no one knows I'm here and no one knows I have asked you to act on Her Majesty's behalf. You are unknown, discreet, logical, loyal, and at loose ends at this moment. It would be a service to the Crown and earn Her Majesty's most fervent gratitude if you would consent to do her this service."

"How can I refuse?"

"Precisely what I told your father. And this is as much as we know: Luddington was last seen heading out of London, toward Wixoe . . . though why I can't imagine . . . three nights ago. So I would begin the search there."

Ismail stood up and held out his hand. "Good luck, my boy. I expect to hear from you soon. Edmund—"

His father acknowledged the prime minister.

A moment later, they were alone in a most uncomfortable silence.

But it had always been thus; his father had been aloof and inaccessible—to him—for as long as he could remember.

And he was a man he never addressed as *Father.*

"I trust Tristan is well," he said finally.

"He is."

"I am well, too."

"That is very evident."

"Then I think we have covered everything. I beg leave to be excused."

"As you wish."

He turned at the door to look at his father and felt enveloped by a familiar feeling of fury and frustration. He had been to Wrentham four years earlier, before embarking on a diplomatic mission, and he had not been back since, and still everything was the same, from his father's habitual reception of guests in his study to the somber and oversized dark suits and elegant white gloves he wore and the impassive expression on his face.

He was inscrutable and unknowable except to his favored older son and heir, and there had never been room in his life for anyone else.

"Good night, sir."

His father nodded imperceptibly.

Declan waited, but there was nothing more, there was never anything more, and he finally stepped out of the room and slammed the door emphatically behind him.

"Have you seen this man?"

He felt like a fool as he posed the question yet again in another of the small inns in still another coach stop along the road to Wixoe.

He still did not know what he was doing, chasing after one of Ismail's feckless pets whom he had insinuated into the queen's cabinet. He was not a Yard investigator and he didn't think he was being particularly discreet either; all he had was a very bad recent photograph and a story that was as transparent as glass.

"No, I ain't seem 'im, guv. What's the story?"

"Money," he said briefly. That always opened them up.

"Oh now . . . money . . . ? Money he owes or someone owin' him?"

"Someone owing him, you might say."

"Now ain't that interestin'. Lemme look at that picture again."

And so it went. He dropped a hundred hints of money and came up with not a clue.

"Have you seen this man?"

It was a strange likeness of Luddington, taken just as he was turning toward the light and the camera, so that his face stood out in grainy relief while the rest of his torso was in shadow.

"Don't look familiar to me. He from around these parts?"

He was weary with sustaining the lie. More than that, he had too much time to ruminate on why Ismail had chosen him for this thankless task. It made no sense, particularly in the context of Ismail's asking in the presence of his father.

And Ismail and his father were not the best of friends.

Yet his father had summoned him at Ismail's request.

"Have you seen this man?"

No one had seen him; no one questioned the lie; no one told the truth.

And finally he arrived in Wixoe.

Wixoe was just what he expected: a small, drab town cluttered with mean little houses, stores haphazardly built along a main street, and a handful of pubs, populated by a mix of rowdy miners, well-heeled investors, families, slumming aristocrats, and persons of dubious reputation.

This was a town with open arms for anyone who had money to spend. Everything was for sale—in shops, on street corners, in the pubs, on the square—and there was an accommodation for every taste and every vice.

It was enough to make a man lose his every appetite.

"Have you seen this man?"

He started that evening making the rounds of the pubs.

"I seen a hundred men this night alone, guv. What's in it for me?"

"Who's to say when money's involved?"

"Ooh now—lemme see that again."

The same lines, the same play. It wasn't working. And he couldn't conceive of what would.

"Have you seen this man?"

It was early evening in the Pig and Poke pub, and the barkeep was being cagey.

"Who wants to know?"

"His solicitor."

"Really," the barkeep murmured. "And how do I know that?"

"The gentleman would know that. Have you seen him?"

"Well, maybe I have and maybe I haven't."

The barkeep waited a moment and then moved away as a customer burst through the doorway.

". . . 'ey—'Arry—whaddya mean the Position Girl ain't on tonight?"

"Just what I mean. Haven't found a replacement for her. Don't know when I will."

"Where's she at?"

"How the hell do I know? Maybe she got tired or bored or she got a better proposition. Maybe one of the boys kidnapped her and married her. Maybe a slaver got her. Who knows? I'm losing barrels of money because she took it into her head to leave me high and dry. Didn't leave me a note or nuthin'. Left her old da, too. Women! Who can understand 'em. Have a beer on me, captain, and drink to the Position Girl."

He slid a foaming tankard across the bar to his customer.

"You say something, guv?"

Declan shook his head. "Not me, guv. Curious coincidence, though, someone else missing."

"You think so?"

"I'll take an ale."

"You got money?"

He threw some coins on the bar.

"Guess your blunt is as good as anyone else's," Harry said grudgingly and drew his ale.

Declan sipped; it was tolerable, but Harry the barkeep was becoming intolerable.

"Got a place to stay tonight, guv?"

"No."

"Mrs. Allnut takes boarders by the night. First street over to your left."

He got up and tossed another coin on the bar.

"Guv?"

He turned back.

"I'll look at that picture again."

Declan tossed it on the bar and Harry picked it up and examined it more closely.

"Naw . . . I don't think I seen 'im."

He took the picture.

"G'night, guv."

He didn't turn back this time, walking straight into the milling crowd congregating outside the pub.

It was like a country fair: Wixoe had suddenly come alive with movement and men seeking surcease in the vice of their choice. There were women on every corner, enticing customers to join them for an evening of pleasure, and hawkers with every kind of merchandise to seduce the idle and aimless.

There wasn't a quiet place to be found, and he began walking toward the location of the boardinghouse as a last resort.

He felt a moment of uneasiness that he couldn't quite define as he mounted the dimly lit steps to the door.

He knocked, the door opened, the landlady admitted him, took his money, and showed him to a small room with a bed, a commode with a washbasin, and a sputtering gaslight sconce on the wall.

He didn't feel any safer in this little hellhole. It was obvious he was never going to find Luddington. And it was also obvious that wasn't a conclusion he wanted to take back to Ismail.

This was a village of lost souls. Anyone could disappear forever. As public a figure as Luddington; as well known a figure as the Position Girl at the local pub . . . and who knew how many others had vanished in the maw of Wixoe's underground life?

*Perhaps Luddington ran off with the girl . . .*

There was a fanciful idea, born both of the comments of Harry the barkeep, who had obviously recognized Luddington's likeness, and desperation.

*Or was it? Harry knew Luddington. The girl was gone. Luddington was gone. And there was a father somewhere . . .*

*Who the hell was the girl? No name . . . the Position Girl, whatever the hell that was . . .*

He began drifting off . . . *the Position Girl . . .*

He awoke to the sun streaming in through the grimy window opposite the bed.

Fierce sun. Late morning. And a preternatural quiet, as if the inhabitants of the town had all gone back to the grave.

He made his preparations and went down to the dingy parlor, where he found Mrs. Allnut sitting in a rocking chair by the window.

"The price of your room entitles you to some tea and scones for breakfast," she said, indicating a table against the wall where there was a pot heating on a candle stand, some cups, cream, sugar, and a plate wrapped in a towel.

The last thing he wanted to do was eat her food, but he needed the tea, and he was surprisingly hungry.

He pulled a chair over near where she sat and brought over his plate and cup.

"Ye don't have to make conversation with me," she said.

"I'm new to town. I need some information."

"That don't come cheap neither."

"I didn't think it would." He laid out some bills on the table.

She took them, counted them, tucked them into her apron, and nodded.

"Have you seen this man?"

She studied the photograph by the light pouring in through the window, and he watched her face to catch every nuance in every wrinkled line.

*She knows Luddington—*

"No," she said, handing the photograph back to him. "I ain't never seen him."

"I see," he murmured, biting into a scone. *Hard as rock and awful to chew.* He sipped the tea, which, though lukewarm, helped. "I was at the Pig and Poke last night. Lots of talk about the Position Girl . . . local girl they said, left her father and just off and went."

She looked at him suspiciously. "That's what they say."

"Ma'am? What is a Position Girl?"

She didn't trust his question. "You never heard of a Position Girl?"

"I never have," he said emphatically.

"What swell place did you come from?"

"London, ma'am. I'd appreciate it if you would enlighten me."

"It's nuthin' special. Men pay for it, girl takes off her clothes and poses for 'em. Anyone could do it. I did it, oh so many years ago. Might've been the first back then, and now there's always a Position Girl at the Pig and Poke. That Mansour girl, she was recent—six months, maybe, after the other one left. They all leave after a while, you know. They get a lot of money, and there's always one besotted man that wants to up and marry 'em and get 'em away from that crowd."

He felt a little shocked. He had never heard of such a thing, in public, where anyone could walk in and watch.

"I see," he murmured.

"Her da—he's a drunk. Squandered all his money right in that very pub; queer how she wound up there, and now she's gone, and the old man's maundering away in his hovel. Who's gonna pay for 'im now, I ask you?"

He shook his head sympathetically and finished off the last of his tea. "I should be going now. I appreciate the company, ma'am."

"I appreciate your good manners," she said, just a little flirtatiously, as she rose from her chair to see him to the door. "You be back again tonight, mister?"

"I don't think so," he said. "Good-bye." He breathed a sigh of relief as the door swung shut behind him.

And now, he thought, the drunk Mansour . . .

Mansour could only live in the meanest section of town, and as Declan prowled the narrow streets and listened at the doors of homes that were no more than sheds and lean-tos, he felt that same vague sensation of uneasiness.

*A fool's chase . . . fitting together two disparate facts . . .*

He asked, finally, one, two, and three suspicious and rude individuals. The fourth was willing to talk to him after he slipped him a couple of coins, and for that consideration he was directed to a squalid cabin at the bottom of a hill, the doors and windows of which were firmly shuttered against the world.

*This is crazy—I'm grasping at fog . . . there's nothing to be learned here . . . Luddington and this girl . . . I'm making stew out of rocks and barley. . . .*

He rapped on the door.

Silence.

Irresistible silence.

*. . . But what if there is something there . . . ?*

And then—a noise . . . a honk—

He rapped again.

A growl . . . something sounding beyond the door . . .

He pushed against the door and was shocked when it swung open. He almost fell into the fetid stench of a small, dark room lit solely by the flaring embers in the fireplace.

And in the far left corner of the room he made out a lumpen shape on the floor.

"Mansour . . . !"

"Who be there?" The voice was slurred and gravelly, barely comprehensible.

"A friend."

"A friend has a drink."

"A friend might have money for you."

The figure struggled to sit up. "What d'ye want?"

He decided to leap into the breach. "Your daughter . . ."

"The bitch—" Mansour fell back on the floor. "Get out of my house! Take your foul mouth with you. The bitch . . . the bitch, runnin' off and leavin' her da hungry and thirsty . . . and you comin' and seekin' the bitch that abandoned me . . . oh God, oh God, I wished I had died in the war . . ."

He started rolling back and forth in anguish, his voice suffused with tears. "Oh, if I'd have died—but he wouldn't let me die . . . he wouldn't let me die, and I was good for nothin' ever since . . . even the drink couldn't save me—my God, my God . . . my tongue aches for a drink to burn away the hunger and the pain . . . the pain—why didn't he let me die . . ."

He was crying, heaving back and forth, in long, loud, gulping sobs.

"Who? *Who?* Who wouldn't let you die?"

"Oh, God, and then the bitch—to hide from the bitch, and she went off and left me and took all the money . . . all the money . . ."

*Goddamn, the man was crazy, out of his mind, delirious with drunken rage—*

"I'll give you money—tell me who—who wouldn't let you die?"

Mansour hiccoughed and burst into a loud, keening wail.

*What do I think—he'll mention Luddington's name? I'm crazier than he is, standing here and trying to make sense out of his babble . . .*

"He should've left me to die . . . to die . . . oh, God, I need a bottle—I need a drink . . ." Mansour's spiky hand crept out from under the covers, doting around for a bottle. "Get me a drink, you—get me a drink and I'll tell you where she went. That's what you want isn't it? You want *her*—they all want *her.* Oh, but she got such beautiful money; she made me a shelf of bottles—look, by the fireplace . . . maybe there's a bottle . . . go on—go on, I would kill for a bottle . . . or did you come to kill *me?* Who are you? *Who are you?*"

"I'm someone who wants to give you enough money to feed your thirst," Declan said carefully, picking his way through the darkness and the clothes and straw and who knew what else—God, rats, dead rats, plates clattering under his feet, empty bottles rolling across the floor—to the fireplace wall.

*Jesus—she had lived here—the girl men paid to take off her clothes*—he felt along the mantel—*dirt, rags, twigs, vermin . . . Christ . . . yes, a bottle—full . . .*

"I found something."

"I told ye; a good girl she was when she was here, tried to keep me clean and tidy, she did—come on, come on . . ." His hand snaked out again, grotesque, gnarled like the claw of a beast.

*He is a beast—look at him snatch the bottle—look at him drink—a half bottle in less than five minutes . . .*

"Ahhhhh . . . ohhhhh—it burns the tongue, it takes away the hunger . . ."

*Time to attack, now—*

"Where's Luddington?"

"What are ye talkin' about? Ye're daft—Luddington . . . I never heard of such a name . . ." He drank deeply.

"Where's your daughter?"

"I don't know. She never came home—goin' on a week, it must be, and took the money with 'er, if it's any of yer business, which it ain't—who you be anyway, stranger?" He drank again.

*Damn, the bottle's almost empty . . .*

"More—I need more . . ." There was a gurgling sound as he finished. "Oh dear God, it's not enough, it's not enough—I still taste it, I still taste it—oh, oh, oh—oh God, just kill me now, kill me now—why did he let me live, why? Why? *Why?*"

"Who?" Declan stumbled across the room, stepping on the awful detritus, to the fireplace. "*Who,* damn you . . ."

"Give me a bottle and I'll give you a name . . ."

*Was* there another bottle? Christ, he couldn't see a thing—yes, one bottle, two—three . . .

He felt his way back across the room and thrust one of the bottles into Mansour's outstretched claw.

There was a gurgling sound and then Mansour sighed.

"Where's my money, stranger?"

The claw nudged him.

He pulled out a thick handful of banknotes and thrust them into the claw.

"Ahhh . . . ohhhh . . ." More gurgling. "I made it go away, I made it go away. Now you go away, stranger. Let me die in peace like he should have done all those years ago."

"Who? Give me the name—who?"

"Oh, he was a sly one. Pick and chose, he did; told me so . . .

and now look at me . . . look—I can't drown the hunger . . . it pursues me like a demon . . . oh God, oh God . . ."

*"Who?"*

"The dreams—the dreams . . ." The gurgling sound again. "Ferenc . . . the devil . . . Ferenc—you can't drown him, you can't kill him, you can't, you can't . . ." More gurgling.

*Jesus Christ . . . the name, all that time wasted for a name he didn't want to hear—he had to get out of there . . .*

He backed out slowly, nudging the refuse out of his way.

"Ferenc comes," Mansour shrieked suddenly. "Ferenc comes . . ."

He was out the door, he was running to get away from the unearthly wail of a deranged man.

He could hear it—all the way up the hill he could hear it resonating in the air, in his mind, in his soul, and as he slowed to a panting walk, he felt that encroaching uneasiness attack his vitals.

In broad daylight. On a wide open street.

*Luddington . . . Mansour—and a trollop who had disappeared, no connection . . . no connection at all—*

It was his last thought.

He felt something heavy bludgeon him between his shoulders, and then across his head.

His legs crumpled under him and in a blinding flash he thought he saw God with the long, flowing beard of his father hiding his barely moving lips—and he was saying something . . . Ferenc . . . Ferenc . . . and then he tumbled headlong into oblivion.

# Chapter 3

She bolted awake suddenly, aware of a definable difference in the stifling, shuddering darkness.

She groped for the edge of her pallet. The stench was, as usual, almost unbearable, and the moaning of the ghostlike voices that inhabited the dark was like an ongoing chorus of doom.

The air was heavy; it felt as if it had weight and she could reach out her hand and grasp a palm full of the moist, thick underlay of it. But she knew she touched nothing.

But there was a difference; something was different. She couldn't tell what, except that the awful rolling and pitching motion had finally stopped, and she had the horrible feeling she was suspended in a limbo of lost souls.

She knew that she was but one among many and that for a week, maybe more—she had lost all sense of time—she had been held prisoner in the hold of a ship before it embarked on its journey to hell.

No, hell was this fetid dungeon where a hundred writhing arms competed for every scrap of rations, every drop of water their captors saw fit to feed them.

Hell was the teeming darkness, the scent of sweat, fear, hysteria, the sound of vicious grunts and curses as the bodies piled one upon the other to gain the least advantage by whatever means possible.

Hell was lying in the dark, in the stench, and not knowing where you were, who you were, or where you were going.

*No, I know who I am—I am Sayra Mansour and I will hold onto that one scrap of certainty, or I will die . . .*

And she felt as if she was one minute short of going mad—

*Surely that wasn't a finger of light slithering into the darkness . . . ?*

Immediately there was a rush of bodies crawling over and around her, clawing, shoving, cursing, crushing her . . . She fought for air, her scream lost in the grunts and howls of the animals trampling her.

*And now I'm going to die . . .*

Cra-a-a-ck!

She heard it, the distinctive slash of a whip, once, twice, three times, and suddenly everything stopped and there was a dead, papery silence.

A tumble of bodies fell on her, in obeisance to a dominating force that was as palpable as if it were hovering above them like a bat.

*I'm going to die . . .* She bucked against the weight, scratching and pinching furiously, fighting the bodies, pushing and shoving with every last ounce of strength she had left.

*I'm going to die . . .* a crush of bodies squirming all over her, frantic, frightened, faceless, serpents in hell—she gasped for air . . . *I'm going to die—*

The sound of the whip whistled through the air, vicious, unexpected, unrelenting; someone screamed, and all the bodies moved in one motion, as if every being felt its sting.

She pushed, one last violent effort as she felt the pressure ease; and then air—suffocating, stinking, precious air. She gulped it like water; she clawed her way to the surface, as if she were drowning, lifting herself from the lumpen weight above her with superhuman effort.

Cra-a-a-a-ck!

The whip sliced through the air again into the preternatural silence.

"And now—" A disembodied voice cut through the air. "And now you understand—you, all of you, are *mine . . .*"

The bodies above her cringed and fell back; she alone moved, wriggling frantically to get free of the dead weight and the fetid smell of the bodies all around her.

It was so dark; they were all animals, even she, feral in her determination to gain just the freedom of her body, pushing and writhing until she lifted herself, pulled herself out from under the tangle of torsos that pinned her.

"Ahhhh—" The disembodied voice beyond the door breathed

a sigh of satisfaction. "The slaves are properly obedient to their master. They understand the purpose of pain. It is well. It is time. The slaves will move, slowly, one at a time, and pass through the doorway. Now . . . !"

The whip cracked again, and the bodies began shuffling toward the thin line of light, almost as if they were on a leash.

She waited and waited until the sound diminished, and only then did she grope her way to the edge of the pallet and feel her way over the side to her feet.

*Oh God, my feet* . . . She could barely stand, her legs felt so wobbly. Her shoes had disappeared days ago. Her dress was in tatters, her hair matted like a rat's nest. She put out an exploratory hand and someone bumped into her and cursed.

"*Move* . . ." A body shoved into her and propelled her forward, toward the light.

She didn't want to go toward the light; she wanted to curl back up into the darkness and never confront what awaited her beyond the door.

Warily, she stepped forward and forward again, in line with the bobbing bodies in front of her, toward the Voice, toward the light.

And then the light, glowing, beckoning just beyond the threshold—she hesitated an instant, her heart pounding with fear, and then she ducked under the doorframe and into the light.

But the light was not freedom. It glowed from a half dozen lanterns hanging from the beams crisscrossing the outer hold area. A dozen black guardians with whips and hostile expressions stood in a line, guiding the captives into this anteroom and toward a ladder.

Her step faltered. A whip cracked and she felt the sting of it against her ankles. She lurched forward and fell against the ladder.

They climbed over her, hoisting themselves up onto the third step of the ladder, and then upward—to what?

She shoved her way to a standing position and levered herself up onto the first rung of the ladder.

*I can't do this . . . oh God, I can't do this—*

She lifted herself again, one bruised foot after another, scuttling up the rungs like a wounded beetle.

And into the light—

A bright white blazing light that pierced her eyes and blinded her with its intensity; she covered her eyes as she staggered onto the upper deck and against the bodies.

"Open your eyes, my pretty." The Voice—the Voice was there—and then the insidious lash of the whip against her legs.

She felt raw, exposed, helpless.

The whip slashed against her hands and she dropped them.

"That's better."

That awful voice that sounded like it emanated from a dead skull, paper thin, whispery with menace.

She opened her eyes slowly and the light almost killed her. She had never seen such relentless light. She could hardly see anything else; it took her a full five minutes to become accustomed to the glare, and only then could she focus, first on the line of women that stood ahead of her on the deck and then on her horrible, improbable surroundings.

The women looked like death—all drawn and pale from the voyage, all in rags and filth, all like animals waiting to attack. And, across from them, another line of muscular black men armed with whips, waiting for the first little transgression.

The Voice stood apart, swathed in a hooded white robe that covered its face, its hands, obscured its sex, and gave it the aura of being something apart from mortal man.

Overhead, a glaring blue sky and a sun that shone down with pinpricks of hot light. To one side of the ship the water met the sky at the horizon in an indistinguishable blue line.

And to the other side a wall of rock, topped with brilliant white buildings, stretched to the sky, a mystical city, with no visible means of access except to those who wielded the power and knew its biding secrets.

The silence was like death, cut only by the sound of gulls and the barest whisper of wind against the sails.

No one moved; no one dared to move with the guardians there and the ominous figure of the Voice standing apart from them, watching and waiting for someone to disobey.

The sun moved higher, burning their faces. The hot air settled on their skin like a woolen blanket. The sweat poured off them, their throats were parched, their tongues thick, their lips and limbs stiff with sustaining the pose of subservience.

It could have been hours or minutes: There was no way to measure how long they stood there with the sun beating down, their heads bowed, their filthy, raggedy bodies in a stance of supplication.

But finally, finally the Voice spoke.

"That's the way, my pretties. There you are, in perfect obedience. You learn fast. Excellent. Excellent. One barely needs to mete out punishment for you to understand. I am well pleased. And if I am pleased, it will go well with you. It is as if you are taking vows, my pretties. In order to succeed in the cloister you must learn obedience to the rule. So it is here. Obedience is everything. Pleasing your masters is everything. Pleasing *me* is your first lesson and you have learned it well. But let one of you rebel and all shall reap the consequences. And so now we will proceed."

The figure walked toward the side of the ship hard by the rock wall and then turned. "You may follow, my pretties."

They followed, with the guardians beside them, prodding them, not one of them daring to wonder where the figure was leading them.

They were like lemmings, Sayra thought in horror. The Voice would demand they jump off the ship and they would do it; they would do anything it said because they were in the grip of a terror too awful to contemplate.

Because, in spite of everything, they still valued their lives—and the Voice knew it, the Voice counted on it, and the Voice was testing them by commanding that they keep walking forward although there was nowhere to walk to.

And then, just as suddenly, there was an opening at the side of the ship just wide enough for a person to fit through, and the Voice ordered everyone to step up.

A palpable sense of dread rippled through the line as the first three women stepped up and seemed to disappear over the side of the ship.

Instantly, everyone hesitated, turning in unison to look at the hooded figure of the Voice. Immediately its head lifted imperiously, and it stretched out its arm commandingly.

No one dared disobey. The next woman stepped up and over and disappeared. And the next, and the next, and the next . . .

And finally it was her, and Sayra pushed down on her feeling of mounting terror and stepped up onto the edge of the plank.

Three feet below her stood a line of guardians waiting at the foot of a stone staircase cut into the rock that wound up the side of the seemingly impenetrable wall.

The one closest to the plank held out his hand; she knelt down to take hold of it and he mercilessly pulled her down onto the rocky ledge beside him.

She landed off balance and fell onto her knees. Immediately he prodded her to her feet and shoved her toward the stone steps.

She fell again and landed on her hands, and the guardian closest to the steps wrenched her upright and onto the first step.

She looked up, ignoring the burning bruises on her palms and knees; the summit was so far above her that those who had already begun the ascent looked like spiders as they laboriously climbed toward the blazing sun.

Her heart pounded with fear; her head spun dizzily as she tried to estimate the number of steps, the time it would take, the chances of escape, and the likelihood that this stairway to the heavens would ultimately lead them all into an unknown hell.

His first thought, when he regained consciousness, was that he should have known, he could have fought, he should have subdued them—whoever they were.

And instead they had trussed him up like a plucked fowl in the dank confines of some moaning, groaning excuse of a ship, and they had fed him like a dog, taunted him like an infidel, beat him like a slave, while they remained like cowards in the shadows.

He could not guess who his tormentors were, and after they throttled his rebellion out of him, he didn't much care.

He was ready to die; he had always been ready to hand up his life from the time he had begun his diplomatic career. That was the danger, that was the risk, and he had willingly sought the danger and lived for the risk.

But this . . . this—

For what?

He lost all track of time. Everything centered around his hunger, his thirst, his remaining as invisible as a ghost as the mystery ship rolled and pitched its way to oblivion.

He was barely aware when it ended. He felt like a stinking, hanging carcass waiting to be flung on the dung heap when they finally came for him.

In the dark they cut him down and he sagged to his knees.

They pulled him upright ruthlessly and wrenched his arms behind his back and tied them tightly, and then they blindfolded him.

He was meat in their hands—they could pound him and pummel him into any shape they wanted—he put up no resistance whatsoever.

And finally—"It is done." It was a disembodied voice, deep and hollow, like the voice of doom.

They lifted him, knocking his legs out from under him, and carried him like a sack of flour.

He braced to meet death.

And then he lost consciousness altogether.

She emerged from that torturous ascent up the rock staircase into a fairy-tale city of pristine white.

The women who had preceded her were lined up against one blazing white wall, each panting and sweating with the exertion of the climb.

The figure of the Voice stood at the head of the line, waiting; its minions, the guardians, were aligned across the brick terrace from them.

*. . . how—?*

She sagged against the wall, her breath ragged, her head aching, her skin raw from the blazing tentacles of the sun.

There was no way to escape it; not the heat, not the prodding whips, not the terror, not the sense that there was no way that any of them were going to come out from this captivity alive . . .

*Oh, but I will. I will . . .*

She clenched her fists against her feeling of helplessness. There were at least two dozen women here, the last of them just emerging onto the brick terrace and almost swooning with exhaustion as they staggered toward the wall.

Two dozen women abducted and taken to some exotic clime for what purpose none of them could imagine.

*It was not just her, it wasn't some kind of plot, some device to keep her quiet about what she had seen at the Pig and Poke.*

*But what it was, she couldn't begin to understand.*

Once again they waited. The ominous silence enveloped them. The sun beat down. The guardians paced alongside them, poking and prodding them to stand up straight, to focus their eyes on the Voice, in prime obedience.

Not a breath of a breeze stirred the air.

No one dared breathe in the stillness.

The guardians stepped away and the Voice moved along the line like a disembodied being.

"Very good, my pretties." Again the raspy, papery voice that sounded like death. "Very good. You are strong. You are not faint of heart. You will need that strength."

The Voice paused, bowed its head for a moment, and then looked up at the line of cowering women.

There was no way to see its eyes or its face. There was nothing visible but the sliver of shadow beneath its cowl-shrouded head. They could not even tell if it was a man or a woman beneath its cassock.

All they knew was that the Voice was heartless; that it would show them no mercy whatsoever.

They waited, trembling in fear, for its next words.

"You are now the chattel of the begoun of Kabir. You have been chosen to be the vessels of his pleasure. What, my pretties? You shudder at the honor? So—you have not learned the lesson. You do not understand perfect obedience. It is well I have discovered this perfidy at the outset. It is very well.

"Hear me well, slave women—you have no autonomy here, no voice, no life other than that decreed by the begoun. Everything you will learn, everything you will do, every breath you take will be directed toward the pleasure of the begoun. You exist for no other reason, and the moment there is one hint of rebellion—one shudder of revulsion—you will die.

"So you will get on your knees with thanksgiving that I have chosen to be compassionate this afternoon in light of your disobedience."

A half dozen whips cracked against the backs of their knees and they fell to the ground.

"Now—" the Voice hissed, "you will recite this prayer: 'I beseech the forgiveness of the most benevolent, generous, merciful begoun for my transgressions.' "

The Voice paused, waiting for them to repeat the words, which came out in halting, reluctant whispers.

" 'And I swear my life and my existence will be dedicated to the sole purpose of pleasuring of the most exalted beneficent be-goun . . .' "

They mouthed the words.

" 'And that I am less than dirt until the supreme one chooses me as the instrument of his pleasure . . .' "

They repeated the words.

" '. . . and my only goal from this moment forward is obedience, acceptance, compliance, and preparation for the holy be-goun's rapturous penetration.' "

They whispered the words as their import sank in.

The Voice nodded, satisfied. "You will question nothing. You have no voice here, no will, no desires, no opinions, no preferences. You will be told what you must do and you will obey. If you refuse, you will die. Obedience is everything. Anything else is punishable by death."

The words resonated in the silence.

The Voice turned its back and bowed its head, and only the cry of a gull wheeling overhead punctuated the ensuing silence.

They didn't dare look at each other. They stared at the figure of the Voice as if it were their sole link to reality.

The silence stretched until their nerves were screaming, and then, finally, the Voice turned and slowly began coming toward them.

They recoiled as if they were one body.

*It isn't alive—it had to be supernatural: it looked like it was floating above the ground, and it's scaring us to death . . .*

"Yes, my pretties," the Voice murmured as it passed them one by one and looked deep into their eyes. "I see your fear and your disgust and your determination to live. Let me emphasize—you cannot escape. Your fate is sealed. Believe it. It is so."

It turned again and made its way back toward the front of the line. Its head lifted, and the guardians fell into place beside them and indicated that they were to move as well.

They shuffled uncertainly in the wake of the figure as it approached the blank white wall of a building ahead of them.

And then suddenly there was a yawning black space in the center of the wall and the figure of the Voice stepped into it, turned to look at them meaningfully, and then disappeared within.

And they understood that they had finally come to the end of the journey, and they had no choice but to follow.

She was burned by the sun, devastated by the finality of the words, and numb to everything that was happening as she moved in her turn into the darkness and down a set of wide, shallow steps and once again into the light.

She had to adjust as she stepped into a sumptuous hallway with a stained-glass ceiling through which the light poured in phantasmic colorations over a tiled floor.

Everything was pristine white, arched, and patterned in the same tile: the walls, the entryway, the benches built in under the windows . . . all cool, white, inviting tile.

She wanted to divest herself of what remained of her clothes and lay down her heated body on those tiles and sleep away the madness of this nightmare.

The figure of the Voice seemed to blend into the whiteness, but its next command was real and shocking.

"And now, my pretties, take off those rags."

They recoiled almost as if they were one body.

The Voice lifted its head as if it couldn't believe that it had seen an instant's defiance. "My pretties insist on thinking they have free will. You have nothing. You are nothing. You are vessels of pleasure, no more, no less. Vessels have no opinions, no feelings, no options. Vessels just *exist. Now*—take . . . off . . . those . . . rags. . . ."

The Voice meant it; the guardians moved menacingly closer, and they understood that there were no choices: They must obey.

Each of them began, reluctantly, to undo the buttons of her bodice, or unhook her skirt, or remove what was left of a jacket.

The Voice waited, and when they hesitated it nodded, and a guardian cracked the whip perilously close to the bare feet of the woman who was first in line.

"You *will* obey."

They obeyed, their tattered clothing slithering over their trembling limbs to the floor until they stood naked—and humiliated.

"Yesssss," the Voice hissed. "Perfect obedience . . ."

It drifted toward them again, inspecting them.

"Filthy bodies," it said finally. "Ugly, fleshy, stupid bodies. Not remotely worthy of the begoun."

It turned to face them. "That will change. All will change. Those abominable bodies will be prepared for the glory of the possession of the begoun."

It nodded toward the guardians. "We will begin."

One phalanx of guardians marched past the Voice to the far side of the hallway and pushed open a pair of massive doors.

Light flooded through, beckoning, inviting light.

*A world of light, tempered by the darkness of subservience . . .*

And once again their only choice was to move; they shuffled forward, conscientiously looking at the floor until they came to yet another staircase.

They descended cautiously, and at the bottom they were enveloped by a blanket of dense moisture as they stepped into a small, steamy anteroom.

The Voice was there ahead of them. "We bathe, my pretties. We bathe all day, every day; we keep our bodies fresh and moist and perfumed for the pleasure of the begoun. Slaves will assist you. You will spend the rest of the day here; I daresay it will take that long to clean you up and make you presentable. You will be fed and you will rest. There will be an interpreter, should you need one. You will each be assigned a slave who will scrub you and attend to you."

It clapped its hands and the guardians moved back and a door opened to admit one black woman whose head and hips were wrapped in a colorful cotton cloth. She motioned to the first woman, who eyed her warily, reluctant to move without the permission of the Voice.

"You may follow," the Voice said, a note of satisfaction coloring its words.

She left, and another woman entered and motioned to the second captive, who awaited the nod from the Voice and then followed her slave out the door.

There was a slave for each captive, women as indistinguishable from each other as the captives were in their nakedness.

Sayra felt herself tensing as the next woman entered the room and motioned to her. *Now the test—she must look at that patronizing, smug ghost of a figure and wait for its approval. It was galling, it was humiliating. It was meant to be.*

And she did not know how to keep the defiance from her expression as she lifted her eyes to the black slit in the cowl and awaited its signal.

It nodded, and she followed her slave through the door and into the cavernous recesses and the sulfurous humidity of the *hamam.*

She did not know where to look first. There were naked women everywhere, splashing in one of the five pools of steaming water, lounging on the tile benches that surrounded the pools, huddling in corners whispering, or laid flat out on tile beds with slaves attending them, rubbing oils and perfume on their bare skin.

The dozen or so women who had preceded her were already immersed in the water, their expressions glazed with a kind of pained pleasure, as if they could not believe this was the final outcome of their humiliating journey.

Her slave motioned for her to step into the nearest pool. She knelt on the cool tile—the walls, the ceilings, the benches, the arched recessed niches, everything was made of that same cool patterned tile—and dipped a hand in the water.

It was skin-crinkling hot. She sat on the edge of the pool and eased herself into it, wanting to obliterate herself altogether in its scalding depth.

Her slave was beside her in an instant, roughly pulling her up and uttering angry, unintelligible words; she read the inescapable meaning in the woman's intelligent eyes: she was to stand still and let the woman attend to her, and nothing else would be tolerated.

She stood; her slave removed a length of material from her waistband and a vial of some kind of liquid she had tucked in with it, uncorked the vial and applied the liquid to the cloth, and then began a systematic scrubbing of her body.

It was not unpleasant to be handled this way; the woman's hands were firm, knowledgeable, purposeful.

When she was done she motioned to Sayra to immerse her body, and then she applied the liquid from her vial to Sayra's hair and washed it thoroughly.

Sayra then submerged herself entirely, and her slave unwrapped the material from around her waist around her as she led her from the baths to one of the tile platforms and motioned for her to lie down.

Here she was given a cool liquid to drink and a choice of sweetmeats from a platter. While she nibbled, her slave rubbed her body with the rough material and then applied oils all over her and wrapped her up again.

She lay back, taking in the scene around her. A hundred women—she couldn't get over it—all unabashedly naked, their bodies glowing against the darker colors of the patterned tile that reached twenty feet to the ceiling.

Everywhere, there were arches framed by marble columns, and private niches recessed from the main room where there were benches, and a place for the copper pitchers, bowls and bottles with the accoutrements of the bath.

She felt her slave working on her hair, combing it and blotting it with another piece of material in a hypnotic motion that made her want to close her eyes and just float away.

The anomaly of it was frightening. The bath was a distinctly sensual experience, heightened by her enforced nakedness, the overpowering scent of perfume, the slick slide of the oil permeating every pore of her being.

The bath was pure self-absorption, a glorification of the very thing the Voice had tried to nullify.

And now she and the others were to be steeped in every decadent luxury, and to compete with every other preening beauty, as they awaited forever the moment that might never come.

It defied all logic that she could be abducted and immured for the rest of her life solely at the desire of this mythical begoun.

She felt faint at the thought of it. Her whole life limited by the boundaries of these beautiful tiled walls. Her whole life charted by the whim of one man, and dedicated to the purpose of seducing him who had the choice of so many already.

This was real. She wasn't dreaming. There was no way out. She had no life; she had no self. She had been transformed into an object on a shelf whose sole purpose was to wait until such time as the all-powerful begoun chose to use her.

# Chapter 4

"My name is Zenaide."

The voice was husky, accented, distinct.

She lifted herself languorously onto her elbows and opened her eyes. The woman standing next to her platform was tall, dark-haired, naked, and adorned with gold around her neck, her arms and her ankles.

She was an older woman, as evidenced by her face; there were wrinkles around her mouth and her dark, hard eyes, and just a suggestion of a chin and some sag to her breasts, and that despite her shapely, well-kept body.

She said the first thing that came into her head.

"I want to leave this place."

Zenaide smiled, a cruel, knowing little smile, as if she had a secret that she would never reveal. "That is not possible."

"Why not?"

"You are chosen, and the chosen ones do not question. They obey, perfectly and completely. You have not yet learned that lesson. It goes hard with those who do not obey. You have been warned twice now. There is no more leniency. There is only punishment if you transgress again. I am Zenaide. You will now tell me your name."

She clenched her fists and levered herself upright. *What lie could she tell? She would never be obedient—never.*

"I am—Mary."

Zenaide stared at her for a moment, and then she lifted her arm and swung it hard against Sayra's face.

She was so shocked, she almost fell off the platform. She felt tears sting her eyes, and a tingling heat stain her cheek.

"This pretty is a one who would face death rather than obey," Zenaide murmured, lifting her hand like a benediction. "So be it."

She felt a cold wash of terror. What was one body sacrificed to the greedy god of obedience? She was nothing; she was less than nothing. But she had to try.

"I am Sayra."

Zenaide's hard, unfeeling eyes settled on her. "There is no more leniency."

*Now what? Now what?* She was frantic with fear, and she didn't know whether to be bold or to kneel before the bloodless tyranny of this woman who now held her future in her hands.

Any choice—*any*—rather than none. She willed her trembling body to a muscle-straining stillness.

"I will take any punishment, but I do not want to die."

Zenaide's eyes flickered with interest.

"I will serve the begoun; I will be compliant. I will not question. I have learned the lesson. I will be obedient."

Zenaide reached out her hand and touched Sayra's hair, ran it through her fingers, and then she relinquished the strands to take Sayra's chin in her hand to tilt her face up so she could see deep in her eyes.

"It would be a pity to kill you. The begoun is partial to slaves with such milk-white skin. Very well. A punishment . . . we shall see. We shall begin again. What is your name?"

"I am Sayra."

"I am Zenaide. I am one of three who will be your guide, your teacher, your interpreter. I will show you where to go, what to do and how to do it; I will instruct you in the art of pleasing the begoun, and if you hold his attention successfully, and if he gets a child with you, I will be rewarded and you will be anointed his *kadin* and spend the rest of your life in luxury. Your sole focus from this moment forward is to attract the begoun and get with child. Do you understand?"

"I understand," Sayra murmured, keeping her voice low and her head bowed, thankful that she had circumvented the consequences of the first test. But attract the begoun? Get with child?

*It's a competition—if there are three, then there are three mentors to guide and instruct the two dozen of us who are newly ar-*

*rived to see which of them can successfully get a slave impregnated by the insatiable dictator who rules this place . . .*

*Barbaric! Uncivilized!*

"Sayra . . ." Zenaide's sharp voice cut through her rebellious thoughts.

"Yes, Zenaide."

"It is time."

"I am ready."

Zenaide snapped her fingers and the slave who had bathed Sayra appeared magically to remove the cloth around her body and to hand her a length of filmy material to wrap around herself.

"This, of course, is only for the first day; the compassionate begoun understands completely that one must get used to one's nakedness. A day is permitted to conceal your body behind the trappings of your civilization. But the begoun yields to no one: The cover is transparent. It is an illusion that preserves your modesty, yet still allows our exalted begoun to feast his eyes where he will."

She motioned, and the slave slipped the garment over Sayra's head. She looked down, and it was like wearing nothing—a film of white netting that floated against her body, settling in every enticing curve, revealing every secret.

She stifled her outrage. "I am ready."

Zenaide led her from the baths into a columned arcade off which there were a half dozen rooms devoted to the care and pampering of the harem slaves: the laundry, the kitchen, the storerooms, the hospital, the cupboards of the jewels, the perfumes and oils, the robes.

At the end there was a massive wooden door that opened onto a small verdant courtyard completely enclosed by the surrounding buildings, which were all encircled by a columned gallery.

"This is one place you may take recreation," Zenaide said. "There are benches, there are trees, and the pool, in which you may bathe to cool off if you desire. It is one of the begoun's favorite places to watch his lovelies. This way is the Hall of the Divans."

She motioned toward another massive door in the gallery to the left of the courtyard, and Sayra followed obediently as Zenaide led her into the next building.

This was a surprise—an interior that was at least three stories high, and open at the center to a roof of stained glass that sprayed multihued light all along a central brick-paved walkway.

There were three tiers of rooms on either side of the hall—dining rooms on the first level, the bedrooms on the second, rooms of worship on the third—all connected and reached by a staircase that spanned the balconies that fronted each of the tiers.

It was a place bustling with women in various stages of undress and communion with other women. There was a group in the dining room and another in the hall feeding from a huge bowl of rice; still others were whispering in close conversation, just barely seen around a corner. There were slaves carrying bowls of food or water, and still others farther down the hall scrubbing the brick paving.

"This is your home," Zenaide said, mounting the staircase on the left. Sayra followed, her head bowed, keenly aware of the curious stares that followed them as they made their way to the bedroom floor.

Everywhere, every wall, every ceiling was tiled, columned or gilded. Every window was covered with ornate latticework that threw a shadowed grid against the wall.

The bedrooms were like barracks; the floors were uncovered, the walls were tiled in a riot of colors and motifs, the ceiling was gilded, the windows barred with the ubiquitous latticework, but otherwise there was no furniture except a row of cupboards along one wall.

Zenaide threw open one. "At night, if you are so unfortunate as not to be chosen by the exalted One, you retire to this room, where you take a mattress and bring it to your allocated space. There are lavatories at the other end of the room, a half level below here, but you must obtain the permission of the Mistress of the Night at the time of your need."

She closed the cupboard door and turned to face Sayra.

"I will remember to do so," Sayra murmured.

"So docile, my pretty," Zenaide said. "You think you are obedient? You think yourself compliant? Oh, you have yet to learn a lesson in humility. But it will come, it will come; because I have chosen to spare you, you must repent in other ways to purify yourself for the moment of ultimate penetration. Yes, it will be so. The exalted One has decreed it. I am his vessel, as you will be, my pretty. We will make you ready. We will make you willing. You will yearn to abase yourself before the omnipotent One and beg him to take your miserable body. It is always the way with the rebellious ones."

*I relish the prospect. . . .*

She bit back the retort. It was so easy to fall into an attitude of submission. It required only that you keep your wayward thoughts to yourself and promise to do things you have no intention of doing.

What was this stupid woman but a zookeeper, holding the whip over a cage of passive women, preparing them for a rutting stag?

She was not afraid of Zenaide now she knew her threats could be tempered by the mere use of acquiescent words.

She had only to bide her time and do as they told her. A simple thing to save her life.

She followed Zenaide out of the bedroom and back down the stairs.

Almost immediately a slave accosted them and whispered something into Zenaide's ear.

She dismissed the slave and clapped her hands. Immediately a tall, hulking eunuch appeared with a whip in his hand.

"It is time, my pretties, to bathe before dinner. All except you, my docile one." She swung toward Sayra. "You will scrub the floors. Front to back of the Hall of Divans. And here is Paik to watch over you. Every square inch, Paik, she shall scrub on her hands and knees, so she will recognize and be humbled by the honor accorded her by the most beneficent begoun."

She clapped her hands again and two slaves appeared with two buckets of water between them. "Take her."

The women gaped as the slaves aligned themselves on either side of Sayra and forced her to move with them down the hallway.

"Do not hesitate to mete out punishment," Zenaide said to Paik. "The begoun could never fault you for teaching humility to a slave who will not obey. You—my pretty—" she called down the hallway. "On your hands and knees—and make sure she does not get up until we return."

And then she and her menage of lady hens disappeared, leaving Sayra on her knees in the waning light, a scrub cloth in her hand and murder in her rebellious eyes.

"It is time."

Faceless voices in the darkness, entering the cell where he lay half conscious in the filth and the matte silence of a dungeon.

They came to feed him; he did remember eating, if one could call stale bread and sour milk food, and he knew in the deepest recesses of his mind that they were speaking a language he could understand, although he could not in his delirium remember what it was or why he was conversant with it.

All he wanted to do was let himself drift down into the darkness and let go, and here they were, at the moment of his surrender, at the dungeon door. He sensed immediately that they were not there to give him sustenance.

"Get him up. The exalted Being does not care if he is half dead. Only if he is clean when he enters the blessed One's presence. Up with him! To the baths; carry him if he will not walk. Quickly now . . ."

There were six of them: two of them on either side, one behind and two yanking at his legs. Finally they just lifted him as easily as if he were on a pallet.

The sixth carried a torch to lead the way, and he could see through his dimmed and bleary eyes stone walls, dirt floors and thick iron bars. Not a window, not a sliver of light. The merest board and rags for a bed, a clay bowl and a cup to eat from. The longest hallway to traverse to someplace called the baths.

He let his body go limp and allowed his captors to bear the burden of his weight. He fought for consciousness and to clear his mind.

He had no idea how long he had been imprisoned thus; he suspected that he might even have been drugged with the foul-tasting milk, which would account for his feeling so hazy and disoriented.

But now—he could smell the fresh air, he could soak in the light, he could almost taste freedom.

"Leave him." The command was as sharp as the crack of a rifle.

They dumped him unceremoniously on a hard, cold floor.

"Send for Shihab who speaks the language."

"It is done."

"You—Udo—remove his clothing. Basu—clean clothes, immediately!"

He felt hands reaching for him, pulling and prodding his western clothing from his body, exclaiming over his rags.

"Ah, Basu—the omnipresent One provides for everything, even the comfort of his captives. Let us make him fit to kiss the feet of his savior. Udo—Basu, in the baths with him."

They lifted his naked body by the arms and legs and tossed him; he landed in a geyser of water and sank instantly into a deep heated pool.

Like a rock. Like he was dead.

*Damn . . . he hated the water, hated losing control; hated fighting an amorphous enemy . . .*

He surged to the surface sputtering and kicking, to hear his nemesis say with some satisfaction, "It lives. It fights for its life. This is good. Ah, here is Shihab. Into the pool with you and tell this vermin that Basu and Udo will bathe him and make him presentable for him who holds life in his hands. Now!"

He treaded water as the three eunuchs waded into the pool. The two were naked; Shihab wore a turban and a loincloth, and he lifted his hand in common greeting.

"Peace, stranger. I am Shihab who speaks your language, and I come to assure you no harm will come to you. You are to give over to the slaves that they may bathe you."

He allowed them to grasp each arm and move him toward the shallow end of the pool.

"Where am I?"

"You are the honored guest of the begoun of Kabir, selim. When you have bathed and refreshed yourself, you shall have an audience with the exalted One. I shall be your interpreter. Anything you wish, you have only to request it of me. What shall I call you?"

He was standing by then, with the slaves rubbing him all over with a harsh-scented soap and rough cloths, and he resisted the urge to push them out of his way.

"Call me Sinclair. Tell me who is the one who brought me here."

Shihab turned to look at his superior. "He is Munir, and of no moment now, selim Sinclair. I am your guide and your mentor from this time forth."

He clapped his hands and the two slaves stepped back, and he motioned to Sinclair to leave the bath.

"Here; the beneficent One has provided clothing that will be a comfort to you. Udo will dry you off and help you to dress. When you finish, you will join me in the anteroom, where you will partake of some refreshment."

He clapped again and the others disappeared, leaving him alone with the slave called Udo and Shihab himself.

"There: There will be no more guards, selim Sinclair. I leave you to Udo's ministrations."

And then he was alone with Udo, debating whether to let the muscular slave dress him or to fight him to the ground.

*If I want to do battle, I must be feeling more myself. It is well. It would be easier not to fight this sod who is responsible for nothing.*

He took stock of his surroundings as Udo began helping him on with his trousers. He had never been privy to such a room in all his travels.

It was cavernous, with marble walls, columned niches and doors and a cool white-tiled floor. There were three pools, each of which was fed by an ornate fountain carved into the marble in the shape of fantasy beings.

There were windows high up in the walls, with ledges and clear glass to let in the streaming sun, which added to the shimmering feeling of humidity.

Here and there a marble bench was situated for the convenience of the bathers, and on one of them his clothes had been neatly laid.

Moreover, Shihab had brought him western dress: dun-colored trousers and a shirt of a light, coarsely woven material that lay against his skin like silk, and a burnoose of the same material to wear over that.

There were leather sandals as well, but nothing approximating undergarments and nothing with which to shave the week's worth of beard stubbling his chin.

Udo looked him over carefully after he had dressed, nodded and motioned for him to follow.

Now he was going in the opposite direction from which they had brought him in, through an ornately decorated door and into a small, rich room furnished with tufted sofas set low to the floor, gorgeous gem-encrusted silk hangings on the walls, and thick jewel-colored carpets overlapping each other on the floor.

And there was light and air from windows that were open widely and shaded with lattice.

Shihab awaited him at the farthest sofa, in front of which there was a table laden with covered platters, a copper pitcher and a coffee service.

"Seat yourself, selim Sinclair. We will eat and talk in the manner of peaceful men."

He sat. "How peaceful to abduct me and leave me rotting in that dungeon?"

Shihab waved his hand as if to dismiss it and began uncovering the dishes of heaped fruits: dates, plums, apricots; breads and walnut paste; lamb fragrant from the oven and rice cooked with broth and milk.

"A mistake."

"I think not."

"Please, the lamb, most excellent. Some wine. Things happen, selim, as you yourself know. But all is rectified."

"How long was I held there?"

Shihab shrugged. "A week, no longer, selim. The fruit—freshly picked this morning. The paste—sublime." He was heaping all of this on Sinclair's plate as he spoke, and he set it in front of him and waited.

His stomach reeled at the smell of the lamb. But to eat was necessary, and to keep his composure was essential.

He scooped up the rice and fruits. "Excellent together, Shihab. The stomach balks at anything heavier."

"Selim Sinclair does not mince words. Of course; it is understandable that after a week—"

"And more, if you count the weeks I was under sail."

Shihab looked taken aback. "As you say, selim. All that time and undernourished. The begoun will be merciful. Please—as much as you can eat."

"Answer some questions then."

"I have told you all I can."

"Who will answer my questions?"

"The all-powerful begoun will tell you all that you wish to know."

"All that he wishes me to know, you mean."

"Selim . . . it is better to be tactful and restrained."

"It is *not* how I am feeling right now."

"When selim's stomach is full he will come to realize the necessity."

He looked up sharply at that and Shihab met his gaze blandly.

"Selim is a man of superior understanding. Enjoy your food. You are a prisoner no more. And when you are ready, selim Sinclair, we will proceed."

It had been two weeks since her public humiliation, and she thought she had become used to walking around stark naked in the company of a hundred women.

She thought. But there were moments . . .

There was too much jealousy, too much anger, too much spite, too much currying favor, too much fighting for position.

Ever obedient, she played the game. She was one of four new passion slaves who were Zenaide's protégés. Three of them believed: there was no escape, there was no other life, no other focus, no other reason for living than to become the chosen of the begoun.

Three of them believed they would die if they were not chosen, and three of them believed they would rot away in ignominy if they could not get with child, and three of them devoutly believed the gods would strike them dead if the child was not a son.

And so they skirmished among themselves: who was the most beautiful, the most talented, the best cook, the best maker of coffee; who had the biggest eyes, the fairest skin, the longest hair, which of them the now godlike begoun would choose first, which of them would not disgrace Zenaide.

"Ah, but see the haughty Sayra who thinks she is above the concerns of mortal women."

"Nay, she is humble, as befits one who strives to be a consort of the begoun," Sayra said, the lies tripping so easily off her tongue.

"But then, how can one command his attention? One must *do* something to make oneself noticed." This from the fair-haired Olga, who was slight of body and short in stature, and whose pronouncement was tinged with its usual tone of desperation.

"One should have only to present oneself," Amalie said, who was taller, well rounded, and seemed very sure of herself in spite of her plain-pudding face.

"One must cultivate one's talents and whatever arts would please the begoun, is it not so?" This was Phyllida speaking directly to Zenaide in a catechism that had been repeated over and over the preceding two weeks.

"We already see where the talents of the pretties lie," Zenaide murmured. "Amalie is the artist, and that will please the begoun. Olga is a magician with food, in spite of the differences in culture, and the begoun most assuredly delights in dining. Phyllida is the musician who transports the begoun to a place of peace. And Sayra dances."

Zenaide looked up at Sayra, who stared right back at her.

"The exalted begoun must enjoy the movements of the dance," she said daringly, not liking the fact that Zenaide had not amplified her talent into something more. God, what was happening to her? She wanted to hear the rest, even more than did Phyllida. So what did that make her, in spite of all her resolution?

"The dance is freedom," Zenaide said. "It is a place to which the almighty begoun cannot allow his passion slave to go." Her eyes flickered again, in that curious way that showed more than mere interest. "One cannot know if he will be pleased or if he will order your death. But you will insist."

Sayra felt chilled. Zenaide had never in the past two weeks indicated anything like this. "It is what I know."

"Then we shall see," Zenaide said. "However, you might try to learn to make coffee or keep the accounts—or something."

"Perhaps—something."

But there was nothing but the proscribed rituals of the day. Baths twice a day, sometimes three. A massage, a nap, two hours of dining and gossip with those among the passion slaves with whom you were forced to make friends, an hour of instruction in the art or talent of preference, during which time they were given robes to clothe their nakedness; two hours of dinner, more gossip; an hour of specialized tutoring in the arts of lovemaking by Zenaide.

"When you are chosen," she would say over and over again, "you will be brought to the holiest of rooms where everything is of the richest and most beautiful; the walls are hung with gold. The bed is furnished with silks and furs and draped in jeweled chains. Here the all-potent begoun awaits you. When you pass the columns you must lie on the floor, facedown in subservience, that the ever potent begoun may know that you are his vessel and obedient to his will.

"Only when he signals to you may you move. If he does not summon you, you must make haste to leave. You must not speak, you must not beg, you must not breathe. You must withdraw as silently as air.

"But when he summons you to his heavenly bed . . . ah, now you allow yourself the joy of knowing you will know the potent begoun as only a passion slave can.

"You will remain prostrate, and you will crawl inch by inch to the foot of the bed where your potent majesty awaits you. Every moment will heighten his desire and yours. The more time you take, the more powerful he will become, the more excited, the more uncontrolled, the hungrier for possession, the more ravenous for penetration.

"Take your time. It is the only time in the whole of your life here that you are ever permitted to make the most glorified begoun wait for that which he desires.

"You lift the cover at the foot of the bed; silken it will be, slippery to the touch. You will crawl up under the cover, up and up and up until you are facedown next to the exalted One in all his glory.

"He will wish to look at you. And if he is bursting to possess you, he will touch you. You will turn on your back and invite his possession.

"You, Sayra. Lay down on the floor, and I will show just how to spread your legs to incite his passion."

They all took turns at this: It was always before bedtime, when the mattresses were laid out on the bedroom floor. And Zenaide always sounded reverent as she detailed their duties. And her instructions always sounded so clinical.

"There, start at the foot of the bed. Now—crawl slowly inch by inch . . . that's right. Now the most rapturous begoun awaits you, examines you, touches you. Now you turn, slowly, away from him. Onto your back. Lift your legs. Higher. Against your chest as high as they can go. Nothing must impede the awesome spending of passion of the exalted One.

"Still higher, Sayra. He will not be denied anything.

"Look you—all must be positioned so that he may see everything, and he can instantly and fully penetrate your nakedness.

"And when he does—such glory! Such pleasure. Such rewards. You will beg for him to penetrate you again. If he is pleased with you, he will take you again and again. And when you leave him, he will deck you in jewels and favors.

"And if his penetration proves a child, he will make you a chosen one.

"And if it is a son, he will make the child his heir and you reap all the prestige and rewards of the *kadin*."

There was a long moment of silence, as there always was, after her recitation, and then Sayra rolled herself to a sitting position.

"Has anyone ever gotten him an heir?"

Again that flash in Zenaide's eyes. "No one. Yet. He exhausts each new crop of passion slaves, and when they prove useless he must of course have more. It is why you were chosen. It is why you are here. You are the best of all of those who have been claimed. One of you will get the heir of the begoun. I feel it. I know it."

Her flat gaze moved from one to the other in the low, guttering light of the candles. "All over the *haremlik*, the mistresses are instructing their groups of new passion slaves. But mine must be the best. Mine must be the ones to command the attention of the begoun and get with child. You will do everything in your power to attain this goal."

She leaned forward and stared at Sayra. "*Everything*."

Sayra stared back. "I understand."

Zenaide got to her feet and moved across the room and began dousing the lights. "Yessss," she hissed, as the candles went out one by one, "I am absolutely certain you do."

* * *

The door was made of gold and it swung open on silent hinges to reveal a room so flooded with light from a three-sided square window bay that it was almost blinding to the eyes.

Arranged along the bay, on a dais, were long, low couches upholstered in silk, four torchieres, and a tandur for both heat and warmth.

Nothing else was needed against the vast expanse of windows that framed the couches. The dazzling light outside, the white of the surrounding buildings against the blue of the sky. The gilded and molded ceiling that looked like a representation of heaven.

Simplicity. Elegance. Restraint.

They stood on the threshold of the reception room of the begoun in the House of the Throne Room, entry to which was signaled by the brass gong outside the gold door.

"If you would be so kind," Shihab instructed him, "one kneels in the presence of the begoun until his signal. Then you may rise and join him. He will indicate where you may sit. It is usual for him to take one of the chairs to the side and for his guest to take the other. The couches are rarely used. The begoun dislikes direct contact with the sun but cannot forswear the traditional reception room of his forebears."

He stepped outside the door, struck the gong once more and said, "The begoun now knows I have instructed you as to what is proper. We will wait."

He stood as still as stone, still struck by the simplicity and the grandeur of the room. *The palace of a tyrant. The kingdom of an autocrat with no laws, no rules, no morality but what he decrees. What manner of man can this be?*

They waited; the room was so enfolding that it did not seem like any time at all had passed.

And they waited.

*Those windows—easy to break, easy to run, if only one can gain access without a guardian.*

*I need to figure out a map of this place. I need something to write with. I need something with weight to use as a weapon.*

He looked at Shihab, who returned his questioning look with a smile.

"The merciful begoun will attend us soon."

*He is so sure, so certain of his place and his allegiance. A man doesn't know where his loyalties should lie these days . . .*

A booming gong interrupted his thoughts, and a retinue of attendants moved slowly into the room from another golden door to the right.

A moment later the tall ascetic figure of the begoun followed, draped in fine-woven cotton, his hands folded under the long sleeves of a burnoose, his head almost fully enclosed by a ceremonial headdress.

Immediately Shihab dropped to his knees and covertly pulled at Sinclair's sleeve to remind him to do so as well.

He bent stiffly, and got down on his knees.

"Munificence."

"Shihab. Our guest?" The voice was deep, almost as if it were buried in his gut and he forced it up every time he spoke.

And Sinclair understood every word.

"This is he."

"Present me."

"My lord begoun, I beg to present Sinclair." This was spoken in the common language, and then Shihab turned to Sinclair. "Sinclair, my pleasure to present the exalted begoun of Kabir."

"I am honored."

Shihab translated.

"You may rise."

The tone was clear enough. "Shihab—on the stool next to me. Sinclair, choose which of my humble chairs suits you."

Shihab translated.

"The beauty of this room suits me," Sinclair said. "The chairs matter not."

"Very well," the begoun said, and seated himself in the one that looked like a truncated wing chair. "You may seat yourself."

Sinclair sat.

The begoun clapped his hands and a cadre of serving girls entered, bearing trays of food, the scent of which almost made him nauseous.

Two more servants brought in collapsible tables which they set up in front of Sinclair and his host, and one each by their side for the food.

The begoun leaned forward, and Shihab began to translate.

"I understand the good Shihab has offered my apologies for the manner in which you were abducted."

"Indeed."

"I am mortified that such a mistake was made."

"It is easy enough to rectify."

"We are of a mind to enjoy your company for a while, Sinclair. You have much to teach us."

Sinclair studied his eyes; the rest of his face and his mouth were almost completely obscured by the headdress, intentionally, he was certain. But the eyes—the eyes were alive, glittering with some emotion: malice? Almost as if he, too, understood every word that was being spoken.

*Oh, possible, entirely possible. How many such pashas had he dealt with in his career who were wily gamesplayers who thought every diplomat was a pawn?*

*But this one—there was a menace about him, an aura of both utter control and complete abandonment—this one . . .*

The silence stretched out as the begoun waited for his response to the invitation.

He knew all about silence. Someone would always break, and it was usually the one who wanted something.

The begoun poured himself a cup of coffee. "We know of your reputation, Sinclair."

He didn't expect that. That was dropping the other shoe way too fast. Or else—this was not part of the game.

"You flatter me," he said carefully, with Shihab translating. "I am sorry that your henchmen were not similarly knowledgeable."

Shihab hesitated, shot him a warning glance and finished the translation.

The begoun waved it off. "Ignorant peasants. How could they know? Come, a drink. Wine. Coffee. Something stronger? I can accommodate any preference."

"My preference is to set a date to leave."

Again Shihab faltered, and then finished the translation.

The begoun's eyes flashed with anger. "It will be at my discretion, and after we have spoken. You must sample the delights of Kabir. Perhaps you might change your mind and wish to stay."

Sinclair said nothing, and the begoun began picking at the tray of food, rare tidbits of meat he could insinuate under his headdress and eat neatly.

"Shihab will show you to your quarters and will attend you for the duration of your stay. Please, selim Sinclair, avail yourself of our hospitality, and let us both learn."

He had no choice. He nodded his head as Shihab translated. "How can it be other than the begoun desires?" he said, the irony coloring his voice and surely not lost on the begoun. "I am, from this moment forward, at your service."

# Chapter 5

"We will dine tonight with the begoun; he has commanded his passion slaves to be present to help him entertain a guest. A treat, my pretties. A feast for the mind and the body. To the baths with you. You will soak the longest, prepare the most thoroughly, smell the most beautiful, look the most enticing—quick! quick! Tonight he may choose. Tonight he may want . . . an opportunity not to be taken lightly. It has been so long. . . ."

Zenaide nudged them on with a suppressed excitement that seemed out of keeping with her usual phlegmatic manner.

She was disappointed to find others were there before them, and another mistress sidled up to her and made a sarcastic remark about her group, nearly getting herself thrown into the pool.

*This is serious, very serious. Tonight he may want you, she said; it has been so long, she said. . . .*

Sayra stood at the shallow end of the pool and allowed one of the slaves to scrub her body with fragrant soap.

*All these women, hoping, craving one thing—*

And into the tepidarium and onto a marble bench where another slave began methodically kneading oil into her body.

She loved the massage and the scents of the oils. She had chosen her own, the one scent with which she would be identified. After two weeks the slaves knew and could choose among the cruets of oil stored in the niches which scent belonged to which passion slave.

But today was different: today the massage was short and there was no repose after. Today each of the passion slaves was commanded to move on to another room recessed behind the tepidarium, where they would be shaved.

The humiliation was complete: There was no escaping it, with five slaves to hold you down and one to do the deed. And Zenaide supervising.

It took so much time, so much careful time; so much control to put the most delicate parts of your body into the hands of a slave who might or might not be skilled at what she was doing.

It was complete and utter obedience to the will of the begoun, who had dictated that no woman should appear before him with an unshaven body.

"And that should be all you need to know to joyfully submit to this ritual," Zenaide said harshly. "Stop crying! Babies, the lot of you. And the stoic who still rebels in spite of her deferential words. Oh yes, Sayra, one can see in your eyes. I was certain you would cause trouble. I knew it. And now it is too late. Go on, all of you. They must still dress your hair and line your eyes and make up your body."

"But surely . . ." Phyllida protested weakly.

"Surely *what,* passion slave?"

"We will dress for company?" Phyllida croaked.

"Why would we do that? The powerful begoun wishes to display the obedient passion slaves who exist solely to pleasure him. All this beauty belongs to him, is subjugated to his desire, crawls to him to beg for his favor. He will hide nothing another man can envy. Go now. There is much more to be done."

Phyllida scuttled away.

"That one will not be chosen," Zenaide muttered under her breath.

"That one is ripe to be chosen," Sayra said. "She is the embodiment of everything you have told us the begoun seeks in his passion slave. She is modest, virginal, beautiful, obedient."

"The new mistress of the passion slaves is, of course, correct," Zenaide said icily. "Nevertheless, you will go on to the next station; there is no time to lose."

Or there was too much time to have the body attended to when there was so little else that could be done to it after the depilitation.

Still, the ritual required it: the head hair oiled and dressed; the eyebrows elongated, the cheeks and nipples rouged; the nether parts gently rubbed with henna to outline the delicate shape. A wisp of transparent material to conceal the lips and mouth. A jeweled bracelet to call attention to the smooth curve of the arm. An anklet for a particularly pretty foot.

Zenaide lined them up and paced back and forth, eyeing them, making little corrections here and there.

"The gong will sound and we will proceed to the House of the Throne Room. You will walk with your heads down; you will not look upon the munificence of the begoun until you are commanded."

The gong reverberated through the Hall of Divans. Each group of passion slaves filed out of the barracks led by the mistress of her group. Each one's head was bowed, each one's arms were crossed over her midriff as she was commanded to accentuate her breasts.

Each one's heart was pounding with a combination of fear and excitement as they filed out of the House of Divans for the first time in two weeks and through the First Court that led to the House of the Throne Room.

From the outside this building resembled a mosque, with its domed roofline that rose several stories high.

Inside, it was rich with color, the floors covered in overlapping rugs, the ceilings gilded, the walls hung with fantastically embroidered cloths, an entrance way to the majestic Court Saloon where the begoun would receive them.

They entered through arched golden doors that were flung open by two eunuchs dressed in royal regalia.

This was the room beneath the dome; the walls here decorated with a golden lotus motif around the arches and in the friezes that spanned the space just below the dome. At the far end there was a bank of windows behind a colonnade of arches. In the center of the left wall there was a cushioned dais centered in a kiosk over which there was a canopy supported by four marble columns.

There was not a sound as they crossed the thick carpeting to the colonnade where, behind the arches and down one step, there were benches furnished with padded seats.

The Mistresses motioned to the passion slaves to line up behind the columns, all two dozen of them, where they would silently await the pleasure of the begoun.

*This is insane.*

Sayra couldn't help herself. She could not resist looking at the magnificence of the room, and the possibility of escape via the windows behind her.

*"Ouch!"*

Zenaide's cruel fingers pinched her back to reality.

*"Troublemaker!"* she hissed, twisting the tender skin mercilessly. "Did you not learn, rebellious one? You may not raise your eyes; you may not look at *anything!* If the begoun had caught you . . . stupid girl, stupid!"

Sayra lowered her eyes and resisted the urge to touch her bruised skin. "I hear you."

"You hear nothing, blighted one. And you shall pay for this as well, disgraceful one. . . ."

Sayra bit her lip. A vessel. A mindless crock; that was what she was. Never to think or feel or desire freedom ever again; to play the slave in this charade to display to the tyrant his wares.

How could she fight it? How could she accept it?

And what would she do if she were the chosen one?

She would not be; she would *not.* She would do something, anything, to make herself distasteful to the begoun.

She had to be more careful. She had to reconstruct the false front she must present to Zenaide; she had not hidden her true self nearly well enough.

And she couldn't give up hope.

She jumped as the gong sounded, and a reedy pipe began to play.

"The begoun in his glory comes!" Zenaide whispered joyously.

The golden doors opened, slowly, reverently. A retinue of slaves entered the room, surrounding two men, one tall, regal and impassive; the other slightly shorter, darker, dressed in a loincloth and a turban.

The slaves escorted them to the kiosk where, at the gesture of the turbaned one, they lowered themselves onto cushions placed at either side of the columned platform.

The slaves retired along the wall as another gong sounded.

This time a cordon of women entered the room, dressed in colorfully embroidered silks and veils, and moving carefully in rhythm with the music. They were followed by the piper and a half dozen other musicians carrying harps, drums and pipes who proceeded to line themselves against the opposite wall.

The women meantime had circled around the room and had formed a gauntlet by the door.

A third gong sounded, and the musician with the drum began a rhythmic beat.

A moment later the figure of the begoun appeared in the doorway, a tall, ascetic, menacing shadow swathed from head to foot in gold-embroidered silk robes.

The cordon of women moved, at his signal, and he followed them into the salon at a measured pace.

As if he wanted everyone to look at him.

And had taken the greatest of pains to make sure they saw *nothing.*

He seated himself cross-legged on the kiosk platform so that the canopy completely obscured the upper part of his body.

*Hiding his face. His expression. As if he were the sum total of his male parts and nothing else. Oh God, what manner of man is this?*

The music faded away; there was a long, full moment of silence, and then the begoun clapped his hands.

The turbaned one arose and turned to the colonnade. "The exalted begoun bids you welcome," he said, translating into several languages deftly. "I am Shihab, your interpreter. We are here to honor Sinclair, guest of the begoun, with entertainment and food. I beg leave to present Sinclair." He turned to the man seated cross-legged on the opposite cushion, who nodded stiffly.

"And now it is the desire of the glorious begoun to be presented to the newest of his passion slaves. We will begin. Nadea."

Nadea, one of the three Mistresses, immediately pushed forward the first girl, and the others meekly followed her out of the colonnade, one by one, their heads bowed, their eyes lowered, their arms enfolding their midriffs.

The begoun showed not a flicker of interest.

"Atiya."

Atiya's group moved forward into the salon, and each of her charges was introduced by name, as had been Nadea's, and still the begoun did not react.

"Zenaide."

Phyllida went first, Olga next, Amalie and Sayra, hanging back a step before Zenaide pushed her into the salon.

This was the worst, bending herself into this posture of submission. She couldn't do it. She wanted to see the tyrant. She wanted to make him reject her so she would be free forever.

She lifted her head, lowered her arms, squared her shoulders and marched into the salon like a queen.

He had never felt such consuming fury as he did as he watched the women captives parade passively by. There was nothing he could do—nothing. They were all subjects of the begoun to do with as he would.

The names were lost on him, and their naked bodies all looked depressingly the same, rouged up, garnished with jewels and utterly sexless.

And yet they were there to entice the begoun. They were there to be objects of passion for the begoun, with no free will, no right of refusal, no other desire than to please the enigmatic despot seated in the kiosk.

He had seen it before, but never flaunted like this in front of him. In other courts, in other places, he had been introduced to the slaves of the pashas in ceremonious entertainments similar to this one; but always the women were dressed, bejeweled, protected in modesty from the prying eyes of any man, even an honored guest.

But this—this was an outrage to the women, a humiliation in any other court to be paraded in front of another man like a prize mare. A brood mare.

He heard the names—"Phyllida . . ." an Englishwoman with some self-assurance in her walk; "Amalie . . ." a rabbit; "Olga . . ." passionate that one, swaying her hips slightly as she passed the kiosk and circled back toward the colonnade.

"Sayra . . ."

She moved out of the shadows of the colonnade like royalty, her head held high, and he couldn't take his eyes off her.

Such dark, flowing hair; her naked body perfect and proud, adorned only by a collar of gold around her long neck; her dark eyes flashing; her long, strong legs; he envisioned them cradling . . . who?

*I want her.*

He heard the muted moans of despair coming in a low hum from the colonnade.

*Jesus God . . . I want her—*

She was too arrogant, that one. The begoun would kill her sooner than bed her.

*And kill him without blinking an eye for his traitorous thoughts.*

She came closer and closer; her eyes focused on the begoun, seeking the secret of he who controlled her body and her life.

And when she came abreast of the kiosk she paused, and her gaze passed from the shadowy begoun to Shihab, whose face was frozen in horror, and finally rested on him.

He met her eyes squarely.

*I will help you. Somehow. I don't know how, but I will help you.*

She read the message in his eyes, in the set of his mouth.

*And I will have you . . .*

He had never wanted a woman the way he wanted her.

*He'll kill us both—but I will have you . . .*

*. . . Sinclair . . .*

*Hope—in his eyes—the hardest, iciest eyes I have ever seen in my life . . . he's English . . .*

Her heart pounded wildly. A gram of hope . . .

She stumbled as Zenaide's hands grabbed her and pulled her behind the columns and shook her.

"Oh, you will be the death of me, willful one. You have signed your death sentence and likely mine as well! How could you? How *could* you? With your honeyed promises and your pleas for mercy! And yet—and yet, you betray me, and now the begoun, in his mercy, will have your life. Trust me, lying eyes—those who do not obey find submission in death!"

"I—"

"You will not speak to me. Your tongue is poison. Your words are bile. And now it is too late—see? The begoun comes—prepare to meet his wrath . . ."

And he was, he was walking slowly across the expanse of jeweled carpet toward them, with Shihab three paces behind him.

The Mistresses and passion slaves sank to their knees, their heads buried in their hands, their whimpers and moans plainly audible.

"Down, you!"

Zenaide pushed her viciously, and she fell onto her knees.

"Do not look—do *not!*"

But she had to, she *had* to . . .

He was almost upon them, and she could see nothing. His face was swathed in white silk and only his eyes, deep set, hooded, burning with emotion, were visible.

He lifted his hand. He pointed.

Shihab whispered, *"That one."*

Zenaide's trembling voice responded. "Oh merciful One, I beg of you . . ."

"The begoun desires the one who throbs with life."

"He cannot—"

"The begoun has chosen."

Zenaide drew in a sobbing breath and grasped Sayra's arm, and pushed her to her feet up into the salon, and then shoved her down to her knees.

"Prostrate yourself before the most merciful of begouns. He has chosen you, ungrateful one. The begoun has decided, disgrace to all women, he wants you."

*Oh dear God . . .*

She moved involuntarily, as if she would rise to her feet and run.

Only Zenaide's iron fingers kept her in place.

"Never in the history of the *haremlik* since I have been a Mistress have I seen the begoun demand a slave who has so flagrantly disobeyed. You have no notion of your fortune, disgusting one. The begoun has given you back your life. But does the daughter of a dung beetle show gratitude? No. None. Nothing. He will kill us both over your stupidity. . . ." Zenaide whispered frantically, her fingers digging viciously into her arm.

"Say something, dung slave. Express your appreciation to your compassionate and forgiving begoun—"

She closed her eyes. She would die. Surely she would just die on the spot if that tyrant touched her. Dear Lord, how could she? How could she? And that Sinclair, with his impassive face and his glittering know-all gaze . . . he was just sitting there, doing nothing, watching everything with those icy eyes that had promised . . .

*What—? She had read in them what she had wanted to see: rescue, release, sanity—*

*They're all insane.*

*I'm insane.*

*I'm standing naked in this autocratic pasha's den of lust waiting for him to kiss me or kill me. . . .*

*What more could he do to her after her flagrant breach of propriety?*

Zenaide shook her. "Daughter of a gnat—beg his merciful forgiveness or he will squash you like the insect you are."

"Tell him . . . tell him—"

"Speak, vermin . . . avoid his eyes; speak to his feet, beg for your worthless life . . ."

Her gaze skittered across the room to Sinclair.

She could read nothing in his expression; he sat stone still. Not a flex of a muscle. Not a twitch of a nerve.

She was alone, dead alone, with the twisting pinch of Zenaide's fingers her only reality.

She swallowed convulsively.

"Tell him . . ."

She looked up at the tyrant who would signal her fate. From that angle she could see more than just the burning determination in his eyes; she could see the desiccated skin of his forehead, his demonic eyebrows, the curve of his cheekbone beneath the delicate fabric that concealed it.

*What manner of man . . . ?*

*A consumer of flesh who would suck the life out of any willing participant and kill her in the end . . .*

*There could be no other course but resistance.*

She took a deep, heart-stopping breath.

"Tell him—I can't . . ."

* * *

Her words echoed and reverberated through the salon.

The silence thickened horribly.

Zenaide moaned and threw herself at the begoun's feet in a torrent of self-deprecating words.

Shihab's eyes bulged and he shook his head wildly as he translated haltingly.

The begoun's burning gaze deepened as his eyes flicked over her with the intensity of little licking flames.

She skewed her eyes away from him to Sinclair, who had not reacted by as much as a flicker of an eyebrow.

She was utterly, utterly alone, and she felt as if her heart was going to drop right to her feet.

"Tell him—" She looked at Shihab pleadingly. "Tell him that in my life before I was a performer. Tell him . . . tell him I was accustomed to remove my clothes for money to drive men to lust."

Shihab translated, his expression revealing nothing; the begoun responded, never moving his eyes from Sayra.

"The begoun says, what has this to do with my desire?"

Now she felt a swooning desperation. "I am suggesting perhaps that the begoun would wish to view a performance . . . as an enhancement to . . . to—"

Shihab translated, and the begoun looked at her speculatively. "The begoun wishes you to elaborate."

She took a shaky breath and swallowed hard. *Elaborate?*

"Men would come to see me and they would pay to see me take off my clothes," she began tentatively, to the guttural underlay of Shihab's translation.

She saw the begoun's eyes sharpen with interest.

*There's something here—something that may save my life. What is it? What? What does he want to hear?*

She bit her lip. *What?*

"In my country, as the all-wise begoun must know, women dress in many layers of clothing. Therefore to see a woman remove her clothing incites a man, excites him, provokes him. And the woman who can do this, the woman who will undress for him—and those women who will simulate or engage in the ultimate coupling—they are the ones who reap the reward."

She could feel how intensely he was listening.

"The begoun wishes to know what do the men do, how do they act?"

"They offer money; the more money they bid, the more clothes the performer will remove until she is naked. And then . . . and then—"

And then she made a mistake: She looked at Sinclair.

Now there was emotion, a kind of judgmental male cynicism reflected in the twist of his lips and the unwavering iciness in his eyes.

She swallowed again. "And then . . . the performance ends. And after, the patron may choose to purchase a woman for the night to spend his energy and his lust."

"And with the women who simulate . . . ?" Shihab asked, in response to the begoun's question.

"She may choose a partner for the night who pays dearly for the privilege. Or she may not. In my country, in this situation, it is the choice of the woman."

Shahib translated to a spate of commentary from the begoun. "The begoun says this is of interest to him."

Her knees almost gave way.

"The begoun says you will perform for him, and he will choose a partner for you, and we shall see if the western ways can incite the exalted One who has experienced all."

Shihab listened again, nodded and translated. "The begoun requires that Zenaide prepare the passion slave and bring her to the reception room in an hour."

He turned to the others. "The entertainments for the evening are canceled. On your knees to the all-powerful begoun."

The drummer began a rhythmic beat. The cordon of women moved to surround the begoun; he motioned to Sinclair, and Sinclair got to his feet.

The cordon moved forward, and Sinclair followed them without a backward glance.

Silence again until the doors closed behind them, and then Shihab turned to the Mistresses of the passion slaves. "You are dismissed." He waved at Olga, Phyllida and Amalie. "All of you. You—Nadea—take them away."

He nudged Zenaide with his foot as the others filed out. "You—fool—on your feet; you have work to do."

"I am at the begoun's command," Zenaide murmured shakily as she maneuvered herself upright.

"And you, slave—you gambled well, but take heed—if you fail to ignite the passion of the begoun, all of our lives will be forfeit. And this time—there will be no way out."

# Chapter 6

"I cannot believe it, I cannot; it is unprecedented that a passion slave should reject the begoun . . . what is the world coming to? A slave dictating to the begoun . . . you!" She pushed Sayra roughly into the courtyard of the Hall of the Divans. "You—what were you thinking? You do not know—you cannot know. . . . An hour to prepare—it cannot be done. How can it be done to the satisfaction of the begoun? Unthinkable. Unbelievable."

She pulled Sayra around to face her. "I told them, you know—no English girls; they never submit. They never last long. They always think they can overcome. And they always die."

She let the stark words hang in the air between them.

"And so what can the puny English pudding show the begoun? *What?*" She shoved again, and Sayra went flying through the door into the hallway of the Hall of the Divans and fell to the brick walkway.

"Camel dung presumes to tell the begoun . . ." She thrust her foot into Sayra's ribs. "A maggot dictates to the begoun . . . a scuttling ant will be the death of us all. . . . Get up! Get *up!*"

Sayra climbed slowly and warily to her feet. Zenaide was screaming at her. Zenaide was scared. And she herself was petrified. What had she done but put off the inevitable? She had bought time, but not enough, not ever, to formulate some plan of escape.

An hour . . . barely enough time to bathe and get herself decked out in whatever she could find in the cupboards of the Mistress of Robes.

No time at all to think about dying . . .

Zenaide was circling her, brushing off the dirt from her body, muttering under her breath.

"Praise Begoun, there are no scrapes. You must go now and choose what you wish from the Mistress of Robes and the Mistress of Jewels. And then to the baths; there is no time to waste. The Mistresses will help dress you. Go now!"

She went, with Zenaide trailing behind her, excoriating her at every step, calling ahead to forewarn the Mistresses to pull out their best wares.

And then, what was there to choose from? Short, spangled, embroidered vests, flowing trousers, silken overblouses, jeweled girdles, golden slippers, transparent veils and skullcaps that tied under the chin. And she had no idea how to utilize these filmy materials to her advantage.

She threw out a half dozen pieces of clothing, some slippers, a head covering, a length of embroidered silk, a vest . . . she would figure it out later . . . and then on to the Cupboard of Jewels, and the Mistress there with a chest full of baubles for her consideration.

Earrings, assuredly; bangles, necklaces, an ankle bracelet . . . she didn't know—she didn't *know* . . . what would entice those burning, knowing eyes, what would bring *him* to life?

She ran for the baths, her slave following and Zenaide gathering up the clothes to bring them to her so that she could dress directly after bathing.

"Inconceivable . . . unthinkable . . . unimaginable," Zenaide kept muttering as she scurried into the bathing room and began laying out the wardrobe.

Sayra stood, frozen, in the center of the pool, with her slave vigorously rubbing her down with soap.

*This cannot work, this will not work; I will be dressed like any other woman he has ever had at his command. There will be no bidding, no excitement, there will be no crowd feeding each other's arousal . . . this is doomed—doomed. . . .*

She stepped out of the pool and up to one of the marble benches, where her slave proceeded to rub her body with fragrant oil.

"There is no time, no time. The gong will sound and we will not be ready, and the begoun . . . begoun will kill us . . ."

Zenaide was voicing her every fear.

"Be quiet!"

"Oooh, a bold one you are, pestilence from the sea. Now you have a moment of the begoun's favor and you think you can order the Mistress of Passion Slaves. You think there's nothing to fear; you think there is no death for those who fail."

"I think if you want me to succeed, you had best be more positive that the begoun will be receptive to my performance," she said brazenly, as her slave motioned for her to sit up so that she could dress her hair.

"No, leave the hair . . . tell her, Zenaide . . ."

"Foolhardy—" Zenaide muttered and translated her words. "Well, there are the clothes. Take what you will."

She lifted up a pair of silken balloon trousers. *She's right, this is impossible. I would look the same as any other passion slave.*

"How much time is there?"

"Thirty more minutes by my reckoning; no more and possibly less."

"Tell the slave to get me a knife and a needle and thread. I must make changes." *Now where did this come from? Desperation? She had no idea what she was going to do, except that she must emphasize the exotic differences between herself and the begoun's other women.*

*The things he knew must not be known about her. She must convert all this film and gauze into something that was as English and constrained as possible.*

*A fool's errand in a half hour . . .*

"Tell her . . ." she directed Zenaide. "Rip open the seams of those black silk trousers and sew them up the front like a skirt. Don't argue; just *do* it!"

Zenaide stared at her angrily and then gave the instructions to the slave. "And what next, your lowly highness?"

She was fingering a length of spangled gauze. "I need some kind of undergarment; this will do." She began winding it around her breasts and up and around her neck. "And that black satin chemise—have her cut down the front of it—neatly—that's right."

She slipped it on over her makeshift undergarment. "Yes. Is that skirt ready? It doesn't need to be fine-stitched, you know."

Zenaide handed her the skirt and she stepped into it. "This will do. I need a belt now—one of those coin chains. And the vest. Thank you."

"The passion slave has taken leave of her senses," Zenaide muttered.

"The passion slave is trying to save both our lives," she snapped.

"You could have done that easily by crawling into the holy bed of the begoun this evening. But you—all of you Englishwomen—you must make things difficult. Always you must make trouble. And always you die . . ."

She ignored Zenaide. "I am almost ready."

"You look . . . you look foreign."

"That is the point. Why give the begoun that which he can command already?" Sayra said as she clipped on the earrings. These were exotic—and real, diamond dangles that glistened like dew. "I think we must pull up my hair." She snapped her fingers and her slave came forward. "Tell her."

Zenaide translated and the slave shrugged.

"I will do it then." Sayra lifted her hair and began winding it into a tight chignon.

"This is forbidden," Zenaide said, her voice tinged with panic.

"Nothing is forbidden for this evening's performance."

"A woman never, ever constrains the glory of her hair."

"Tonight she does," Sayra said grimly, searching around for something with which to pin her thick tresses. "Here—" She found a stickpin. "Push this through." She pantomimed what she wanted the slave to do. "Ouch! Ahhh . . . it will have to do. Now—"

She stood up. She was absolutely layered in clothing—the skirt, the undergarment, the chemise that was belted with coin belt, the gold-embroidered vest.

"I need slippers now, and something to wind around my neck."

Zenaide handed her what she required without comment.

"I am ready."

The gong sounded.

"You are reckless and irresponsible and we all will die," Zenaide said as she led the way from the baths.

The gong sounded then, as if to underscore her words, echoing with an awful clarity through the *haremlik* and startling them both.

"It is done," Zenaide intoned. "Pray for the mercy of the begoun."

The torchieres were lit in the reception room, and the flickering light cast eerie shadows all over the walls.

Sinclair and Shihab stood by the door, awaiting the gong that signaled the arrival of the begoun.

"This is unprecedented," Shihab whispered. "For most holy Begoun to request the carnal pleasures of the voyeur—this is . . ." He stopped short; he didn't know what it was, except so unusual that any eyewitness to it might well be marked for death, and he was chilled by the thought.

"But the woman," Sinclair said. "The woman is accustomed. In my country she is no better than a trollop, a whore, a doxy, available to any man who has the money to buy her."

*The bitch, the utter knowing, flaunting bitch, and how the hell she got herself to Kabir and in the begoun's harem was perfectly plain: She wanted it, she wanted all the carnal pleasure she could handle, and what better place than where a woman was a slave to one man's desire?*

*She was perfect. Ripe. Ready. A body made to be possessed. Loving her nakedness. Wanting to arouse every man in sight. Provoking. Wanting it. Never getting enough. Made for the harem, where that body would be used just the way she wanted it.*

*He should have known. What would such a creature be doing among the passion slaves unless she was there purposely? Unless she wanted the opulent life of the odalisque. Unless her erotic fantasy was to be naked and waiting for the carnal possession of he who ruled the harem.*

*He hated her, and he hated his impulse to want to rescue her. She was no better than she should be: a woman who removed her clothes for money in another life, so that men could ogle her and lust after her. She could make the choice, and reject them or spread her legs for them as she desired.*

*And she must have desired. This was no innocent kidnapped from the bosom of her family.*

*This was a wanton. He should have seen it in her eyes, and in the voluptuous way she strutted before the begoun.*

*She loved her nakedness. She had loved seducing the begoun with her lascivious words. And she would love showing herself off to him.*

*An English rose, all soft beauty and pointed thorns; let a man take her whom she did not desire—and she would prick and he would die. . . .*

*He was a fool to have seen only the soft petals of urgency and need unfurling in her intelligent eyes.*

*Now there was only one need, one urgency—his own—and he knew exactly what he had to do. . . .*

*All those windows . . . surely there was a way—*

A gong sounded, and he suddenly became aware of Shihab's scrutiny.

"Ah, Begoun comes soon," Shihab whispered. "Selim Sinclair would do well to concentrate his efforts on the exalted One. Selim is far, far away in places he should not explore, even in his most secret thoughts."

"I have no idea what you are talking about."

"Selim's mind wanders, wishing, desiring, planning for what cannot be. Kabir is a city in the clouds, selim, and to think one can escape it is merely to desire death."

"You speak in riddles."

"Take warning, selim; there is no way out short of jumping a thousand feet from the seawall. And even then you will never escape the wrath of the begoun."

"This is of no concern to me—but out of curiosity, tell me how this is possible . . . if one is dead."

"Begoun will make sure to retrieve your body, selim, and then—Begoun will *eat* you."

The gong sounded again, as if to underscore his words; somewhere beyond, a drum began a slow dirge of a beat.

Moments later two eunuchs entered, carrying a platform covered in red silk, which they set down in the middle of the room.

A third eunuch entered, his arms piled high with embroidered pillows which he strew around the platform before he and the other two exited the room.

And then there was silence, a hard, thick silence tempered by Shihab's shocking words and his own hardheaded disbelief.

"When our exalted begoun enters," Shihab whispered finally, "you will approach, make your obeisance and seat yourself as he commands you. This is a special honor accorded you by the exalted One. Begoun permits himself so few of the secular pleasures."

*So few of the secular pleasures . . . and yet this self-styled ascetic pasha had the reputation of a glutton, feasting on the voluptuous nakedness of a hundred beautiful willing women . . .*

*And tonight, this one in particular . . .*

He felt his groin tighten and forcibly pushed his proprietary feelings away.

A third gong sounded, a low, reverberating, mellifluous note to herald the approach of the begoun.

He felt Shihab's elbow against his ribs; he looked across the room and there, framed in the doorway, backlit by a luminescent glow and accompanied by the drum dirge, stood the begoun, swathed in gold and shadows.

He moved slowly into the room, almost as if he were floating inches off the ground, attended by a naked eunuch who reverently held the hem of his robe.

He paused midway into the room, as if he was waiting to be acknowledged, and Shihab fell to his knees, pulling Sinclair unwillingly down beside him.

The begoun spoke, and Shihab lifted his head.

"The all-seeing, all-knowing exalted One welcomes selim Sinclair to his presence to share the treasures and pleasures of his harem."

Sinclair raised his eyes. "Tell the begoun I am honored."

Shihab translated, listened, and listened once again as the begoun issued his commands.

"Begoun requires that we crawl to the pillows beside the throne chair, Sinclair. You will be seated next to the all-powerful One and you will be permitted to share all. Do not protest this. It is a test of compliance."

"What is not?" Sinclair muttered, hoisting himself onto his knees to follow Shihab's painstaking progress across the wide expanse of jewel-toned rug.

"It is so little to do for the privilege the exalted One has granted," Shihab panted, motioning to the pile of pillows beside the gilded throne chair as he climbed onto his pile. "It is done. Begoun is well-satisfied at this mark of respect."

Sinclair folded his legs under him and looked up at the shrouded figure which had followed them step by slow step.

*How far to go? Those eyes—those burning, knowing eyes . . . I know he understands all, as I do when Shihab translates. A test for me—a test for him . . .*

"A man who commands another to crawl to him deserves no respect at all," he said brutally, staring at those impenetrable eyes.

*"Selim!"* Shihab cried in horror. "This is blasphemy! I cannot—I will not translate this gross violation of the exalted One's hospitality. I do not know what to do, what to—"

The begoun spoke, his glittering eyes boring into Sinclair's equally icy ones.

"Begoun says . . . Begoun says. . . . he thanks you for your kind words," Shihab translated, overcome with amazement. "Begoun says we will now enjoy the pleasures of the evening."

The eunuch helped him into the throne chair and then took his place behind the pillows where Shihab and Sinclair were seated.

The begoun spoke again.

Shihab clapped.

The drum began once again, this time in an urgent, pulsating rhythm, accompanied by the reedy pipe, from somewhere beyond the doorway.

And then *she* appeared, silhouetted against the doorway from which the begoun had entered.

She walked slowly and deliberately into the room, around the platform and in front of the begoun and his guests, swinging her hips, exaggerating her walk so that they could fully appreciate how tightly she was clothed.

It was a little drama—she swayed and strutted, all the while wiping her face, pulling at her collar, lifting her skirt, waving her hand in front of her face as if she was so hot, she didn't know what she might do.

. . . perhaps remove her gold embroidered velvet vest? She shrugged out of it and tossed it across the room.

Oh, but it was still not enough—she tore off the shawl she had tied around her hips at the last moment, threw it over her shoulder and then breathed deeply.

But she still was so hot; she ripped the collar of the chemise to bare her collarbone and just the shadow of her breasts above the concealing underwrap.

She could not get cool enough. She sat down on the platform, lifted her skirt and proceeded to painstakingly remove her slippers to bare her feet.

Oh it helped; just a little, it helped. The cool air against her naked feet.

She stood up, stepped off the platform and simultaneously tore the chemise off her body.

Now she stood before them clad in the makeshift skirt girdled with the coin belt, the long golden chain swinging against the tight underwrap that concealed her breasts.

Her head fell back, dislodging the stickpin. She crossed her arms over her breasts and began pulling at the wrapping, and pulling, clawing to find the tucked-in end of it so that she could pull the constraining cloth away from her body.

She found it; she held it up triumphantly, and she slowly unwrapped the cloth, pausing for a heartbeat before she pulled it away from her straining breasts.

And then she lifted the material and let it drift to the floor as she bared them to her audience's avid gaze.

She walked toward them, her arms crossed under her midriff to lift her breasts, her hips thrusting forward in an exaggerated manner so that the skirt slipped downward by small fractions as she moved.

When she came close she removed her arms and wound the chain around her neck and under her breasts, and she lifted her arms to thrust them further forward, and she began shimmying her whole body.

The skirt slithered downward; the coins on her golden belt made little chinking sounds as she contracted her stomach and writhed her hips to work off the last piece of clothing.

She was hot, oh so hot, and her nipples were taut with longing, and the skirt was the only thing impeding her way to the lover she desired.

It slipped into a pool of black at her feet and she paused, her arms over her head, her hair tumbling now all around her shoulders, so that they could see all there was to be seen.

And then she turned and moved to the platform and climbed

onto it, one leg extended, her back to them, so that they could appreciate the long fluid line of her back as it curved into her hips and buttocks.

And then she was up on the platform, reveling in the lush feel of the silk as she rolled onto her back and then her side to face them, her one leg angled upward so that nothing was hidden from view.

Over again onto her stomach, her upper body lifted to display the outline of her breasts and stone-hard pointed nipples.

Up on her knees next, her breasts swinging between her arms, the tips of her thrusting nipples brushing the sensuous silk-covered platform.

Slowly then, pivoting on her hands and knees to show off her legs and the cushiony curve of her buttocks.

And finally curling into a ball so that all they could see were her buttocks and the enticing cleft between.

She did not move; the air was thick with lust and desire. She knew what it felt like—steamy, wet, sweaty. It was so silent, she could hear the shaky indrawn breath of one of them—or all of them. She could feel the pulse of arousal, the hard-driving male need thrumming in the air.

But this time no one was bidding; this time she had played for an audience to whom she could not say no.

She bit her lip and wriggled her body.

She heard the voice of the begoun.

Shihab translated.

"Sinclair—undress you and take her."

She felt a jolt of pure terror. Sinclair of the icy eyes who had watched her every move with rampant male skepticism . . . dear Lord—

. . . *take her?*

She heard the soft slough of material as it was removed, the pad of his feet as he came closer and closer, and finally the tight grasp of his fingers as they dug into her hips.

Strange male hands handling her; her body began trembling, she couldn't help it. She had never been touched like this—ever—and he would never believe it.

She turned her head so she could see him; his face was expressionless as stone, and then he leaned over and cupped and covered her body so that he could just whisper in her ear.

"I won't hurt you."

"You will," she whispered. *He had—another he—once in the dark . . .*

"Begoun commands. I will be in and gone before you know it."

*How like a man . . .*

"You will not get in," she hissed.

"I'll try or die, harem whore."

"Then he'll kill us both," she swore as she felt him probing between her legs, pushing, pushing, painfully pushing, and finding no hot passage to paradise.

"And he will, harem bitch, especially if he finds out you lied to him."

"I told no lies."

And she probably hadn't; but he didn't have time to find out if she was a virgin vixen or the best pretender on the planet.

*Jesus—almighty . . .*

"You're going to tell a whale of one now. Up on your knees and spread your legs, whore; I'm going to slip between them, and then you're going to moan and groan and writhe as if your life depended on it, and I'm going to pump you and hump you and get us both out of this mess, and I hope I never see you again. *Now,* bitch—move it for all you're worth. . . ."

She moved—she felt him guiding her body backward against his, and him slipping between her legs so that the shaft of him rested against her shorn cleft; and then he began a slow, steady rhythm, cushioned between her thighs, stroking her nakedness with arrogant surety.

"Love it, harem whore—show the impotent bastard you love it—" She heard his hard, rasping whisper, she felt her body responding to the way he was handling her—the hard heat of his hands pushing her and pulling her, and sliding all over her buttocks and hips with an urgency all out of proportion to the pretense.

Or was it a pretense?

The feel of him handling her—the hot, hard stroking of his

naked male root against the virgin nakedness of her—the voluptuous sense of the angles of him against the softness of her . . .

She moaned, she writhed against him, she sought to contain the mystery of him as he pushed like a piston between her legs, as she felt the long, stabbing thrusts of him caressing the naked innocence of her; she reached for him, she bore down on him, she felt the long, strong pleasure of a man in the throes of seeking his pleasure.

It could not be more.

He wished it were more; her skin was so soft, he wanted only to feel it. Her response was so natural, so giving; he felt her movement, her excitement, her seeking his thrusting shaft; he felt the unfurling of the petals of the rose as she pushed herself against him willingly, soft, dewy, enfolding, hot from the sun . . .

*Like the harem whore she is; like she's been trained to do. Pretending to love it. Pretending to want it, when all she wants to do is arouse men beyond their capacity to think . . . that's what a harem bitch does. That's what a harem bitch is . . .*

He felt her movement as she shimmied beneath his hands, the chinking sound of the coin belt underscoring each thrust of their bodies. He heard her soft, fluttery moans deep in her throat. He felt her nakedness, all his for the taking . . .

*. . . anyone can take the harem whore; that's what she's here for; that's what she's trained for . . . to strut around naked and to spread her legs for whoever wants her—there could be a line of men waiting for her, and she would take them all, the bitch, because that's what she wants. . . . that's what she came for—to be a whore in a place where nothing is forbidden . . .*

*. . . smart harem bitch, living in luxury with all the men at her feet she could possibly ever want . . .*

*. . . and all she cares about is making them want her by flaunting her naked nipples . . .*

*. . . she made me want her—made me insensate with wanting her . . . the bitch—never again . . . never, ever goddamned ever again . . .*

*. . . I don't want her—*

*. . . I just want to . . .*

*—with a harem whore . . .*

He jammed himself against her, over the edge, spewing and

pumping into the nestling curve of her thighs, against the wet heat of her womanhood, right there, naked, willing, he didn't care—he wanted to ejaculate all over her, to mark her with his scent and his seed.

He collapsed onto her, pushing her down, wiping himself against her so that she was so covered with him, no one could question whether he had fully possessed her.

"Don't move, whore. Pant. Groan a little. Make him think you were a full participant in the event . . ."

She felt his hot breath against her ear, and a stirring resentment of him that superseded every other feeling.

She took a deep breath and sighed.

"Better. You are definitely excellent at what you do."

"And what is that, Sinclair?"

"Faking it. Faking everything, I wager. . . ."

She felt like slapping him, but she was flat on her face, and he was lying against her, his lower torso pinning her, his manhood quiescent.

"But here we have excellent proof that a man may fake things as well, Sinclair."

"The only proof we have is that I can command my body to save us from this jackal's hell. Don't expect mercy next time."

"There will be no next time."

"Shhh . . . he clapped his hands."

The begoun spoke, his words muffled by the way they were lying.

Shihab translated.

"The begoun says the performance was intriguing, though he has never seen the like. He is pleased by the masterful possession of the passion slave by Sinclair. I must inspect the passion slave now."

She started shaking all over again.

"What is he going to do?"

"Examine you, of course," Sinclair said heartlessly. "Surely you expected this."

"Who knows what to expect from this madman," she muttered, even as she felt tears stinging her eyes and Sinclair lifting off her so she could roll over and sit up.

"The passion slave will remain on her back," Shihab said.

She levered herself up onto her elbows.

"What are you going to do?"

"I must ascertain that Sinclair has indeed spent his seed in the vessel of the passion slave."

"He means spread your legs, whore. But you don't care for whom you spread them anyway, do you?"

She could have killed him. He had gone from being a ray of hope to being the voice of doom. He had condemned her without knowing her circumstances. He thought she was a liar. He thought she had come here willingly. He thought she *wanted* to be here.

He lifted himself off the platform, and for the first time she got a look at him naked.

He was tall, so tall; his shoulders were ropy with muscles and his back was long and strong and tapering down to his narrow hips and the tight curve of his buttocks. His legs were long and corded with rock-solid sinew, and when he pivoted to face her she saw the firm strong root of him nesting in a thatch of dark, wiry hair between his legs.

She was so captivated by the sight of it that she was barely aware of Shihab standing tentatively beside her, staring at the evidence of ejaculate all over the lower part of her torso.

"The seed is spilled," he pronounced.

*. . . from that—to this—how fascinating . . . I want to touch him . . . he thinks I'm a liar; he saved our lives . . .*

The begoun spoke again.

"Begoun is much taken with the performance. He will see it again, tomorrow, at his pleasure."

Her head jolted up and away from the entrancing sight of Sinclair's maleness.

*"What?"*

"Begoun is well pleased with the passion slave and his honored guest. He will have more, tomorrow."

The begoun spoke; Shihab answered and then turned to Sinclair questioningly.

Sinclair looked first at Sayra, then at Shihab and finally into the opaque eyes of the begoun.

"How else can one respond? It is an honor to serve the begoun and service the passion slave."

The begoun nodded and drifted across the floor toward the door with his eunuch following. A moment later he was gone.

"An excellent choice, selim," Shihab murmured only after the begoun had exited. He clapped his hands.

Immediately, Zenaide appeared from what hidden cubicle Sayra could not guess.

"Take her away until tomorrow," Shihab directed, as if she were an object to be lifted and put back in a closet or a drawer.

"Begoun shall be served," Zenaide said reverently, pushing her out of the reception room above her muttered protests.

And then there was silence—blessed silence—and the scent of lust and culmination.

Shihab turned to Sinclair and bowed.

"And so, selim—it was not so unpleasant to obey the command of the begoun after all, eh? Dress yourself. Such expending of energy deserves a healthy meal. We dine with much happiness tonight. Begoun is pleased and his will has been served!"

# Chapter 7

"Merciful Begoun that he did not kill you for your insubordination," Zenaide muttered as they raced across the courtyard to the Hall of the Divans. "Oh, you live under some lucky star, you dungfish from the ocean, that you have survived the wrath of the exalted One and incited his curiosity. Blessed Begoun that his foresight encompasses all that comes before him with compassion and even-handedness—even a mere woman."

Zenaide pushed open the doors, and immediately the other women rushed forward and surrounded them, babbling away in a tumult of languages, with Amalie, Olga and Phyllida shoving everyone out of the way to get to her first.

"What was it like?" Olga, wide-eyed.

"Did it hurt?" Phyllida, certain.

"Were the lights on?" Amalie, breathless.

"What did he look like?"

"Where did he touch you?"

"Did you do everything Zenaide taught us?"

"Was it good?"

"What did it feel like—the penetration—?"

"Did you feel anything?"

"Was he pleasured?"

Zenaide pushed them away. "Shoo—shoo! There is nothing to tell. This unruly cow managed—merciful Begoun—to beguile the exalted One. Let it be a lesson to all of you: the eternal begoun appreciates imagination and a certain crafty boldness. And that is all you need to know."

"Will he reward you?" Phyllida, this time her eyes gleaming with mercenary lust.

"It is too soon to tell," Sayra said warily, taken aback by the onslaught of questions and avarice she saw in their faces.

"Enough! It is not seemly to make such inquiries. The honorable begoun moves in his own time, at his own pace. But I will tell you"—Zenaide looked around at the crowd of them, and particularly at the several other Mistresses of the passion slaves, as she spoke and then translated—"that the almighty begoun is so besotted, he has requested my clever passion slave for this coming night."

The crowd of women shifted and murmured excitedly.

"She is a rarity among passion slaves, one our merciful begoun seeks for a second night of pleasure. Learn well from this, you who listen. What rewards cannot be obtained when one is clever and obedient at the same time? Search in your hearts for when it might be your turn, and know you that it was *my* passion slave under *my* guidance whom the exalted One desired for more than a night."

She turned to Sayra. "You now—to your bed. You will be sequestered as a mark of favor of the begoun. It is inconceivable—and yet it is . . . he would wish you not to be contaminated by the comments and questions of the others. Come now; there is a private closet, and a slave to do your bidding. I can count on the fingers of one hand how many passion slaves have occupied this room."

Sayra followed her out of the Hall of the Divans and into the garden, where the air was fresh and sweet and moist with the all-saturating heat.

And there, a dozen yards along the wall of the doors to the Hall of the Divans, was a smaller door with a latticed window. Zenaide pulled it open and motioned for her to enter.

Here was another brick-paved corridor, but at the end of it was a large square room hung with silk and tapestries, with thick overlapping rugs on the floor and a soft mattress covered in satin in one corner.

In front of this was a low table on which there were covered dishes, and there were pillows on the floor, and soft candles everywhere.

"Begoun must be pleased," Sayra murmured, utterly dismayed

by the opulence of this sequestered room. "Or is there a secret entrance where he will come to ravish me?"

"Foolish bitch. The merciful begoun needs no secrecy. He will have you at his will and you will crawl to him at his pleasure. There is food there for you, and your body slave, who is Mirza, will come presently and bathe you. All this, you stupid sow, because the exalted One was ravenous for something new and different and it was your good luck to provide it. Next time—well, who of all those sullen pigs would have the imagination to divert the jaded senses of the all-knowing begoun? Only the English sows, and they are *always* troublemakers. Eat your food, malcontent; you will need your strength. Do not make trouble, and do not retire before Mirza bathes you."

Zenaide stared at her for a long skeptical moment. "I do not understand the wisdom of the begoun, but then—it is not my place to understand, only to obey . . ." She shook her head, "—and still it is inconceivable . . ."

She left Sayra then, standing in the middle of the luxurious room. The door closed emphatically behind her, and Sayra sank to the floor, into the silky pile of the carpeting, on her back, staring at the gilded ceiling and the fretwork on the windows.

*The pleasure of the begoun—a mystical thing, enacted by whom? Whoever happened to be his guest for dinner?*

*I cannot believe this is happening . . .*

She rolled up into a sitting position and scuttled across to the table and lifted one of the covers on the dishes.

*Lamb . . . ummm—oh, and fish . . . and rice and fruit . . .*

She was ravenous suddenly, shoving the food by the fistful into her mouth, as if all her attention to that one task could block out all thoughts of anything else.

*Not hardly.*

She sank onto her haunches and poured some wine from a squat little pitcher.

*What am I going to do tomorrow?*

*And what if he wants—he wants . . .*

*I won't think about it. He won't. He can't. And that arrogant stallion will never . . . if I have to kill him . . .*

*If I have to do . . . what I did—*

*No!*

She climbed onto the mattress and reached eagerly for a piece of lamb coated with ginger and almonds and stuffed it into her mouth.

*No! I will dress, I will do—anything—to get out of this place . . . anything he wants . . . I'll be his harem whore if that's what he wants, I'll do even that . . .*

She licked her lips. . . . *even that* . . . Remembering the feel of his hands against her nakedness.

. . . *didn't grab her by the hair and pull her to the floor in the dark recesses behind the stage at the Pig and Poke . . .*

. . . Remembering his stroking, knowledgeable fingers as he caressed her buttocks. . . . the weight of him as he covered her . . .

. . . *didn't throw her to the ground and heave himself over her, his trousers undone, his manhood lunging, ripping apart her dress . . .*

. . . Remembering the tentative feel of something hard pushing at her authoritatively, prodding, probing, pressing . . .

. . . *thrusting between her legs—hard, unmerciful, dry, ripping, tearing . . . hurt—her groping hands shoving him, feeling for something, anything . . . her screams muffled by his huge, hot, sweaty hands . . . the scent sweat and lust; she knew it in her dreams . . .*

. . . Remembering the length of him, thrust into the cushion of her thighs, seeking her heat, seeking to save them . . .

. . . *in a floorboard, a loose nail, rusty, creaking, desperate, yanking it, bucking off the feel of the invader; his snarling threats, her trembling hand lifting it . . . so slow, so slow, up and over; and him never noticing the movement of her arm, up and over slow and over . . .*

. . . Remembering the urgent pump and pound of his body against hers as he drove himself to completion . . .

. . . *the spew of blood as she attacked him, driving the nail into the throbbing veins of his neck . . .*

. . . Remembering the spew of his seed, sticky, wet . . .

. . . *sticky, wet . . . over—*

. . . *over—*

. . . *safe—*

. . . saved—

She closed her eyes. . . . *not a virgin—*

*Not a whore.*

*Safe—*

*Until the next time . . .*

"Oh . . . and here is one who has lived to tell the tale."

The voice was low, throaty, knowing.

She looked up. Her body slave, a towel on one shoulder, stood at the door, tall, slender, naked, her skin the color of rich coffee, her hair streaming down her back, and cradling a pitcher of water against one hip.

"You are Mirza?"

The woman nodded.

"You speak my tongue."

"At the will of the all-merciful begoun am I here and at your service, treasured one."

But she said the words in such a way . . . as she hovered by the door. "The exalted One's chosen must command me," she amplified.

"You may enter."

She dropped to her knees and began the slow crawl toward the mattress.

"Mirza . . ."

"It is the custom, treasured one. I do not mind."

"It's ridiculous."

"You speak so and yet you live . . . Begoun must be overcome with passion."

Now Mirza was before her, on her knees, her intelligent eyes assessing everything about her.

And she stared back, trying to read into that ironical tone and those lively eyes whether Mirza was sincere or whether she was trying to tell her something.

"There will be a second night."

"Praise Begoun!" Mirza exclaimed, and dropped her head to the carpet. "A miracle that all may live. Who is this lamb of sacrifice who has so captivated the heart of the exalted One?"

"I am called Sayra."

"May you live beyond tomorrow," Mirza murmured, almost like a prayer.

"I visit Begoun again tomorrow."

"Merciful Begoun—can it be so soon? What can it mean? The treasured one has so bewitched and entranced the almighty, all powerful begoun that he cannot go one night without you? Oh, treasured one—guard your secrets . . . there are those who would kill for them."

"There are no secrets. There is only a bath and then sleep."

"How can one sleep after having seduced the unobtainable One?"

*. . . harem whore . . .*

*Unfathomable reaction.*

*. . . what if she were a spy for the begoun . . . ?*

She shivered.

"My understanding is that you are to bathe me . . ."

"And to watch over you, treasured one, that those disposed to jealousy and rage cannot harm you."

"Nonsense." And it was—all these intimations of cat-fighting; if only they knew . . .

*. . . harem bitch . . .*

*The opaque and omniscient begoun watching, watching, salivating at every thrust and moan, at the sounds and the scent of someone else's sex permeating his space, lapping up every prurient moment of his naked slave submitting to the male root of his choosing . . .*

*That was power—*

*And he was going to wield it again . . .*

"The treasured one will allow me to tend to all her needs."

"As you wish." Sayra lay back against the pillows and watched as Mirza poured the water into a dish that was attached to the pitcher on the underside, and in which apparently there was soap and a fresh cloth with which she would bathe her.

A soft cotton cloth skimmed her body as Mirza deftly washed every inch, and under her arms, between her legs and buttocks, down to the soles of her feet, thorough and light as a moth wing.

"The treasured one is beautiful, out of the common way. Begoun must be beside himself," Mirza murmured, keeping up a hypnotic commentary as her hands worked magic on Sayra's skin. "A second night. An event that will be retold for millennia in the lore of the harem. A second night to tempt and tease the unknowable One. What must one learn when one has the almighty One at her beautiful feet? What vast knowledge of the ways of men can be garnered from bringing the all-powerful One to his knees? Oh, would that the treasured one be gracious and share her secrets before she finally receives her just reward . . ."

The words had lulled her; she was floating on a great puffy cloud of pleasure and only those words . . . "finally receives her . . . just reward . . ." pierced through, like little jagged bolts of lightning.

*Zenaide had talked of the rewards of pleasing the begoun. Living in luxury for the rest of one's life . . . what else could it have meant?*

*And yet—there was that challenging, ironical tone in Mirza's voice. To be read how? What was real?*

Her eyes popped open. "What do you mean?"

"Ah, treasured one . . ."

" 'Just reward' . . . what does that mean?" She struggled to sit up. "You said, when you entered, that I am a one who lived to tell the tale. What did you mean?"

"I meant nothing, treasured one. I meant . . . I meant . . . it is not easy to surrender oneself to the desire and the will of the exalted One. There are those who faint at the prospect. Who go to his bed screaming for mercy. But you—treasured one—you are not such a one, and I am proud to serve you."

She resumed her cleansing. "The unobtainable One will come love you and then we will all be free."

*Now what did that mean? . . . We will all be free . . . here is a one who lived . . .*

"The glutton who desires all women could never savor just one," Sayra said brashly.

Mirza stopped her movement. "But one doesn't know. There has never been a one who pleasured him so . . . at least in my lifetime here. There are stories, of course, just as your night with Begoun will become the stuff of legend. But I will vouch for it; I was the honored slave of the treasured one. My name will go down in history."

She pushed, and Sayra turned over onto her stomach. Mirza began the soothing strokes of her cloth down Sayra's back.

"And if one does not please the begoun?" Sayra murmured lazily.

The stroking stopped; there was a pause, almost as if Mirza were debating how much to say, and then she said stiffly, "One thing that can happen is that one is relegated to the status of body slave."

Sayra felt the chill. "You were sent to him."

"He rejected me. I had not the chance. I have fallen from grace forever."

"And what is another thing that can happen?"

Mirza turned her head. "I have no knowledge."

*Evasion . . . so there is something—something . . .*

"Mirza—"

"Ask me not."

"I ask you."

Mirza's eyelids fluttered; her expression was pained.

"Does not the water feel delicious against the skin of the treasured one?"

"I am chilled," Sayra said, and she meant it. Her skin felt constricted; she felt as if she was on the edge of a precipice, and there was a shadow behind her that would send her over the edge.

"I will fan you," Mirza said, getting up and removing the pitcher, the bowl and the towel. "And the treasured one will sleep."

"Tell me, Mirza."

Mirza lifted one of the hangings on the bed wall and removed a huge paper fan and then crawled her way back to the bed.

"There is nothing to tell, treasured one. I know nothing . . . except . . . except"—her voice faltered, and then she finished in a whisper—"the whereabouts of those women are unknown as well."

*. . . unknown . . .*

*How many women had passed through the harem doors and utterly disappeared?*

She was shaking; she was lying on that soft, luxurious bed in the dead of night, a body slave sound asleep at her feet, a candle guttering in a pottery bowl, and she was shaking as if she had a fever.

*I'm doomed. There is no way out of this. Women have died—*

*and I am one who has lived to tell the tale . . . dear Lord . . . for how long? For the next five minutes?*

*He sends his minions around the world to find flesh for him to devour . . . and he's never satisfied—*

*Oh, God . . .*

She couldn't sleep. It was impossible to sleep. Every shadow seemed like a threat. The slightest movement from Mirza sent her imagination skittering.

She swung her legs over the edge of the mattress and levered herself into a sitting position.

*I have to get out of here. . . .*

She reached for the squat pitcher to pour herself some wine to moisten her mouth.

Nothing . . . but she couldn't have drunk it all; she must have slept, and Mirza could have taken advantage of it. . . .

She was going crazy. All she had to do was open the door and walk out.

She got up and padded across the room, her heart pounding wildly, the shadow of her body preceding her like some ghostly presence.

For an instant the door looked as forbidding as the entrance to a prison.

*But this room isn't a prison. . . .*

She grasped the handle and pulled.

*. . . or is it . . . ?*

Her heart fell to her toes.

There was a guard at the door, his huge, muscular back to her, immovable as a mountain.

She closed the door slowly and leaned against it, feeling as if the walls of the room were closing in around her, too.

There was nothing, nothing—a huge high-ceilinged room, perfectly square, its ceilings molded and gilded, its windows placed out of reach, so high even a ladder could not reach them. And no other furnishings but a mattress and a small oblong table.

*Food brought in. Slave walked in.*

*. . . and knew that a fan was hidden behind the wall hangings . . . What else was hidden behind the wall hangings?*

She reached out her right hand and felt for the material adjacent to the door, and lifted it.

*. . . a wall, plaster and pitted with age—damn—no wonder they covered it up . . .*

*. . . but still—*

She began walking down that side of the wall, her hand slipping along the silk, feeling for any irregularity.

There was nothing.

She turned to the perpendicular wall and slowly moved her hand up and down the hangings.

*. . . how possible is it that the only thing behind the hangings was the fan?*

*What do I think I'll find? A rabbit hole?*

*. . . a—crack . . . ?*

She scrambled behind the silk—and there, midway between the door wall and the window wall, was a door fitted precisely and evenly into the plaster, white as the plaster, with a little brass fitting incised into it.

She recoiled.

*A door . . . to where?*

She touched the brass fitting.

*Real . . .*

She poked at it and pulled up a little brass hook that just fit around her finger.

*Oh, God . . .*

*Pull it? . . . Push it? Drop it and run . . .*

*. . . nowhere to run . . .*

She lifted the hook and pulled.

The door moved, swinging toward her silently as sin.

Darkness beyond, and a matte flat scent spiraling out toward her, as if it was reaching for her.

*And she wanted to go . . .*

*Anything, anything to escape—*

The darkness beckoned her, and she envisioned just walking into it and finding oblivion.

*. . . but what would she find—really . . . ?*

*. . . in the dark . . .*

*. . . what if it were the doorway to hell . . . ?*

*. . . what if it were the true, secret, only way out . . . ?*

*She had to try—there was nothing left but to try . . .*

Still, she was scared down to her toes. And it was so dark—

She wheeled around to her bed. There—that . . . all those columns of candles . . . she grabbed two, a fat chunky one and a taper, and lit them both in the wavery shimmer of the floating candle.

She used the bowl to prop open the door and set the fat candle in it, and pulled the silk hanging over the door and out of harm's way.

Then, lifting the taper like a torch, she stepped over the threshold and into the darkness.

She was in a narrow tunnel walled in stone with a curved ceiling and a cool stone-paved floor that angled downward, almost as if it was forcing an intruder to move forward.

She took several tentative steps.

*This is insane. I'm insane.*

*No, the whole situation is insane—*

She took a deep breath to calm her pounding heart and kept moving. Anything was better than standing still.

*Yes, I'm walking in a dead dark tunnel stark naked, looking for a way to escape a tyrannical pasha who devours women as if they were sacrificial lambs . . .*

*Does this make any sense?*

She held the candle higher, bracing herself with one hand as she crept along the tunnel.

*She was the sacrificial lamb—hadn't Mirza said . . . not a woman had pleased the begoun in her memory . . .*

*. . . of course—Mirza wasn't very old . . .*

*. . . "the unobtainable One will come to love you," she had said, "and then we will all be free . . ."*

*. . . because otherwise—we'll all die . . .*

She swallowed convulsively.

Maybe it was the air. It was thick, suddenly, and dank, as if some unseen force was sucking it out of the tunnel.

There was nothing else, just darkness and clamminess, and then a faint smokiness as she moved deeper into the tunnel.

*I am crazy; this is such a gamble . . .*

The scent of smoke intensified, and then suddenly, way before her, she saw a slim finger of light.

*. . . daylight . . .*

*Or a cruel joke . . .*

*One or the other depending, on the whim of the begoun.*

She stopped abruptly at the thought—and caught herself as she just missed toppling down a short flight of steps.

*Oh, my Lord . . . f a person weren't looking and just heading for daylight and freedom—*

It smelled like death, suddenly. There was a cloying scent in the air, distinctly unpleasant; she started panting, taking short, sharp breaths to avoid inhaling as she crept slowly down the steps and over to the opposite wall.

The light was brighter here, and as she edged toward it, she could see that it emanated from a wooden torch chinked like a sconce into the stone wall.

*Freedom around the corner . . .*

*. . . or death . . . ?*

She was just at the edge now, barely able to breathe in the malodorous air, barely breathing at all.

She froze as she heard noises around the corner.

She held her breath; she heard her heart pounding like a parade drum in the silence.

She waited, with rising hysteria, for death to claim her.

And there was nothing—but the ominous sounds of something thrashing around beyond the light.

"Who commmmmmesssss?" The voice was deep, guttural, hissing like a snake.

Her bones melted from pure fright. She couldn't move. She couldn't do anything. She pictured the monster in the shadows savoring his sadistic pursuit, and reaching out finally to claim her.

*. . . naked . . . stupid . . .*

"Is it one of my prettiessssssss?" Its voice was a gurgle, deep in its throat. "They promised me some prettiesssss . . ."

She was going insane—the voice was speaking English.

She swallowed the lump in her throat.

She had to look. She had to *see.*

She plastered her body against the wall, as if it alone held her upright, and she eased her head around the corner.

And back again.

*A joke . . . a prison . . . a light leading nowhere but to an empty space with bars closing off one end, and a shadowy figure rising like a monster from the flames . . .*

She felt faint . . . from the odor, and her fear, and that ungodly voice . . .

"Who . . . who are you?"

"Aggggghhhhh . . ." A gurgle. "English, are you? They sent the Englishman, didn't they? Didn't they? Yessss? Yesssssss . . ."

She couldn't move, she couldn't; her limbs felt like water, and she would just collapse into a puddle if she so much as twitched.

"Tell him, my pretty . . . tell him that Luddington is here. . . . Tell him—the masters arranged it allllllllll . . ." A deep inward asthmatic breath. "Tell him—Ferenc lives . . ."

Her muscles jerked involuntarily as she heard the name.

"Tell him—Ferenc is everywhere and he'll never get out aliiiii-iveeee. . . ." Its voice rose to a crescendo. "Aaaaggggghhhh— the hunger . . . it never stops—you can't kill it—you can never get enough . . . aaaaggghhh. . . ."

She saw him fall to the ground; she heard a noise, a slurping noise, a sound like gnawing, as if he were a dog with a bone.

She dropped to her knees and crept around the corner . . . closer . . . ten steps closer . . . it was all she needed . . . she could see it clearly, too clearly, the blood, the bones . . . a skull—

She screamed—a heart stopping scream of pure terror—and she ran—an animal operating on instinct only, she ran, scraping her feet on the steps, dropping the candle in her fear and ferocious need to escape—racing up the canted floor of the tunnel as if it were level.

And behind her the demented hissing voice of the monster, his voice rising to a horrific shriek: "Ferenc comes . . . Ferenc comes . . . Ferenc comessssssssssss . . ."

# Chapter 8

She felt as fragile as a porcelain doll.

She hadn't slept; her eyes felt grainy, and her body trembled involuntarily as if she was cold.

She flinched from Mirza's touch as Mirza awakened her.

"Ah, treasured one—" Mirza murmured. "You have not slept. It will be said that I have not done my duty. . . ."

*No, you haven't—you've done the begoun's duty, but that will end, that will end.*

"You will bring me something to eat and drink," she said sharply, "and then we will sit and talk."

Mirza stared at her. She stared back.

"I am at your command," Mirza said, bowing her way out of the room.

And then she was alone.

She didn't want to be alone. It had been bad enough to lie awake the rest of the night with the knowledge of the secret tunnel. She still couldn't believe what she had seen, what she had heard.

She didn't know how she had gotten out of the tunnel. Her hands were scraped raw from rubbing against the walls as she felt her way back to the room.

And all night long all she could hear was that voice, and all she could see was the blood dripping from the monster's hands and mouth, and all she could think about was all the *treasured ones* who had appeased his hunger.

*Why was she thinking like that?*

*Because the debris at his feet looked like . . . bones—*

She wasn't hungry. Her mouth felt dry, her skin felt like bisque—cool to the touch, brittle in strength.

*I have to get out of this place . . . that man—that Englishman . . . Sinclair, his name. Icy eyes. He is not of a temperament to put up with this much longer. He must help me escape.*

She bit her lip.

*How can I use him?*

*How far would I go?*

She might have no choice about that, either; she was absolutely certain the sexless begoun would hand her over to Sinclair once again, and this time there would be no way to prevent the inevitable.

She knew it. But that man had been fully and functionally aroused by her performance. So it was only a question of seducing him, so that he would save her, too.

She felt chilled again.

*Surrendering twice, all in the name of survival . . .*

The door opened, and Zenaide entered, carrying a tray.

"Merciful Begoun—finally you understood the awesome power of the almighty One. Mirza tells me you did not sleep. Let me look."

She marched straight to the bed, set the tray on the low table and pulled Sayra to her feet.

"There are circles under your eyes. Hmmph . . . we do have much work to do. But the reality is now evident: The begoun commands all. You are but a flea in the universe, a life form useful in the moment and easily crushed when your part is played. Praise Begoun—it is a hard moment when the passion slave comes to realize that her life is dependent on the will of the beneficent One. . . ."

"On the whim, you mean," Sayra muttered, wrenching away from Zenaide's clawlike hands and sinking onto the mattress. "I'm hungry. This is a lot of nonsense and I don't want to listen to it."

"The passion slave feels just a little potent, does she, because Begoun has chosen her for a second night? Ah, but the second night is the hardest, lowly one."

"One only has to hope that Sinclair is the hardest," Sayra interpolated rudely as she uncovered the tray. The scents almost made her sick. Fruits, almond paste, some kind of bread, sweet coffee . . . she picked up an apricot and bit into it.

*Like soft flesh . . .*

She choked.

Zenaide watched her. "Let me pour your coffee, treasured worm. I am not so easily fooled as Mirza."

*So Mirza told her I wanted to talk.*

"The only one easily fooled is the passion slave," she retorted, taking another bite of the apricot and ignoring the proffered cup.

Zenaide set it down. "The Mistress of passion slaves is not a servant. Mirza said you wanted to talk."

"Oh, you have said enough, mistress. There is nothing more to talk about."

"You are very wise not to pursue this further. Your sole function is to prepare yourself to receive the rapture of the begoun. We need to do much work." She clapped her hands and the door opened. Mirza appeared, followed by the eunuch.

Mirza dropped to her knees and began crawling across the floor, her soulful eyes focused on Sayra.

"Take the tray," Zenaide directed the eunuch. "And you—filthy piece of refuse—get off your knees and take the treasured vessel by the hand to the baths. Enough of this nonsense. Begoun's will be served!"

She lay facedown on the marble bench and several work slaves hovered around her, kneading her flesh, rubbing her with scented oil, massaging her, warming her skin, her thoughts, her desire.

They were so smart, the work slaves. They knew how to prepare a passion slave for her work. Every part of her was subject to their knowing, stroking hands.

This was different than before. Before, she had not proven she could command the attention of the begoun.

Now—

Now she was a *treasured one*—for however long *that* designation might last—

*Long enough to make a plan.*

*One hour . . .*

*No, one day—just one day . . . enough to talk to him . . .*

*Long enough to . . . I don't know what . . .*

*I have to make sure the begoun asks for still another night—How . . . how?*

She felt languid, sleepy; the horrific images of the night before receded as the work slaves' magical hands seduced her into a light, mindless sleep.

*Just for a moment . . . just—to forget . . .*

*No, she couldn't forget . . . not a word of what that monster had said—*

"Let me see you." Zenaide, standing over her, her voice as sharp as an incision.

One of the work slaves rolled her over and Zenaide inspected her face. "Very good. The circles are gone. Your skin feels soft and warm; I instructed them that you should soak for two hours. And now the lotions and creams. Yes, the slaves have done excellently well. Don't move. Mirza will bring you a choice of garments. Praise Begoun, the undisputed One has requested his passion slave favor him with the dress of Kabir tonight."

"As he wishes," Sayra murmured, turning onto her stomach again.

"As he *wills,*" Zenaide corrected sharply, clapping her hands again.

Mirza appeared, her arms full of silk, gauze and velvet.

Zenaide held each garment up before her. "What say you?"

"Remember I must be able to easily remove each garment."

"I forget nothing, treasured butterfly."

"No, you don't. Let me see." Her imagination raced. Something different, yet the same. Conceal and reveal, that was the whole trick of being a Position Girl. Men were the same, whether they were in a pub in Wixoe or a luxurious pasha's castle.

What she had to gamble on was that Sinclair was the same as well.

"Black, I think," she said finally as Zenaide spread several garments on the tile floor. "Some veils. That headdress. Those silk trousers. I want something to cover my face. Some jewelry, too . . . bracelets—a necklace . . . let me look at the trousers."

Mirza held up the garment, which was made of a fine translucent silk and was girded at the waist and ankle with jeweled bands.

*Now how do you make the common dress of Kabir into something seductive and out of the ordinary?*

*Just as you did to make the skirt—you cut . . .*

Her heart started pounding. This was daring. More than daring. This was flouting the begoun's custom.

"I want the trousers cut, Mirza, so that the only part of me that is covered is my legs. Do you understand?"

Mirza looked at her blankly. Zenaide sent her a skeptical look and translated her words.

"Are you sure, treasured vessel?"

*No, she wasn't sure . . . not of anything, but she must seduce Sinclair into a fury of desire for her.*

*. . . with all that entailed . . .*

"I'm sure," she said resolutely. "One must be the same, yet different. Why would the most exacting of begouns want that which he can have already?"

"Ah," Zenaide sighed, nodding in agreement as she waved at Mirza to do her bidding. "You have come to that understanding as well. I am well pleased with your insight. The imperious One is indeed fastidious and demanding. And yet . . . the one whom he claims will be the queen of eternity . . ."

*Won't she just—dead in the jaws of the monster in the tunnel . . .*

She shivered.

"Ah, treasured chalice . . . the thought is so seductive, is it not?"

*She's mad; I have to escape. . . .*

"Forever the chosen of the sovereign One, forever in his bed, awaiting his rapturous possession. Praise Begoun to live such a life of unremitting pleasure!"

"Until there is an heir . . ."

"Yes, until the child. And then, a life of luxury and leisure. There can be nothing more a woman could want."

*You think not? Stupid old woman . . . dear lord—they're all insane, all of them . . .*

"You have crossed a boundary no other woman in my memory has crossed—a second night with the most particular One. Our names will be legend in Kabir, treasured receptacle. Only you know what you must do. I will provide whatever you need."

*I need some answers. . . .*

"What about the others?" she asked curiously. "Phyllida, Amalie . . ."

"They remain pretty English peaches with no imagination or taste. I venture to predict they will eventually become body slaves. They will not be tried, treasured receiver, and so they will never fail."

"I see . . ." Sayra murmured. Immured forever, sisters in sins that would never be committed. "I want some water now, and then to sleep."

"The treasured vessel may have anything she wishes." Zenaide clapped her hands, and a line of slaves came marching into the tepidarium with trays of food. "Anything," she whispered as the trays were set down before the marble bench.

"Anything," Sayra murmured so that only Mirza could hear, "anything but freedom . . ."

She slept. And finally it was time for her to dress. The tepidarium was empty by that time of all slaves except Mirza, whom she had requested.

*Anything . . .*

The garments were laid at her feet, and Mirza was brushing her hair.

"I could not help," Mirza whispered. "I must tell all. The walls have ears."

"Even this?" Sayra asked, looking at herself in a hand-held mirror.

"No, this I will not tell."

Her eyes met Mirza's in the mirror.

"Then tell me this . . . what of the passion slaves who have failed?"

Mirza's eyes grew rounder. "There can be intercession. I was a one. A eunuch in favor with my mistress of slaves . . . the others—oblivion . . . I cannot say more."

"And will you tell?"

"I will not tell. If they watch, it seems only that I request instructions from the treasured one . . . tell me what you would have me do."

"He will never find favor with any woman." She caught herself, she hadn't intended to say that. And Mirza looked positively terrified.

"He will find favor with you, treasured one. He has never requested a second night. He will come to love you, and you will save us all."

*. . . the burden of it . . .*

*Dear Lord . . . save me—*

"I will dress, and then you will summon Zenaide."

*Cut-out trousers and layers of veils. What else was there to pique the interest of the oppressor who could not be seduced?*

*But the Sinclair—oh, he was another matter altogether . . .*

*He was going to save them both . . .*

"Ahhh, the treasured vessel is beautiful, mysterious . . . praise Begoun . . . how can he not succumb?"

Zenaide at the door, beckoning to her. "Come . . . your audience awaits . . . the drums are beating; the heart of Begoun quickens as he imagines the delights to come. . . ."

They were walking through the garden now, toward the Hall of Thrones.

"How discriminating, the all-knowing One—only Begoun knows what is best, what is right for Begoun . . . and every chosen one heretofore has been a tragic mistake. Oh, we rejoice in the good fortune of the treasured vessel. No other one has ever been so called. Praise Begoun she has come among us. . . ."

They entered the Hall of Thrones to the pulsating sound of the drum.

"Hurry—" As they raced to the entrance to the throne room, which was shrouded by a curtain. "Listen to the drums. They are pounding with the message of Begoun's desire. Now, treasured vessel, *now* . . . ." She held back the curtain. "Your second night. Now—Begoun awaits you. . . ."

"Selim Sinclair—she comes . . ."

He could hardly miss her as she posed provocatively against the curtain, swathed in layers of gauze with jewels at her ankles, hips and neck that flashed through the material as if it was transparent.

She was transparent. She was just waiting to slide out of that gauze and present them with her naked body.

And he would wager a feather to a farthing that the begoun was going to hand her off to him again.

And this time he would show no mercy.

He watched with shuttered eyes as she slithered into the room—different today, pretending she was a whore of Kabir, looking as exotic as an English rose as she pranced around the room in a flurry of delicate material.

How soon then before she needed to strip herself naked for them? How long could she bear the feel of silks and gauzes against the skin that yearned to be bare?

How long could *he* wait?

She paused before him, shimmying to her knees before him, her whole body shrouded but for her glowing, knowing eyes.

She danced away from him, and immediately a length of gauze slipped from her shoulders. A turn, and another length of gauze pooled at her feet.

Now only her hair and face were covered with silk; and her breasts, wrapped around again, and a short skirt over the transparent trousers.

She climbed onto the platform, wriggled her body and turned to face them. Slowly she lifted her hands to untie the material that was wrapped around her breasts. So slowly it fell away from them, as if it wanted to cling like a man's lips.

She slowly rolled to her feet, the silk still in her hand, and unfastened a clasp around her waist, and the short thigh-length skirt pooled at her feet.

And she was naked—and she was not.

Her breasts were bare; her face was covered but for her eyes. Her legs were encased in the thin filmy silk of the trousers. And between her legs, nothing—no modesty whatsoever. The whole of her femininity starkly outlined against the dark frame of silk.

*Goddamn her . . . I want her now . . .* He felt it, the charge of his manhood the moment she revealed her nakedness.

*And look at her—squatting, spreading her legs to show herself off. Pulling the silk enticingly through as if it was caressing her instead of what she so artfully desires.*

*. . . playing with it . . . a whore to her soul . . . she was never as innocent as she pretended . . . sliding it between her legs like a lover . . .*

*Wrapping it around her breasts . . . rubbing it on her nipples . . . enticing her men like a whore . . . learning new tricks in the harem, the bitch . . .*

He wanted her. He wanted to pound her right through the platform. He wanted to tease her and taste her. He wanted to make her forget any other man she had ever seduced. . . .

And now she was walking toward him, still rubbing her nipples with the silken cloth.

He could inhale her scent—harem lotus, thick, sweet, voluptuous—he could see her eyes, flashing with arousal, and she was coming to him, to him, as if she knew, as if she were demanding . . .

Crouching before him, her legs spread, her naked nipples just within reach of his hand . . . moving as if she wanted it, wanted him . . . snapping the silk that had caressed her sex against his cheek, and then a breath of a whisper—"Save me . . ." before she dropped to her knees in obeisance before the begoun.

And then turned to reveal her naked buttocks in the enticing silken frame before she crawled back to the platform.

She paused there, in preparation for climbing onto it, her head touching the floor so all they could see was her naked bottom, and then she lifted herself onto the platform and curled herself up once again so the light played on her buttocks. And then on her stomach, her knees, so she could crawl around to face them; on her haunches then, and her hair unveiled in a wild tumble down her back; on her knees in a bold stance so that her nakedness was clearly visible to them.

And then the silken length reappeared in her hand, reminding them of the erotic use to which she had put it.

She waited in the thick, charged air of the room. She leaned backwards, bracing herself on her arms, and reached for a pillow from a pile of them behind her. Levering herself upright again, she insinuated it between her splayed legs and lowered herself slowly onto it.

*Oh, the bitch knows what she's doing. She knows what she's doing to me . . . "Save me"—I wouldn't save an inch of her for anyone else. I'll devour her so there's nothing left . . . who else but a bitch would ride a pillow . . . Jesus . . .*

The begoun stood up abruptly and barked a command.

"Begoun says—enough! Begoun commands you to strip off what is left of her clothing and take her."

He was out of his cotton shirt and trousers in a heartbeat, and he walked slowly toward her.

She watched him, every step, every spurt of his unruly manhood that pumped out before him as if it were reaching for her.

"No mercy, whore . . ." He pitched his voice so just she could hear him.

She writhed her hips teasingly and her eyes kindled. "I have to talk to you."

"You've already said everything a whore needs to say. You're going to get what you want. . . ."

"I want to get out of here. . . ."

"Who cares? You're where you belong, whore, and I'm here to take full advantage."

"I have to talk to you. . . ."

"Your nipples say it all, bitch. Get ready . . . he's waiting . . . he wants me to take you full bore. . . ."

Her eyes changed, for just a second. He was at the edge of the platform, ready to push her on her back and penetrate her every secret.

"Listen—"

"No time . . . Get over here. . . ." He reached for her.

"Luddington . . ." she whispered desperately.

He froze. "Shit . . . damn—don't say another word . . ." He could feel himself wilting . . . just a fraction, with all her luscious flesh his for the taking. *Damn, damn, damn . . .*

He climbed onto the platform and eased her down on her back. "Don't say anything . . ."

"You have to . . ."

"I don't *have* to do damned anything," he growled. *Except ram myself into you and pound my way to oblivion. Jesus. Damn it . . .*

He felt himself spurting again at the thought of it. She was his for the taking, spread out before him like a delectable feast.

And the begoun was waiting.

He buried his face between her legs. He heard her frantic shriek—"*What are you doing?! What are you doing?!*"

He felt her body straining against the invasion of his tongue and he pulled her more tightly against it.

She was so soft and wet and musky; her scent permeated his pores. Her body bucked against him, exciting him all the more.

She cried and moaned, her body writhing this way and that as she tried to negate her feeling of helplessness.

His hands were tight on her thighs, pushing them apart, delving with an insatiable ferocity into the very core of her.

He couldn't get enough of her. He wanted to contain her. Her body was sweet, liquid, hot, luscious . . . innocent—he was the first to take her this way, and he relished the knowledge and dismissed the contradiction.

She was his; in this long, slow, swollen moment, as she hovered on the brink of discovery, she was utterly and completely his. He possessed her the way no other man ever had before, and no other man would in the future.

She was full and ripe, and she was feeling him, suddenly, feeling the expert pull of his tongue and lips against the most intimate part of her.

She stopped bucking and started bearing down, easing his way, sinking into a languid acceptance of his possession of her.

*The harem whore wanted what he alone could give her.*

*Good.*

*And he would give it to her so she would never forget; he wanted her to know, to feel, to remember his carnal kiss for the rest of her days.*

She screamed; he felt her body shiver and contract as he made the ultimate contact. He pushed himself into her, sucking on her, kissing her, pulling her culmination from her in frantic gasps and groans.

And then her hands tried to push him away, and she began kicking him and moaning, "No more, no more . . ." and he eased himself away from her and crawled up beside her.

He felt like jamming himself deep inside the hot, wet heat he had just tasted and damn the consequences.

She was too beautiful; her eyes were closed, almost as if she didn't want to see what had happened, and her body was flushed, her nipples taut with lingering need.

He leaned over and licked the nearest pointed tip and then closed his mouth around it and sucked lightly.

"Omigod . . ." she breathed.

He relinquished the pressure enough to speak. "They're still watching. We have a long way to go, harem whore. You talk. I'll play. You taste good, by the way. . . ."

He took her nipple in his mouth again and she gasped. A ladylike gasp, as if even this sensation was a complete and total surprise.

*Jesus . . . He was going crazy if he was rhapsodizing over the nipples of a whore in a harem . . .*

*But God, she was delectable . . . and too innocent for words—*

*The begoun would devour her . . .*

She was moaning with pleasure, her body arching against his mouth, seeking his insatiable tongue.

"*Talk . . .*" he hissed.

"Oh, God, I can't . . . what you're doing . . ."

"Ignore it . . ."

"I can't . . . He's . . . a monster . . . in a cell . . . tunnel—he said . . . he said the masters arranged it . . . he said . . ." She shuddered. "He said—to tell you . . . Ferenc—lives . . . oooohhhh . . ."

He took her then, with his fingers this time, inserting them boldly between her legs as deep into her as he could push into the wet heat of her.

"Oh, God, what are you doing?" she whimpered.

"Saving you . . . saving us . . ." he muttered, rooting after the other breast.

*Us . . . he'd said it . . . shit—he couldn't let himself think He had to put on such a show that he would gain them another day. That was all he needed, another day.*

"Moan and groan, whore, you know how to do that. . . ."

"Isn't it enough?"

"Nothing is enough . . . spread your legs. I want him to see everything I'm doing. . . ."

"What more does he want?"

"I can't guess; all I know is I'm bursting for you. . . ." He pulled at her nipple. "God . . . I don't care what you are—I have to have you. . . ."

She made a small sound in the back of her throat as he removed his fingers and climbed over her.

*Gorgeous face. Full lips. I want them . . . I want her . . .*

He pushed, and she opened to him; he thrust . . . and he was home, deep inside the wetness and the heat and the essence of her that still lingered on his lips.

*Heaven—*

He didn't have to demand her response; it was there, real, pulsating with need. He could have spent himself right then.

But he was aware of the audience that wanted to savor his possession of the whore. They wanted to see every last intimate detail. They wanted him to jam himself inside her with long, plunging strokes, and they wanted to see her writhing in ecstasy and begging for completion.

And he would make her. He of all of them could make her beg. The harem whore begging for his size and his sex to fill her, to excite her, to bring her to screaming rapture the way neither of them could.

He would take her with him. She would be his alone. Naked for him. Open for him. Waiting for him. Willing for him. Begging for him . . .

*Your harem whore . . . that body, those nipples . . . her luscious sex . . .*

He rode her hard; he couldn't get enough of her. Her hips bucked and shimmied under him; her eyes were wide open, reflecting a dozen different emotions . . . all out of an innocence he could not ascribe to her.

"Beg . . ." His voice was hoarse, his body dripping from his exertions. "Beg me for your pleasure . . ."

"You're crazy . . ."

"You're putting on a play, whore. Get the words out . . ."

"*You* want to hear the words—"

"You're goddamned right I do. *Do it . . . !*"

He was particularly pleased when she caught her breath at one long, slow lunge and then began panting and moaning, "Oh . . . oh, please . . . oh! . . . oh! That feels so good . . . more—give me more . . . oh! You're so big . . . it feels so good—more . . . more—deeper—oh! oh! Fill me up . . . give it to me . . . make it pleasure me—"

He believed her. She was very good at begging; he believed it, she knew how to do it—no innocent here . . .

"Ohhhhhhh . . ." Her groan was loud and long and violent as he began his frantic last thrusts to completion. "Ummmm . . . ahhhhh . . ."

"Jesus . . ." he muttered. "Bitch . . ."

"Hurry . . ."

"The hell . . . you're going to come if it takes me all night—"

"So big," she moaned. "So hot . . . so . . ." She drew in her breath suddenly, explosively. "Oh my God—!"

She was feeling it. She was feeling every long stroke, every hot thrust. Her body changed, her rhythm quickened; she pressed down on him urgently; her body began shifting to meet his every movement.

She was with him, and he reveled in it. He rocked against her, strong as a mountain, the peak against which she was climbing to explode against the sky.

Any minute . . . her body pulsated with need and knowledge and comprehension that it was he who would unleash her shattering culmination.

It was coming, it was coming; he felt her stiffen, widen and let go—in a guttural wail that chilled him with its erotic intensity.

Her body convulsed against him, once, twice, three, four times in a frenetic seeking of the ultimate pleasure, until the ballooning feeling broke inside her, gushing like a geyser to the rhythm of her moans.

He rocked against her, giving her his hard strength, feeding the pleasure with short, hard strokes that he ceased the moment she shook her head.

"Another minute . . ."

"I can't . . ."

"You have to—"

And he wanted it; he wanted to explode inside her and leave his seed soaking into her very vitals. He wanted it.

It took one long, hard thrust, and he was gone, over the edge, into ecstasy, drenching her body with all his need and all his sex.

And she looked up at him, in the throbbing aftermath, and she whispered, as if nothing had happened, "Luddington . . . the monster said— . . . he said—Ferenc is everywhere—he said . . . he said—we'll never get out alive. . . ."

# Chapter 9

*So this was the feeling, this was the way . . . all that pleasure encompassed in the unfurling of a woman's soul . . .*

She lay as limp as a rag doll against the pile of pillows with him sprawled, spent, beside her, his unruly manhood still as long and strong as an iron pole.

The air was saturated with the scent of their sex; the silence was thick, ominous.

Finally, the begoun spoke, Shihab translated. "It is time for me to ascertain that selim Sinclair has spent his seed on the passion slave."

"Let him do what he needs to do," Sinclair whispered, turning his face to her so that the movement of his lips was barely visible. "God, I hate this. . . ."

"Do they watch you all the time?"

"Except when I relieve myself."

His eyes kindled. "There's that much at least . . ." he began, as Shihab stepped up onto the platform and knelt beside Sayra.

"It is well; Sinclair has expended himself upon the passion slave."

He listened as the begoun spoke.

"Praise Begoun, he is much taken by the passion slave's performance and selim Sinclair's stamina. He commands you to strip the passion slave naked and take her again in the way of master and slave."

She caught her breath. Sinclair had no such reservations.

"I am pleased to service the passion slave in whatever way the begoun directs," he said, rolling up to a sitting position, his jutting manhood as imposing as if he had not depleted himself in her ten minutes before.

He levered himself onto his knees and straddled her legs. "What the hell is he talking about?" he whispered.

"You do your part," she hissed back, "and I'll do mine."

And he did; she had no choice in the matter. He shifted her so that their voyeurs would have a complete view from the side of this performance. He lifted her and slipped the gauzy black veil with which she had caressed her body under her.

And then he slowly worked off the crotchless silk trousers, bending over her, his long fingers stroking her, his voice barely above a breath.

"I think we'll get another night. I'll figure something out. Where was Luddington?"

"Imprisoned in a secret tunnel behind the wall hangings in my room. They isolated me. I'm one of none who has held his interest for more than thirty seconds."

"Keep wriggling like that—he likes it. I like it."

"I can tell. I can't see anything else but your . . . your—" Words failed her.

"You're not supposed to see anything else; I want you to only . . ." He insinuated his fingers between her legs and under her body to caress the crease between her buttocks. ". . . look . . ." as she writhed under the expert caress of his fingers, "at . . ." which came forward in a long, deep stroke over her sex, ". . . me—" and up to gently stroke one tight, taut nipple.

And then he ripped off what was left of the silken material and tossed it at the begoun.

"Get ready . . ."

"I—" *Magic fingers, long and strong, working on her, feeling her, brushing the tight cleft of her sex, seeking her . . . was she ready? Did she not know all the secrets of Eve ? And still he could seduce her . . .*

She wasn't even prepared for the feeling of silk sliding between her legs and gently pressing against her womanhood as he pulled it out from under her—and tied it around his neck.

*All the scent and sex of me—*

"Now . . ." he breathed, spreading her legs.

Immediately she angled them, lifting them upward against the hard wall of his chest. As he leaned forward into her, she rolled her body toward her breasts so that all that was visible was her treasured vessel, which she offered for his insatiable erotic pleasure.

"Jesus . . ." He took a deep breath, reared back and mounted her—just rammed himself inside her, pinning her, blind to her, remorseless in her as he began his pummeling ride to ecstasy.

It was what the begoun wanted to see—the receptacle, without a face, a personality, without consideration or kindness or thought for anything but his own self-indulgent pleasure—a wet, hot place to shoot his seed, nothing more, nothing less.

He knew it—she knew it, and she even took some perverse pleasure in the thumping, pounding feel of him using her the way pashas had used their slaves for millennia. He rode her wildly, his hands feeling her crazily every which way, out of sight of the eyes of the watchers, feeling her in places she never would have dreamed that pleasure lurked, stroking her, urging her . . .

And her body responded; her body knew what she did not, that pleasure was everywhere, in the most unexpected places, in the most incredible situations; pleasure was there, furling within her and spreading to her vitals.

He towered over her, on his knees, rooted in her, pumping forcefully into her body, feeling the power of having her completely and utterly his, naked for him, hot and wet for him, tight for him, barely able to hold him or contain him.

This was possession, pure, erotic, voluptuous lust. This woman, this body whose scent enveloped his senses as he tested his virility against her willing, wanton body . . . this one, whose token he now wore . . . this one he wanted for his own passion slave . . .

The thought of it—the thought of her waiting, willing, wanting, offering all of her naked self for him to spend his lust for her—he caught back a groan, he contracted his body in one last powerful thrust and he took her, pouring himself into her in an unabated torrent of need and desire.

Into silence.

A long, attenuated silence. He stayed rooted in her, poised on his knees, with her legs braced against his shoulders.

They didn't dare speak; her eyes were shuttered, he didn't know what she was thinking—

And she didn't know what to think. This was the end result the tyrant envisioned for all the women who crawled into his bed.

She couldn't envision anything but the feel of Sinclair's thick, hard manhood deep between her legs. It was the only real thing: his forceful, naked possession of her.

The begoun spoke. Shihab translated. "Praise Begoun—the consummation is perfection. The passion slave is subjugated. Sinclair is her master. The incomparable One is pleased, and commands that the passion slave return on the morrow."

The begoun spoke again, and Shihab translated. "Merciful Begoun—tomorrow the imperious One wishes to examine the root of Sinclair's power. You will come to Begoun naked, selim, and you will talk of things that only men can speak."

"It is my honor to serve Begoun in whatever way I can. Perhaps Begoun wishes to . . ."

"Selim must understand: All must be in cleanliness before it is presented to Begoun. I am certain selim can accommodate both Begoun's wishes and the passion slave's obvious desire."

"It shall be as Begoun wishes."

"Begoun wishes to keep this powerful image of the passion slave and selim joined together. You will uncouple after the exalted One retreats."

"It shall be so."

The begoun rose, his naked eunuch following him, and once again he moved silently, this time coming closer to the platform to inspect the scene, his sharp, expressionless eyes taking in every nuance, and then floating away toward the curtain until he disappeared behind it.

"Praise Begoun," Shihab whispered, falling to his knees. "Another night. It is a miracle. . . ."

Sinclair began easing himself away from Sayra, his eyes dark with some kind of emotion that she could not read—or did not want to read.

*He doesn't want to leave me. He wants to stay within me and take me again. His manhood is still so hard, like a rock. I still feel him there. I'm soaked with him there . . . I want him there—*

He mouthed something to her—"Tomorrow . . ."as Shihab insistently pulled him away.

"Selim—"

"Yes . . .

Shihab clapped his hands.

Zenaide appeared.

"The passion slave has been requested for another night."

"Merciful Begoun!" Zenaide cried, dropping to her knees. "Yet another night!" She murmured something to herself and got to her feet.

"Come, repository of the seed of Begoun. Tonight you are holy . . ."

She sat up slowly, her body aching from his voluptuous use.

"Tonight you will be celebrated. Tonight you have proven the worth of all passion slaves."

Sayra eased herself down from the platform, feeling a spurt of ejaculate trickle down her leg. She touched it, smearing it on her skin, loving the feel of it—thick, sticky, the residue of his erotic coupling with her.

Instantly she wanted him. She could picture him, long, strong, thick, hard, hungering to possess her.

*Nothing like before; nothing like the penetration and the assault when she had managed to get away from her attacker. Nothing like . . . blood then, too, but no culmination . . . nothing for him.*

*Something for me.*

*The easing of* his *way to possess me . . . who could have known I would surrender to the whim of a tyrant and find such pleasure?*

*I want him right now . . .*

She drew in a hissing breath. *If she were going to die—she wanted him now . . . all night, deep inside her, covering her, feeling her . . . when life comes short, pleasure is all the sweeter—*

*Tonight I have proven the worth of the passion slaves . . .*

"Tonight," Zenaide said, as Mirza opened her bedroom door, "tonight, the passion slave is queen."

"Praise Begoun—you are a man of strength and prowess, selim. Such a one may rule the harem in concert with the desire of Begoun."

"I am honored to have pleased the begoun and serviced the slave to his satisfaction." *I could service her again this minute. . . .*

He was still naked, and even as the thought entered his mind, he felt himself elongating, hardening, thickening with voluptuous need.

"Selim is powerful in his manhood."

"I could take her again, and again after that. She is willing and hot for a man, as Shihab has seen with his own eyes."

"Never has there been such a willing slave."

"Such hot, wet womanflesh; and did you hear her beg? Did you see her entice a man beyond endurance?"

"I saw her tempt selim beyond a man's control."

He was losing control, he was so engorged with wanting her; he could barely maintain his composure and carry on this conversation between men.

"What is a man's control when he is tantalized by such a passion slave? There is a one who loves to be naked."

"I saw it myself, selim. The way she moved, the way she exhibited her body. She couldn't wait to spread her legs. And when selim mounted her she willingly submitted to the power of his virility."

"Selim is still hard as iron with no naked passion slave on whom to spend his lust."

"I will find you a passion slave."

"I want *that* one. I refuse to fight an unwilling slave who does not want to be possessed. We know this one wants it. Thus I want her."

"Yet again . . . that one?"

"Just the thought of her arouses me. Just talk of her makes me hard with lust for her. Just to mount her and discharge my seed. What more could a man want?"

"These are matters which you must discuss with the perfect One."

"Look at me—my manhood is ready to explode," he whispered hoarsely, ignoring Shihab's attempt to divert him, gauging his reaction to his words. Was Shihab a man? Did he lust after the forbidden? Even if only to watch?

"Give her to me. Let me seduce her; stay with us and watch

everything. Let yourself be seduced by her nakedness, but I promise you, I will be the only one to mount her tonight."

"Even you cannot maintain such hard male strength," Shihab murmured. "You must save yourself for tomorrow."

"No, you sit beside me now as I embed myself in her; you learn the secrets of a virile man. I have done all that is required of me. Now my lust to possess her is all I can think about. Let this be my reward; I ask nothing but to service this passion slave for as long as I remain hard and hot for her."

Shihab looked at his hard, jutting flesh. "It is dangerous to yearn for a passion slave."

"She is nothing but a vessel in which to ejaculate my seed. A willing receptacle for any act I desire. A man could die happy possessing a slave like that."

"Begoun has said selim may have any reward he chooses."

"I choose to spend myself upon the passion slave."

"Begoun's will be done. With the exalted One's indulgence, I will give her to you."

Sayra lay reclined against a mountain of pillows, reveling in the wet feel of his male discharge trickling between her legs.

"Praise Begoun," Mirza murmured, "you are drenched with his seed. Let me wipe you."

"Don't touch me," Sayra said sharply, and then, at the sight of Mirza's face, she modified the tone of her voice. "Leave me covered with the evidence of his possession."

"Oh, treasured vessel, he has implanted his seed. Such joy, such rapture. Begoun in all his male glory. Such power. Unimaginable. Unthinkable among mortals. Only Begoun knew the answer—he was waiting for the treasured vessel to present herself to him. Praise the treasured vessel—" And she fell to her knees.

"This is ridiculous, Mirza. Get me something to eat." *Get me Sinclair. Am I not queen? Can I not command to be bedded by him? To have to wait . . . to have only the memory of the feel of him between my legs . . . this is unimaginable—the power; the strength . . .*

*I want it . . . I want him, now, hard, hard and quick. And then all over again . . . how could I have come to this—a passion slave to the soul—his passion slave, whenever he wants me . . .*

*If he would only come now—*

*But how can he? Only the eunuchs enter the harem. And the begoun . . .*

*Never Sinclair . . .*

*If only he knew—*

*If only I could forget the sight of him all hard and hot for me . . .*

She made a little sound at the back of her throat as she envisioned him standing naked and ready, long and thick and strong as a pole. *Ready to take me, to pleasure me . . .*

She felt breathless with arousal. *Just the thought of him . . .* her body twinged. *Just the memory of his penetration . . . so forceful, so powerful*—her body reacted. *For just a minute his masterful possession—rock hard and quick and gone . . .* She melted against the pillows. *I would be his harem slave forever . . .*

The door swung open and Zenaide entered.

"Begoun commands," she said briskly. "Up you go."

That shocked her out of her sensual reverie. "What? What?"

"Come . . . there is no time to waste—you may not prepare."

She pulled Sayra from her bed of pillows and pushed her out of the room.

She was swamped with fear. "Where are you taking me?"

"Where Begoun commands."

"Tell me where . . ."

"Fear not; the treasured receptacle is queen. Only Begoun can command."

"I cannot refuse."

"Treasured receptacle is wise. She is wet with Begoun's seed. All is well."

They were now in the Hall of Thrones, crossing through the throne room and out into a courtyard which, in the course of events, would never be seen by a passion slave.

Zenaide paused before an ornate outside door in the wall and knocked. There was an answering knock in return.

"You may enter, treasured receptacle. This is the purview of men; I may proceed no further, nor may any woman, save by Begoun's command. Praise Begoun, you are a one."

She bowed and dropped to her knees as the door slowly swung open.

Shihab's voice commanded her from within.

"The passion slave may enter."

She slipped over the threshold and closed the door.

She was in a room amazingly similar to the one from which she had come, high-ceilinged, draped with bejeweled silk and thick carpets underfoot, flickering candles. There was a satin-draped mattress heaped with pillows, and a small table on which was a platter of sweetmeats, a pitcher and the candlesticks.

Shihab reclined on the bed, watching; and Sinclair stood directly in front of her, stark naked, his rampaging manhood jutting toward her.

His glittering gray eyes swept her body with a savage possessiveness, and she felt a thrill of pleasure that she was naked and her nipples were hard and he wanted her and nothing could impede his inevitable penetration.

He came to her in two steps and pulled her over to the nearest wall, and pushed her against it.

"Now, passion tormentor—" He positioned himself before her, his naked male self poised to take her; he lifted her left leg and braced it high against his body, and then he drove himself into her without any preliminaries whatsoever.

She swooned at the sensation of his forceful possession. She couldn't think, she didn't care. *He's between my legs, that's all I care about—that I'm naked and wet for him and he is naked and hard between my legs, how potent is that one ineffable part of man, how vigorous, how unknown . . .*

She felt the tremor that racked his body. The stiff points of her nipples scraped his hairy chest. His body rocked against her. She felt him throbbing deep within her, and his massive effort to maintain control.

She reveled that she had brought him to this: a pure naked lust to possess her no matter what the cost.

"I am your passion slave," she whispered.

"You're my harem whore," he growled. "Nothing more, nothing less."

She made a hissing sound. "I'll make you spew so long and hard you'll be drained for a week."

"You can't make me do anything."

"Watch me . . ." She braced her back against the wall and swung her right leg up and around him so that the only thing that was supporting her was the wall and the strength of his powerful male root. "Take me now, Sinclair. Let me feel you driving between my legs . . ."

She felt his shudder, and his long, strong fingers grasping her buttocks.

"I'll take you . . . I can't wait to take you . . ." He began pushing against her in long, strong strokes, building his rhythm; deep, thick, luxurious strokes that plumbed the very core of her . . .

"Hurry . . ."

"Oh no, oh no—" they were whispering, panting as he reared back and jammed himself into her, and came in a long slow spuming release.

And he stayed deep within her, joined with her, against the wall.

"This is crazy . . ." she murmured, barely on a breath.

"We'll figure it out later."

"Why is *he* here?"

"He is learning to be a man."

"He won't live that long."

He smiled faintly. "He has granted dispensation. I wasn't nearly done with you."

"Any old passion slave would do, Sinclair."

"I don't get hard for any old passion slave." He felt himself spurting to life again. "I get hard for you."

She groaned deep in her throat.

"I'm hard for you now."

She swallowed convulsively. "I feel you."

"You're so tight and wet; how could a man not get hard for you?"

She made another sound. "I get wet only for you."

"That's what I want, harem whore, only me. And no other man getting hard for you."

"I wanted *your* hardness between my legs tonight. I couldn't wait. I thought I would have to wait."

He was rocking against her now, gently, rhythmically.

"You're waiting now."

"I feel you now, so deep and long and strong all over again . . ."

He drew in a hissing breath. "*I* can't wait. I want you now."

"Take me—"

And he did, contracting his body against her, pushing her against the wall, pounding his lust into her to her cries of pleasure, seeking her release in the maelstrom of his own.

And she came—she pitched over the edge into a gush of sensation that mirrored his own, a long washing drench of release that carried her with it into a cataclysmic completion.

And then, without breaking his connection with her, he lifted her, and motioning to Shihab to make room for them, he carried her to the bed, laid her down and covered her.

"And so, passion slave . . ." he whispered.

"A respite . . . ?" She sighed, wriggling against the rampant length of him. *Still there, still rigid, still deep and thrusting . . .*

He moved against her. "Just let me . . ."

"I can't stop you—"

"And you don't want to, do you? You love it—you're a born passion slave . . ."

"Only for you—" she murmured, her body moving almost involuntarily, seeking him, rubbing against him, tempting him with her undulating hips. "Only for you . . ."

He suppressed a groan. *Whoever moved like this, tantalizing him, torturing him, making his weary manhood elongate just by her erotic movements, goading him beyond his endurance . . .*

*. . . no, he could handle a passion slave—he could handle that naked willing body forever . . .*

"Master to slave, harem whore . . ." He shifted himself onto his knees. "Do it. Roll over for me—it's what he wants to see. It's what you want."

She lifted her legs against his chest and he grasped her thighs and began rubbing them as he eased her upward and over. "You know what I want, Sinclair."

He pushed himself into her. "Hard enough?"

She groaned. "Yesss . . . yes—" She felt his hands on her buttocks, lifting, pulling, pushing, all the sensations all over again, the rhythmic pumping, his long fingers caressing, probing, the languid, hot haze of possession as he took her with powerful potent strokes, on and on and on and on and on . . .

She felt wet, liquid, centered solely on the pistonlike drive of his virile sex. She didn't have to move; she just had to be the receptor of all the shimmering, unfurling ecstasy that he could pound into her insatiable core.

She heard herself begging, she hardly knew what she said; her whole body was swollen, fecund, yearning for that one inexorable break that would send her senses careening.

He towered over her, ferocious in his possession of her, his body lathered, his grunts a counterpoint to the rhythm of his thrusts.

He wanted to go on forever. Her body rippled under his, demanding more and more and more; voracious, tenacious, wet, hot, brazen . . . he couldn't get deep enough, hard enough, go long enough to appease her.

*Mine . . .*

He felt himself stiffening.

*No one else . . .*

He felt it coming.

*Wet for me . . .*

The whole of his focused force bearing down on her . . .

*Hard for her . . .*

He exploded, ramming himself deeply within her, exploding, his body shuddering as each hot spurt discharged with the force of a gun.

He heard a hoarse, soughing groan, he heard *her* long drawn sigh of pleasure; he felt himself inundated in the sticky ejaculate of his culmination, and he couldn't move, he couldn't move.

"Selim is truly a potent man." Shihab, his voice cracked with disbelief. "I will report to the perfect One that selim has spent himself three more times upon the slave."

"Who says I am finished with her?" he said, easing himself away from Sayra and sinking down beside her.

"Truly, you are a virile man, selim."

Sinclair looked down at Sayra's flushed face. "I have never seen a woman so willing to spread her legs."

"She is a temptation to all men, selim. Any man who saw her thus would desire her."

"Including you, Shihab?"

"I am immune to the charms of the passion slaves, Sinclair. Yet even she could seduce a one such as I."

He smiled grimly and slipped his hand under the pillows and withdrew the gauze veil which he had taken as a token. "I believe she did," he said pointedly, his gaze resting on Shihab's protuberant member, pressing urgently against his loincloth.

He rolled over onto her and then to a sitting position so he could straddle her legs, and he began gently wiping his ejaculate from her body.

"Please don't," she whispered. "I like the feel of it."

"I want the scent of you . . ." He looked up at Shihab. "See how she begs?" He held up the veil. "I will tie this . . ." He draped it over his turgid manhood, sliding it downward over his shaft so that he could feel the full, potent sense of her without possessing her.

His eyes met hers, challenging, daring; he felt her body shimmy as she reacted to the sight of his hand working the filmy veil all over his manhood deliberately, tauntingly, watching it stiffen like a ramrod as he finally tied it tightly at the base of his sex.

"I will wear the scent of your sex *here.*"

She made a helpless sound at the back of her throat.

He moved toward her mouth. "What else will the passion slave part for my pleasure?"

She groaned and centered him so she could lick him.

He shuddered. He wanted her to take him like that, right there, right then, but that was not the way of the harem. A man's prowess was measured by his potency and his stamina, not whether a slave would pleasure him in obverse ways; that was too easy. A man needed to prove he could penetrate the slave, maintain his erection and discharge his seed.

Anything else was superfluous here.

Shihab got to his feet.

"It is enough. I will tell Begoun you have spent yourself three more times upon the slave, and I will summon Zenaide to return the passion slave to her quarters."

He never moved his eyes from Sayra. "As you will."

"Goor guards the door," Shihab said, just a thread of warning underlying his words, as he opened it and withdrew.

Sinclair waited until he closed the door behind him before he climbed off Sayra and sprawled himself next to her.

"This room . . ." she whispered. "This is so like mine, every detail, the furnishings . . . it makes me wonder—"

"Wonder out loud then. The best I've been able to do is get another set of clothes from that bastard."

"I wonder . . ." she started shivering. "I wonder if there is another secret door . . ."

He jumped over her and out of bed. "Where? Which wall?"

"The far wall."

He started walking the length of it, from the window wall, ripping away the silken hangings as he went.

And there, at the midpoint, almost directly opposite the bed, he found the fitted door.

"There's not much time," she said tentatively as he strode back to the bed, reached under the pillows again and pulled out a shirt and a pair of trousers made of a light cotton drill.

He tossed her the shirt. "Put it on." He slipped into the trousers, and then dumped the tray of sweetmeats and grabbed a candle.

"Ready?"

"No."

"Good. Show me how to open this thing."

She was beside him in a minute, grasping the little hook, lifting it and pulling. He set the tray on the floor to wedge the door and then stepped over the threshold.

"It looks like a tunnel, maybe going toward that cell from the opposite side."

"I don't want to know."

"You can't stay here. If Shihab returns . . ."

"And sees the open door, he'll lock us down there forever."

"Then we'll have to be faster than he. Come . . ." He held out his hand. "I want you with me."

"A dispensable passion slave," she muttered, stepping gingerly into the tunnel.

*An indispensable slave to my passion . . .*

He held the candle high and led her into the darkness.

It was eerily the same. Everything the same, as if the male side of the harem had to balance exactly the female side.

The rough walled tunnel. The canted floor. The sense of evil.

And as they proceeded farther and farther, the choking, cloying scent.

The thin halo of light defining a corner.

*I'm reliving a nightmare . . .*

She pulled his arm. "Steps ahead . . ."

He lowered the candle and the steps were there, waiting to trip the unwary and send him crashing, headfirst, into oblivion.

They edged their way down the steps toward the light.

The odor was almost unbearable now.

And muffled noises that almost sounded like . . . like what? *Someone speaking . . .*

They both thought it; neither of them wanted to say it.

They could almost make out the words.

". . . most High, anointed and exalted One, I bring the passion slave to do your bidding . . ."

*Shihab . . . !*

They crept closer to the corner of the wall.

The noise was inhuman, underscored by a frantic feminine voice begging . . . for what?

Sinclair handed her the candle, dropped to his knees and peered around the corner.

*Jesus God . . .*

Luddington, on a bed of bones, blood dripping from his mouth, stroking the innocent flesh of the passion slave who lay limply in his arms.

And the high-and-mighty Begoun, his pale skull face and red-rimmed eyes revealed at last, his pointed, bloodstained teeth poised to bite the neck of the terrified, struggling passion slave, one of the other three who had been in the charge of the mistress Zenaide.

# Chapter 10

An unearthly scream shattered the air.

And then she was right behind him, peering over his shoulder, seeing the horror he was seeing, the monsters, the piercing, the blood . . .

*"Omigod . . ."*

He pushed her out of the way violently. "Don't make a sound . . ." barely breathing the words.

"Dear God, what was that?"

Another earth-shattering scream . . . and then a guttural sound that was utterly inhuman . . .

"Let's get out of here."

He grabbed her hand and the candle, and they ran . . . up the steps, down the tunnel, like the chapter of a book she was rereading. But with a difference. Those screams, that noise, the odor, the voices . . .

*Dear Lord . . .*

They ran.

Her voice stuck in her throat; her heart felt as if it had stopped.

*Murder . . . she had witnessed murder.*

*Again.*

*Blood . . . blood all over the place . . .*

She faltered, her knees wobbling, and he grasped her hand and pulled her. His strength. His determination.

He yanked her over the threshold, kicking the tray out of the way and then swinging the door tightly shut and wedging the tray as best he could at the threshold.

"Jesus . . . we have about two minutes. Shihab saw us."

"The slave . . . who was she?"

"Don't think about it now."

"What—what *was* that? What are you doing?"

He was burrowing under the pillows, and a moment later he pulled out another shirt and a pair of trousers, which he tossed to her.

She stepped into them without a word as he opened the outer door a crack.

"Damn—the eunuch is still there." He shut the door and quickly scavenged the room. "How heavy do you think these candlesticks are?" He picked one up and hefted it. "It will have to do."

He reached up and pulled down one of the wall hangings. "Jesus, I wish I had a knife . . ."

She watched in terror and fascination as he tore at the material.

"I want those jewels. We need . . . " . . . *We* . . . his words petered out as he picked up a candle and set the flame against the material. "We have thirty seconds, I swear." The silk flamed up, and he carefully burned enough of a hole so he could quickly douse the flame and rip the material apart.

He tossed the jeweled piece to her. "Wrap it around your waist and get over by the door."

"What are you going to do?"

"We're breaking out of here tonight . . ."

. . . *we* . . .

He wasn't even thinking; she was there, she had seen, she would be food for the gods before morning, he was sure of it, and that he would not last until midnight.

. . . *we* . . .

"Shhhhh . . . "

The silence was ominous.

They heard a thumping at the secret door. Footsteps beyond the outer door. Voices whispering. Silence again. Mere minutes ticking by. Their hearts pounding; their lifeblood pumping furiously, almost in denial of the reality they had witnessed.

"Any minute now . . ." he breathed. Shihab had seen them. And Shihab was the high priest of death. He would welcome them with open arms and feed them to the voracious Begoun, who roamed freely through his city of flesh and immortality.

*. . . the masters arranged it . . .*

*. . . Ferenc is everywhere—*

*. . . Ferenc lives . . .*

*. . . in the corporal bodies of Luddington and a gluttonous pasha—*

*. . . in the soul of a besotted wreck of a man in an obscure seaside town . . .*

*. . . on his father's lips in a dream—*

*Had it been a dream—? He couldn't remember now; it all seemed like a dream. Nothing was real but the woman and the taste, the feel, the scent of her enveloping him.*

*That—and freedom . . .*

*He could think about it all later . . . he was certain all the pieces would come together later—*

*If there was a later . . .*

He felt her trembling. "Shhhh . . ."

"He'll kill us."

"He always intended to."

Not reassuring words.

They jumped at the sharp rap on the door.

"Selim . . ."

Shihab, his voice bland, deferential, a little uncertain when Sinclair did not respond.

"Selim . . . ?"

The knob turned, the door opened, and Shihab cautiously inched his way in. "Selim . . . ?"

Sinclair didn't move until he was across the threshold, and then he swung the candlestick like a cricket bat and cracked it against Shihab's face as Sayra quickly shut the door.

Shihab went down like a sack of flour, and Sinclair dropped to his side.

"He's out; nose broken, lots of blood to feed his cohorts. No weapons. No jewels. Quiet now—" He rose to his feet and pulled her to the opposite side of the door and opened it.

The eunuch Goor stood guard, his back to the door.

Sinclair crept up behind him, slowly, stealthily, noiselessly.

*The man is a goddamned mountain; I have to get him in just the right spot.*

The silence was stultifying. His caution was nerve-wracking. She watched from the threshold, ready to run at the instant.

Sinclair moved, one step, two steps, a hesitation, a third step, interminable minutes as he eased closer and closer to his prey.

She stifled a sound. *Surely the evil ones were coming . . . ?* Her heart sounded like a drumbeat in the silence.

And then—

Cr-a-a-a-ack! on the side of the neck, and Goor keeled over. Sinclair stared at her over his prone body, the bloody candlestick still poised in his one hand, and then he held out the other.

She took it, stepped over the eunuch, and they ran.

They didn't know where they were going, but they ran, through the courtyard and into the throne room, where her discarded trousers lay draped on the begoun's throne.

He paused for a moment, staring from the jeweled waistband to the window and back again. "Are they real?"

"I don't know."

"Grab it."

She swooped down and picked up the torn trousers as he leapt up onto the sofas and examined the windows.

"Stay back—" He swung the puny candlestick against a pane—once, twice and again before it shattered. At that rate it would take an hour for them to break enough glass to make a sizeable hole.

And what was out there anyway? Blue sky. Whitewashed buildings in the distance. A small terrace outside the window and nowhere to go . . .

"The gong . . ." He raced into the anteroom, brushing away the insidious memory of Shihab's words . . . *selim's mind wanders . . . planning for what cannot be. Kabir is a city in the clouds . . . and to think one can escape it is merely to desire death . . .*

He grasped the mallet—*I desire life, you bastard*—up onto the sofas again, and a long hard swing into the glass—

And it shattered into a thousand pieces—

"Get out of the way!"

He was like a madman; anything to escape—he punched at the shards, showering glass outside the throne room and within, all over the sofas and the floor.

"Let's go—"

He leapt out the window into the blazing late afternoon sun. He could hardly see, the light was so glaringly bright, the sky so blue.

They were like pygmies against the interminable sky.

They were on a terrace that was surrounded on three sides by a low stone wall.

And there was nothing else except buildings in the distance, and no possible way to get to them, and below them, hundreds of feet below, glassy waves of water, lapping gently against the rocky foundation of what looked like a fortress.

*A fortress. A place to immure their captives and perpetuate their unholy cause.*

*Kabir—a city in the clouds, Shihab had said.*

*Hell on earth . . .*

A gong sounded, once, twice, three times—they heard voices then, and a concerted march of bodies from almost everywhere, above them, below them, behind them—

She looked around wildly for any possible means of escape, but there was nowhere else to go—only back to the arms of the bloody begoun or over the edge into the backwash of the sea . . .

She was going to die now, for sure—

He leapt up onto the stone wall as the begoun's minions converged in the throne room.

"We have to jump."

"I can't . . . I can't swim—"

"Jesus—shit—you're going to have to now, passion slave: Make a choice—food for Begoun or fodder for the fish. . . ."

She felt close to hysteria and reached for his hand. "I hate you."

"I'm saving you; I'd think you'd be a little more grateful."

"I'll think of a way to properly thank you later."

"You'll have to . . . here they . . . coooommmmeeee—" And he jumped off the ledge and pulled her with him.

*A thousand deaths . . .*

They cut the water with an enormous splash and sank down, down, down, to a place from which she was certain she would never return.

Her arms were flailing wildly, in deadly desperation.

*Oh, God, where is he? Where is he?*

She sank helplessly into a void: water suffocating her, pulling her, seeking her . . .

And then, just as she thought her lungs would burst and he was gone forever, she felt herself being hauled up and up and up into blessed fresh air, into life, into a minute of freedom.

She opened her eyes to the vastness of the sea around them and to his sardonic expression as he paddled them toward the rocky foundation some hundred yards away from where they had jumped in.

"Oh, God—there's nowhere to go . . ." Her fear swamped her, she felt herself sinking again, she heard his sharp command to kick her feet somewhere faintly in the distance.

She kicked frantically and felt her body rise, and his fierce grip guiding her toward an outcropping of rock they could hang on to.

She grasped the rough surface desperately, while he swam around in a circle to get a sense of what they were up against.

"There's always somewhere to go," he murmured as he surveyed the odds with a skeptical eye. But even he felt a little daunted by the expanse of water that seemed to reach to the darkening sky. "I just don't think we can find it tonight."

"Oh, dear Lord . . ."

"They'll probably send out some small boats to try to find us—but they're not going to be able to do anything much in the dark. Consider this: there has to be some launch point—maybe on the other side . . ."

"The other side—? The other *side?* You can hardly see where this side ends, for God's sake—what do you mean, the other side?"

"Listen, slave woman, *you* begged me to save you. I'd be on the other side right now if you weren't here to slow me down."

"I'm going to die," she moaned. "I know it. I just know it."

"You're not going to die; you're going to hang on just as you are. There's enough of a ledge here so you could even sit, if you don't trust yourself in the water."

"I don't; I'm scared to death."

"I'll lift you up then." He grasped her hand and pushed, and she scuttled up onto it.

It was hardly a ledge—it was just a slope of surface rising from the water, barely enough room for her to align herself against the fortress wall with her feet dangling in the treacherous water and him right beside her, hanging on to the outcropping with his hands, his elbows, his upper torso.

That, and impinging death everywhere she looked.

She swallowed hard. "What happens after sunset?"

"We hang on."

"Or slip away."

"We won't."

"You're so certain. How can you—how can you be certain of anything, after all this?"

"I'm certain I want to live," he said inflexibly. "Even if it means hanging on to this rock by my teeth. What about you, passion slave?"

The words sounded odd as he said them. He had known her in every intimate way it was possible to know a woman, but she was a passion slave no longer. Nor was she the woman whom he had bedded at his whim.

And now those rules of erotic possession did not apply.

"We just leave all this, leave the monsters to dispose of all those lives with impunity?"

"We leave all this."

"All those women . . . Phyllida, Olga, Amalie . . . it was Olga, wasn't it?"

"I don't know Olga."

"It was Olga," she whispered. "I saw her eyes before he bit into her . . . oh, my God—before he killed her. And they are just feeding his bloodlust. What manner of man is this? What is he that he can steal women and pretend to enslave them when all he intends is to kill them to feed on their lifeblood?"

"Is that what happened to you? They kidnapped you?"

She answered, almost as if she was reliving it. "There was blood all over. Just like in the cell. I saw them fighting while I was performing. I saw one attack the other, and then the blood. So much blood. And later it wasn't there, and Harry—the barkeep—he swore nothing had happened."

"Harry? The barkeep? Where?" he interrupted.

"At the Pig and Poke—in Wixoe. They got me there. They got me and I never saw them coming. . . ."

"Jesus . . ." he swore.

*The Pig and Poke. Where she performed; she had even explained it to the begoun, and he hadn't listened, hadn't connected.*

*The Position Girl. The daughter of the human detritus in the shack.*

*The first time—or was it?—he had heard the name, Ferenc.*

*Ferenc comes, off the bloodstained battlefield to rescue mortals who would have rather died.*

*Ferenc lives—*

*Ferenc is everywhere. . . .*

*. . . The masters arranged it . . .*

*Goddamn hell . . .*

"Who are you?" he whispered. But he knew already.

"My name is Sayra . . ."

"Sayra—" He rolled the name around on his tongue. "Sayra. I know who you are—you're the daughter of the town drunk, Mansour."

Crashing reality, coming right on the heels of the blue-dark sky. She could hardly see him. She didn't know him. And yet to him she had surrendered her soul.

But that was over. He knew her father, that liquor-sodden bastard who was content to live in rags and shacks and dine on whatever vermin he could exercise himself to catch?

*He knows who my father is. What else does he know? What else could he know?*

*Does he know a man named Ferenc saved my father's life on the battlefield almost twenty years ago? Does he know my father aches from a killing hunger he cannot control?*

*Oh, Lord—oh, Lord, I wanted this man; I willingly gave myself to this man—for what? To find out he's part of it—whatever it is?*

*Oh, no, no no—I will not die here, I won't . . .*

Bit by bit darkness fell. The silence between them lengthened. The horror they had witnessed took on a stunning fearsomeness.

Every noise, every lap of a wave represented a threat.

Every now and again they could hear a voice in the distance. A shout. A bird wheeling overhead—looking for a carcass to pick?

Her shirt dried, and the upper part of her pants, and her hair. The sultry air was like thick cotton against her skin. She rolled up the sleeves of the shirt and doused her arms with water.

And then, suddenly, there was a ray of light around the far end of the fortress. Voices following it, and the light—no, more than one light—two, three, four . . . coming closer—something moving . . . the voices talking among themselves as the lights, in tandem, came closer and closer . . .

"The search party," Sinclair said, his voice expressionless. "Four of them. Begoun has decreed we must be dead. They have only to recover the bodies and bring them to Begoun and he will dispose of them and reward them greatly."

"You understand them?" *No, no—no—still more conspiracy . . . ? He had been able to translate everything the begoun had said? He had known . . . ?*

He ignored the question as self-evident. "We are going to get one of those caiques."

*. . . we . . .*

*—the daughter of Mansour . . .*

*. . . blood on the wall in a pub in Wixoe . . .*

*—the hell—*

The lights were coming closer, revealing the shadows of the men on the caiques, four on each: two to row, one wielding the lantern, one shouting instructions.

"Get *down* . . ." he hissed suddenly, pulling at her leg so that she toppled into the water against him. "Shhhh . . . hold on—there . . . don't move—don't make a sound—"

He clamped her hands to the rock he had been hanging on to, and then suddenly, terrifyingly, he disappeared.

*Oh, Lord . . .*

The lights came closer. She just knew one of the oarsmen or the slave with the lantern would see her . . .

*Maybe not—*

*. . . trust him?—*

Her fingers felt numb. The lights came closer, swinging out into the water and back again in a circle toward the fortress wall.

*No choice—*

Closer still.

She was breathing too loudly; they would hear her, hear her heart, smell her fear . . .

Closer still, their voices reverberating off the water, words that only Sinclair could understand . . .

*How could he . . . ?*

*Betrayal . . .*

Her breathing panting gasps as her fear escalated. They were coming abreast of the rock now, the lights swinging back and forth, back and forth, over her head, a fifty-yard radius around the boats and back again.

*Too near that time . . .*

*. . . oh, God . . .*

She took a huge breath and ducked her head under the water just as the circling lights grazed the rock ledge to which she clung.

And up again, gasping for air, certain they had seen her . . .

Down again, as the light swung around again, almost as if they thought they had seen something but weren't sure . . .

Up again, choking and sputtering as the caiques moved slowly past the rock.

And then suddenly a shadow rose from the water and grasped the truncated end of the nearest one and pitched it upward and over.

Instantly one light went out—shadows crashed into the water, screaming for help.

The caique upended itself again; a shadow barely visible raising an oar against the lantern-lit sky, and then it hunkered down within, and a moment later the caique was bobbing precariously next to the rock, and his strong hands were lifting her numbed ones from the ledge and heaving her bodily up onto the deck.

"Keep down; they've turned—they're coming back for the others. That should delay them—unless they leave them to drown . . . entirely possible—are you all right?"

"Yes," she gasped, her hands feeling the wooden flooring to make sure it was real, and then him—to ascertain that *he* was real, he was there, and this really was happening, the caique was moving and the lights really were receding in the distance.

She climbed to her knees and then wished she hadn't.

There was suddenly no light anywhere and they were heading into a deep, unfathomable darkness, with no idea where they were going or where they might wind up.

Heat. Bright light. Her body floating. Airless. Soundless.

*Heaven . . .*

Something over her head . . . she struggled awake, her arms flailing.

"Hey—"

A voice . . . she shook herself like a puppy. *His voice.*

She pulled the thing away from her face. *His shirt.*

She eased herself to a sitting position.

The sun felt like a furnace.

"Rinse the shirt off and put it over your head."

He was draped in the length of jewel-encrusted silk he had ripped from the harem wall, and he was perched at the back of the caique and he had been watching her sleep.

She hated the idea, but she did as he told her.

"We don't know where we are, do we?"

"Not a clue."

"Or if there will be land any time soon."

"No."

That was as bald as anyone could get. No false hopes. They could die out here as easily as they could have at the hands of the begoun. And just as painfully.

"I don't suppose you know anything about navigation?"

"I can figure out east and west," he said.

"And—we are going?"

"North, actually."

"And you know that much because . . . ?" she asked irritatedly.

He hesitated for a moment. "I think Kabir is located in the Strait of Makhmara. I think we're headed toward the Turkish mainland, hopefully somewhere near Istanbul."

"And you've been awake all night figuring this out."

"Well—reading the stars, actually. But it's all of a piece."

"Because—" she interpolated as she suddenly comprehended the how and why, "of the language they spoke? Because you understood them. *All* of them—Begoun included?"

He didn't have to say anything; that part, now, was perfectly obvious.

"But how . . . how do you come to know the language, Sinclair?"

He turned his head slightly so that he was looking out over the water and away from her. "I am the younger son of a peer, apt in language, logic and tact—or so they told me when I was up at Oxford. I am—or was—in diplomatic service."

"Looking for someone named Luddington."

"On a mission to find him."

"Shocking what you found instead. Did you need to bring him back?"

"No, I think he needed to get me out of the way."

That shocked her.

*. . . the masters arranged it, he had said . . . tell the Englishman . . .*

She looked at his grim expression and she knew he was remembering as well.

"I see." But she saw nothing at all. Just the boundless reach of the sea. And the man who had breached a harem on a mission.

*A man who knew her father . . .*

*Who spoke the language—*

*Who willingly possessed a passion slave at a begoun's command . . .*

*Who knew the monster in the cell . . .*

*Who did what he had to in order to get what he wanted—*

*A dangerous man, his sights set on survival . . .*

*Who might sell her in some bazaar in Istanbul—damaged goods—a woman who had willingly surrendered herself in a harem bed . . .*

*She couldn't believe it, even now.*

*It had been a dream. A lifetime ago, already.*

*He wouldn't abandon her.*

*He would say she could always earn some money spreading her legs.*

*He would say she was good at that.*

She didn't know which she feared more—death at sea, or living death at his hands.

She stared at the sea—no, the Strait of Makhmara—that reached unendingly to the sky.

*Ferenc is everywhere . . .*

*Ferenc comes—*

He kept his gaze determinedly due north.

The sun was a bitch, glaring off the water like a mirror reflecting light. The heat was thick, sulfurous, heavy against the skin.

He made her remove her own shirt, douse it in the water and drape it over her head, so he could retrieve his own.

"This damned silk is hardly any protection; the color is too dark, and it dries too fast. Don't act like a virgin. I've seen you, and I can handle your nudity. Besides, you'll be cooler this way."

Only he didn't know if he could maintain his composure at the sight of her. He reacted instantly; he would come to life even if he was at death's door, he thought irritatedly as he rearranged himself so that her taut-tipped breasts weren't directly in his line of vision.

He wanted her. Insanity in the midst of the baking heat—the sultry heat; rank barbarism.

He felt primitive. He wore her token still around his elongating member, and he could have sworn that her scent still permeated it, still enveloped him.

*The lesson of the harem: Possess the slave, own her forever; take her when you will. A rutting bull, seeking surcease. Her willing body, enslaved by the possession of his pumping, thrusting manhood driving her to screaming pleasure . . .*

*That—now . . .*

He shook himself violently, took one look at her lush, naked breasts, and heaved himself over the side of the caique in one explosive movement.

The water was tinglingly cold.

*Perfect.*

His driving urgency shriveled.

*Can I ever look at her without wanting to be enfolded by her?*

He swam around the caique and back again.

No land in sight. Sun and water as far as the eye could see.

He had allowed himself to drift far too long.

He eased himself back up onto the flat end of the caique and, deliberately avoiding her huge, dark eyes, he picked up the oar and resolutely began paddling.

It was time, he thought, to find some direction.

Nightfall.

And with it suffocatingly hot air with not a breeze to relieve it.

He stayed at the back of the caique, languidly paddling the water to keep them on course.

She lay toward the bow, cushioned by both shirts folded up under her head, her naked body draped with the trousers, which had been soaked in sea water.

There was moonlight, faint and riding so far above them, she could barely see him. But she was so aware of him.

It was her nakedness. She could feel the urgency in herself, almost as if removing her clothes had made her a passion slave once again, alive only to the possibility of his need to possess her.

But of course he needed nothing. Unto himself and keeping secrets; that was Sinclair.

She could just see the line of his broad shoulders as he dipped and dragged the oar.

She was breathless with excitement, imagining him there, the muscles flexing on his broad bare chest with every precise movement; the strength of his hips anchoring him as he twisted and turned and dragged the oar first on one side and then the other.

*His hips anchoring her . . .*

She drew in a faint, hissing breath. *The lesson of the harem: A woman knows nothing until a man has possessed her in all her nakedness.*

*And then—when she knows everything, she can have nothing—*

Her body twinged.

*If he was naked, I could see him . . . I could tempt him—*

*I could feel him . . .*

She could feel herself succumbing to the urgency and to the

contradiction of it. How was it possible, in such a situation, at such a time . . . ?

She didn't care.

She wanted the moonlight caressing her heated body as he watched. Nothing hidden from him. Everything offered to the moon and the stars and the inevitability of his possession.

Like that. Just like that.

She writhed impatiently under the moon.

She heard the harsh intake of his breath and knew he was watching her.

She wanted him to watch her. To want her. To come to her.

She felt the faint, covert movement of him removing his trousers, and she shivered with anticipation.

He was bursting for her.

"If we were still in the clouds, I would take you with no compunction," he said hoarsely, "but you are a harem slave no more, Sayra."

"Oh, no, I am a passion slave still, in my body and my heart. If you want a passion slave, Sinclair. If you want her, take her. She is your passion slave, and she has no other name, no other being beyond this moment of possession."

"Is that what you want?" he asked roughly.

"It is all I know how to be, Sinclair. You have made me; you were the first, and you wear my veil as a token of your possession of me. I am naked for you, waiting for you . . . wet for you—"

He dropped to his knees and pushed her legs apart.

"I can't . . . stop—" he groaned, and pushed himself into her gently, so, so gently into her enfolding heat, to embed himself as deeply as possible so that she could feel the bone of his hips against the soft curve of hers.

"Don't stop," she whispered as he buried his head in the curve of her shoulder.

"Don't move. I want to stay just like this. Just like this."

Cradled in the soft rocking motion of the caique . . . making soft little movements now and again . . . undulating her hips against his, seeking to pull him deeper still . . . listening to the water lapping against the caique . . . moaning as he pushed himself against her . . . reacting to the twisting dart of pleasure as he murmured, "Passion slave," against her ear . . . angling her legs to give him the fullest penetration possible . . . his long fingers playing idly with her right breast . . . his whispered words, "Such a hard nipple," sending her into a spasm of pleasure . . . and finally his mouth covering that taut, tingling nipple and sucking . . .

She moaned, grinding her hips violently against him.

. . . such unimaginable sensations . . . her body writhed with pleasure as he pulled and licked and sucked on her turgid nipple, and murmured disjointedly against her taut skin, "Passion nipples, passion slave . . . passion . . ." as if he was losing himself in the abandoned response of his sucking on her.

He kept on and on and on; she wanted him to take the whole of her breast in his mouth; she wanted to give him everything, everywhere. She couldn't give him enough; her body arched against him, begging for more, her hands working convulsively in his hair.

Unbelievable pleasure, shooting like a comet down to her very vitals. Her body vibrated around him; he was the hot center around which she revolved, the hot core, thick and hard, and her pleasure spiraled around him as he delicately fed on her engorged nipple.

Just that, just the nipple, and the hot essence of her enfolding him, and her moans and sharp, quick movements against him. Just that. A passion slave with passion nipples that begged to be sucked.

He could not get enough of that lush, hard nipple. It fit into his mouth as if it was made to be there. As if everything about her was made for him.

Passion nipples, feeding his frenzy to possess her. He couldn't move; she was writhing and moaning so frenetically against him, begging, begging him, loving it, wanting it . . . and he—wanting her never to forget the sensation of his mouth sucking her passion nipples . . . wanting her to beg for it, beg for him, beg for the completion that only he could give. . . .

He pulled at her passion nipple one more time; he felt her stiffen, felt her bear down on him, felt her whole body shuddering out of control, one spasm after another, incandescent with pleasure as she wrapped herself around him and totally surrendered to his mouth, to his hot, hard male possession, to the wanton in herself.

He lifted his head; he wished he could see her face, could hear her soft, soughing moans.

"Is the passion slave ready to be possessed?"

She drew in a long, gasping breath. "Take me . . ."

In four short, driving thrusts he gave himself to her; with a long, keening cry that echoed over the water, he spent himself in a drenching release that wrung him to his very core.

He did not remove himself, he lay coupled with her quietly after, attuned to the feel of himself enfolded within her, the water, the sky and the certainty that he wanted her for his passion slave forever.

# Chapter 11

She awakened alone under a tent of clothing propped up by the oar, and immediately she panicked.

*"Sinclair . . . !"*

She batted away the shirts and scrambled to her knees. *Oh, Lord, I'm alone; he washed overboard—nonsense, he can swim—nothing anywhere—just water, water, water to the sky—and an evening of stardust that seems like a dream . . .*

*Calm . . . calm yourself—*

"Sinclair . . . !" She crawled sternward and peered over the flat edge; he was there, kicking, pushing, his long, strong body propelling the caique with a furious impatience that was immediately reflected in his expression as he looked up and saw her.

"Get back—get covered; it's dangerous in the sun . . . *do* it—"

"You, too."

"Soon. Go on . . ."

He had to conserve his breath; she was stark naked and she could already feel the sun shimmering on her bare skin. She grabbed the shirts and trousers and dunked them in the water and then donned one shirt and draped the other over her head.

No help; the deck was burning hot as well, and she shimmied into the trousers and huddled under the shirt, and felt the swifter movement of the caique as he pushed it northward.

A short time later she felt him heave himself up behind her, and heard him panting as he slithered heavily onto the deck.

"I need that shirt—now . . ."

She doused the shirt again and tossed it to him, and then unbuttoned her own, shrugged out of it, wet it again and put it over her head.

"Did it help?" she asked after a lengthy silence while she stared at the unremittingly blue expanse before them.

"I don't know. I just needed to do something."

"And you always take action."

"Don't you?"

"What's going to happen?"

"We'll survive."

*. . . we . . .*

*Always talking about "we," as if she would be with him forever. But she was a passion slave no more . . . and he did not know what she would be if ever they got back to England.*

Nor did she. He was so confident. Even in the face of a sun-scorched, limitless horizon where blue merged into blue and nothing else could be seen for miles, he was so certain.

And she was certain of nothing. After one had been a Position Girl and a passion slave, what else was there? She couldn't begin to imagine what would happen when and if they returned to England.

*She would go back to Wixoe, back to the Pig and Poke, and he would go back to London, to his other world, and resume his life as the dashing Honorable that he was.*

*And marry someone suitable and set up his nursery . . . and it would be as if all of this had never happened.*

*Those high-stepping peers were very good at pretending nothing happened.*

She couldn't look at him. She was thinking too far ahead anyway. There was nothing to say they wouldn't just drown an hour from now, or a day. . . .

*. . . we'll survive . . .*

*. . . we—*

*By the force of his will and his strength alone . . .*

*They had gotten this far.*

*And the others . . .*

*Were not nearly as strong or determined.*

*And they would die.*

*Were dying . . .*

"The monsters survive," she murmured.

"We can't do anything about that," he said brutally.

"Even now there is a ship somewhere bringing new slaves, new blood—"

"And a ship with two who escaped."

"Whose story would sound like . . . like . . . a ghoulish fairy tale—"

"It's none of our concern."

"None? *None?*"

"None," he repeated ruthlessly.

"But Luddington . . ."

"I found him. There's nothing more. I don't think about the why and the how of it. He is what he is and where he is by his own design, and nothing can ever be done for him."

"And Ferenc—?" She shuddered as she said the name.

"There is no such a one. It is a legend, a name designed to throw fear into those who are superstitious and uneducated."

"He saved my father," she whispered, "on a battlefield twenty-five years ago. . . ."

"Your father was mistaken," he said coldly. "And it's not for discussion, not now." He stood up abruptly, shucked his clothing and dove back into the water.

*Effectively ending the questions and the conversation. Those bluebloods surely knew just how to do it.*

*And why was she thinking about him like that? Because civilization could be just over the horizon? Because nothing was certain beyond the next moment and the next? Or because she knew he would abandon her at the first likely moment?*

She stared straight ahead, biting back her tears. *Abandoned . . . and changed forever . . .*

She felt the caique surge forward as he began a strong, rhythmic kick.

Nothing out there; nothing.

All this effort, futile. The sun would broil them and the sea would claim them. There could be no other ending.

This was nothingness—all blue and a blaze of light and heat and regret . . .

. . . drowning in regret . . .

Something had changed. She was barely aware of it. What . . . ?

And then it was there—a distant but definitive line bisecting the horizon, and they were coming closer and closer . . .

*"Sinclair . . . !"*

But he was halfway into the caique already, and panting with exhaustion. "I know . . . I know—"

Closer still as he grabbed the oar and began paddling furiously. They could see all of it then—the land, and the hazy outline of low-lying buildings that seemed to rise from the shimmering mist of the sun-washed shore. Fragile fishing boats bobbing gently at anchor. Clouds scudding suddenly across the sky.

His strength propelling the caique through the water with superhuman energy.

*. . . we will survive . . .*

*. . . soon—*

*Almost . . . almost—there . . .*

The storm came out of nowhere—darkness suddenly superseded the sun, and the wind whipped up from the water, tossing the caique this way and that.

And then the rain came, pelting them, drenching them, a fury of pounding water, and all he could do was push her down onto the deck and cover her with his body.

The caique rolled on the roiling waves. He shifted his weight above her to one side and the other to weight the fragile boat to keep it afloat.

*Any minute, over and gone . . . dear Lord . . .*

She swallowed water. The storm swallowed her words.

*. . . we will survive . . .*

*He will—*

The caique heaved downward into a dark, rising crest of water that broke over the bow and almost washed them overboard.

*"Jesus . . . hang on—hang on . . ."*

*I can't . . . I can't—*

She fought with the water; she grabbed for anything solid and fought against the upending cant of the caique as he maneuvered himself forward and back above her to combat the rolling waves.

The rain poured down in sheets. They could see nothing but

the bow of the caique plunging and heaving into the roiling water.

And they couldn't hang on; they couldn't.

She felt herself slipping and sliding, her fingers numb from the tension of trying to hold onto the rain-slicked sides of the caique.

She couldn't, she couldn't . . . she felt the caique lifting on the force of a wave, lifting up and up and up, as she slipped toward the stern, and then out and over into the pounding waves.

She felt him grasp her leg as she frantically fought the water, fought him as if he was the enemy and not the storm.

The caique floated upside down riding the waves a dozen yards away, and he was desperate.

He released her—she sank—he dove under her and lifted her from below to the surface with his arm around her midriff.

She was coughing water, utterly petrified with fear, but even in her near hysteria she understood not to fight him, that he wouldn't let her drown.

He was fighting the water and the pelting rain, and hauling her limp body beside him as he worked his way slowly and methodically toward the overturned caique.

He was so strong. In the heat of his battle with the elements she could think of nothing else except that it was his will and his determination that would save them.

She had lost her shirt; she could see it and the drifts of bejeweled silk floating away beyond reach.

But he was getting closer and closer to the caique through sheer dogged physical power, pulling and pulling, reaching and pulling—and—reaching one more time—seizing the flat edge of the stern, hanging on and hanging on while he caught his breath.

And then, slowly, he hauled her alongside him so she could grab on, and then they just held on as the caique pitched and rolled.

They were never going to make it, never. She wasn't strong enough; the storm was too violent, everything was lost anyway. . . .

*"Don't let go . . ."*

She heard him under the pounding rain, she saw him kick off, and she felt as if her heart had stopped.

*Doomed . . . just doomed—*

She hung on with every ounce of strength in her. She wouldn't look; she couldn't look.

The rain poured down, pelting her like little fists; the caique rolled like a drunken sailor, with the wind gusting behind her and pushing her farther away from Sinclair.

She felt the pure terror of utter helplessness; she felt as if she ought to just let go and have done with it.

She clung tighter, choked with fear. The water was unpredictable, buffetting her every which way. She couldn't feel her fingers or her legs as she kicked futilely to maintain some kind of balance as the caique tipped crazily up and down.

*. . . we will survive . . .*

*I must survive—*

*To do what?*

*It might be better to die than to wind up in the hands of whatever awaited her—a woman alone—on shore . . .*

*Oh, God, she had to stop thinking this way—*

*Oh, dear Lord—what was that?* as she felt something touch her and she panicked, her hysterical scream lost in the wind. She involuntarily relinquished her hold and started thrashing around wildly.

He caught her up again, by her arm, and grabbed hold of the caique with his free hand. Then it was his strength supporting her, supporting them, and she went limp with relief.

They rode with the wind for an interminable amount of time. And then suddenly it seemed as if the wind abated, the sky lightened and the rain subsided.

Immediately, he thrust the caique upward and held his breath as it fell back once, twice, and then the third time tipped and dropped over into the water, deck side up.

He maneuvered it to the flat end of the stern, and with the last of his waning energy he heaved her up onto the deck, and then levered himself up behind her and fell heavily onto her prone body, heaving and panting as several small faceted stones fell from his mouth, drained beyond measure.

And they floated.

He made no effort to move, other than to sweep the stones securely into his hand.

And then they lay still and silent, as the wind died down and the rain changed into a fine drizzle, and the caique drifted.

She had never known such peace, with the now gentle swell of the waves cushioning them, the weight of his exhausted body enfolding her so that she saw and knew nothing else, and then the sudden break of the rays of the sun through the clouds, almost as if heaven were calling them.

Peace—her battered body at rest finally . . .

. . . *fragile but still alive* . . .

And what to follow?

She thought they might have slept; but he awakened instantly as the caique nudged bottom, and levered himself upward on his hands.

"Oh, shit . . ."

She followed his gaze.

A dozen faces hovered over them, surrounding the caique and blotting out the sun.

He made sure she was covered before he helped her out of the caique, while answering what seemed to be a barrage of questions, in their language, from the agitated onlookers.

Finally he turned to her.

"We are in the village of Tafiq, two days' travel from Istanbul. They don't like naked women, and they don't like strangers, especially those who arrive by boat. They're taking us to the amir's house, and one of them is getting you something to wear so you will at least maintain the *appearance* of modesty."

"How convenient you understand everything."

He squinted at the sky. "Almost everything."

"So diplomatic," she murmured, wrapping the shirt around her tightly, very aware of the disapproving looks of the men who had stayed to guard them.

There was no other word for it. They hadn't moved a foot off the beach, they were surrounded, and two of the men had gone off to announce their arrival to the chief and to procure the appropriate clothing for her.

And now their guardians were silent—so silent that it was unnerving. The sun beat down on them, and the sky, so violent and gray an hour before, was now a hot serene blue, and connected to the horizon with no divisible line whatsoever.

As if Kabir did not exist.

*And how do we know we haven't stepped into another den of monsters?*

She shivered.

*They were alive, that was all that counted.*

*Unless . . .*

*Oh, no—*

She looked up to see the two other guardians returning, one of them carrying some kind of covering for her.

He handed it to Sinclair, who unfolded the two pieces and slipped them over her shoulders and her head, and fastened the veil over the lower portion of her face.

"Hold these." He slipped the jewel stones into her hand, closing it tightly and tucking it emphatically under the burnoose. "And don't open your mouth."

"I wouldn't think of it," she said drily.

He motioned to the two who seemed to be the leaders that they were ready to be brought into the presence of the chief of the village.

They entered a whitewashed building a short distance away.

Here, out of the sun, it was as cool as a tomb, with the only light filtering in through a window cut into the stone wall above the entryway.

Their escort withdrew, save for the two men who had announced them, and the one murmured a word or two to Sinclair, who translated.

"The amir will be with us presently."

"I could have guessed."

"You are not supposed to talk."

"Sinclair . . ."

"I know. But at least they didn't attack us. There's something . . . something about the way they reacted when I said we had come across the strait." He paused a moment, as if he was trying to define just what the response had been.

"I told them—but they didn't believe me . . ."

* * *

The amir was seated on a brocade divan in the main room, before a fireplace and beside a table on which his number-one wife had set a plate of fruits and nuts and several pitchers. He looked as dry and mottled as the walls of his home.

"This is Amir Hammadi. He says you are permitted to stay while he questions us. Be seated," Sinclair whispered, lowering himself to the floor and pulling her with him. "He offers food and drink, but you will take yours with his wives after we talk."

"Passion slaves," she murmured, feeling a flash of anger; these women were trapped, too, every bit as constricted as any slave in Kabir.

He was drinking water from a clay cup, and he choked.

"Selim—"

Hammadi addressed him; she recognized that word, and Sinclair immediately turned his attention to him.

He spoke quickly in answer to something the amir said, and then the dialogue went back and forth like lightning.

And then there was a pause.

"What does he say?" she whispered.

"Shhhh . . . he says no one returns from Kabir."

"Right, because the monsters *eat* them . . ."

He had heard that before . . . *where? Where?*

"*No one.* And he wants to know what proof we have that we've been in Kabir."

"Because otherwise—what? *He'll* eat us?"

He gave her a baleful look. "Or execute us as spies . . . an immodest half-naked woman and an Englishman, after all—give me one of the jewels. . . ."

"Oh, no . . ." She clenched them tighter: their passport, their wherewithal; he had risked his life to save even these several stones, and she didn't see how he could just hand one over to this creaking desert chieftain whom they could surely outwit.

"Oh, yes . . . a gamble, admittedly, but easier in the long run."

She gave him the smallest stone; clear, faceted, sparkling in his hand, even in the dim light.

Hammadi took it and examined it closely, his expression inscrutable, and then he spoke again, his voice calm but with just a thread of excitement running through it.

"He wants me to explain exactly what happened," Sinclair translated, watching interestedly as Hammadi handled the stone before he launched into the story, with Hammadi interrupting him periodically for clarification or to ask questions that sounded impossibly suspicious.

And she had to sit, her head bowed, her arms folded, sunk into the faintly foul-smelling *yashmak* and listen to the babble and never interject one word.

*Trust him . . .*

*Trust—*

*Myself . . .*

Hammadi was staring at the jewel as Sinclair spoke. Now he was quiet, tuning the stone in his thick brown fingers, turning their fate in his hands as surely as if he was some kind of fortune-telling mystic.

And when Sinclair was done there was a chilling silence.

*Even Hammadi doesn't believe it—how could anyone believe it?*

And then he spoke.

"He has never seen the like of this jewel," Sinclair translated. "He says legends tell of the wonders of the city of Kabir, where only the dead survive. He wishes for us to be examined. You will go with his first wife and, by my request, you will return when she has ascertained whatever it is he wants to know."

He rose up, held out his hand, and she placed hers into it, with the remaining jewels, transferring them to his keeping.

A woman appeared just outside the door of the room and motioned for her to follow.

She looked at him pleadingly. He shook his head slightly.

*Do what they want. It's our only chance.*

She had no choice.

She left him, exiting the room silently as a nun.

Five women stripped her, their fingers like so many little bothersome flies, puffing, unfastening and pushing.

And when she was naked the head wife, gorgeously dressed in embroidered silks and glittering gauze, gesticulated patiently until she understood that the ladies wanted her to lie on the padded cushion on the floor.

The second and third wives, who were less opulently dressed and wore no makeup, knelt beside her and began a scrupulous examination of her body, poking and prodding her, and going over every inch of her body with their hands, and with comments she could not understand.

When they were done they dressed her carefully in the garments of a woman, replacing the burnoose and *yashmak,* and with much comment and ceremony, they escorted her back to the room where Hammadi awaited her.

Sinclair was seated precisely where she had left him, his expression unreadable, as she slipped into the room and folded herself down next to him as the first wife reported to Hammadi what she had found.

"What in heaven's name was that all about?" she whispered.

"They were looking for the mark of the *strix.*"

"Oh . . ." She reined in her exasperation. "And did they humiliate you, too?"

"They did, and they're not done; they just don't believe me, and the only saving grace is that I can speak their language."

"What did the wife say?"

"She says there are no marks, nothing irregular anywhere, and her body has been prepared in the way of the harem." He sent her a flashing, knowing glance. "He cannot believe it."

"Why?"

"Shhhh . . . there's more, There is the trial of the horse. Jesus. Listen, they're going to take us outside on the sands. They are at this moment choosing two boys—virgins—to mount two white horses which they will ride out onto the shore and gallop past us."

"This is crazy—*why?*"

"To prove we are not lying. That we are not of the living dead."

"*What?*"

"This is their test. This is their way."

"I don't understand."

"The horses will shy away from us if we are . . . one of the ones they think inhabit the fortress of Kabir. But we show no signs, no marks, no asymmetry. The amir is willing to believe. The others—not. And so they will test us. They are ready now."

He levered himself to his feet and held out his hand. "We must do as they want."

"I understand." But she didn't. All this mumbo-jumbo about Kabir. And that nonsense about the living dead, and the dead surviving. The only ones who would survive were the monsters; *they* would live forever.

The sun was a red ball sinking into the horizon as they made their way to the edge of the water. Nothing beyond the horizon except monsters—and nightmares. How could anyone believe—?

But then, superstition ran rife everywhere . . .

She kept her head bowed as two ancient men delegated by the amir positioned her on the beach. Out of the corner of her eye she saw Sinclair a dozen yards away from her. Far enough away so that a horse could pass between them.

*A horse, for heaven's sake . . . monsters and horses—and he didn't blink an eye or explain a thing.*

She marveled at her own patience.

But nothing seemed real anymore; not her kidnapping, not the horrible journey and the awful Voice, not her nightmare sojourn in the harem, not even the monsters, or their escape from Kabir.

What was real were two children on horses silhouetted against the waning sun, waiting for the signal to begin the final trial.

A crowd had gathered on the ridge above the sands. Men only in small knots at intervals, some of them venturing down onto the beach, quiet, so quiet; not a murmur among them.

Nothing except the horses stamping with impatience. And Sinclair, still as stone, certain as the sunset that whatever this test was meant to prove, they would come out the victors.

The amir lifted his hand and swung it down in a chopping motion.

Immediately the horses surged forward, racing across the sands from a hundred yards away, building up speed and momentum that could only be halted by supernatural means.

Closer and closer they came, their hooves turning up a smoke screen of sand that blurred the edges of the critical motion of the horses and obscured the crowd.

Any minute now the horses would fly by the two of them,

standing still as statues at the edge of the water—or they would rear up, shy away and brand them as monsters forever.

She held her breath; she could feel the swirl of the sand as the horses and their riders pounded closer and closer. She closed her eyes. Anything could happen, anything. This was a world where rules and morality did not apply.

Irrationality reigned: the horses tore past them, not faltering for a moment, and in the aftermath, with the echo of their pounding hooves resonating in the shocked silence, the amir raised his arm again and the muttering crowd dispersed, until the only ones left on the beach were Sinclair, herself and the man who still held their fate in the palm of his hand.

# Chapter 12

And then she was sent away with the women to be fed, bathed and made ready, should Sinclair call for her in the night.

"This is abjectly unfair; I don't understand anything."

"You don't have to—yet."

"You're brutal."

"I am, and you like it."

"I don't like you," she snapped. *Oh, and what would he say to that? One of a thousand things, like—*

"You like being alive," he said coolly. "You like a lot of things I've done. Go with the women. I will call for you later."

"Perhaps the amir will offer you one of his wives."

"Oh, a definite improvement over a passion slave," he murmured. "Go now. By tonight I'll know more."

*Or maybe he would know that having her with him was a detriment, and he could move a lot faster if he just left her in the amir's harem. . . .*

*. . . where she belonged—*

*Oh, nonsense—her mind was going, it was . . .*

She lowered her head and followed the amir's first wife down a narrow corridor and through a thick oak door into the *andarun,* the women's quarters.

There was no one to translate here, only the eager gestures of the first wife, pantomiming what she wished her to do.

She pointed to herself: "Asha."

"Sayra."

Asha spoke again, a torrent of words and gestures, motioning both to the other wives and making dismissive gestures toward Sayra, by which she finally comprehended that Asha wished her to follow the other wives through yet another door, a courtyard, and finally into the *haman,* the bath.

Asha waited expectantly as the other wives attended to their respective duties of oiling the water, laying out the towels and finding clean clothing for the guest.

Sayra slowly removed the *yashmak,* the burnoose, and the robe they had given her, and stepped boldly into the water, to the nodding approval of Asha.

Another barrage of words as she gave instructions to the wives, which ended by her clapping her hands.

Another woman appeared, a servant by her dress, who carried in her hands soap, a washcloth and a comb, and it was she who waded into the water to attend to Sayra.

Asha approved. The other wives tactfully withdrew, and Asha gave further instructions to the slave, who then began vigorously washing Sayra's hair.

Now Asha was silent, watching with her veil removed and her bright dark eyes taking in every nuance of Sayra's appearance.

Sayra watched her just as warily from the depths of the bath as she floated to allow the slave to rinse out her hair.

Who, after all, could be counted on as an ally? This woman was sharp, pretty, intelligent; she could see it in her eyes. The kind of woman who ruled, perhaps not kindly, but one who was definitely obeyed. One who had the wit to scheme successfully to become first wife.

Who gave every evidence of accepting the verdict on the stranger—that she was what she appeared to be and nothing more ominous.

Except that everything else was ominous and phantasmagoric.

For all Sinclair knew, the amir was a monster, too. . . .

No, no, she wasn't going to think like that. They had come this far. They would find out the answers. And then they would leave. Surely that stone-sized jewel could buy them transportation of some sort . . . ?

It was nervewracking not being able to speak or understand Asha's ongoing stream of words. But her gestures were clear: The slave was to wash her body and her hair, comb her hair until it dried, massage her with oils, make sure she was fed, and then prepare her for the night.

She was a little unsure what that meant, but it became clearer after she had eaten all she could of a greasy dish of lamb and rice and drunk some wine that was served to her in the bath as the slave soothingly combed through her hair.

Asha appeared, issuing instructions again.

She was to get up, get dressed in the gauze overdress that had been provided and follow Asha into the *andarun*.

Here there was a rabbit warren of rooms, the largest one of which was a common room where the wives and the children gathered.

Farther along there were bedrooms that were furnished with thickly padded quilts laid out on the carpeted floor and covered by another layer of quilting.

Beyond those rooms was a larger one, the size of the common room, which was richly decorated and furnished with thickly upholstered divans, several large tables and some small footstools.

Asha motioned her to one of the divans.

She sat, noting with dismay that on the tables there was an assortment of what could only be described as paints, as well as brushes, towels, hair decorations and jewelry.

Asha spoke, pointing to the paint pots, and Sayra shook her head violently. It was obvious Asha wanted to paint her—paint her face or her body or both in the manner of the amir's wives, to make her more attractive to *her* amir, and she wasn't going to take no for an answer.

She clapped her hands and two more women entered the room—wives or slaves, Sayra could not tell.

Asha gave them instructions, and one immediately disappeared to shortly return with a bowl of water, while the other knelt next to Sayra and examined her hands and her legs, and said something to Asha.

She watched suspiciously as Asha moved toward her and sat down next to her and splayed out her hands.

They were covered with a painted design, quite beautiful and quite beyond her experience in terms of the sensual power of such a thing.

Asha spoke, waving her hands, pointing to her face, her lips, her eyebrows, which had been painted across the bridge of her nose.

She shook her head violently and pointed at her hands. They could do her hands, her feet if they wanted, as Asha revealed her intricately decorated feet, but they couldn't touch her face. She would fight them if they tried to paint her face.

Asha understood. She didn't like it, but she comprehended that the stranger's custom might be different from hers; Sayra could hear it in her voice as she pointed emphatically to her hands and feet once again. Asha threw up her hands and gave her instructions to the slaves.

And then Asha withdrew, leaving her to the silence and the hypnotic, reedy sensation of the first wet brush of paint on her skin, and the feeling that only a slave could fill in the lines.

She lay sprawled on a divan half asleep, her body lulled by the feeling of the wisping line of the brush all over her body. She didn't know, didn't care where they painted. She had only wanted them not to stop.

But eventually they left her and she succumbed, her eyelids heavy from the mesmerizing movement of the brush.

*For just a moment I'll just . . . just—*

And it seemed like only a moment had passed when she became aware of someone gently shaking her.

Asha again, voluble, her hands flying, pulling at her, commanding her by the tone of her voice to rouse herself.

She struggled awake—and then she saw . . . ornately painted bangles around her ankles and wrists; artistic concentric circles radiating outward from between her legs, framing her most private part; and she bit back a cry of dismay.

Asha thrust the gauze dress at her and she slipped into it frantically, and then the burnoose and the *yashmak,* and then, by Asha's direction, she followed her, silently and shaking with despair, through the honeycomb of hallways into what she had to assume was the men's quarters, and her assignation with Sinclair.

Asha paused before a doorway in front of which was a little niche. She spoke in whispers now, her hands graphically describing what she wanted Sayra to do, and then she demonstrated by removing the *yashmak* and placing it in a little cupboard built into the niche.

She undressed and folded the clothing and put it in the cupboard, and then stood with her chin raised, waiting for the next instruction.

She knew what it was: Asha wanted her down on her knees and crawling into the room, and she expected by her actions that Asha would understand that she refused.

But Asha expected to be obeyed. She pushed her unceremoniously down to the floor and then scratched on the door; on hearing the bidding from within, she pushed it open, kicked Sayra's buttocks viciously with her foot, and then stood impatiently with her arms folded until Sayra moved forward, toward Sinclair, who was sprawled naked on the divan, on her hands and knees.

He murmured something dismissive.

Asha demurred.

He answered, his tone more commanding.

The door closed with a sharp bang as Asha obeyed.

"Who comes?" Sinclair demanded, not moving from his supine position.

She paused, not knowing whether to rise or stay on all fours, or what he wanted or what he saw. All she saw was his lower torso illuminated by the soft candlelight as he lay reclined against a mountain of pillows, his legs spread wide, his manhood towering hard and high above his belly, and the luscious weight of his scrotum nestled invitingly between his legs.

*I want that; I missed that . . . even a day—one day . . .*

"Who comes?" he asked again.

"Your passion slave," she answered huskily.

He levered himself to a sitting position, with one leg angled outward. "Come to me, passion slave."

"Willingly," she whispered, and still on her hands and knees, she crept forward toward him. She knew what he saw and she knew he was powerfully aroused by the sight of her body moving sinuously toward him, her taut-tipped breasts just barely brushing the floor, the elegant line of her buttocks undulating enticingly with every movement.

She felt like a cat who was about to lap up the cream. She

knew what she wanted. She came right between his legs and buried her face there, feeling the rough scape of his pubic hairs against her mouth as she rooted for the taut balls of his scrotum.

Just that, just that . . . just that . . . she didn't know why she wanted that, or how she knew to want that, but she wanted that, rough and smooth, pliant and tight against her tongue.

She surrounded him, pulling him wholly into her hot mouth; she felt his hands in her hair, cupping her head, pressing her tightly against him.

She sucked at him hungrily, hard and soft, licking and tasting him, moving her tongue all around his luscious balls, her fingers working convulsively against the base of his manhood.

She felt his tumultuous response; he couldn't get enough, he thrust himself against her hands, his body juicing up in spite of his efforts, his ejaculate seeping down all over her hands.

He was coming, coming, coming. He couldn't stop it, he couldn't save it; her avid mouth moved, how she knew to move, at just the right moment, how she knew to smear the lush liquid of his passion all over her nipples, how she knew to bend her voracious mouth to the very tip of him, to take him just so into that wild, wet mouth and pull and suck just there, just there . . .

He exploded—into her mouth, all over her hands that held him firmly and tightly against her succulent tongue . . . all over, all over—

"Passion . . . slave," he groaned, pushing himself into her mouth and letting her suck until he could bear it no more. "Jesus . . . God . . ." He pulled away violently and pulled her up hard against him and rolled them both back onto the pillows.

She was on top of him, his shaft positioned between them, all hot and sticky and hard as a rock.

"Selim has spent his passion," she whispered.

"Am I hard? Are you hot? Selim has barely begun." He rolled her over so that she was on her back and he was poised by her side. "How beautifully they've painted you," he murmured, his fingers tracing the circular pattern that swirled downward from her hips. "How hard your nipples are. And wet with my juices. How wet are you, passion slave?"

"I'm wet for you." She sighed as he brushed her throbbing cleft with his expert fingers.

"Let me feel how wet."

She parted her legs and arched her hips, and he slipped his fingers deep within her, and she lowered her body and bore down on the tight, hard feel of them deep in her core.

"The passion slave is hot and wet and wanting," he murmured, as he worked his fingers expertly in rhythm with her undulating hips. "Tell me what the passion slave wants."

"I want you, hot and hard and deep between my legs."

"I am there."

"You are here," she whispered, grasping his jutting manhood. "And you are so hard . . ." She ran her hand all over him, squeezing and stroking him in exactly the right places as if she knew, as if she had always known.

"Hold me there," he commanded her, bending his head so that he could take one of her stiff, pointed nipples into his mouth.

Her body twinged violently as she arched up against the heat of his voracious mouth, her hips writhing against the erotic invasion of his knowing fingers.

And then she was lost in the inviolate pleasure of his greedy sucking; every sensation settled in that one taut, lush pleasure point, and he knew just how to play with it with his tongue, his teeth, his lips alternately squeezing and sucking at it.

He played with her, his fingers thrusting into her with the ferocity of his body as she shimmied against the intensity of feeling he pulled from her breast.

This was unimaginable: his mouth, his fingers, her greedy hands all over his massive maleness as he sucked and pushed and thrust into her, all together, all one, her body, his oh-so-long fingers, her hands, his granite length, his mouth, her nipple, her legs angling to give him everything he sought—and more, more, more . . .

. . . more . . .

More, shimmering at her center suddenly, between her legs and at the very point of her nipple . . .

More, as he somehow intuitively knew . . .

More, as the sensation expanded and expanded like a balloon, outward, upward, thick, creamy, all at the tip, in her hands, in his mouth, coming, coming, intensely slow, filled—too filled—and then suddenly exploding into a thousand fragmented sensations that she strained to capture in her hands.

"Passion nipples," he whispered, his lips against her breast. "I'm going to explode if I can't take you."

"I want you to explode. Explode for me. Between my breasts, all over my nipples. Do it . . . I want it—I want it all over me—"

He climbed onto her, straddling her hips, positioning himself so he could thrust between the lush mounds of her breasts.

She wrapped her hands over him, pushing him down tightly against the valley between her breasts.

"Now—" she whispered, and he began thrusting. She arched against him, holding his long length, feeling his strokes, and at the final moment, when his urgency propelled him, she cupped one breast against the underside of his shaft so he could feel the caress of the stiff pleasure point of her nipple.

And he came, and he came, and he came, explosively, convulsively, uncontrollably, spewing himself all over her breasts, her shoulders, her hands, her mouth, and just when he thought she had wrung every last ounce of pleasure from his body, she lifted her head and pulled him into her mouth, and sucked him until he felt the last welling spurt of pleasure and he came again in her mouth.

"I have done my duty," she murmured in satisfaction as he collapsed on top of her. "I have drained selim to the point of exhaustion."

"I will be hard for you in an hour," he growled. "I am getting hard just thinking about possessing you again."

"Let me feel if you are getting hard." She insinuated her hand between them where already he was elongating in sensuous little spurts she could feel as they talked. "Oh . . . !" He was full-blown hard and his body rocked against her as she enfolded him in her hand.

"I got hard for you in a minute, passion slave. I want to embed myself inside you and feel your heat and wet surround me. Let me," he whispered, "let me possess you. Now. I can't wait. I'm hot for you . . . feel how hard I am for you—"

"I feel it. I want it." She spread her legs, undulating her hips invitingly, and he nudged her, inserting the thick, ridged tip of him precisely between her legs. "Yesssss . . ." she sighed when he didn't push further. "Oh yes . . ." as he stayed poised just that way.

She moaned, feeling the thickness of him, the hardness of him and the power in him.

He lifted himself onto his hands and splayed his legs so that her thighs straddled his widely.

"Look at me."

She eased herself onto her elbows and loved what she saw: the connection between them, his hard strength half in, half out of her hot, enfolding, feminine core.

"This is the possession of a passion slave. You were made to be a passion slave. You want this. You love this. You need it between your legs just like this."

"I love it between my legs."

"You want it."

"I can't wait for it."

"You love a man's hardness."

"Whenever I can get it, selim."

"You've got it now, passion slave."

"Then let me feel it," she taunted him. "Where is this hot hard *man* who wants to possess me?"

He drove himself into her as she watched. "Right between your legs, passion slave. Right there," as he pulled back and thrust again. "And there," and again, "and *there,*" as he rammed into her ferociously. "Tell me you don't feel that. Tell me you don't live for that . . . tell me how much you want it . . ."

She could barely breathe, she was so insensate with pleasure. She loved his words, his sex play, his pumping humping body forcefully charging into hers so she could see every movement in and out, in and out, long, strong, potent, hard as a rock and the bedrock of his being.

She couldn't do a thing but let him take her with his relentless, primitive desire to possess her.

"Feel it."

"Oh, I feel it," she moaned.

"Love it."

"It feels so good . . . so hard—"

"Want it . . ." He drove into her again. "*My* hardness. Mine. *I* get hard for you. *I* possess you. *I* live between your legs—"

She groaned. "You . . . yes . . . yes—"

And somehow, again, he climaxed, a shudder of sensation washing through him and ejaculating through his most potent part.

"Don't move . . ." she whispered as he made to withdraw himself. She held out her arms. "Stay inside me," and he lowered himself gently into the cradle of her arms, her body, her passionate surrender.

She felt his fingers tracing the intricate painted lines on her body.

"They have truly made you a woman of the harem," he murmured, his hands moving freely, intimately examining every inch of her body.

She lay still, reveling in the sensation of his handling of her.

*Because after all, someday the games will be over; the pleasure will end. We cannot keep this up forever. It is only for this place, this life, the world of a harem slave who is subjugated to her master.*

Even as she thought it, she felt his hands on her buttocks, lifting her, positioning her so her legs were braced against his chest and she was readily available to him.

And then she felt him push himself into her, deep, deeper, his naked, focused force hard and hot and *there*.

He towered over her and deep within her and he grasped her legs to balance himself as he began his rhythmic drive to completion.

And she loved that, too, that passionate driving connection of his body to hers, that she was there for him, wet for him, and the moment he penetrated her, wanting him in her as hard and deep as he could go.

He took her with the same unbridled passion, cramming himself, ramming himself into her hot, willing body in a fury of lust, desire and desperation.

And he unleashed himself in a wrenching, spurting surrender

that drenched her with his seed, and then he fell on the divan beside her.

She lay there, awash in his juices, inhaling the scent of their sex, a passion slave to her core, with her master asleep beside her.

She slept.

At some time during those hours he pulled her tightly against him, her back to his front, and wound his arms around her so that his one arm lay over her breasts, his other hand cupped her feminine mound and his manhood nestled just between the cushion of her thighs.

So that when she awakened with subtle little stretching movements and began wriggling against the hands that confined her, she immediately felt the unmistakable signs of his arousal.

"Don't move," he whispered, as if she could help the sensual tightening of her body as she became more and more aware of him. "I'm getting hard for you."

"I feel you," she whispered back, "I . . . feel you," as his fingers delved into her welcoming fold, and his hardening length jutted out between her legs.

She grasped him with both hands and shifted her body so that she was straddling his rigid length. "I have you . . ."

"I have *you,*" he murmured as he cupped her right breast and stroked the burgeoning nipple with his thumb.

She made a moaning sound at the back of her throat; her buttocks ground against his hips and she arched herself against the massaging caress of his fingers on her erect nipple and the feel of his quiescent fingers filling her womanly core.

The sensation was unspeakably erotic; she rode him, rubbing her fingers all over the thick, ridged tip of him as he played with her nipple and crammed his fingers tightly inside her.

She felt him there; she felt the shimmering pleasure of his caressing her nipple, and the lush knowledge of his powerful shaft under her writhing body. All of that, and his whispered words, and the feel of his virility in her hands, and that he could arouse her with a touch, a word, the sight of him naked and primitively erect for her . . . all of that, all of it—

"Passion nipples . . ." He breathed the words against her ear and she spasmed with pleasure. "*My* passion nipples, *mine—*" as he rubbed and squeezed the one gently, so gently it was almost unbearable because she felt the sensation to her very core.

"So hot for me . . . so fast for me . . . ride me, passion slave—" as she bore down on his granite shaft, ". . . take me—" as her hands convulsed all over the protruding head of his penis, ". . . come for me—" as her body vibrated with the pure hot tension of her tumultuous slide toward release.

And then it was there, crashing violently inside her, her body gyrating wildly against him, her hands everywhere she could grasp him, squeezing him, stroking him, pulling at him, demanding that he climax in her hands.

He held himself back, though he was almost not able to do it. She was too potent, her pleasure too powerful to be denied. He restrained himself with the greatest difficulty until the storm force of her culmination ebbed away and she was floating in the aftermath.

Then he gently removed his fingers and inserted himself into the hot velvet center of her.

"Oh . . . !" A tiny gasp, a sensual sigh, his both arms around her now, his male self rooted where it belonged, deep within her, enfolded by her, granite hard for her.

"Don't move," she whispered, loving the feel of him like that, back to front, and the knowledge of how hard and long and strong he was to possess her that way.

"I don't have to move; you do all the moving for both of us, passion slave." And it was true; already her body was responding to the feel of him inside her with those attenuated feminine movements calculated to entice him to climax. Her one hand moved delicately over his thigh with soft caresses, and the other sought to capture the sensation of his connection to her as she delved between her legs to find him.

". . . ohhh . . ." Just that, that one wondrous sound as her fingers grazed the joining point between them.

He moved then, so she could feel the sensation and the power of his possession, and her searching fingers grasped him at the base of his male root so that she was connected to him there, too.

". . . ahhh . . ." A throaty sound of pure pleasure as she surrounded him with her fingers.

He crammed himself against her, against those knowing fingers that tested his prowess. "Let me possess you, passion slave," he whispered in her ear. "Feel how hard I am. Feel how I want it . . . how you want it. Let me—let me . . ." as he rocked against her. "Let me . . ."

She wanted to let him. And she didn't want to relinquish him. Not yet. Not yet.

*This is the power . . . this is a woman's power, that a man wants her so desperately all the time in all ways . . . this is where potency lies—in complete surrender and equal pleasure . . . yes—yes . . .*

"Yes . . ." she breathed. "You're so hard for me. I want it . . ." She slipped her hand away. ". . . I can't wait for it—" She writhed against him. "I want to feel it. . . ."

He undulated against her, pushing himself tightly into her so that there was not a breath of space between his body and hers. And then he rocked against her gently, with no thrusting motion. He wanted her to feel him filling her, all of him, every last rock-hard inch of him.

And they lay this way, with him pushing and rocking and her wriggling and shimmying, seeking his heat and his hardness, and neither speaking until she could stand it no longer.

"I'm aching for you."

"And you're so wet for me. This is possession, passion slave—a man's hardness deep inside you bringing you pleasure without his moving an inch, and making you want it, making you beg for it, making you helpless in your need for it. Isn't it? Isn't it?"

She couldn't answer, she was so insensate with the feel of him inside her and the corded strength of his arms holding her tightly, and the harsh sensuality—and truth—of his words grating against her ear.

This was possession—naked and wanting forever . . . where was her power now?

His arms gripped her tighter. "Tell me you want it."

"I want it," she whispered without hesitation.

"You need it."

"I need it."

"You need *me*. . . ."

"And you need *me*—" she murmured brazenly.

"We'll see, won't we, passion slave?" he growled, and then he nudged her forward so that she rolled onto her stomach, and without disconnecting from her, he lifted her under her hips so she was perfectly placed for him, and without another word, he took her.

Like a piston he moved, hard and hot in a ramrod rhythm, driving himself to completion.

The sensation was intense: She was with him all the way, her buttocks shimmying with every stroke, pushing against him, enticing him in the erotic way that only she knew how; she knew. Every powerful stroke was but a concession she pulled from him that his need to possess her was more potent than hers.

She knew everything. But a passion slave was trained to know everything—

He grasped her hips as he began the inexorable plunge to completion. It was like falling; it was a waterfall of pleasure, taking him by surprise; a spume of drenching sensation from head to toe in the backwash of her shuddering release.

He eased her down, and then himself, still joined with her, and even after this awesome spending of his desire, still wanting her.

She felt him playing with the hair curling around her ear and she lifted her head slightly.

"Shhh . . . I think they're watching us—"

She groaned. "No . . ."

"We have to get out of here."

"I've heard that before. Why do you think—?"

"Curtains moving. Noises. I only just noticed because I wasn't asleep. This evening was probably a test, and they can make of it what they want, depending on their sexual practices, but I have a feeling it won't come out positive for us."

"After all this . . ."

"You have no idea."

"And, of course, you have no time to tell me."

He shot a cautious glance around the room. "I don't think I do, actually." He lifted himself away from her. "Jesus. I'm still hard."

She rolled over to look at him and stretched out her hand. "Come to me then. . . ."

He looked down at her and his unruly manhood strutting so proudly in blissful ignorance of an impending crisis. "Where are your clothes?"

"There's a cupboard just outside the door. I put them in there before that tyrant made me get down on my knees."

"I like you on your knees—but not right now. All right. We have to get your clothes. Or you can wear mine, whichever is easiest."

She sat up and then lay back again. "I'm just drenched down there, Sinclair."

"I have something . . ." He got up and went to the small table where his clothes were folded neatly. He lifted them and pulled out a small oblong of material, one end of which was tied in a large knot.

He held it up as he came back to the divan. "Angle your legs." He knelt down next to her and began wiping her with the cloth, whispering, "I tore this off the divan cover. Hold still. And no, he didn't find the jewels."

"What were they looking for—on you?"

He didn't answer. He sat up, staring at the painted design on her body. "Shit. All right—" He held out his hand and pulled her to a sitting position.

"What? What?"

"Shhhhh . . . better?" He was whispering again.

"Yes. But *what?*"

He took the oblong of cotton and tied it swiftly around his neck and was immediately enveloped by her scent.

"We've got to get out of here." He grabbed his own clothes and pulled them on.

"Come . . ." He took her hand, blew out the candles and felt his way toward the door. "Shhhh . . ."

He opened the door slowly and eased his way out into the niche. The cupboard was right there, to his left, just as she had said. He opened it and pulled out the folded clothing and handed it to her.

While she dressed, he scouted the passageway.

There was no one guarding them, but there were voices coming from the amir's receiving room.

*A conference on the mating habits of the living dead . . .*

*Jesus . . .*

She was adjusting the *yashmak* as he made his way back to the room.

"He's got his advisers with him down that way. We have to go the other way."

"The adornment room is down that way, and the bedrooms."

"Then we'll have to be quiet. Let's go."

They tiptoed down the passageway, which was lit by wall sconces, past a half-dozen closed doors and into the eerie silence, until they reached the room where she had been painted.

"There."

They slipped in, and he closed the door behind them, enclosing them in darkness.

"Damn; I should have taken a candle. Any windows in this place?"

"I don't know. I never noticed."

"Stay by the door. I'm going to feel my way around. . . ."

He moved away, and she tried to envision the room as she had seen it when she was brought to it. She remembered the divan where she had lain, and the two servants, and the mesmerizing feel of the brushes wisking over her legs and arms.

But nothing about the room . . .

"Can't even hide out until morning," he whispered, all of a sudden by her side. "There's nothing, just wall hangings." He opened the door and they ducked into the passageway. "We don't have time to figure it out. We'll have to go out the way we came in."

They catwalked back in the opposite direction, past the bedrooms, the room they had shared, past the connecting passageway that led to the baths, closer and closer to the voices, which sounded contentious and loud.

He pulled her close so he could whisper in her ear. "They want to come after us. They say the horses proved nothing. They say we indulge in mating practices that prove we are liars."

He moved forward slowly and stealthily as the voices got closer and louder in argument.

"Get down; flat down on the floor. We're going to crawl by that door. Get down—*now.*"

She dropped to the floor instantly, following his lead.

The doorway was five steps away, no more, and the voices within were shouting.

He moved then, on his hands and knees, quick—quick, his head down, his movement tight and flat to the floor.

He motioned to her, and she hiked up her burnoose and stretched herself as low to the floor as she could. At his signal she moved, just as the amir slammed something down on a hard surface and shouted into the babel of voices.

She got to her feet, he grabbed her hand and once again they ran.

He wasn't even sure the outer door wouldn't be locked—if they were what the amir thought they were. Then they would be invincible, and there would be no point—

They were at the door, he was pushing the door, when they heard a voice behind them.

She whirled. The first wife, about to open her mouth and scream.

He reacted—he dove at the woman's legs, knocking her over so that her head struck the passageway wall and she fell limply to the ground.

"Unconscious. Hurry—" He was at the door again, lifting the bar, pulling it open so she could run into the cool early morning air.

He closed the door behind him. "The stables. Those horses—no idea where . . ."

They raced toward the end of the compound closest to the water.

Nothing, not a sound . . .

"Quick . . . around back—they'll be coming for us any minute . . ."

They crept around the side of the main building of the compound.

Now they could hear—shouts, excuses, the sound of pounding feet as the search inside began.

There was waning moonlight to guide them in and around the maze of buildings in the compound. It was easy to hide in the shadows as they made their way slowly and cautiously to the opposite end of the property.

Easy and nervewracking, with every sound sending chills up and down her spine.

He stopped them.

"Shhh . . ." He cocked his head, listening, inhaling the scent in the air. "This way." He crossed from one side of the compound to the other, melting into the shadows again.

She waited one moment and then followed.

"The stable." He didn't need to tell her; she had caught the scent as well. But they were at a rear wall, with no access and only one direction in which to go.

They edged their way slowly, cautiously, toward the corner they could not see in the shadows.

And it was there, suddenly, and they were around it and running toward the entrance.

"Thank God for the moon," he muttered, as they disengaged the doors and pulled them open. "I hope you can ride."

"I can't," she whispered tremulously.

"You're going to have a short, fast course then. Stay here." He disappeared into the blank darkness.

She heard the horses react as they sensed the disruptive presence. She heard him cursing as he fought to bring out the horses. She couldn't imagine how he would get them in the dark, but he was a man who could do anything.

Even outrun demons.

It was taking so long, so long. In the distance she could hear the amir's men, their voices distant, angry, fading in and out of earshot as they ran around the compound.

The horses were restive and noisy as Sinclair rooted among them, stamping their hooves, blowing, neighing, surely being heard by someone in the compound.

"I'm coming . . ." his voice knifing out of the blackness.

And then he was there, already mounted, holding his hand out to her.

"Slower this way, but better than your falling off."

He was so strong; after everything he still had the strength to lift her singlehandedly up onto the stallion in front of him.

"Get your legs over; we're going to ride, and hard."

She shifted her body and swung her leg over. She felt his arms come around her and his hands entwine in the horse's mane.

She heard the shouts in the distance as he maneuvered their mount out of the shadow of the stable and into the moonlight.

They were a hundred yards away from their pursuers as he urged the horse on.

It leapt forward at his signal in a burst of power that almost unseated them both, and it raced up the ridge overlooking the beach with the speed of the wind.

Someone was behind them. They heard the pounding of hooves out of rhythm with their own, and he pushed their mount harder, to greater speed, to farther distance.

The horse sprinted and picked up speed, dashing across the ridge, up and down the swales of sand as if they were hard ground.

She hung on for dear life, the strength of his arms the only thing keeping her from falling off.

They were outrunning their enemies. Faster and faster into the blackness they went, with only the certainty of Sinclair and the instinct of their mount to guide them.

An interminable time later, Sinclair reined in the lathered horse and slowed him down to a walk and finally to a halt.

"We'll rest here."

Here was in the middle of nowhere, close by the water, far enough away from Tafiq that the amir could not catch up with them.

He stripped off some material to tether the horse and then sank wearily onto the sand; she folded herself down next to him and they stared out at the water, where there was a lightening toward the east, the first sign of dawn.

"They'll expect to find us now," he said suddenly. "They'll be searching at first light."

"Why? What do they think they'll find?"

"Corpses. They think they'll find living corpses asleep in the sand. Do you know anything about that? Do you understand what was happening in Kabir? And that they went so far as to paint your body with the markings of the owl, the mark of the *strix,* because there was nothing else, not a mark, a sign or a symbol. That's why they ran the horses: a horse with virgin child riding it is supposed to shy away from approaching anything supernatural. But it didn't matter—because we escaped from Kabir, they will believe what they believe. They believe that we're of the living dead . . . that we're ghouls who rise from the grave and walk by night . . . monsters . . . blood-suckers—vampires."

# Chapter 13

*Monsters again . . . blood-sucking ghouls—in secret cells in a fortress in the middle of nowhere. . . .*

She felt faint, hysterical, and there was no time for histrionics.

"I'll tell you the rest as we ride. We have to keep moving. They'll be out by sunrise because ghouls hide from the sun, and they will think that we won't have had time to find some resting place. Do you understand?"

She was trembling, consumed by the horror of it, and by the confirmation of all she had experienced in Kabir. "I . . . I understand."

The sky was already streaked with pink and a hint of the sun edging up over the horizon. They couldn't wait much longer.

"I think we should go."

She repressed every question, every hunger. He operated with such certainty. He seemed to meet each problem as it came and solved it the best he could. He had had the foresight to steal the jewels, gotten them off Kabir, evaded the amir, liberated their transportation, and now the next problem was getting to Istanbul. One thing at a time. One decision at a time. And slowly and inexorably the thing got done.

They headed northeast, because by his reckoning that was the approximate route toward the city.

They rode fast at first, aiming for distance from Tafiq, and the horrors of Kabir.

But as the day heated up and they veered further and further from the water, and they passed no other villages where they could barter for food and drink, he called a halt to rest their mount, and they found some shade and huddled there to escape the shimmering sun.

After a while he ventured out and discovered a little pool of water where they could drink and refresh themselves and then it was back in the shade while they waited out the torrid midday heat.

"Tell me now," she said after a long revivifying silence, "tell me what they were looking for. Tell me what it means."

She was ready, she thought; she thought she felt secure enough now that the amir's men would never find them; she was confident, even, that Istanbul was within reach, and so nothing evil could ever touch her again.

He squinted at the sun, trying to calculate how much longer they would have to remain at a standstill. A day would not be nearly enough time to talk about what had happened—or a month—or maybe even a lifetime.

He wondered how fortunate he was that the amir had chosen to speak before his advisers became bloodthirsty about testing the strangers.

He knew too much—or perhaps not enough.

"This is what the amir told me," he said finally. "More than twenty-five years ago, after the war in the Crimea, an itinerant photographer from Rumania came from Istanbul to photograph the villages along the Strait of Makhmar. He had been on the battlefields; he had witnessed bloodshed—he had defied death. He thought he was immortal. The amir said he was a strange one who stayed secluded by day and went out among them at night. And when he wished to photograph them, he would cover himself with a drape and walk among them with his apparatus, sometimes posing them, sometimes taking photographs of the landscape.

"And sometimes he invited them to sit in what he called his studio, which was the room he occupied in the compound by invitation of the then amir, Begoun al-Raouf Bazouk, who was particularly intrigued with both the process and the photographer's talk of eternal life through the medium of the photographic process.

"He spent innumerable hours with Bazouk, taking pictures, discussing theology and philosophy, and the theories of war, death and the nature of loyalty.

"He had saved many men on the battlefield, he told Bazouk, and now he would give many men immortality in a different way.

"He stayed three months and after he left the bloodletting began.

"The amir knows because his beloved, to whom he was betrothed, and who was coveted by Bazouk, was the first of the victims they found. Dead, drained of blood, utterly, totally, a husk of a corpse. And then others—night after night, he said—as a monster prowled among them.

"And when they discovered it was Bazouk—they forced him into exile in the fortress from which he can never escape, and where he made a world for himself that provides him with everything he could want.

"They thought—they were hoping—he had somehow died, even though they knew from eyewitness accounts of those who saw the ships offloading their human cargo, that he was alive, and that he was feeding off of slave labor and slave lives.

"No one has ever come back from Kabir. This is the legend. Anyone who survives must be a revenant, a *vrykolakas,* with extraordinary powers.

"With us, they were looking for the bite marks that indicate a victim has been transformed into a creature of death; and when they didn't find that they started testing us for an aversion to light or water; the shying of the horses, and if we had resisted biting into the organs of animals—meat they told us was . . . tests all for the walking dead.

"They could not take the chance. If we lived, it meant the horrors of the fortress were real, and that the ghouls are of their blood and that we would only continue the never-ending bloodletting.

"And if we died—and if misfortune struck the village—we would have been the cause. They would have killed us just to prove we could not die. Either way, we would have become part of the legend of Kabir."

"And the name of the photographer?" she asked, dreading the answer, knowing the answer because some of the story was so familiar.

"You know it already."

"Ferenc," she whispered. "Oh, dear Lord—Ferenc comes . . ."

It explained everything—and nothing. The monsters lived, and would go on feeding off the living, and no one could stop them.

And it didn't explain how an emissary from the queen had come to be among them.

*The masters had sent him,* he had said. *Ferenc comes . . .*

A photographer from a land rampant with folkloric monsters. Walking with impunity among men. Infecting them. Destroying them. Preying on innocence wherever he found it.

If they could find Ferenc, they might understand why Luddington was there. How Luddington became one of them. What he would tell them when he returned to England.

What could he tell them? It was beyond imagination, beyond comprehension.

And yet they had seen it with their own eyes.

He had changed their course; they were pushing now more northwest, toward the city of Tellal, closer to the Bulgarian border.

And now they were coming on small towns and villages, which they skirted in order not to raise suspicion. But he wanted desperately to make Tellal by the following day.

They rested outside the village of Desir, and deep, deep into the night he went on a foraging mission to find food and water.

He knew all the tricks; he had spent some years in Istanbul in the diplomatic corps, and before that in and around Bandara and Salkha in covert activities that were unorthodox, undocumented and disavowed by the government.

Stealing food was easy. And there was always a well somewhere in the center of a town. Desir was larger than most, which meant the compounds were more far-flung and no one would inadvertently come upon him in the dead of night.

And he knew how to map a strange location, so he could find his way back anywhere. Moreover, the moon was his ally this night, so the only variable was how long it took to procure the food.

This night it was easy: a nearby home, meat drying on a rack in a window. A bowl of fruit on a table. A plate of chopped eggs. A bucket from the well—he was done in a mere half hour and wending his way back to their night site.

She was huddled against a tree, with the horse tethered nearby, and she was in shadow, trembling like a leaf.

"The night is eerie now. Everything . . ."

"Shhh—take the dipper and drink some water. I found some fruit, eggs, some meat. It should be enough. And we want to give to the horse. Then you can sleep."

"I don't understand all the things we know. Why did Asha give me to you?"

"The monsters don't mate. It was another test of aversion. They watched everything, and God knows what they deduced from it."

"I'm scared to death. Aren't you?"

"I don't know what I am. I just know what we need to do. We need to find out about Ferenc, whether it is a legend or it is real. And then we'll know what to do next."

"I want to go back to England," she whispered.

"We'll do that, too," he said, and he was so certain, she believed him.

They came to Tellal the next afternoon, in the height of the noonday heat, on foot, with their exhausted mount limping beside them.

"We can barter him for some money and some transportation. There is a train that goes to the city of Lestra, on the Black Sea, and from there we can travel by boat to Dalmas on the Rumanian coast. Two days at the most."

He knew everything. She could contribute nothing except questions, fears and a willing body that, in the throes of their exhausting travels, he did not want.

It was better that way. Getting it over with before they returned to England. *If* they returned to England.

The glissading sensuality of their last night together—who could hope to relive such explosive passion again and again and again?

Traveling together put enough of a strain between them. He was as focused on getting where they were going as he had been on pleasuring her. Nothing would deter him. It was as if he was on familiar territory and he knew exactly what to do. And all she could do was follow.

The bazaar first, with the horse. Allowing the merchants to compliment its lines, and tentatively feel out whether he was willing to sell. Never letting them bargain down because the animal seemed worn out. Assuring them it would recover within the hour and they would be aghast at what a jewel of a horse they had purchased.

The back-and-forth went on for what seemed like hours, and in the end he came away with a roll of money and two pairs of boots, one of which he made her put on immediately.

"It is good. An excellent price including the boots."

"If a man has the skill and the language."

"You know I have the skill, passion slave."

Her body twinged at the vibrant tone in his voice. "And I *speak* the language," she murmured throatily.

"And I'm always hungry," he countered, his gaze kindling as he caught the gleam of desire deepening in her eyes above the veil.

They were already at the stalls of the foodsellers. "We'll take our own. Which means we'll need some kind of pack and something to carry water."

He shot a question at one of the merchants and then translated: "The train to Lestra. On the other side of the square. Leaving in an hour. Maybe more. Maybe in five minutes. Nothing is ever certain. Is that all? Then let's go."

It was an hour at least, among animals and garrulous men, and silent women who always seemed to be veiled and waiting.

Three hours, stop and go, on the train to Lestra, its buildings marching precariously up the steep side of a mountain that sloped down to the sea where, at the dock, there was a rickety steamship office and a line for tickets that seemed to stretch for miles.

"We buy the tickets, we spend the night here, however we can find accommodations. The locals sell rooms. Or we can stay down at the dock. Loading on will take time. And two days over water."

And it was just as he said. Only hotter, smellier, more inconvenient, more crowded, with not an inch of space to move and a distinct sense that anyone on board might kill from irritation alone.

There was no sleeping, and it was now clear why Sinclair had brought their own food: nothing was provided over the course of the two days: not water, not a biscuit, not a sanitary place to relieve oneself.

And all of these travelers were prepared and they all seemed accustomed to it.

But not she. Not she. To her it was eerie, scary . . .

It was like—too much like—the voyage to Kabir. Her fear increased tenfold as the ship tossed and rolled and the passengers argued and fought all around them.

Then it was several hours before they could debark, and when they finally climbed into daylight she had all she could do to walk down the gangplank when she wanted desperately to just stand and gulp in the fresh air.

He pulled her unceremoniously down onto the dock. She was shaking so hard, she could barely take in her surroundings.

Except there was nothing to see—just the endless water, green hills and the terminus of yet another train, and two hundred passengers trying to crowd onto it all at once.

They took the train, hopping onto it moments before it left the makeshift station, and paying their fare with an exorbitant amount of Turkish *dinari* for the bone-rattling ride to Dalmas.

And another several hours later, into civilization. A real city with real houses, real hotels. Real food. Real everything.

He knew exactly what to do, where to go to exchange what was left of his *dinari* for roubles, and which inns catered to travelers, and it was obvious he was well-versed in this language and the particulars of this country as well.

She could have a bath brought to the room. The innkeeper would provide breakfast and hot water, and one of the servants would haul it up the stairs for a fee.

All of this he arranged, and then they were shown to the room, which was on the second floor and contained a bed, a dresser, a washstand, an armoir, all of oak, and a rag rug underfoot.

"First things first," she murmured, tearing off the *yashmak* and the burnoose. "Burn them."

She stood before him in the gauze overdress and the incongruous boots. The dress of a woman, and the symbols of a monster painted in feathery stripes all over her torso and legs, and clearly seen through the flimsy material of the dress.

She felt tainted suddenly, unclean, unclear. "It won't wash off, will it?"

"Eventually."

He could be brutal; she turned away and sank onto the bed, feeling overwhelmed and close to tears.

"What now?" she said, biting back the urge to give in to all those untenable emotions.

"Money, clothes, food, in that order. Rest. And tomorrow—"

"Yes?"

"Tomorrow we go to church."

She was restive; the room was hot, too hot. She felt too unsettled, nothing had calmed her, not a bath which did nothing to remove the paint, nor eating, when she couldn't bring herself to swallow anything for fear it was an *organ* . . .

She wished he hadn't told her that; she wished he hadn't gone off and left her by herself, huddling in the lumpy bed with just a sheet around her and a pitcher of water and an overfilled plate of food she could not eat.

She pushed it around in the plate. Some kind of cornmeal mixture accompanied a stuffed vegetable . . . and some unidentified meat . . .

He had gone to try to sell one of the two remaining stones. They would need money, lots of it, to go in pursuit of a phantom. And money to get them back to England.

She was beginning to think they would never get back to England.

But he made everything seem so simple. With the money, he would outfit them with everything they needed for travel; they would spend the night in Dalmas, visit the local church, and then continue on by train to Bucharest in the morning. And why Bucharest?

There were universities in Bucharest, with scholars who could answer questions, and it seemed like the rational place to start hunting a monster.

He had come back not too long after—with money, with clothes, with food, and a suitcase to carry it all.

Resourceful, he was, and she wasn't in the least grateful.

The dress fit perfectly; it was white and light, appropriate for the summer, the heat, her flaring resentment. Undergarments to go with it. A change of clothing—a similar garment; more appropriate shoes because they might be doing a lot of walking. A hat. A brush. Toiletries.

A rational mind on the hunt for the irrational . . .

But everything that had happened was irrational, unbelievable, inconceivable.

He ate the cornmeal, the vegetable, the meat, without compunction.

And now he lay naked beside her as she tossed and turned and dreamed of monsters climbing in through the windows.

But the monsters were forever immured in a fortress. There could be nothing else. And so perhaps it had been a nightmare, after all. And this Ferenc would prove to be nothing but a legend, a man—*a man*—who had saved lives, had saved her father's life in the heat of the battle so many years ago.

She felt his hand on her thigh, and immediately her fears receded and her body reacted.

*No monsters—only passion, and that unfurling, consuming desire . . . he has only to touch me . . .*

His hand skimmed her yearning flesh, insinuating itself perfectly between her legs. His breath was warm against her ear. His whispered words were perfectly plain.

"I want you—let me mount you. Let me take you."

She felt as if her bones were melting.

"Be my passion slave tonight. Forget civilization. These past nights—I wanted you and there was no place, nowhere for you to feel how much I wanted you—"

She groaned as he moved her hand and wrapped it around his jutting erection.

"Now you can feel it. Now you tell me—tell me you want it . . . I want your words and I want your body naked and willing. . . ."

She was hot just listening to him, her fingers running all over the forceful thrust of him, teasing him, fondling the ridged tip of him, liquid for him, waiting for him.

"Tell me," he hissed against her ear, and she turned her head so that her lips met his.

"I will be your passion slave tonight. . . ." she whispered, and a moment later she felt his delicious, welcome weight as he pushed her legs apart and mounted her, lifting up her legs and forcefully pushing himself into her and spending himself almost instantly with the fury of a man who could not wait to possess her.

"This is what the passion slave does to a man," he said harshly. "She makes him dream of the delights of possessing her until he cannot restrain himself, and once he mounts her, he loses all control."

"You would take your passion slave *every* night?" she whispered, aroused by his instantaneous surrender.

"I would mount you every night, a dozen times a night, to make up for all the nights I could not possess you. I am hard for you every minute of every night. And I think my passion slave understands that very well."

She made a sound—of acquiescence, of submission, she did not know.

"I need you between my legs every night," she whispered. "I need you hard like that for me every night."

"I am always hard for you, passion slave. Feel me up anytime you want. Anywhere you want."

"I feel you now," she sighed.

"Do you feel this?" He thrust himself into her.

She groaned.

"And this—and this . . ."

And that, and on and on forever; she was sliding on a haze of languid pleasure. It hovered, the feeling, inviting his thrusts, teasing him, pulling him to the brink, testing his mettle.

He met the challenge; he was her master, there was nothing she could do to tempt him to surrender.

She would have to capitulate first. And the moment she understood the feeling broke like a storm, pouring tumultuously over every hard place, skeining over the softness in her, rippling into all her secrets, and catching his straining, gushing release in its backwash.

He stayed buried in her, panting, his arms wound tightly around her, his lips just grazing her ear.

Her body vibrated against his with tenuous little seeking movements. She inhaled his scent, thrilled to his shuddering breath at her ear, and to the filling force of him at her center, which thickened and lengthened with her every movement.

"Are you hard for me now?" she whispered, gyrating her hips in overt enticement.

"What do you think, passion slave?"

"I think you want me again."

"And I think you can't get enough of my hardness, can you—can you?" He withdrew himself suddenly, abruptly, and moved away from her.

"I need it," she whispered.

"I know it, and I'm going to make sure you get it." He was standing at the edge of the bed, and he reached for her and pulled her toward him so that she was lying horizontal to the foot of the bed, with her legs at the edge of the mattress.

"I want to see it."

"I don't want you to see it; I want you to feel it—every last hard inch of it—when I put it where you want it most. . . ."

She lay very still, shuddering with excitement. The dark surrounded her, and the scent of sex. And the erotic anticipation of the moment when he would take her.

But he didn't take her with the forceful mastery she expected.

He spread her legs and lifted them against his hips. And then he moved against her and pushed himself into her slowly, sensually, and paused.

"You feel it."

She moaned.

He pushed again and paused. "You feel it."

She groaned.

He pushed again and paused. "Tell me how hard it is."

"More . . ."

"I'm not moving, passion slave. Tell me how hard."

She shifted her body, trying to bear down on him. "Please . . ."

"Begging for it, passion slave?" He pushed again and paused.

"All those promises . . ." she murmured, wriggling and shimmying to press herself fully and wholly on his shaft.

"That's my promise, passion slave. All the hard, hot sex you can handle."

"I can handle it," she said grittily, undulating against him. "I can handle every hard inch of you."

He drove himself this time, a forceful thrust that embedded him deep within her.

"You've got it now, passion slave."

She writhed in pleasure. "Oh, and I feel it, all hard and throbbing and just waiting to give itself to me."

"It's waiting to give *something* to you. . . ."

"Don't wait—" she whispered, lifting herself against him, demanding his heat, enticing his rippling possession of her.

It was all she wanted, and she thought she had never felt him so deeply, so intensely.

He held her legs, so that her body was canted upward in their joining. The position gave her purchase to move in ways she could not when she was pinned to the bed.

And it gave her the most erotic sense of his possession of her, as if he were the center of the world, and her sex, her pleasure, her life all radiated out from him.

And then his thrusts—this time long and slow and compellingly hard against the softness, the enfolding heat of her.

She had never felt that hard-soft oppositeness so fully; she had never understood so completely how complementary were the differences, how perfect.

In the dark. Feeling only that one long, strong hard part of him that had already enslaved her. Wanting it. Pumping for it. Knowing she would beg for it. Making those unintelligible little sounds of pleasure at the back of her throat in rhythm with his thrusts . . .

She didn't want it to end. But there was an urgency suddenly in him, and then, deliciously, in her; she couldn't wait, he wouldn't let her.

Every nerve ending in her was taut with expectation. Her body twinged, spasmed; she ground her hips down onto him hard, hard, hard.

He came back at her, driving into her again and again and again, shifting her hips to take him more fully, more intensely.

"Is it hard enough for you, passion slave . . ."

She couldn't answer; she was thrashing around on the bed,

pumping wildly, her whole body suffused with a violent need for completion.

And it was there, just there, just one more thrust, and one more—she could feel it coming; she could feel all the strength, the power, the force of him focused on that one shimmering, expanding point of pleasure.

She almost didn't want to give it up. She didn't want to . . . want to—want . . . she wanted—

He wanted . . .

In the dark they exploded together, their bodies grinding violently against each other in a shattering, heart-stopping culmination that left them both breathless.

And then—a stillness, a silence; he lowered her, kneeling on the side of the bed, saying not a word because there were just no words to say.

He didn't lay down next to her; he remained joined with her, not an inch of his power diminished, and there was no possible way to ignore him *there*.

She angled her legs and pushed herself downward to embed him more deeply.

"The passion slave is still not satisfied."

"A passion slave is always ready to be possessed by her master," she whispered primly. Shakily. He was grinding his hips against hers, still deep and hard within her, tormenting her, tantalizing her.

"Is she?" he murmured.

"Always naked, always willing."

"Is she?" Gyrating tauntingly now.

"Always . . . wanting—"

"Wanting *what,* passion slave?"

"The . . . hard part . . . the brutal, hard part—" she gasped as he slipped himself out of her with a suddenness that was explosive, and then nudged himself back into her with that same slow, pushing, pausing movement.

"Brutal . . . ?"

"When you're not between my legs . . ."

"Brutal for me, too. Brutal wanting you and not being able to possess you. But tonight . . . you are my passion slave and I will have you as often and as many ways as I want. . . ."

She felt him climb onto the bed and over her, supporting himself by his hands and knees so that he was directly above her, not touching her body, not connected to her in any way except by the hot, filling length of him joined with her.

In the dark, where she could see nothing, only *feel*—

Feel *him* . . .

Feel *it* . . .

*Want it, long for it—she didn't care . . . her nakedness was his to do with as he wanted—she was his for the price of the unspeakable pleasure he could give her—and she needed it . . . she would beg for it—*

She braced her legs against the mattress and lifted herself to meet him more fully.

*Heaven between her legs, thrusting, filling, slipping in and out of that hot, enfolding sheath that wanted to contain it there forever . . .*

*Heaven . . .*

*Feeling—*

Once again there was nothing else in the world but his pounding, potent manhood, wringing every ounce of shattering pleasure out of her body.

In the dark. And then him, panting, lying down beside her, his heartbeat thudding like a drum, his lathered body just touching hers, the scent of their sex permeating the room.

*Heaven . . .*

*Bone-melting heaven—*

"Passion slave . . ."

Two hours later . . . perhaps less? She awakened instantly at the sound of his voice, so raw with sensual need. She reached out her hand to touch him; he was all there, reaching for her.

"Are you naked and willing?"

"A passion slave is always naked and willing," she whispered, her fingers caressing his bone-hard shaft, sliding all up and down its hot, throbbing length. "Especially when her master is so hard for her."

"How long did it take, passion slave? Only long enough to imagine how I want to possess you this time. And instantly I was hard for you."

His words, in the dark, with her hand fondling his ramrod manhood, made her wet with excitement.

"Tell me—" she whispered.

"Climb onto me, down on me . . ."

She caught her breath.

". . . sit on me—"

*Oh, God; oh, yes . . .*

She was up and straddling him in an instant, poising herself over him, seeking the bulbous tip of him and then slowly lowering herself until she felt the nudge of it against her feminine fold.

She gasped as she pushed further and he was there, and his hands were cushioning her buttocks, guiding her, settling her, pushing her downward and downward until she encompassed the whole hard length of him and she could only feel him pulsating wildly in her hot, wet core.

And then his hands—all over her, feeling her buttocks, her crease, her thighs, moving to her ribs, her breasts, her nipples—

Oh, her nipples—she bent forward to give him her taut, tingling nipples, and she felt him, she felt him so hard, so deep, she felt his fingers rolling and stroking her nipples into two hot pleasure points, and she felt as if she was going to expire from the pure excitement of it.

But her body knew differently. Her body was rippling, undulating, grinding against his urgently, enticing him with the response of her nipples, tantalizing him with the way she danced around his hot male root.

She rode him. She rode him up and down and all around. She reared back to seat herself more fully, to feel him more deeply, and then she leaned forward to taunt him with her nipples, to let him feel and fondle them yet again before she once more pulled away to torment him.

And he was driving himself against her, reaching for her, fondling her buttocks, her hips, her breasts, taking them into his hands finally as she teased him once again, and taking one lush pleasure into his mouth.

Her whole body melted around him. This was what he had intended to do: to suck that hard, pointed nipple and drive himself into her until they both couldn't stand it anymore.

He couldn't get enough of her nipples, or her body gyrating tightly against his urgent thrusts. This was what he had imagined; this was what he meant to do—to lick and suck her luscious nipples into utter, complete surrender to him; this was what she was made for: his body, his mouth, his hot . . . hard—volcanic eruption . . . spuming like a geyser—on and on and on . . . his body spasming wildly, thrusting upward against her violent push down, her cry of pleasure as she came drowned in the tide of his release—

Everything noticed and not noticed—in the dark—as she collapsed against his chest.

No energy to move; he remained as always embedded within her.

And this time, finally exhausted, they slept.

What woke her up she couldn't imagine. He was sound sleep beside her. There wasn't a sound in the room. Not a sound from the street.

Everything eerily silent . . .

And yet, and yet . . .

There was something . . . something—

She swung her legs over the bed and padded to the window.

Fog, hovering like a sentient presence, the street barely visible, a street lamp shining hazily like a beacon from below.

She climbed back into bed and huddled against the rock-solid wall of Sinclair's chest.

There was nothing—her imagination only . . . a nightmare she couldn't remember.

She turned on her side, felt something clammy at her neck, and jacked herself up into a sitting position in terror.

As real as . . . something . . . she felt it—she touched her neck. She *had* felt something . . . her heart started pounding—

There was a thickness in the air, and a chill, as if the fog had drifted into the room, palpable, musty—in motion . . . ?

And then suddenly—it was gone, and with it, the dankness that had permeated the room.

And then—and then . . . something blocking the window . . . outside the window . . . ? Splayed against the window—

Her heart stopped; she just knew her heart had stopped. She couldn't move, she couldn't breathe . . .

Something was outside the window . . .

And then suddenly gone . . .

She lay stiff and still, like a corpse. Whatever it was, it could easily come get her, and not even Sinclair could rescue her then. . . .

Mighty Sinclair, sleeping like a felled oak—

She awakened hours later, as the first light of dawn was visible through the window, and she lay very, very still, slowly and carefully taking stock of everything before she moved.

Nothing at the window.

Nothing in the room.

Sinclair half awake beside her.

A businesslike rap on the door and the innkeeper's voice informing them that breakfast would be at the door within the half hour.

Normal things. As normal as things could be on the first leg of a journey to find a monster.

# Chapter 14

Once there was something definitive to do, the horror receded. She found comfort in the mundane tasks of washing and dressing, with Sinclair volunteering to help her.

"Whoever would have thought that *dressing* a passion slave would arouse a man so?" he murmured, as he knelt naked at her feet and rolled up her stockings and attached the garters to the pristine cotton drawers that encased her lower torso. "Who would have thought . . . ?"

It amazed her, too; she felt the same excitement that he wanted her, and an intriguing sense of the power of concealment. Only her breasts were bare, and laid out beside her was a camisole and the light white dress she was going to wear. The shoes were on the floor beside him, but he made no move to put them on her feet.

Instead, he was fondling her legs, all sheathed in the white cotton stockings, and growing more taut with desire by the moment.

"I want you . . . I'm hard for you . . ." His voice was rough with that intense need, and he rubbed himself against her stockinged foot. "Let me take you—"

He had only to speak—her body reacted as if he had caressed her, arching sensually, her legs angling in overt invitation.

He moved toward her, pushing her back onto the bed, his rampant male root seeking her through the slit in her drawers; he hovered over her as he eased himself into her and then he eased himself back on his knees, with his legs splayed wide and her legs draped over his thighs.

She wanted to stay like that forever, with him towering over her, connected to her solely by that driving, insatiable male part of him.

"Always ready, always willing," she whispered.

"And your master always stone hard for you, always wanting you . . . clothed or naked, wanting you . . ." He took her then, he was wild for taking her, with the sunburned line of his body pounding against the bright white of her underclothing; it incited him to see her dressed that way, with the nakedness of their joining concealed by her clothes.

He wanted to rip them off. He wanted nothing between him and her naked surrender; and he loved the mystery of it, camouflaged, but penetrated easily and solely by his ramrod desire.

"Passion slave . . ." His voice was raw, shaken with emotion as he drove against her and she met his every vigorous thrust with sensual abandon.

"Your passion slave," she whispered. "You named me . . ."

"I named you perfectly, passion slave. You spread your legs for me instantly at my command."

She moaned. "I want to feel it more."

He pushed himself deeper, grasping her legs and pulling her more tightly against his hips. "Feel it, passion slave. Feel it hard and tight inside you."

She gasped. "Yes, yes . . . more . . . yes—"

"Is it hard enough for you?"

"Yes . . . oh, yes . . ."

"Deep enough for you?"

"So deep, and *so* hard . . ." she was almost incoherent with pleasure, writhing against him, seeking him in torturous, tantalizing moves that meant to entice him to capitulation.

"Ah!" as he shifted and plunged deeper.

"Oooo . . ." as hips writhed against the white cotton concealing their fused bodies.

"Ummmm . . ." as he crammed himself more tightly against her.

"How can a man not succumb to a passion slave?" he muttered. "She has every womanly art at her command, and there is nothing her master can do about it. . . ."

"Ohhhh . . ." She whimpered as he moved and began vigorously thrusting.

"I need to possess you . . ." he groaned, grasping her thighs tightly as his forceful strokes took on a torrid rhythm that made her breathless with excitement. "I need it, I want it . . . I'm hot for it, hard for it. . . ."

He drove and he drove and he drove, each lunge a perfectly measured stroke in exactly the right place . . . so right—she felt her body writhing out of control . . .oh, no—

She felt herself heaving and grinding against him—oh, no—as pounding waves of sensation claimed her, pulling her under, sending her spiraling into a fathomless sensual oblivion.

She rocked against him violently, trying to escape her destiny; instead she pulled him with her, once, twice, three times, and over—he rammed himself into her and gave himself in surrender, the master at the feet of his slave.

She felt as if she was drowning in the aftermath. There were no nightmares in this room: there was only life. Her body flowed with his ejaculate; he lay beside her limp and wrung out and not quite willing to move, and there was a calmness between them she did not know how to define.

That was shattered by a second knock on the door.

"Breakfast," he muttered, rousing himself. "No, don't move yet. I want to blot some of that . . ." He got up, went across the room and rummaged among his neatly piled clothes, and came back with the oblong of cotton in which he had tied the jewels.

There was nothing tied into it now: There was only one stone left, hidden somewhere among the things he had bought for travel.

He began wiping her gently between her legs; the cloth was soft there, and a symbol of something—she forgot what. She felt so tender there from the forcefulness of his lovemaking, and it was wondrous that he understood that.

A few moments later he gave her a towel to put there, and he turned away to slip into his trousers so he could open the door to take the breakfast tray.

He brought it to the bed, where she was now sitting, and he laid the tray beside her. "The usual: fruit, eggs, biscuits and honey, coffee."

"I'm starving." She took the cup he handed her and a biscuit.

"We have much to do." He was dressing rather than eating,

and it was strange for her to watch him envelop himself in the trappings of a gentleman.

*But that's what he is—the son of a nobleman, accustomed to the finest, at home in society, on speaking terms with the peers of the realm . . .*

It took no time for him to dress, and suddenly he was a stranger in a black frock coat and she didn't know him. Suddenly she just didn't know who he was.

"Your turn," he said easily, handing her the camisole and her dress. "I'll play maid if you like."

"But you know what can happen," she murmured.

"It's happening right now."

"And yet—we have much to do. . . ."

"A man must be stronger than his impulses," he said, taking a handful of dates. "It's the civilized way."

She slipped the camisole over her head and tucked it into the drawers. It felt so strange being encumbered with underclothes; heavy, confining.

She pulled on the dress. He had purchased the simplest clothing possible, with the minimum of lace, flounces, tucks and fasteners.

But the high collar choked her; the belt that spanned her waist felt constricting. The shoes felt a size too small.

Everything else went into the suitcase after she brushed and pinned up her hair, including the boots. That he would carry, with their spare clothing, the toiletries, and the water and food he would procure later.

She looked uncertainly toward the window as they were preparing to walk out the door.

It had been nothing—a nightmare, born of the unpalatable truths that Sinclair had revealed to her. Simple, sense-making . . . and never to happen again.

She closed the door firmly behind her and followed Sinclair down the stairs.

She was shocked when she caught sight of herself in a mirror as they entered the reception foyer.

She looked every bit as much a stranger as she had thought Sinclair, an elegantly postured stranger dressed in white with her hair piled and pinned to the top of her head, her complexion pale and her eyes and brows dark and stark against her skin.

And he—a step ahead of her—so tall, so severe in his dark suit, so purposeful; he passed out of her sight and around a corner before his image barely registered.

She followed slowly to find him counting out the money to pay for their room and in discussion with the innkeeper, after which he took her arm and directed her toward a corner of the foyer near the door.

"I asked him for some food and water, and for directions to the church. He said there's a funeral today and the priest will not be available to talk to us. A little girl was attacked and killed last night."

She felt a cold wash of fear. "Attacked . . . ?"

"Murdered. Found by the water, her neck broken and marked with two puncture wounds, and her blood smeared all over her body. . . ."

The monsters were everywhere, and she felt a dread certainty that there was nowhere to hide.

Already the townspeople were milling through the streets on their way to the church, and as she and Sinclair stepped out among them, she could sense an explosive underlay of anger and fear running through the crowd.

"We have to get out of here," Sinclair whispered after he had listened to the passing conversation for a moment. "They're saying, after the funeral, that they're going after every stranger in Dalmas, and they're going to find the fiend who did this."

"Dear heaven . . ."

"Back inside—" He pushed her through the door and accosted the innkeeper again, and then he returned to her.

"He says the train station is a half hour from here, in the valley, and we're just in luck. He has a carriage and driver available to take us—for a price."

"As if he didn't charge you enough for the food and water," she said darkly.

"And I'd pay quadruple to get out of this place now. I think it's going to get very ugly."

A half hour later they debarked at the station.

It was obvious this was a terminus: There was a large stucco building to accommodate the ticketing office and waiting travelers, there was a roundhouse, several trains out of service and four pairs of tracks radiating away in the distance.

And the next train departing for Bucharest wasn't for three hours.

He bought the tickets, a whole compartment, because he didn't want a sleeping car, with its open bunks shielded only by curtains and accessible to anyone; nor did he want anyone sharing the compartment with them.

"You're scaring me . . ." she whispered.

"The threat is real: You can't tell who might be a murderer."

"A monster, you mean."

"Someone capable of that, let's say."

"And I thought we left them in the fortress. . . ."

"We don't know anything for sure."

She shivered. "But it could be—"

"We don't know anything about what it could be," he said firmly. "So the best thing is to take precautions. We'll be on our way in a couple of hours. We have food and water, and we can isolate ourselves in that compartment until we reach Bucharest."

"She was smeared with blood, you said . . . and puncture wounds—"

"Probably third-hand information from superstitious peasants. We don't *know.*"

"No, we just take precautions."

"Which I would do anyway in the normal course of events," he said evenly. "It's a complete waste of time to jump to conclusions. We'll be in Bucharest in a day or two. We'll find out more then."

*Monsters, monsters everywhere—who was a monster? Could he be a monster? Could he?*

It was late afternoon before the train steamed into the station. It took another hour for the off-loading, the refitting and the turnaround, and then they boarded, along with a hundred other passengers.

The compartment cars were at the front, the sleeping cars after, and the bench seating at the rear.

The sky had clouded by then, as if there was a storm brewing, but inside the compartment it was rather cozy, and rather hard to imagine four people crowding themselves into the narrow leather seats.

A half hour after that they were on their way.

The beginning of the journey held some interest for her. The surrounding countryside was lush and fertile. As the train rocketed through the valley she could see massive crenellated castles intermittently perched on cliffs that swooped down to great swales of farmland with trees, hayricks and thatched houses dotting the landscape.

And graveyards, with bone-white gravestones, and trees hovering over with leaves like predatory fingers.

She felt as though the mountains on either side were looming, and up on the peaks monsters were waiting.

The sky continually darkened, as if they were traveling toward midnight. And mysterious footsteps clumped by their locked door, so that it sounded as if the monsters lurked just beyond as well.

She caught herself up. She couldn't keep doing this to herself. She was being fanciful. Susceptible. Everything else had been a bad dream.

She could have dreamed it.

And she was making far too much of the incident in Dalmas. More likely the child had wandered to the water's edge at night and had been caught in the undertow, and pierced by some detritus floating in the sea.

A small seaside town like Dalmas, with so many strangers using it as the nexus of their journey . . . of course the townspeople would want to put blame on something external, exotic, supernatural.

All the elements were there, and the rational explanations, if she didn't let herself veer off into absurd speculation.

And somewhere in Bucharest, someone knowledgeable would be able to tell them the whole thing was preposterous and pure, ungrounded superstition.

They ate. There was bread and cheese and fruit and cold chicken. Water to wash it down. A healthy amount left over for breakfast. And then they slept, exhausted and in their clothes, on each of the two leather benches.

In the morning things seemed less ominous. They had passed out of the valley and were traveling toward their first stop, Ferezhti. There they took a rest stop while passengers loaded on, and a vendor hawked food and drink from the station platform.

The conductor who had checked their boarding pass at Dalmas inspected the ticket once again and announced the next stops would be Sibiu by dinnertime, and then Bucharest in the morning.

An hour later they were on their way.

He seemed preoccupied. She looked at the scenery and covertly studied him.

*A stranger. Civilization had turned him into a stranger, and it felt as if there would never be another dark night of passion.*

There was too much light and too much motion; the shades were up to emit the light from the windows across the passageway, and there was a constant stream of travelers moving from one car to another.

They were still traveling through the rural countryside, with the clustered roofs and church spires of the towns they passed off in the distance.

There was still that hovering darkening of a threatening storm. And a sense of urgency as they hurtled closer and closer to Bucharest.

"What are you thinking?" she asked him.

He sent her a speaking look from beneath his brows. "I'm thinking how much I hate clothes."

*Nothing about monsters; everything about life.*

"Why is that, Sinclair?" she asked.

"Because a man feels obligated to remain a gentleman when he dresses like one."

"I'm not sure what you mean."

"You know what I mean," he said, unfolding his legs so that she could see the very evident bulge between them.

"I see what you mean," she murmured, feeling that anticipatory tension seizing up inside her.

*No mysteries, no darkness, no shadows. Only life.*

"And there's nothing I can do about it."

"What would you like to do about it?" *As if she didn't know . . . as if she didn't feel the pulse of wanting it, too—*

He smiled tightly. "What do you think I'd like to do about it? But there are no passion slaves on a train to Bucharest. Only a lady whose sensibilities must be taken into consideration."

"And who defines those sensibilities, Sinclair?"

"The gentleman always does, my lady."

"Can the lady not make her . . . wishes known?"

"Then she is no lady."

She smiled, a knowing, cat-lapping smile. "Then perhaps she is a passion slave."

"If she is . . . *if* . . . she is still constricted and constrained by her clothes and by her circumstances."

*. . . a passion slave is always naked and willing . . .*

"She is willing and ready," she whispered, "in spite of the circumstances."

He held her eyes as he got up, pulled down the shades over the door and held his hand out to her.

She took it and he pulled her down onto his lap, so that she was sitting on the heat of his passion.

"Not shocked . . ." he murmured, eying her mouth.

"I hate clothes, too."

"What about kisses?"

"I don't know about kisses," she whispered. "Passion slaves are not taught to kiss. . . ."

*. . . and he had never kissed her . . . What was a kiss, after all, compared to the lush sensuality of his erotic penetration . . . ?*

"I will teach you," he said raggedly, and he slanted his head and fit his mouth against hers, startling her as his lips met hers.

*. . . oh so different . . . this press of skin on skin—so . . . refined . . . so restrained . . . a gentleman to a lady—delicate as a rose . . .*

He pulled away. "A kiss."

She wasn't sure, but she felt—there must be more. "How you kiss a . . . lady."

"A gentleman doesn't bother with those niceties otherwise."

"And if it were not a lady? If it were . . . a passion slave—?"

"Is it? Are you? Am I kissing a passion slave?"

"I am always a passion slave, no matter how I am dressed," she whispered. "How does a gentleman kiss a passion slave?"

*. . . oh, so differently . . . oh . . . !*

This was possession once again, this was pure physical, elemental domination of her mouth, her tongue, a wet, hot roll of sensation inside her mouth as he took her as forcefully as he claimed her body.

*. . . this . . . this—*

He took her breath, her lips, her tongue, a dark invader deep in her mouth, endless in her soul.

*. . . kisses . . .*

She couldn't think; she never expected that the raw heat of his kisses would send her body out of control.

Or that every time she pulled away from him he would claim her again, calling her to him with the husky words "passion slave—" that she was powerless to resist.

And who could have dreamed of the voluptuous delights of a kiss?

She could feel him, beneath her clothed bottom, elongating subtly, as if their erotic talk had not aroused him nearly enough. And her own body, already languid and wet for him, tensing with each wanton foray of his tongue, and little darts of pleasure assaulting her very vitals.

He knew how to kiss a passion slave, and she shut out the desire to know how many others he had kissed this way.

He was kissing her now; he was hard for her now. There was nothing else—nothing beyond the kiss and the eroticism of his possession of her mouth, and their isolation in this little heaven. . . .

This kiss was endless; she gave herself to it, she responded to it, she knew implicitly just how to kiss him back, how to make demands, how to submit to his masterful tongue.

*She knew everything now . . . and kisses could not sate her surging desire. Only one thing . . . and yet she kissed him as if she couldn't get enough of his hot, dominating tongue.*

*She couldn't . . .*

He pulled away to look at her face, her swelling lips. "A passion slave is born knowing how to kiss. . . ." He took her lower lip between his teeth and tugged, and immediately the darts spiraled downward, settling pleasurably, unexpectedly, so that she undulated against him. "There was never a one like you . . . you arouse me unbearably and I need to possess you—now."

"Tell me how . . ." she breathed, reaching for him.

*. . . clothes—she hated clothes; they hid him from her, as they concealed her from him . . .*

"It is easy for a passion slave. Lift your dress—yes . . . straddle my legs . . ." as he unfastened himself and his manhood sprung to lusty life. She touched him, and she almost succumbed right there to the sight and the feel of him, knowing that in moments that the massive, erotic male essence of him would be embedded deeply in her.

She climbed over him, letting him guide her against the swollen crown of his rigid staff until he nudged his way between her legs and the split in her drawers, found her welcoming fold and pushed his way emphatically into her hot, wet sheath.

And then he eased her onto his lap, with her legs on either side of his thighs. And he was there, all hard and throbbing and *there*. . . .

"A passion slave never closes herself off to her master," she whispered as she reveled in the feel of him. Had it only been this morning? It was too long, too long to go without his hard possession of her.

And he felt it, too. She could see it in those eyes, burning now with the lust of desire.

"And will this passion slave always find a way to receive me—no matter where, no matter when?"

She undulated her lower torso against him. "Are you not where we both want you to be?"

"I am where I want to be, between the legs of a hot, willing passion slave."

"And I have what I most want between my legs," she whispered in answer, and she felt the thrusting spurt of him as he reacted to her words.

"You are always so hot and tight."

"And you always fill me so completely."

"Don't move."

"I wouldn't try . . ." she sighed, because it was perfect sitting on him, her body pressed tightly against him, naked and dressed in the most erotic way, as if his possession of her were the one item she needed to complete her wardrobe.

The subtle rocking of the train added to their arousal, an element they could not control.

She leaned into him, shimmying downward; he slanted his mouth over hers and took her, took her mouth, took her body, jamming inward and upward forcefully in total mastery of her melting heat.

Oh, and then—what was there? Sensation, total hot, naked sensation she was helpless to resist, and more, that she craved; this hot, hard man, surrendering to the wet, soft, undulating lure of her . . .

"I love the thought of penetrating your clothes." His voice was barely a breath above her lips. "I love the thought of you dressed and naked for me. I feel you surrounding me, naked and clothed. I can't stop myself. . . ."

He had buried himself within her to the very root of him. "I can't stop wanting you. . . . This is insane—a passion slave on a train spreading her legs for me . . ."

"And what are you doing to me?" she whispered, holding on tightly to him. "You don't know what you're doing to me. . . ."

"Tell me . . ." His lips touched hers. "Tell me what I do to you—"

"I want it . . . just as much—"

"Yes . . . ?" Another light touch against her lips.

"I love it between my legs. . . ." She was answering every kiss, every touch. "I need it there—I can't wait to feel it there. . . ." She melted against his lips, seeking his tongue. Just like that. Just . . . like—that . . . as he thrust upward in rhythm with her telling kisses.

Like that—she didn't have to move; she didn't have to do anything except part her lips and welcome his seeking tongue and his masterful stroking, and both were part and parcel of each other—his hot, commanding tongue and the dominating thrust of his body.

Just that . . . like that—she opened herself to him, she unfurled for him, her heat welcoming his, tantalizing him—she was so close, so close . . . her mouth was violent on his, all of her seeking him in the most primitive, elemental way.

His passion slave, his . . . that was what she was, made to pleasure him, and be pleasured in return . . .

No . . . made for him to pleasure . . . white hot and raging out of control all over him, riding a billowing wave of turbulent sensation—no control, nothing, tumultuous, churning, cascading downward, ever downward, like the tide rushing in and crashing on the rock-hard shore.

Rushing to meet the wet, hard shore . . . as he pushed against her and pushed, and pulled from her every last eddy of pleasure before she drowned in the lusty undertow of his explosive, mindless release.

Now the air was suffused with the scent of their sex.

She sat across from him, all primly and trimly arranged; it was early evening, and he had broken out the remainder of the food they had purchased in Dalmas.

The bread by then was almost stale, but neither noticed. The cheese had melted; the fruit was hot and slightly sour. The chicken was gone; the water was warm.

Sibiu was an hour away. They ate ravenously as the miles sped by and darkness fell.

There were candle sconces on the wall of the compartment; he lit one and it cast a shadowy glow over them.

She sipped the water, savoring it as if it were champagne, choosing not to think of anything beyond the next moment, and the flaring look of arousal in his eyes.

The train steamed into Sibiu shortly thereafter.

Enclosed in their cocoon, they listened to the bustle of passengers and vendors, on and off, off and on, voices, footsteps, shouts, the wail of the whistle as the train got set to depart, more noise as those who were not passengers raced for the exits.

And then they were moving again, slowly, the wheels grinding, the mournful sound of the whistle reverberating to the skies.

The pulsating rhythm of the wheels echoed the slow acceleration of a different kind of hunger between them.

"I need a name for you, passion slave." He was lounging against the corner of his seat by the door, merely wetting his lips with the water.

"I have a name," she said tartly.

"It's not enough of a name—Sayra, a proper name, a lady name. *Not* the name of a passion slave. Not a name that when I address you will arouse you and make you ready for me. I need a name. . . ."

She loved the idea of a passion name, but she wouldn't let him know it. "My name is perfectly fine. You ought to use it sometime."

"You are most decidedly *not* a Sayra when you open yourself to me."

She swallowed, hard. "What am I then?"

The air thickened. "Paphia, Cypria, Jezebel, Lai . . . Messalina—you are all the women who fearlessly give themselves to the men they want . . . you are Messalina—a queen and a courtesan . . . and every man she meets at her feet. Yes . . ."

She caught her breath; he saw it, his eyes kindled. She turned her head and lifted her chin.

"Messalina . . ."

She loved it. A powerful courtesan, sexually voracious—insatiable in her hunger, possessed by anyone who wanted her . . . a slave to her passion—what better name for a passion slave?

"Excuse me?"

"Messalina . . ."

"There's no one here by that name."

"There's someone here who is hungry for pleasure. Her name is Messalina. She is a passion slave. And there is a man who is hard for her. He was told Messalina willingly gives herself to the man who wants her."

*Messalina . . . queen of passion and desire . . .*

"Tell me how much he wants her."

"He has been watching her for this hour, cursing the gods that have clothed her naked body. He has been imagining the shape of her perfect breasts beneath her dress, yearning to caress the hard points of her nipples, aching to get beyond the layers and layers of her skirt to her hot, naked skin, bursting to bury himself deep within her. That is how much he wants her."

Her body responded, almost as if it wanted to pull toward him, as if it couldn't wait for his touch, his possession.

And she loved the game. She wanted to play it all night long.

"He does not want her enough. Let him wait."

"Cruel Messalina."

"The more you wait, the more you will want me."

"If Messalina knew . . ."

"What should I know?"

"How hard I am for you."

"I *would* like to know that," she murmured. "Let me see." *So imperious. So perfect.*

He held her eyes for a long, sensual moment. Then he unfastened his trousers and pulled his erection free.

She caught her breath. He was so magnificent, so rigid, so luscious.

She lifted her chin. "Hard enough. Let me look for a while."

She liked his darkening expression, and she could have sworn he elongated even more.

"Looking will not bring you the explosive pleasure you crave."

"I like looking, Sinclair. I like the contrast between your clothed body and the most naked male part of you."

"Touch it, then."

"Messalina is not ready to touch. Or to be possessed. She wants to *look* at you."

"I can't take this. . . ."

"You named me, Sinclair. I am the courtesan queen who dictates where and when you may take her."

"Lift your dress so I can see you."

She smiled insolently. "Maybe." *Such heaven, he was so thick and stiff and hot with wanting her, she could almost imagine the gorgeous moment of penetration.*

"Do it, Messalina."

She shrugged. "What can you see, after all?" She lifted her skirt to reveal her prim and proper drawers, and she deftly slipped her hand into the split between her legs to emphasize what was there that he could not see.

"If you stripped them off, no one would ever know."

"I have done what you wanted, Sinclair. You are naked and I still have the pleasure of looking at you without revealing anything."

"I want to feel you."

She shuddered at his sensual words. "I want to keep looking at you."

"Let me feel you. Strip off your drawers. I need to feel you."

"I love looking at you, Sinclair." She did; he was long and strong and so forcefully male. She wanted to reach out and run her hand all over his jutting manhood; she wanted to do more than that. . . .

"Messalina . . ." His voice was ragged with tension. "I need you naked and under me."

*Oh, yes, I want that, too . . .* "Come and get me, Sinclair."

He needed no further invitation. He reached for her; he ripped off her drawers, her stockings, her petticoat, her dress, tearing every piece of clothing off her body with a restrained violence, until she was completely naked.

"When a man is hard for you, Messalina, don't play with him too long."

"I like playing with you," she murmured as she felt his fingers probing and then insinuating themselves between her legs.

"And now I'm going to play with you, as long and as hard as I want. . . ."

"I love how you're playing with me," she moaned.

"Then turn toward the seat. On your knees, Messalina. Perfect." He lifted her slightly, removed his fingers and, with one virile thrust, he took her.

She groaned, a long drawn out sound of ecstasy. The nakedness of him embedded in the nakedness of her. So perfect. So perfect.

"Messalina . . ." He was all over her, he covered her, his lips nipped at her ear. "Never deny me."

"Messalina never denies a man who is hard for her. . . ."

"I am the only man who is always hard for you, and don't you forget it . . ."

"You make it so hard to forget—"

He pushed at her. "This is how I always want you . . . naked under your clothes and aching for the moment of possession."

"I'm always yearning for you," she whispered. "Take me now—"

He did not hold back. His strokes were even, strong, rhythmic and emphatic, as if he were claiming her forever.

His hands played all over her body, stroking her belly, caressing her taut nipples, cupping her breasts, his body pumping like a piston.

She was braced against the seat, covered by him, claimed by him, utterly lost in him and the pounding waves of sensation as he drove them inexorably toward completion.

And when it came it took them by surprise, catching them both in one long, simultaneous and ferocious climax that left them drenched and utterly spent, and he collapsed on top of her, covering her, still thrust deep within her, and they gave in to the fulfilling silence.

They couldn't sleep. He was sprawled on his bench, his quiescent member nestled against his trouser leg.

She sat opposite, still naked, her back against the window wall, her one leg propped against the back of the seat and the other angled downward, over the edge of the seat, her foot lost in the shreds of her clothing on the floor.

She was exhausted. But she still felt aroused and volatile, the passion slave in her element, naked to the man who existed to possess her.

She loved how he had taken her; she loved her wanton name. She loved the fact that he was still dressed and she was not. And she loved it that every inch of his male essence was visible to her.

It was all she needed for the moment.

She lay back against the wall, her arms pushing against her breasts so that her taut nipples stood out against the dark leather of the seat.

She knew he was looking at her. She wanted him to never stop looking, to never stop wanting. She wanted to arouse him all over again, so she could watch his potent manhood rise to the challenge.

She wanted . . .

She wanted to be his passion slave forever; she wanted to think about nothing else but the all-consuming pleasure of his possessing her.

She wanted . . .

She wanted to just stare at his gorgeous maleness all night. She wanted to take him in her mouth and feast on him.

She wanted—

The air was positively steamy with her wanting. And he knew

it. She could see in those hot, icy eyes that he knew it, and he wanted to prolong and protract her wanting.

And, she thought, she could play that game as well.

She girded herself to resist the overwhelming eroticism of him sitting there, watching her, his response to her naked body measured in the ever-increasing spurts of his unruly manhood.

It would be so easy to succumb. But Messalina could make him wait for as long as she wanted. Messalina was in control.

She hid nothing from him, but with every subtle, deliberate movement of her body he seemed to elongate still more.

He watched her. The air grew thicker, the tension almost palpable.

She stroked her breasts and watched the hot desire flash into his eyes. She writhed around on the seat to try to make herself more comfortable and she saw his manhood ripple in response.

She crossed her arms over her midriff in the submissive posture of the passion slave and she saw him clench his jaw as the gesture threw her breasts into prominence.

He wanted her again.

He couldn't have her—not yet, not yet.

She was a slave, a courtesan, a queen, and as of this moment she ruled him. And she was not ready for him to mount her.

"And when, Messalina, will you stop arching and stretching and writhing around as if that bench could give you the pleasure you crave?"

"Oh . . . I thought—I was certain that you were totally wrung out and I didn't wish to disturb you for the sole purpose of pleasuring me," she murmured, just a little disingenuously.

"The likes of a Messalina can never drain my resources. But I will exhaust yours. I will have you again this night, Messalina, and again, if it suits me, and still again, in a dozen ways I can think of, and by the end of this night we will see who is totally wrung out from pleasuring whom. . . ."

She gave him a skeptical look.

"You tell a good story, Sinclair, and heaven knows it is all too easy to arouse a man when one is naked. So what is the point?"

"This is the point," he said bluntly, stroking himself slowly and purposefully. "This is where we start. And this is what we do . . ."

He was over her in an instant, feeding himself to her, and she resisted, smiling up at him in that insolent way she had. She took him in her hand instead, pumping him and pumping him while he braced himself against the back of her seat and enjoyed the view of her taut tipped breasts and her facile hands exploring every hard inch of him.

"Definitely the point," she murmured, slanting a look at him, and then opulently licking the thick-ridged tip of his shaft, and then taking that, just that succulent part of him into her mouth. ". . . ummmm—"

He felt her lips and teeth squeezing and sucking at him, he felt her hands sliding up and down his stiff length, playing him like an instrument, pulling every last note of pleasure out of him until he could hold himself back no longer.

And she took him; she willingly took him and tasted his passion until she couldn't draw another drop, and he sank to his knees in front of her.

"So you think you've sapped Samson's strength, do you?" he muttered. "A passion slave knows nothing of a man's raw hunger. Spread your legs, Messalina. I need to feed on your hunger. . . ."

He didn't give her a minute; he buried himself between her legs in the ultimate carnal kiss, taking her with his tongue, delving into the mystery of her deeply and tightly and inexorably until she was helpless in his hands.

She unfurled her sex for him; she opened herself to him and she gave him all he wanted and more, and she bore down on the magic of his invasive tongue and reveled in the sheer naked primitiveness of his possession.

Everything centered down there. There was nothing that wasn't down there, and he knew it; he played it, he sucked at it and kissed it, and teased it and taunted it until she was ready to scream and beg for mercy.

It was wet on wet, a luscious, swirling wetness, pulling, lapping, thrusting, settling deep, deep within her velvet cleft, and ultimately seducing her into an undulating dance of exploration.

She felt as if she was writhing around the stiff point of his tongue, seeking the ultimate conclusion, needing it, wanting it, and he knew it and wanted her to beg for more.

And then there was no more—there was only the bone-crackling, radiant heat of her climax, incandescent as lightning and breaking over her like fire, flashing hot, raw and then a starburst of unspeakable sensation that rippled away into memory.

He released her slowly, inevitably; he was aroused and huge with wanting her again. He lifted her legs onto his shoulders and softly and deliberately inserted himself into her heaving body.

"And so, Messalina, we're not done yet. . . ."

She wouldn't let him see she was utterly spent. He was unflinchingly at the ready, and so would she be.

"I was hoping you weren't done," she murmured in that same insolent tone of voice.

But her body was canted in such a way that she could feel all of him, and the brush of his trousered legs against her buttocks. It excited her all over again; her body reacted with that telling twinge, and she was ready again for his volatile possession of her.

This time he didn't prolong it. He held her eyes and lifted her under her buttocks, and he took her with short, pumping strokes that left her breathless.

All of him, all of him, all of him surrendering to the naked mystery of her; he would never know why, he would only want to bury himself within her and drive her to sensual excess.

And she wanted it. For all the play and talk, she wanted it again . . . and again and again. No other man, no other sex, him alone, driving and driving until she was mindless with wanting everything he could give her.

He was like a piston, stoking her up, fully focused on one thing—his hard, hot possession of her—and not letting her forget it.

Nothing long and luxurious here—this was male domination pure and simple, and she reveled in every lunge of his body.

He knew it. "Not . . . done . . . yet—Messalina . . . insatiable—"

"Oh I am, I am; are you enough for me?"

"Enough and more . . ."

And he was, he was, all there and pulsating and hard and slowly and inexorably taking her over the edge.

And when she fell it was on a dazzling slide of heat and sensation that rippled all over her body, dancing on her skin and coalescing in that one pleasure point between her legs over and over and over and over . . .

He was coming, too, in short, thick thrusts, holding back and holding back, just holding back until he could hold back no longer and he ejaculated in a long, low, wrenching spew of seed, flooding her, giving her his pleasure, claiming her forever.

And then slowly, in the aftermath, he lowered her to the floor so that he could remain within her.

And she thought, somehow, there was a drift of fog in the compartment, and then the light suddenly went out.

He grasped her tightly and pulled her closer.

"Not done yet," he muttered hoarsely, but there was no more time for that; a minute later there was a screaming, grinding sound, and then they could feel a bumping, rolling sensation—and then, just as suddenly, the car was tilting on its side and slowly going over, following the lead cars that had mysteriously and inexplicably derailed from the track.

# Chapter 15

Everything was shrouded in fog.

They were standing with a hundred other passengers on the graded bank beside the track, staring at the hulks of a half dozen cars and the engine tripped sideways on the slope.

She rubbed her hand over her eyes in disbelief. How they had retrieved their suitcase, gotten her dressed and climbed out of their compartment, she would never know.

It was him, all him, all calm and purposeful, without fear, understanding the physics or whatever it was that enabled him to twist and turn and support and lift . . . and finally get them to safety.

And he wasn't at all discommoded by the thick, heavy fog that apparently had obscured a critical turn and sent the engine careening off the track.

He had been listening to the angry tirade of the passengers and the tempered responses of the crew.

"The engineer estimates we're about twenty-five miles outside the city. Some of the conductors are going to try to find help—they'll try to round up enough wagons for us to continue on to the nearest station. That's going to take time."

He paused and listened again. "He invites passengers to go with them if they so desire, and find their own transportation into Bucharest."

She couldn't see his expression, but she didn't hesitate. "Let's do it." Anything was better than standing and waiting, even forging into the deepest darkest abyss of night trailed by a damp, hovering fog that blurred the landscape.

They set out immediately, four others beside themselves and

four conductors with four lanterns that swept the foggy countryside, searching for a house, a barn, a light.

They walked for miles, for hours, within sight of the tracks on the theory they would eventually come to some town or village.

The fog clung to them like a wet shirt. The landscape was barren; if there was a farmhouse within the distance, they couldn't see it.

One of the conductors and Sinclair finally decided to hike off toward the east to see what they could find.

"I'm coming with you," Sayra said.

"That's not sensible."

"I'm not staying with strangers whom I can't understand."

He held the lantern over her. "You're a mess. Look at your dress, your boots. It's not going to get better."

"I don't care."

And she didn't; she would walk in bare feet if she had to. She could see by his expression that he didn't care to argue.

They went on.

There was something so bleak and forbidding about the countryside even in the dark. It was almost as if it was inhabited by ghosts. There was nothing for miles except barren fields and gravelly farm tracks that led off to nowhere.

They kept walking. They kept their silence.

Time merged into the fog and the endless countryside. Sometimes it seemed as though the mist was lifting and the sky was lightening. But then everything would blur again in the shrouding fog.

It was almost as if they were fighting the fog, and Sinclair was the only one of all of them who was determined to win.

They walked on. Another half mile gone by his calculation; he was leading now, and she was behind him, her feet aching, her bones chilled from the dampness, and the others behind, talking in low voices.

He swung the lantern in an arc suddenly. "There—there . . . a light—"

Two of the men shouted something at him and took off at a run.

"Damn . . . come on—" He grasped her hand and pulled her,

and the others followed, hesitantly at first, and then pounding behind them.

The first two had reached the farmhouse and were shouting up at the light when Sinclair and the others reached them.

They were answered by an angry voice, two, and then there was a contentious back-and-forth as the farmer seemed to refuse to come talk to them.

Sinclair stepped forward then, the voice of reason, and within moments a hoary old man opened the door.

More conversation, in lowered tones this time, with Sinclair holding out a handful of banknotes, which the old man eyed doubtfully before taking. And then he gestured for them to follow him.

In his barn, which was a hundred or so yards from the house, he had horses in stalls and two rickety wagons.

"Here's what we've decided," Sinclair said, speaking first to the group and then translating for her. "Those of us who want to go on to Bucharest will take the one wagon; the conductors and any who wish to go back to the train will take the other. The gentleman guesses the train went off the track at Bereshk, which is about five miles west of here, and he has offered to alert his neighbors that help and transportation is needed. We think that everyone can be on his way before noon tomorrow. But those of us who urgently need to get to Bucharest before that are welcome to join us. The gentleman will provide directions."

A half hour later, after several neighboring farmers had joined them with wagons, water and food, and that caravan had set off for the train, Sinclair moved out the second wagon and hitched up a second pair of weary-looking horses.

He had a few more words with the farmer, and then he handed Sayra the lantern, climbed up into the seat beside her, said something to the four passengers who had elected to come with them and snapped the reins, and the wagon finally lurched off into the cavernous darkness.

They got lost twice, and two of their companions grumbled that the train passengers might reach Bucharest before them, but as the first light of dawn pierced the dank drifts of fog, they reached the outskirts of the city and turned onto a broad boulevard that seemed to cut right through its center.

"The gentlemen wish to debark at the first hotel. They say they'll find their way from there."

"Not too soon, if you ask me," Sayra muttered. "I don't suppose they offered to defray some of the money you laid out."

He shrugged. "Why would you expect that?" He turned and spoke to the passengers, and about a half mile on he stopped the wagon and let them off. "This is the Hotel Buchova. It will do for them." He accepted their gratitude in lieu of money and moved the wagon forward before they finished speaking.

"That's that. Now—" He turned to look at her. In daylight, in the wavering morning sun, she looked like an impoverished waif, with her grass-stained dress and thick walking shoes, her smudged face and her hair in disarray. "I think—I think . . ." But he didn't complete the thought and she couldn't tell at all what he had in mind as the wagon moved slowly forward.

Everything seemed in disarray in the sunlight. They had come from the isolated and empty countryside into a modern city with tall buildings and shops and clean paved streets—and those who were abroad at that hour were looking at them as if they were itinerant peasants who had lost their way.

Maybe they had; monsters didn't exist in civilized cities. Women weren't passion slaves or given a love name in honor of sexually voracious courtesans.

This was the part that would turn out to have been a dream.

*Think of it: herself in tatters riding like a queen, a courtesan queen, through the stately streets of Bucharest in a wagon that could fall apart at any moment, pulled by two horses that looked as if they were ready to collapse from exhaustion. . . .*

*Who would ever believe it?*

*Or what she and Sinclair had been doing five minutes before the train derailed.*

*Impossible—utterly impossible . . .*

*Arabian Nights . . . a figment of her overactive imagination—*

"We stop here," Sinclair said suddenly, drawing up under a canopy where a uniformed gentleman awaited them at the bottom of a shallow flight of marble steps.

He rounded the back of the wagon and spoke courteously to Sinclair, even though his whole manner reflected his disdain.

But a moment later he was helping her out of the wagon and onto the red carpet that led into the lobby, as if she were a queen.

Within fifteen minutes she was lying in a gilt-footed bathtub filled with steaming water and the lavish scent of lavender.

Sinclair was a man of action, there was no doubt about it. He had installed her at the Hotel Queen Europa, and he had left her almost immediately, presumably to get rid of the wagon and horses, and to shop for some clothes because both of her beautiful white dresses were ruined.

*. . . Remember how? Remember?*

*And yet—there was not a mark on her body, no stain of impurity; instead she felt clean, light, buoyant. The monsters couldn't touch her here; they were going to find out the truth: that the monsters never existed except in superstitions that had no basis in anything real.*

*And then they were going to go home.*

*Home . . .*

*Wixoe.*

*Even the name was ugly.*

*Wixoe-on-Ly-y-y-me . . .*

She closed her eyes. She truly didn't want to think about Wixoe and going back to the Pig and Poke. Too much had changed. She had changed. She was never going to understand why someone had abducted her that night.

Or whether she had imagined all that blood . . .

She caught her breath. . . . *all that blood—*

*Like the monsters . . .*

*. . . no . . . !*

She hadn't thought of it at all—not since she and Sinclair had talked about it . . .

*And he had known who your father was . . .*

*No! I won't—I WON'T . . .*

She twisted her body and levered herself up out of the water.

*I won't . . .*

*There are no monsters . . .*

*There is no collusion. It's just . . . it's just . . .*

*Coincidence.*

She grabbed a towel.

*It can only be coincidence.*

She rubbed herself briskly, from her toes to her hair.

*I'll ask Sinclair.*

*Easy as that . . .*

She wrapped the towel around her and went into the bedroom, a large, beautifully furnished room with a plush carpet underfoot and floor-to-ceiling windows overlooking a prominent square. There was a table and chairs in front of the window, and she sank into one of the chairs and stared out the window.

It was early morning now; the fog had long ago dissipated and the sun was so bright that she couldn't imagine shadows anywhere.

Below her there was life in the city, an ongoing parade of carriages and humanity on their way somewhere.

*Just as we will be when Sinclair returns.*

*. . . if he returns . . .*

Now her imagination was really running away with her.

*Stop it! He could have left you in Kabir, at the mercy of those monsters. He could have sold you in Tellal. He could have abandoned you in Dalmas. And yet, here you are . . .*

*And good for something too—*

*No. Good for nothing but . . .*

She jumped as she heard a key in the lock and the door swing open.

And he was there, his arms loaded with packages that he dumped onto the bed.

"What a morning. They're bringing up some food, by the way. I hope you're hungry."

She eyed him warily. "Always hungry, Sinclair."

He looked her up and down. "No more than I." And she knew he didn't mean for food. "All right. Here's where we are: I sold the horses and wagon to some gypsies for a handful of rubles and a palm reading."

"Truly? And what kind of fortune did they see for you?"

"The usual nonsense: long life, many complications, money—an inheritance, they said; a woman whom I will marry, death. Many deaths, actually. The whole thing is ridiculous and absurd.

Anyway, there are clothes in those boxes for both of us, and a new suitcase, with a shoulder sling, which will make things a lot easier. And I converted the last of the jewels to cash. We're going to need it. We are not staying here the night. As soon as I clean up, we're going to the church of Santu Maré. I'm told the abbé is the one to talk to, and I made an appointment before I came back here. So—"

*So* . . . she was at the bed, opening the boxes, before she let something slip she might regret. Inside the first box she found a traveling costume of striped seersucker with pleated trim. In the next was a dark blue crepe walking suit and some underclothes, and in the next, a pair of walking boots.

*So* . . . She lifted out the walking suit and the underwear.

*Messalina does not wear undergarments . . .*

*So—*

*It is clear—that is now over with and the next part of the journey begins.*

She carried the clothes into the bathroom.

*So . . .*

*When a man enters civilization, his passion slave ceases to exist.*

*But does his passion?*

When she emerged, dressed, he had packed and was waiting for her, dressed himself in a new dark cutaway suit, and she saw the answer to her question in the determined look in his eyes.

*Passion still exists—*

*But monsters do, too . . .*

The Church of Santu Maré occupied one square block on the boulevard on which they had entered the city. The spires could be seen for miles, the sun glinting off the golden crosses that topped the pinnacles.

It was hewn from marble and embellished with beautifully detailed friezes of religious scenes. There were a hundred steps leading up to its golden front door, and inside it was as cool as God's hand touching a penitent's forehead, and the arched, painted ceiling reached inexorably toward heaven.

They walked slowly down the marble-floored aisle toward the altar, awed by the grandeur and the richness of the church. There was such a mystical majesty within that it didn't startle them when, as they reached the first pew, a priest appeared seemingly out of nowhere and bowed to them and spoke.

Sinclair answered, and the priest motioned for them to follow him as he led them around the altar and through a door that led to a passageway so reminiscent of Kabir that Sayra's heart started pounding involuntarily.

The priest was talking, indicating the arched door at the end of the passageway.

"The abbé awaits us in there," Sinclair said as the priest bowed and left them.

He knocked on the door and it swung open to reveal a huge paneled room with a wall of windows and a large desk, behind which sat the abbé, who looked up and then bade them enter.

The room was curiously dank in spite of the sun pouring through windows and the warmth of the abbé's greeting as he rose to meet them.

He offered his hand. Sinclair bowed and touched his lips to his ring and Sayra did the same, after which the abbé gestured to a bench under the window and indicated they should sit.

"The abbé wishes to know what necessitates an appointment to speak with him," Sinclair translated as the abbé spoke. "I will tell him we have come in search of the truth of the one called Ferenc."

The abbé stiffened as Sinclair explained.

"He says there is no such one," Sinclair translated and proceeded to ask his questions. "We have heard, and we have seen, that there are those who believe he lives. Tell us the truth of it."

"The Church does not condone superstitions."

"There are those who believe the dead can rise and walk again."

"The Lord died for your sins and rose again, my son. There is no other."

"There are those who believe the risen dead feed on the blood of the living."

"We symbolically drink the blood of our Lord, my son. There is no other."

"It is said that Ferenc was of Rumanian extraction. A photographer of men at war who had gone to the Crimea, perhaps never to be seen again."

The abbé shook his head. "There is no such one. This is all a figment of your imagination, my son; there is nothing supernatural about our Lord's resurrection—there is truly nothing more to be said. We rise after death in God's hands only, and our Redeemer will be there to meet us."

"And yet," Sinclair said patiently, "I am told that it is the custom of your country that graves are routinely exhumed at intervals in order to ascertain that the deceased has not become one of the living dead."

"Our *Lord's* grave was opened, my son. You must not confuse that with the ravings of the disbelievers."

Sinclair looked at Sayra. "We will learn nothing here." He turned back to the abbé. "Thank you for your time, abbé."

The abbé rose first and they followed, as he guided them to the door.

"Go in peace, my son."

The door closed behind them almost instantly as they stepped into the passageway, which felt positively claustrophobic after the musty expanse of the abbé's office.

"Damn . . ."

"What was *that* all about, Sinclair? And where did all that grisly opening of the graves mumbo-jumbo come from?"

"I was *very* busy this morning; I went to the university library, which is a hotbed of information. I thought if I had some local folklore to counterpoint any disavowals, the abbé might be more forthcoming."

"No, he seemed only to be protecting himself. And he never asked why you wanted to know or who you were."

"When I made the appointment I told his secretary I was an archaeologist. They, of course, are legendary for asking questions about obscure subjects." He took her arm. "Time to implement Plan Two."

"Is there a plan two?"

"No." He looked down at her, his icy eyes kindling. "But we'll think of something. . . ."

He opened the door to the sanctuary and they entered the hushed sanctum.

It was impossible to think of anything temporal in such a spiritual place. They skirted the pews to examine the statues of the stations of the cross that were encased in niches on the outer walls, and the luminous paintings that lined the vestibule.

And then he felt a presence behind them like a shadow and he wheeled around to find a figure clothed in monk's robes, his face, his features obscured by the hood, standing by the door.

The monk lifted his hand, signaling them to silence.

"Ferenc," he whispered. "You must go to Brother Giurgiu, at the monastery at Berenjevic." He was opening the vestibule door as he spoke. "*Today.*" He slipped behind the door and closed it.

Sinclair jumped for it, and yanked it open.

The sanctuary was empty. The monk had utterly disappeared.

Berenjevic was farther west, toward the Transylvanian Alps. Which meant another train ride, deeper into uncharted territory.

"Why should we believe a mysterious monk?" Sayra asked finally. Surely the question had to be asked. He was just jumping on the information with no qualms, no hesitations.

Sinclair was scanning train schedules. "Because he was the priest who took us to the abbé. And the abbé knew just what I was talking about and chose not to answer my questions."

"And a priest in the guise of a monk did."

"It's obvious he was listening, that he knew the abbé was being evasive, and that *he* thought it was important enough to risk the disguise to tell us. So I think it's important we travel to Berenjevic . . . today."

Their train was scheduled to Budapest and would stop ten miles outside of Berenjevic, and they would hire a carriage from there.

Hours on the train. This time they took the bench seats to save money, which meant crowds and noise and conversation on his part with strangers.

"They do take this walking dead business seriously," he whispered to her at one point as she stared out the window and ignored the babble around her. "They believe it implicitly." He turned back to the elderly woman to whom he had been speaking as she amplified something she had said.

*Monsters . . . there was no getting away from the monsters—*

They arrived in Berenjevic in the early evening, the only passengers to debark at the rustic station.

There was a traveler's rest there, and a driver and carriage that always met the train. The trip would bring them into the village at dinnertime, and the driver suggested they might want to stay over at the hotel.

Sinclair was adamant that they wanted to go on to the monastery, and the driver balked. They would have to hire another carriage, he told them; his sole charge was to bring travelers from the train station to the village.

The trip took them through some raw countryside and into the musty dusk of a summer evening. The village itself comprised a web of winding streets and picturesque houses set in a wild, isolated community that was interdependent and insular.

They could see it immediately as Sinclair set about trying to engage another carriage to take them to the monastery: People turned away, or else they looked at them suspiciously.

"They say the monastery was abandoned over thirty years ago. There is only a caretaker, no one else. There is no reason to go. No one wishes to take us."

She felt their fear; she felt her own. There was something eerie about the whole thing: an abandoned monastery and a monk who was a repository of secrets.

And no one would go there.

She didn't want to go there.

Sinclair persisted. Was there no one, for a substantial sum of money, who would take them to the monastery?

There was finally one, a brawny young man who obviously had been goaded by his friends, and he wanted lots of money.

Sinclair imposed a condition: He would have to wait for them.

That scared even him.

"He has to take precautions," Sinclair translated. "He will do it—for the money—but he needs precautions."

"What does that mean?"

"He said he needs a half hour. And then we'll go."

They got something to eat in the meantime, some cold chicken, bread and wine, and by that time Radu, their driver, had returned with his caleche, and his security measures.

"This is nonsense," Sayra muttered as she allowed Sinclair to help her into the carriage, which was bedecked with bells. "And what on earth is he wearing around his neck?"

"It doesn't matter. All he needs to do is get us there."

By then it was dark; the heat was dense and the moon was high. In the distance they heard the continuous howling of dogs as the carriage headed out of the village.

And then they were at the mercy of the moon, the lanterns swinging from the driver's perch and Radu's sense of direction.

They were deep in the woods, suddenly, following a track that only Radu could see. The wailing of the dogs was incessant.

The track started to rise upward and the air grew clammy and cool. The overhanging trees were more intermittent here, but the branches reached down like ghostly fingers and brushed their hair and faces.

It was macabre, the density of the darkness, the musty air, the beaming light from the jouncing lanterns, the bright white moon throwing the looming trees into shadowy relief, the destination an abandoned monastery.

And the silence. And the dogs. And the sullen uncommunicativeness of Radu.

She was shivering. The air was getting cooler, but she felt it settling heavily against her skin, almost like a blanket.

As the carriage climbed higher and higher, the moon became brighter, the trees thinned out still more; and then suddenly, as they came around a curve in the road, they saw the monastery silhouetted against the moon and the sky.

Unearthly. A rockpile of a mausoleum perched on a cliff high above the trees, a torch illuminating the massive oaken door as if visitors were expected . . .

A shadow moved over the moon and Radu cried out and jerked the horses and the carriage jolted to a stop.

"He won't go farther," Sinclair translated Radu's tirade. "The omens are against us. He will return the money. . . .

"No—you must honor your commitment: You must take us and you must stay. He says he didn't prepare fully enough. He says he will only consent if we agree to use protection.

"—What do you mean? He says he means what everyone knows—those who rise from the grave dwell here and at night they walk the land and claim their victims.

"—Then it is imperative we speak with Brother Giurgiu. He

says the brother is one of them, and no one returns from the monastery alive.

"—We'll take precautions. He says he fears it will not be enough. He didn't prepare fully.

"—We'll have to take that chance. We must speak with Brother Giurgiu."

There was a long silence after Sinclair reiterated the urgency of their quest. Radu looked up at the moon. The shadow was gone. There was a peculiar quiet; the howling of the dogs had abated. The air was still, thick, cool. The moon shone brightly like an incandescent light.

Radu moved to the boot of the carriage and took out a package.

"He says—for us. He was certain we would not know to prepare. He brought garlic for us to wear around our necks. And crucifixes. And grain for the track and the pathway. Take it. Put it on. And then we'll help him spread this stuff wherever he wants it."

It took several minutes to spread the grain along the carriage track and up the driveway to the monastery.

They walked the rest of the distance, guided by the light of the carriage lamps, so they could distribute the grain all the way to the oaken door.

As they approached, they could see a cross incised into an arch carved into the stone above the door. But, shockingly, there was also a cross burned into the door itself that was filled in with hardened tar.

Radu stopped abruptly when he saw it, and then he insisted they say a prayer before they went farther, and when he was satisfied Sinclair picked up the thick rope beside the door and pulled it to summon the monk to admit them.

The door opened slowly, so very, very slowly, creaking on its hinges as it swung back and revealed a black hole.

And then he was there, an apparition, tall, skeletal, ascetic, dressed in white robes, his skull face impassive, indifferent, his burning black eyes taking in everything with one inclusive glance.

Sayra cringed; it was like looking at Medusa and being frozen by her poisoned spell. It was like looking at death without the rituals of consolation.

She wanted to run, even if it meant racing toward oblivion.

Radu was on his knees, muttering prayers.

And Sinclair was impervious. "We seek Brother Giurgiu."

The monk's gaze swept over him, taking in the cross in his breast pocket, the pouch of garlic tied around his wrist, the grain scattered at his feet, and then moved on to Sayra, who stood still as a statue, and finally Radu, who remained on his knees in prayer, crossing himself fervently.

"I am Brother Giurgiu." He addressed Sinclair in a voice as deep and dark as a dungeon. "Why do you seek me?"

"We are told you know the truth about the one called Ferenc."

"There are many truths," Brother Giurgiu said. "We can discuss them. Enter."

He moved aside and they stepped gingerly over the threshold into the darkness, which was suddenly lit by a kerosene lamp that appeared in the monk's hand.

"Follow me."

He led them down a passageway.

*Always passageways,* Sayra thought mordantly, shaking violently with fear. *Monsters couldn't live without them.*

They emerged in a small room that had been a chapel. There were two rows of pews here, and a leather-upholstered oaken chair on a dais facing them. There were niches in the wall that once might have contained religious statues. And there was a large simple cross cut into the stone wall above the dais and a torchiere on either side, which the monk lit with the flame from his lamp.

Then he sat himself on the chair and gestured for them to take the pews. "Ask your questions," he said to Sinclair through tightly clenched teeth and barely moving lips.

"This is what we know," Sinclair said, alternately translating for Sayra and carefully articulating what they needed to know. "We heard of one called Ferenc from this country who took his talent for photography to war some twenty-five years ago. From there he was said to have wandered through the Balkans and Turkey, apparently documenting post-war life in those countries and—apparently—infecting a chosen few with his . . . blood lust."

The monk stared at him.

"We seek Ferenc," Sinclair said baldly.

"There is no such a one."

"But there was. By all accounts there was, and it is our understanding that you have knowledge of that one."

"There was," the monk conceded. "And he came and he *infected* the order until all were gone except one. I am the one. And I am one of his kind, and so he made me. And that is what I know."

"There must be more," Sinclair insisted. "Where did he come from? How did he become what he was?"

"He was the seventh son of a seventh son who led an immoral life and ultimately committed suicide. And so his soul was opened to the blandishments of the devil, who came to him in the guise of a bat and changed blood with him, and thus he became what he was, and rose to walk among the living, seeking souls to infect with his unholy lust.

"He came, when he was untried, to Berenjevic, seeking innocent flesh. The brothers did not know, could not conceive, did not use their holy preventatives. He killed them. He cared not about converting them to his kind, only blood and death. He left for the war, seeking unlimited carnage on which to feed. And he left his only victim, me, in a netherworld between man and beast, paralyzed by the power of the religious symbols of the monastery.

"I know not where he went or how he subsists. I know only how he left me: an immortal savage who is less than human and more than a man, and I must repent into eternity."

"So he, too, is eternal."

"No, he can be destroyed. But the methods are violent, vicious, unconscionable to a religious mind. Yet sometimes, even I—yearn for surcease."

"He lives . . ." Sinclair murmured.

"You must destroy him," Brother Giurgiu whispered. "He is the pulsating heart of darkness. When he stops feeding no one else can be nourished. When he dies they all will die."

"Then you will die."

"But they all will die, they all *must* die. . . ."

"How many can there be?"

"As many as he has infected . . . anywhere, all over the world . . . the living dead walking among us—"

*Ferenc comes* . . . Sayra heard the words; she saw the blood-dripping jaws of the man called Luddington, she heard his voice as raw as rusted metal . . . *Ferenc comes—*

*The monster lives and goes with impunity among us. . . .*

"Tell me how," Sinclair persisted.

"No—you know already, and now I have given you what you could not find in a book: The *vircolac* lives. Ferenc lives. Find him and destroy him and all the living dead shall perish."

The monk's dispassionate words resonated in the room, underscored by the hum of Radu's voice chanting prayers behind them.

"How will I know him?"

"You will know him. You have always known him. He will wreak such destruction, such carnage, you cannot help but know him."

"He has already," Sinclair murmured. "But why him? Why not you?"

"The *vircolacas* slept for a millennium before him. He was chosen. His evil is unparalleled. He has had the opportunity to wander the earth; we will never know the extent of his contamination. But when you destroy him they all will die.

"As for me, I am bound to Berenjevic; the symbols of my religion contain me. I feed where I can among the vermin, but everywhere, everywhere, the crosses constrain me; I am eternally at war with my feral nature. You come to me armed with the instruments of protection, the first to give me hope. Find him and destroy him, and then I can rest in peace."

"Tell me how."

"You know everything. I can tell you no more. It is time for you to go." And they could not help but feel the urgency in him.

"Ferenc is among us . . ." Sinclair said, trying again.

"You will know. You must leave now."

The monk rose from his chair in a preemptory motion.

"Tell the penitent over there it is time to go."

It was Sayra who did that, on shaking legs, barely able to comprehend the whole of what the monk had told them; Radu got to his feet blindly and stumbled out of the room.

"He will not know what he heard in this room this night," the monk said, holding up the lamp. "Only you will remember. Only you will take action."

They entered the passageway.

Suddenly something scurried by at their feet. The monk stopped, the light wavered, he looked downward, as if something beyond his powers were tempting him; then he moved resolutely forward until he reached the door and opened it.

They stepped out into the flickering light of the carriage lamps.

The monk looked down at the grain at his feet and then up at Sinclair. "Go in peace," he whispered. "I go to my hell."

# Chapter 16

They came to Calais after four long, arduous days of travel—from Berenjevic to Budapest, to Vienna, Munich, Paris and finally Calais, and the boat train to Dover.

But it had really felt like they were running as far and as fast as they could, running from the monsters. And there was no way to outwit them; the whole trip long, she had felt as if they were with her, hovering, waiting to strike.

Her sense of dread was all-pervasive. As they came closer and closer to Dover, she felt the onset of panic. They were going to Wixoe, and she didn't want to go to Wixoe. She didn't want to go anywhere near a place that reeked of her father's excesses and her intemperate past.

But Sinclair had decided, and she couldn't understand why unless he intended to leave her there.

And why not? He had another life in London, and she just knew the top-lofty son of a peer would find it very easy to leave a passion slave to the sin and slime of the Pig and Poke.

There was the real fear: He would abandon her and return to London and she would have to go back to the Pig and Poke and her father's stinking hovel.

He had been silent the whole journey, almost as if he had crossed some invisible boundary between the Balkans and Western Europe that had transformed him from the intrepid adventurer into the controlled and self-contained man whom she had first seen when she had strutted into the begoun's reception room.

She had no idea what he was thinking; she was almost afraid to ask.

*Sinclair knew everything, the ghoulish monk had said. He had said he was one of them. Ferenc was the lifeblood. Destroy him and they all would die . . .*

*Monsters everywhere . . .*

*Boxed in by symbols and light and water and bells. Able to wipe away memory and time at will and prey on superstition . . .*

*Yet they were real, blood-leeching beings imprisoned in limbo, in a hell not of their own making—*

*Brother Giurgiu, an innocent victim. And Radu, an innocent bred on legends and fables who would never know he had been in the presence of the reality . . .*

*And after that Sinclair had decided they were going back to England.*

They stood together at the railing of the boat train as it sailed into a thick fog that obscured everything but the outline of the oncoming cliffs.

"Are they there?" she asked suddenly. "Do you think they're there?"

He squinted at the misty coast. "I don't know. I just don't know. But that *was* Luddington . . . and they did send me after him. And the fortress was real. What happened to us was real."

"We don't have to go to Wixoe," she said tentatively.

"We do," he said, and her heart fell. "We have to. Your father—he was the first one to speak of Ferenc—we have to talk to him. . . ."

*. . . we . . .*

"But you can never trust anything he says," she murmured. "He is always in a drunken stupor."

His eyes flickered. "We have to try."

"He's demented." *She* had to try; she didn't want to go anywhere near him. And if they didn't go to Wixoe, he wouldn't be tempted to leave her there. "He could have imagined everything."

"He didn't imagine Ferenc. How could he have known?"

She didn't have the answer because she, too, had heard the name during her father's ravings and had never known what to make of it.

"And then we subsequently heard the name in the dungeon of a Turkish fortress, and in a monastery in the Transylvanian Alps? No, your father must know who he is and what he is," Sinclair said.

He was certain of it. The photographer who had fed his bloodlust on the battlefield and the man who had rescued the drunk Mansour—they were one and the same; they *had* to be. And Mansour might just know more, perhaps something he didn't know he knew; something that would explain why someone had to be sent to find Luddington and wound up in the fortress of a vampire in the Strait of Makhmara.

The fog made it difficult for the ship to maneuver into port. When they finally debarked they were exhausted; it was already late afternoon and Wixoe was another hour away.

Nevertheless, Sinclair elected to hire a carriage and go on there, rather than take a room at a hotel in Dover.

There was an urgency about him now; they were so close, so close to getting some answers, he would not be deterred.

He drove with the recklessness of someone who knew the territory, and as if the devil were at his heels. Time suddenly was of the essence; he was racing daylight, monsters and his own private demons in a dizzying flight toward Wixoe.

She hardly had time to absorb the fact that they were barreling past familiar landmarks and back into her past.

She felt like covering her eyes and pretending she had never been there. But he knew exactly where he was going; she didn't have to tell him a thing. It was as if it were imprinted in his mind. And it scared her all the more to think he had been there, and not very long after she had been abducted.

And then suddenly they were coming into Wixoe, and it was every bit as garish and destitute as she remembered.

They passed the Pig and Poke; the doors were open, the men already pouring in to have a drink. Outside, a sign board announced that the Position Girl would be performing tonight.

*The Position Girl . . .*

*She would always be the Position Girl . . .*

*And Messalina . . .*

*And his passion slave—*

She felt a sinking feeling in her belly as he manipulated the carriage down the narrow streets toward her father's hovel. And the ghosts. And her father's hell of his own making.

What had he been to her but the man who had given her life

and whom, in recognition of that debt, she had taken care of as best she had been able.

She hadn't thought of him for seconds from the time she had been taken, barring the time Sinclair had mentioned him in Kabir and now—and now—she felt a dozen contradictory emotions as Sinclair steered the carriage closer and closer to her home.

Nothing had changed. It tore at her heart. This was the place that had spawned her. No wonder she had no qualms about taking off her clothes or surrendering to the whims of a bloodthirsty despot in order to survive.

And she *had* survived; what could be said of her father?

Sinclair reined in the carriage and looked around. The sun was lowering too fast, and suddenly everything seemed different; the streets, the hovels, the whole idea of seeking out this deranged man.

"This *is* the street . . . ?"

"Such as it is," she said uncertainly. But something about it even looked dissimilar to her.

And then suddenly she realized what it was, and she felt a clutch of fear.

"The house is gone, Sinclair."

"*What?*"

"Look, over there—the house is gone. And it looks like . . . it looks like it was burned to the ground."

They searched through the remains of charred debris. There was hardly anything left. It looked as though there had been an effort to remove whatever was possible to cart away.

Her father, of course, had gotten out. He had to have gotten out. She couldn't think differently; it was too awful to imagine.

*Him drunk, unaware . . . no!*

"There's nothing left," she whispered, close to tears for that man, that unheeding, uncaring, selfish tosspot. "Nothing . . ."

"Was there ever anything?" he asked practically, brutally, nudging a heap of ashes with his whip. They crumpled, and a little puff of wind blew them away.

"No," she said stonily. "And now there are no answers."

He pushed aside another mound of charred rubble. "Jesus . . ."

"Somebody has to know what happened. We have to find out what happened."

"We will," he said distractedly as he kept poking at the ashes. "We will. I stayed at a boardinghouse near the pubs when I came here. Mrs. Allnut's place . . ."

"Yes, I know her."

"We'll go there. She'll tell us."

They turned the carriage around and headed toward the main street, into the hurly-burly of the evening crowds.

"It's worse than I remembered," she murmured. More than she remembered—swarms of men seeking surcease in drink and women, streaming in and out of the pubs, and as they got closer to the Pig and Poke, she could hear the Position Girl chiding her customers.

". . . gentlemen, gentlemen . . . that ain't no compliment to a girl—you got to fork it up now if you want to get the best view . . ."

*. . . the blood . . . the blood—*

*. . . everything that had happened since was drenched in blood . . .*

At her direction, they stabled the horse and carriage and walked back to Mrs. Allnut's boardinghouse.

He rapped on the door, thinking that the place looked seedier than he recalled.

The old woman answered his preemptory knock.

"Well, well, well—it's the posh gent what didn't know about position girls, and 'e's gone and got 'imself one in the meantime, 'cuz 'ere comes Miss Hoity-toity Mansour on 'is arm." She opened the door wide. "Want a room, do you? Mrs. Allnut always 'as just what the gents want. 'Ere, in the parlor, and we'll talk business."

He remembered the parlor, and the closeness of the air and the spartan furnishings of the rooms.

"So you've come back, dearie. Wondered what 'appened to you, especially after that business with your father."

Sayra swallowed the lump in her throat and managed to get out, "What business?"

"Well—you went and disappeared, and there wasn't no one to be with 'im and 'e started . . . well, you know what 'e started—"

"I don't know—" she whispered, the dread of what she was going to hear gathering in a knot in her stomach.

"They was scared of 'im, that's why," Mrs. Allnut said, with just the faintest undertone of sadistic glee. "They was turnin' up dead, you know—and someone saw 'im, that's the thing. Dead people all drained out like someone sucked the life out of 'em. They didn't know what to make of it. It scared 'em. It was like 'e was a monster or something.

"By the way—did you say you wanted a room for the night?"

"We want a room," Sinclair answered her question brusquely, his gaze never wavering from Sayra. Sayra was shaken, disbelieving, didn't want to hear anymore. Not another word more. He reached out his hand and took hers. "What do you mean, like he was a monster?"

"I mean 'e was stalkin' the neighbors and killin' 'em is what I mean, takin' their blood and leavin' 'em like mummies. That's what I mean. And then there was someone who said as how it was a monster and it had to be destroyed, and the only way they could think to do it was to burn 'is shack down around 'im."

"Oh no-o-o-o-o . . ." Sayra moaned.

Mrs. Allnut continued on inexorably. "And even after that, 'orrible as it was, they still say they seen 'im walkin' by night, so what was the point, I ask you?"

"What was the point?" Sinclair asked.

"The man's dead and 'e's still alive—" Mrs. Allnut whispered. " 'E's 'iding now, comin' out when all's quiet and everyone's asleep. There's some as said they seen 'im and heard 'im. The dogs howlin' at the moon. Animals missin'. Rats and all. 'E's out there. And 'e's comin' to get you . . ."

"Mrs. Allnut." Sinclair, no nonsense now.

"And you 'is daughter—born of 'is blood . . ."

"*Mrs. Allnut—*"

"Sir?" She slanted a disingenuous glance at him.

"The room includes breakfast, as I remember."

"That it does, and 'appen 'as it that the one you 'ad last time is available to you."

"That will do fine. We need some rest. We've traveled a long way to get here."

She led the way up the steps. "And where was Miss Sayra anyway, disappearin' like that from the pub and no one knowin' where she got to?"

"She had to go away."

"If she'd've been 'ere, naught would've 'appened to 'im. She'd've stopped 'em. 'Ere's the room."

He took the key and swung their suitcase behind the door. "Thank you, Mrs. Allnut." He closed the door in her face.

They could still hear her as she made her way down the hall. "Never no thanks for nuthin' from the gentry. Takes everything for granted. Doesn't believe the dead can walk. Ohhh, I hope the monster gets 'im—after 'e pays me my money, that is; I hope the monster gets 'im. . . ."

She had painstakingly undressed to her underclothes, and now she lay under the dingy cover, shivering. He slipped into bed beside her and wrapped his arms around her.

"It's horrible," she whispered. "They killed him. And they didn't know anything. They killed him because he was a drunk."

He let the words lay between them for a long while, and then he said, "They killed him because he was one of them."

Her whole body stiffened, as if she was warding off a blow. "No!"

"He was one of them. He was exactly what they thought he was. He told me himself—he was rescued on the battlefield in the war so many years ago. You know by whom. You know why. He has always been one of them. He has always been a vampire."

*"No!"*

"He kept talking about the hunger . . . did he ever talk about the hunger to you, Sayra? Blood—he hungered for blood. . . ."

"No . . . !" She tried to writhe out of his arms. "I won't listen to this; I won't. This whole thing has infected your brain. It's not possible. It's *not* and I won't listen to you—"

"Shhhh . . . you know it's true . . . you know it . . ."

Her body crumpled. "Then what am I; what am I?"

"His daughter—and your mother's; she had to be expecting before he went to war—she had to be. . . ."

"Oh, God, this is such insanity," she moaned. "I can't believe this; I can't. I thought we left it in Berenjevic. I thought it couldn't touch us here. I thought it was safe. . . ."

"Nothing is safe—"

"Are you safe?" She spoke in a whisper.

He considered her question for a long, long moment, so long that it scared her all over again. "No, I'm not safe."

She let out a shuddery breath. "He was one of *them*. . . ."

"Shhhh—it is the only possible answer. . . ."

"Answer to what? To *what?*"

"To the questions I wanted to ask him. Should have asked him, if only I had known."

"You mean *I* should have known . . . I'll never forgive myself—"

"*Shhhh—*" He stroked her hair. Silky midnight hair. Silken body. Silken soul. She could never have conceived of such monstrousness.

Neither could he.

"Try to sleep, Sayra. In the morning we'll go as far from here as possible; we'll go to London. . . ."

. . . *we* . . .

"In the morning . . ."

. . . *we* . . .

She felt his hands stroking her and the horror slipped away.

. . . *we* . . .

His voice murmuring, low, reassuring, in rhythm with his magic hands.

. . . *we* . . .

She slept.

Tea in the morning and stale scones just as before. Mrs. Allnut accepted her money and looked at him keenly. "You won't be back."

They drove down to the ruins of the hovel, and Sinclair helped her down from the carriage so she could walk around what remained of her past.

Finally she traced a cross in the ashes, and he said a few words of prayer, because it was certain no one else had mourned the passing of the drunk Mansour.

And then they climbed back in the carriage and headed for Dover, with her crying quietly into his handkerchief.

From there another train, and she thought she never wanted to ride another train as long as she lived; she sat in a corner and all she could do was alternately shed tears and stare out the window.

*Too many trains. Too many monsters.*

*Too much silence. He had deduced it all and never said a word.*

She felt the tears coming again.

*Figured it out—made the connections from a chance meeting with her father to finding a vampire monk who confirmed it all . . .*

*He knew everything, the monk had said it as though he had some psychical powers and had divined it from Sinclair's very soul.*

*He had to have surmised by then what her father was. And so he had known what they were going to find when he had decided to return to Wixoe.*

She stared out the window, tears streaming down her cheeks and she wasn't even aware of it.

It was a bright and beautiful day for a change—a cloudless blue sky, not a hint of dark clouds or mistiness; it was the kind of day that belonged in a world where there were no monsters.

*Of which her father had been one . . .*

*Why had she not known? Why couldn't she remember a minute before she had been mysteriously abducted and taken to Kabir? No, she remembered the blood—all that blood, all over the walls, and no one else had seen it. No one. Only her. And then they had grabbed her . . .*

*Bloody dripping walls . . . she had told Harry and he had dismissed it, said she had imagined it. Or she was going crazy.*

*And then they had snatched her.*

*They—who?*

*She was going crazy.*

*All that blood . . .*

*Dripping from the unholy jaws of the begoun, and that Luddington—all over the cell, the floor, the walls . . .*

*. . . the walls—*

*The walls.*

She shook herself. There was so much she didn't know.

*. . . you know everything . . .*

"How did you know to seek out my father?" she said suddenly, and she saw that he was deep in thought and that she had startled him.

"I didn't. I was looking for Luddington. It was Mrs. Allnut who talked about the fact that you were gone. I went to him because I didn't know what else to do; because it was odd that Luddington was missing and last seen in Wixoe and you were, too. And then they got me and shipped me off to Kabir."

*Got him, too . . .*

*Took him to Kabir—possibly on the same ship as she*

*. . . tell the Englishman the masters sent me—*

*. . . dripping with his bloodlust, the monster had warned her . . . no—that was Luddington—in a cell in an island fortress, in collusion with a fiend . . .*

*A fiend himself . . .*

*In Kabir . . .*

*. . . the stronghold of vampires . . .*

*. . . shipped him off to Kabir—*

She closed her eyes in despair.

*It couldn't be connected. Her father, Luddington . . . Sinclair—*

*All the blood . . . all over the walls—*

She couldn't get the blood out of her mind.

*And then it was gone, as if some unearthly force had just sucked it up . . .*

*. . . oh—my—God . . .*

*No . . . nononononono . . .*

*Oh, dear God—*

*Think about it . . .*

*Blood all over the walls; two men wrestling at the rear of the pub—oh, God and one had looked familiar . . . dear Lord, she remembered—and no one else saw them, and then suddenly blood everywhere, just everywhere . . .*

*—and by the time she got off the stage not a drop to be seen . . . ingested by a fiend who had committed murder in plain sight for the sole purpose of feeding on his victim's blood . . .*

*And left not a drop, not a clue . . .*

*And no one noticed. And Harry denied it.*

*. . . And only she could tell—*

*If one of the men was who she thought he was—because now she could truly identify him.*

*Or did it matter? Was it solely that she had seen the blood on the walls and told someone? Told Harry, who told her there had been no altercation, no fight, no murder; no blood.*

*That she was mistaken—and then didn't trust her? Had he been a collaborator . . . ?*

*Were they everywhere?*

"Why do you think—" she started, but her voice stuck in her throat. She swallowed hard and went on, her voice raspy with the horror of her conclusions, "Why do you think we were both abducted?"

His expression hardened. "I think they took me to get me out of the way for some reason. What about you?"

"I think—" she almost choked on the words. "I think I saw something I wasn't supposed to see."

"What did you see, Sayra?"

"I think—" She drew in an anguished breath. "I think—I saw Luddington in the Pig and Poke attacking a victim . . ."

She told him, in painstaking detail, about the performance, the men, the blood, the aftermath. Harry. The abduction.

Her conclusions.

He was riveted by her words, his mind racing. She could see it. She could feel it. He pulsated with a kind of excitement like a bloodhound on the trail of a scent.

*. . . the trail of what . . . ?*

"Are you sure it was Luddington?"

"No—yes . . . I think so—"

"Not your father?"

*Her father? Had she forgotten about her father already in the torrent of useless tears and repentance? Could it have been—?*

"Oh, God, I never thought of that . . ." she whispered. "I don't know. I don't think so. Maybe—"

They stared at each other, the implications of any or all of those possibilities sweeping them away like a flood in a storm.

The wail of the train whistle startled them.

"Victoria Station," Sinclair murmured. "End of the line. Beginning of—what?"

And then it was just a rush of humanity racing toward the exit while they chose to wait until their car had emptied before they made their way to the platform.

It was crowded, a crush, faces blurring as they hurried by looking for a hack, or meeting friends and relatives.

They walked slowly toward the end of the platform, in no hurry at all. She found herself looking at faces, looking for monsters.

But who could tell who among them was a monster?

"Ho!"

A voice behind them, and several passengers turned and then kept going on their way.

"Ho-o . . . Wrentham . . . !"

Sinclair stopped abruptly and turned.

A portly man was striding toward them, his face obscured by a broad-brimmed hat, his body covered by a swirling cape, his arms outstretched.

"Wrentham, my boy," he said, reaching to take Sinclair's hands. "Only way to get your attention, you know, calling you Wrentham. We won't tell Tristan. I do wish I had known you were on this train. We could have traveled down together. All of us," he added, eyeing Sayra with undisguised interest. "Introduce me, my boy. Who is this luscious morsel?"

Sinclair's eyes had gone icy and his whole body tensed, and he had the distinct feeling that everything was obverse and nothing was what it seemed. And if that was true, he had to do everything he could to protect Sayra, using any means at his disposal.

He didn't even think twice about it.

"Let me present you," he said coolly. "Sayra, this is Sir Ronald Luddington." *Luddington, whom they'd left at the fortress with blood dripping from his jaws . . .* "Luddington, permit me to introduce . . . my wife—"

# Chapter 17

"Sayra—"

She felt Sinclair's hand on her elbow; she could not have moved on her own if her life depended on it, she was shaking too hard, so he briskly propelled her down the platform, with Luddington by his side.

She heard them speaking, but she was sure it was some foreign language because she didn't understand a word of it.

Before she knew it they were out of Victoria Station and Luddington was hailing a cab, and they were crowded together, knee to knee, in a bouncing, jouncing hansom heading into the teeming streets of London.

She didn't even know where they were going.

She stared at Luddington. *It wasn't Luddington, it couldn't be Luddington . . . How could it be Luddington?*

*This man was whole, plump, burstingly alive, his pale, red-rimmed eyes as guileless as a child's, with not a stain of blood on his soul that she could see . . .*

*He looked nothing like the creature in the cell. Nothing . . .*

*And dear God—there was Sinclair talking to him as if everything was normal as pie . . .*

Their conversation sounded like so much gibberish to her.

She met his icy eyes and read the message in them: *Don't say a word. . . .*

*She couldn't say a thing; she was totally paralyzed, and on top of that she just couldn't in the least come to grips with his introducing her as his wife.*

*His wife . . .*

*His—wife—*

*The words were just not comprehensible.*

*Wife. What was a wife? To a son of a peer?*

*A wave of coldness washed over her.*

*This was insane—a spider's web of lies and deceit that could only wind up entangling them in its sticky strands . . .*

*Or were they both pretending?*

*No, she was the pretender . . . and all of this was going to come crashing down on her when they arrived at their destination.*

The cab turned on the edge of a lush park and continued down a broad avenue that narrowed into a semicircle of elegant columned town houses overlooking the greensward and stopped at the very last one.

"Terrace Circle," the cabman announced. "Wrentham House."

They went up the shallow marble steps between the Doric columns to the massive polished doors; and then a brisk rap of the brass doorknocker and a preemptory ring of the bell, evidence of Sinclair's impatience, and his familiarity with this beautiful stately home on the edge of a bucolic park.

*Whose home then? His?*

The door opened slowly and a cadaver of a butler appeared in formal dress.

"Mr. Declan." The voice was wavery, even a little shocked.

Sayra was a little shocked. *Declan—his name; he hadn't told her his name, or anything about his home—and this was his home, and this ancient old man was one of his retainers. . . .*

"Holm," Sinclair acknowledged brusquely. "Is my father about?"

The old man tottered after him as he pushed his way into the entrance hall and swung their suitcase into a corner.

"He's having his nap, Mr. Declan. With orders not to be disturbed."

"Nonsense. Go and tell him I have returned; Luddington's with me, and I've brought home a wife."

"Your . . . w-wife, Mr. Declan?" Holm looked appalled. "I—Congratulations. Please go into the library and I will awaken Sir Edmund and tell him."

"Do that. Come along, Luddington. You must help me toast my wife."

He led the way into the library while Luddington removed his hat and cape and handed them to Holm and then joined him, and she trailed behind both of them, gaping at the interior of the house and its luxurious furnishings and appointments.

*This was wealth, the like of which she never could have conceived. Yet another terrifying layer over all.*

*She didn't know how she was going to cope. She didn't have an inkling what Sinclair intended.*

*And she didn't know how this fleshy country squire could be the flesh-devouring monster of the fortress.*

*Or why there was such an all-pervasive air of chilliness, of unwelcome in the midst of the lovely symmetry of the house.*

"The best port." Sinclair was at the tantalus, turning the cut-glass goblets and reaching for a decanter. "Ronald—" He handed a goblet to Luddington and poured one for himself and lifted it. "To Sayra—my beautiful wife."

She started and looked up at him uncertainly. He nodded imperceptibly, and she forced herself to smile as Luddington murmured, "She *is* beautiful, Declan. But you've always had such excellent taste. Tell me where you met her."

Sinclair gestured to one of the two settees by the fireplace. Sayra gratefully sank onto one of them, feeling as if her legs were about to give out, and Luddington positioned himself by the fireplace.

"We met—in the Balkans," Sinclair said blandly.

Luddington's gaze flickered. "Oh, truly, my dear boy, whatever were you doing over there?"

"Oh, you know, one is always at the mercy of the Foreign Office. A little affair, easily handled . . ."

*"Declan . . . !"*

They all turned toward the door, and then Sayra's gaze skewed back to Sinclair.

He was as tense as a bowstring, vibrating with emotion. He didn't move a muscle, didn't go forward to acknowledge the man on the threshold of the library.

"Sir . . ."

"So—" His father moved into the room and made his way over to Luddington. "A wife, eh? *And* Luddington. A coup, my boy."

"I was sure you would think so," Sinclair said.

"Ronald," his father said, extending his hand, and Sayra was startled to see it was gloved. And that Sinclair's father was not nearly so tall as he or Luddington; he was buttoned up to his chin in an all-enveloping jacket, he had a long, flowing beard and mustache, and he spoke slowly and deliberately, as if he were barely moving his lips.

Yet he radiated an aura of power that was almost intimidating. Sayra felt positively daunted by the energy that emanated from him as he came to her and held out his gloved hands to take hers.

"My dear." He looked at Sinclair. "She is exquisite. This was so sudden. How often I begged him to find someone and set up home and nursery. How like Declan to do the unexpected. You are very unexpected, my boy."

"I live to surprise you, sir."

His father shot him a sour look and then turned back to Sayra. "Welcome, my dear."

He laid his cheek against hers, so cold, so white that she shivered involuntarily.

"So, we're drinking a toast, are we? Declan—?" He motioned for a goblet. "There. To your lovely bride—what is your name, my dear? My boorish son neglected to tell me—in addition to everything else he has ever neglected to tell me."

"She is Sayra," Sinclair said shortly.

"Sayra, then. To Sayra. Lovely Sayra, and my unexpected son." He lifted his goblet and took a sip. "Sayra, Sayra, Sayra—the first Wrentham bride. Well, have you had time to make any plans—where you'll live . . ."

"I haven't had time to do much else but complete my mission," Sinclair said impassively. "And I'll figure out the rest later."

"So—where were you married?" his father asked as he set his goblet down. "And when?"

Sinclair set down his glass as well. "In a little church in the Transylvanian Alps, presided over by a Brother Giurgiu."

"How exotic," his father murmured. "We must send for Tristan. We'll have a celebration."

"It's not necessary."

"I beg to differ. A lovely bride. A successful mission. And here is Luddington to share my joy. Of course we must. I'll send word to Ismail as well. He will want to know. He would have wanted to be the first to know."

"Yes," Sinclair said dourly, "he would."

"It is settled. Now—Sayra, my dear, my son has elected not to stay at Wrentham House for the last several years. I hope you may convince him that his place is here, with Tristan and myself; we have all the room in the world, and the family should be together now that he has brought home a bride. I assume you'll wish to go to your apartment, Declan, so Luddington will bear me company while I make the arrangements. Come, Ronald. We have much to do before dinner."

"And much to talk about, I warrant," Sinclair muttered after his father and Luddington had withdrawn from the room.

Sayra eyed the closed door. "He was talking about the prime minister."

"Oh, yes, he was."

"I don't understand."

"I'm just beginning to. He didn't blink a damned eye when he saw Luddington in the room. Didn't twitch a muscle. Acted as if it was just what he expected. The bastard . . . he knows—Jesus Christ . . . he *knows* . . . and he knows *I* know—"

He paced toward her slowly. "He didn't come downstairs to do his fatherly duty. He wasn't shocked at the news of our *marriage*. He didn't even ask for extensive details. What father wouldn't ask for the relevant details? And he started planning a celebratory dinner there and then . . . why? *Why?*"

He was face to face with her now; she could feel her blood congealing and she just knew she wasn't going to like his answer. Things were not what they seemed. Luddington was a monster and Sinclair at least had not forgotten that.

He took her hand. "This is why: My father's sole purpose was to get Luddington out of here."

They stared at each other.

"So where are they?" she whispered.

"I think we'd better find out."

They bolted into the entrance hall. It was dark as a tomb.

"Upstairs—"

They raced up the stairs, encountering darkness everywhere—down the hallway they went with its Turkistan runner that stretched its full-length—and in and out of the doors along the hallway into dark, shrouded rooms that hadn't been occupied in years . . . and finally they burst into his father's study.

Here was the only light: the bright circle of lamplight shining on his father's favorite leather chair that still showed the imprint of his body.

There was no one there; only the musty scent of emptiness permeated the room.

"Goddamn . . . son of a bitch—"

"This is scary, Sinclair. . . ."

"Shhh . . ." he whispered. "Anyone could be listening. Come . . ."

Down the stairs they ran and into the parlors, the dining room, the kitchen and pantry, and then back into the library after finding all the rooms but that one in darkness, with no trace of occupation, not even the kitchen, and not even Holm anywhere to be found.

"This is eerie. . . ." She spoke barely above a breath.

"Shit . . . I took a chance and look where it got us. . . . We have to get out of here."

He grabbed the suitcase on their way to the door and they surged out into daylight and fresh air and drifting patches of fog obscuring the sun.

He lived in a flat on St. James Square, but as a precaution he took rooms at the Royal Crescent Hotel and registered them as husband and wife, using an assumed name.

She was still shaking; she felt as if she couldn't stop shaking. This was all too much. Husband and wife. And monsters everywhere, even in Sinclair's patriarchal home.

There was nowhere anyone could be safe.

And there was no one who could tell them the truth.

So she would just hide in this sumptuous room and let Sinclair deal with the monsters. They were his monsters anyway. She just happened to get in the way.

She stood by the window, staring out onto an elegant square.

But she must never forget she was the daughter of a monster who had lived in sloth, slime and an alcoholic stupor for all the years she could remember, drowning his unholy hunger lest he unleash it on her.

And for that reason they had killed him. They hadn't known for sure; they hadn't. Only she and Sinclair knew—knew almost everything.

Almost.

And now they knew that his father must be aware of exactly what Luddington was, and it was the most damnable complication.

He didn't have to say it. She could see it in the way he prowled the room.

"Perhaps *we* are dinner," he said mordantly, plucking her train of thought out of the air. "All right. Enough of this."

She whirled on him. "You're so right. This is insane. I'm suddenly your wife; a monster we thought was immured in a fortress halfway around the world winds up on our train from Dover; my father was in reality a ghoul; a vampire monk in a monastery believes you are the agent of destruction of all monsters. Oh, and now your father . . . Sinclair, I swear I'm about ready to—"

"We have to get ready for dinner at Wrentham House," he said impassively. "You'll need a bath, and to freshen up. You've been sleeping in that dress for days. Wear the blue crepe; the hotel can get it ironed for you. I need to get you a ring—don't look at me like that, Sayra. We'll play it out and see where it goes."

"I've seen where it goes," she said, her voice laced with a bitterness she didn't try to suppress. The only thing she didn't know was where it was going to end. She was useful to him now—but after? Men like Sinclair dropped women who complicated their lives like chips on a card table. And what was she but a complication?

"You haven't nearly seen where it is going to go," he murmured. "And I don't think we have any choice. Do we? . . . Do we—Messalina?"

She closed her eyes as relief flowed through her like water. "No," she whispered. "We have no choice."

When they drew up to Wrentham House that night the whole place was ablaze with lights.

*What was different?*

Holm opened the door immediately, almost as if he had been

waiting for their arrival. "Mr. Declan. They're all in the formal parlor."

The parlor was at the back of the house, overlooking the garden. It was a huge room, painted in a soft, silky ivory, with ornate moldings picked out in gold and a massive marble fireplace overhung with a gold leaf mirror that reached to the ceiling.

The highly polished floor was covered in soft-colored Oriental carpets, but the brocade-covered sofas and chairs were stiff and excessively elaborate by contrast.

Sinclair's father was standing by the fireplace, talking to a distinguished-looking man dressed wholly in severe black, as Holm paused at the door to announce them.

"Mr. Declan and his wife, sir."

"Ah . . ." This from the gentleman in black who immediately rose from his seat and came toward them. "Declan, my boy."

She knew exactly who it was: She had seen scores of pictures of him, but she was shocked at his appearance in person. He was shorter than she had imagined, thinner, paler, with a mane of snow-white hair brushed back from his broad forehead, sunken cheeks and sharp, glowing black eyes.

"Ismail," Sinclair said. "This is Sayra."

"Sayra," Ismail murmured, reaching for her hands. "Come in, my dear. Let me look at you. Declan, why didn't you tell me? Or telegraph me? I would have come to you."

"To Rumania?" Sinclair said skeptically. "Really?"

Ismail looked startled, but he recovered quickly. "Anywhere, my boy. Any time. Come sit down." As if he was the host and not his father.

But his father seemed content to sit in the shadows and let Ismail take control. And how could anyone stop him, anyway?

They sat by the fireplace. Holm brought sherry.

"Tristan will be here soon," Ismail said, pouring them each a glass and handing them around.

"And Luddington?" Sinclair asked carefully.

"A bit under the weather," Ismail said. "He sends his apologies, of course; and since Gaspard is in the kitchen he is beside himself that he's not up to it. We will dine royally tonight, and it's only right: This is a stupendous occasion, Declan. A bride. I don't believe Edmund ever thought to see—well, let me offer the toast: to Declan and the first Wrentham bride—Sayra—welcome, my dear."

"Thank you," she whispered, lifting the goblet to her lips. She barely tasted the sherry. She understood nothing about this evening and all the undercurrents swirling around her, or why they were pretending that Luddington did not exist.

"So," Ismail said, pinning her with his incisive, glowing black gaze. "Tell me the whole—where and when and how . . ."

Sinclair intervened, then, smoothly, easily. "Actually, we're in your debt, Ismail. Had you not sent me . . ."

"Of course," Ismail murmured, delicately interrupting him. "But where . . . ?"

"The . . . trail led elsewhere. We met in Bucharest, where Sayra had come through another set of circumstances. We found a little monastery in a small town nearby where the priest was willing to perform the ceremony. Imagine then the irony of finding that Luddington was on the very train we had taken from Dover."

"Luddington is often befuddled," Ismail said dourly. "Of course, when I gave you that commission I thought matters were extremely grave; I had no idea that Luddington had a drinking problem and that is why he disappears at inconvenient intervals and sends everyone into a tailspin. Well, no more. We know the truth now. And it will be addressed; I would offer you my apologies, but it is obvious that your time abroad was not wasted. Not in the least."

"And it sounded so critical at the time," Sinclair said.

"It is amazing how those things turn out to be nothing in the end," Ismail agreed easily. "Of course, you know that already, even though that's small recompense for the time you spent—but then, you met your lovely Sayra, so of course you'll forgive us and forget the whole affair, won't you?"

Sinclair met his sharp gaze blandly. "Who is to judge a man's recompense, Ismail?"

"That's very generous," Ismail said as he refilled his goblet. "And you may be sure I will call upon you for other signal services. But perhaps not until you and Sayra are settled in someplace."

"They are welcome to come here," Sinclair's father said from deep in his chair. "I would prefer it."

"Would you, sir?" Sinclair now, taking his own refill. "I can't recall your ever expressing a preference before where I was concerned."

Sayra felt the sting of his words and was appalled at his rudeness.

*He is not your husband.*

*Ah, yes, the voice of reason. Not your husband. Didn't put an insanely expensive ring on your hand and whisper the words: With this ring, I thee wed . . .*

*Not him.*

*How many sides were there to this man?*

*And what was this script they were enacting to rewrite the truth about Luddington to make it plausible . . . what audience was listening?*

*Or was it a warning, and was Sinclair flaunting it?*

*She could not decide.*

". . . wouldn't you, Sayra?" His father's voice sliced through her thoughts like an expert blade.

"I'm sorry?" She turned to him politely.

"I asked if there was any reason you would not consider taking up residence at Wrentham House."

She felt an immediate stab of anger that Sinclair had opened her up to this without any preparation.

She looked up at Sinclair and smiled through clenched teeth. "Truly, it's my *husband's* choice. And whither he goest . . ."

He smiled back grimly. "Perhaps we should consider it."

"We'll consider it then," she said, making the decision, for what it was worth.

"You belong here, my boy," Ismail said.

"We'll consider it," Sinclair said impassively. "And perhaps Tristan should be consulted."

"By all means, consult Tristan."

Sinclair wheeled around as they all looked toward the door, caught off guard by the voice whose timbre was so startlingly similar to his own.

And there he was: so tall, dark, muscular and burningly alive, with the same light eyes that kindled like flames, so different from Sinclair and so much the same.

But there was something so much warmer about him, as if he had no hard edges whatsoever, as if whatever one saw was the person he was. He had such presence and such vitality that he utterly filled the room, and none of them noticed that there was a woman with him who trailed in after him with a supreme confidence that matched his own.

He headed unerringly toward Sayra, as if her presence drew him like a magnet, and he took her hands.

"I'm Tristan, of course, Declan's reprobate brother and the nominal heir. By the way, that gorgeous creature over there is Evelina. Now—what did you want to consult me about?"

Sayra stared at him, mesmerized; it was like looking at Sinclair, but without the arrogance and the reserve, and with all the angles filled in with humor and élan.

He just barged in and took over and she felt her bones melting under his warm, probing gaze, and she thought that it was possible that she was finally and irrevocably falling in love.

# Chapter 18

He was witty and charming, and he entertained them effortlessly.

Except Sinclair wasn't charmed, but Sayra barely noticed that because all of Tristan's formidable personality was focused on her. He practically carried the conversation by himself, and he completely ignored Sinclair's mocking gaze, which never left Sayra's face, and Evelina's noticeable irritation.

Ismail and his father just sat back and watched, almost as if Tristan's antics were the appetizer course.

"And of course—Evelina. You must be curious about Evelina," Tristan said finally. "Evelina is a dear friend of the family."

"Dearer than that," Evelina interposed silkily, pinning Sayra with her curiously pale eyes, and Sayra thought instantly that that was more than she wanted to know.

"She and Declan . . ." Tristan amplified.

Sinclair said nothing. Sayra avoided looking at him while she tried to examine what her reaction was to this information.

She didn't like it. It meant that the phantom life she had conjured for him before Kabir actually existed. And it meant that there was a definite chance she would never be part of it.

She looked down at her ring and felt instinctively that Evelina's eyes followed hers.

It was a huge ring; too ostentatious, she thought, but it was obvious he had done that for a purpose. No one could miss it: a bright, glittering square-cut diamond, four carats at least, flanked by a pair of smaller, triangular stones set on a wide gold band.

"Lovely ring," Evelina murmured, and Sayra didn't miss the underlying message: . . . *It should have been mine* . . .

"But that was so long ago," Tristan said, watching them as if they were an experiment he was conducting.

"One hardly remembers," Sinclair said brutally.

"Declan!" Evelina, horrified but coy.

She was so beautiful, in a haughty, pale, blond way. She had porcelain skin that was flushed now, and the palest blue eyes that were faintly red-rimmed, as if she had been crying, and Sayra was sure that she used some kind of kohl on her lashes and lids because her eyes were so prominent in her pallid face.

She wore the palest blue, dripping with ecru lace from her neck to her hem, so that she looked like a fragile doll that a man might want to hold in his arms and protect forever.

*Nothing like a passion slave. Everything like a well-bred woman who would never surrender to such fleshly pursuits . . .*

*Which, really, did a man prefer?*

She couldn't help it: She felt a kind of envy of such a woman who would never be a slave to any man.

*But she would never know such transcending excitement, desire and consummation either . . .*

*Which, really, did a man prefer?*

*Which did a man like Tristan prefer? If she could even half believe the way he was looking at her, she would think he wanted to devour her right then and there.*

"Tell us something about *you,* Sayra," Tristan coaxed her.

She smiled deprecatingly, while she frantically searched for the most palatable way to present the lie. "There isn't much to tell. I come from a small seaside town. My father . . ." *Oh, she didn't expect that lump in her throat when she mentioned him . . .* "my father is recently deceased; my mother died when I was a child. I was . . . ummm—studying abroad when I met . . . S—Declan . . ." *and she almost tripped over his name—why, why, why had he not coached her, prepared her?* ". . . and the rest you know . . ."

"Summed up in two sentences, beautiful Sayra. I hardly think there's that little to your life."

She shrugged. *The less she told him the better; a man like Tristan would be fascinated by the mystery of a woman.*

"And what were you studying abroad, my dear?" Sinclair's father now, a startling voice intent on what promised to be a cat-and-mouse game between her and Tristan.

She flashed a speaking glance at Sinclair. "Religious icons of the Balkans."

"Which makes me wonder exactly what Declan was doing in Rumania," his father said.

"I was following Luddington, of course," Sinclair said blandly.

"Ah, Luddington . . ." Tristan murmured. "He specializes in turning the whole bloody council top over tail, and what does it turn up but that he's a flaming drunk—and how many times have you had someone from the Foreign Office chasing after him?"

"Ah, but look at the jewel Declan unearthed in the process . . ." Ismail said, his eyes skewing toward the parlor door. "Ah, here is Gaspard. Dinner is served."

The dining room was across the hall from the formal parlor. Pastel colors again dominated the room, from the eggshell blue of the walls, which could have been designed solely to set off Evelina's dress, to the pale finish of the table and chairs, which were covered in ivory silk, and the carpeting here, which was a combination of blue and ivory.

There was a breakfront along one wall with an array of covered dishes on warming trays. The table and chairs were centered under an elaborate chandelier; there was no other furniture in the room except the gilt-framed paintings on the opposite wall.

Ismail and Edmund sat at opposite ends of the table, and Tristan and Sayra, and Sinclair and Evelina across from each other.

Gaspard entered, with his assistant, and began the service: oyster stew to start, removed by roast quail, rolled leg of lamb with marrow sauce, onion custard and potato puffs, and finished with meringue cake and chocolate souffle, coffee and tea, and cognac after in the library.

Now conversation was at a minimum. The dinner was exquisite, the meat and fowl perfectly cooked, melting on the tongue, the desserts heavenly.

Food of the rich, like nothing Sayra had ever eaten before.

*This is Sinclair's real life; this is his custom. And Evelina is perfectly placed to be the wife of such a man.*

*There are no monsters here.*

*There are NO monsters.*

*There is only the reality of what will come . . . he can never, ever choose someone less than Evelina. How could his father permit it?*

*They were being too polite about it. She could see the affection in Ismail's eyes—the Prime Minister!—it was a wonder she was not tongue-tied; she was intensely envious that Evelina could converse so easily on a variety of unimportant subjects as the meal progressed.*

*They were all looking at her, too—at the inappropriate blue crepe, creased once again, and dowdy in comparison to Evelina's more elegant evening dress—what were they thinking? What could they be thinking about this Banbury tale about a sudden marriage overseas?*

*But then—Tristan was looking at her in that enchanting way, and every coherent thought fled from her mind.*

"I was just thinking about that," he said, as they prepared to leave the table. "Religious icons . . . an amazing subject for some-one as beautiful as you to pursue. Why?"

"Oh—" *And how to explain that? More lies. Drowning in lies. She swallowed her uncertainty. Best to bluff it through . . . if she could.* "I was interested in folklore and how religious symbols supposedly ward off evil spirits and . . ." she stopped suddenly as she realized what she was saying, looked at Sinclair and then fin-ished, "other supernatural happenings."

"How fascinating," Evelina murmured as they made their way to the library. "You must tell us more."

They seated themselves around the fireplace as the waiter cir-culated with decanters and goblets, and a maid set out a coffee-pot, cream and sugar.

*Now what?*

*No, there are no monsters. All I'm going to do is elaborate on the lie.*

They were all looking at her so expectantly, including Sinclair, but she couldn't tell by his expression whether he was going to let her wade into this quicksand by herself or he was going to throw her a rope.

*How stupid to jump in with both feet. Or had she wanted to gauge their reactions to assure herself that everything was normal and their fears—her fears—were unjustified?*

*Always, when they were surrounded by normalcy, she felt as if everything that had gone before had been a nightmare.*

"Evil spirits, you said." Tristan now, poised on one of the two settees, leaning forward as if he wanted to totally absorb her.

"Supernatural happenings. It all sounds eerie to me. Give us an example."

*Example—he wanted an example? She felt panicked; what could she say that would make some sense and not bear any connection to the monsters?*

"Well—" She felt as if she was floundering, as if they could see right through her. ". . . in Berenjevic, for example—the driver of our carriage—he wore charms—a little bag of garlic, a crucifix—he had bells all over the carriage . . ."

"How odd," Evelina said. "Why, do you suppose?"

"Protection, I would think. The crucifix particularly, and prayers. He was always saying a lot of prayers . . ." *Oh, she needed help now* . . . ". . . wasn't he, Declan—*dear?*"

"As if he was a priest," Sinclair confirmed, taking pity on her. "A lot of superstitious nonsense the ignorant used to defend themselves against ghosts and spirits . . . and the living dead who rise up at night."

"Oh, my goodness—living *dead?*" Evelina shuddered delicately. "We just cannot have this conversation over coffee. It's too . . . supernatural—"

"We'll do it next time," Tristan said. "Over tea. Soon. Tell me, are you at St. James, Declan?"

"No, actually we're not," Sinclair said.

"Ah, of course—you're still newlyweds and you need your privacy. And we wouldn't dream of keeping you, would we, Evelina?"

She shot him a dark look and then smiled at Sinclair. "Not in the least."

"Ismail?" Tristan asked.

"But I must be going as well," Ismail said, levering himself out of his chair. "I'd be delighted to take you where you're staying."

Sinclair studied him for a moment. "If it wouldn't inconvenience you."

"Beautiful women never inconvenience Ismail," Tristan said, offering his arm to Sayra. "Come, beautiful Sayra. Let me help you down the steps. Let me speak to you of springtime. Let me tell you how lucky my brother is to have found you."

Edmund and Evelina remained in the doorway, silhouetted against the light. Tristan walked them to the carriage step.

The air was moist, oppressive, tactile against the skin.

"I want to see you again—soon," Tristan said, kissing Sayra's hand. "And of course you, too, Declan."

"I can see you are most anxious for my company," Sinclair said.

Tristan waved them off without another word; the carriage rounded the crescent and Wrentham House disappeared from sight.

Ismail folded his hands across his midriff. "Tristan is charming, but he can be wearing. Now tell me, dear boy, where did you say we should take you?"

"We're staying in town, of course," Sinclair said. "Take us to the Palace Hotel."

"Why? Why did you tell him to take us there?" she demanded when they were finally on their way to the Royal Crescent.

"Because of Luddington. Because we can't forget what he is . . . and what my father knows he is. And we don't know why he's protecting him."

"Protecting him . . . !"

"We saw him . . ."

"Sometimes I think we imagined what we saw. It seems like a lifetime ago."

"Two days ago we discovered your father was killed because of what he was," he said heartlessly.

She buried her head in her hands as the hansom cab drew up in front of their hotel. "I can't believe this. What are you saying?"

He was silent for a moment. "I don't know what I'm saying."

They hurried through the lobby to the elevator, and up to their fourth-floor room.

"Believe what you want," he said, as he turned the key in the lock. "But no precaution is too excessive."

"I can't believe this is real anymore."

"You believed it was real two days ago. You believed it was real this afternoon when we couldn't find anyone in my father's house. It was very real in the fortress. What don't you believe?"

"That Luddington could somehow get to England from Kabir and contaminate everything," she whispered.

"He's here. He's being protected. When you saw him committing murder they kidnapped you and shipped you to Kabir. And it isn't too much to assume that when your father got out of hand they inflamed the villagers and arranged his murder. They are here, Sayra. And I think Ferenc is here."

"Oh, dear Lord—" *They—they . . . they—pressing in on all sides—the formless, shapeless "they" with blood dripping from their very vitals . . .*

*He was scaring her, scaring her badly.*

"And that's why I didn't tell Ismail where we were staying. Not until we know something more. How do we know who is the enemy?"

The words resonated between them, and he thought they were exactly what he had been trying to say:

*How did they know who was the enemy?*

Sayra moved slowly around the room, picking things up, touching things. *How did they know anything?*

She felt very, very tired; sparring with Sinclair's family had drained her. She wanted to lie down and sleep forever, and she felt ridiculously awkward about disrobing because they had not slept together for a week and she felt disoriented.

She stared at her flashy ring.

"You didn't have to pretend to marry me," she said suddenly.

"You didn't have to say yes," he murmured. "Look at how you captivated Tristan. You could have the whole of London at your feet, every man crawling to you and begging for your favors. My brother would be first in line, I promise you."

"Nonsense." She turned away from him, knowing it was true and what the look in Tristan's eyes meant: She had seen it often enough in Sinclair's.

"What, do you think men can't sense the voluptuousness in you? I promise you, they can. Every man can. And if every man knew what I know about you—you would not lack for a man in this lifetime, Messalina. You could have them all."

"Ridiculous."

"So why, then, are you suddenly so coy with me?"

"This is so strange."

"It has nothing to do with us. We're apart from anything that goes on outside this room. This is our haven; this is the place we find heaven. This is the place where my brother, for once in his life, will *not* intrude. I saw how he looked at you, how he wanted you. But he can't find heaven. Heaven is *mine.*"

She felt the tendrils of desire curling all over her body as he spoke. "Heaven is for the taking, Sinclair."

"Oh, no, you are drunk on power tonight, Messalina. I have been hard for you for days, but perhaps I am not the lover you would choose now."

"For *days,* Sinclair?"

"*You* are not so naive, Messalina."

"Perhaps I am; perhaps I need to see some hard proof—"

"Messalina can have anything she wants . . ." He began unfastening his trousers, and in an instant he released his ramrod member, and she almost swooned as her wet, hot need for it assaulted her vitals.

He read it all in her face. "Undress for me, Messalina. I want you naked—I need you naked . . ."

She needed to be naked for him; she could not wait to strip off her constricting clothing.

But slowly. One piece at a time. Strutting back and forth for him, teasing him, tantalizing him, torturing him, as she brushed her silky stockings against his manhood, as she shimmied out of her skirt, and her drawers, as she bent her head to unfasten the buttons on her shirtwaist and enveloped him in her hair, in her mouth. As she slowly and excruciatingly removed every last piece of clothing while he watched, and his jutting manhood thickened and pulsated with his volatile desire to possess her.

She leaned against the desk in the corner of the room, totally naked, her legs apart, her breasts quivering, her nipples taut, totally consumed with her erotic power.

*This is my place, naked and waiting for him to fill me—this is all, this is what has been missing, this is what I want—all I want—I want him, now, all that male prowess inside me, contained by me, pleasured by me . . .*

"So, Sinclair . . . you are there and I am here—"

"And now the naked Messalina wields her power . . ." he murmured.

"I can go to sleep, Sinclair. It's not that I *need* your hardness. I love looking at you. Perhaps that is enough. I can do without a hard male root between my legs."

"I don't think so, Messalina. You're shuddering with excitement. You can't wait to feel me between your legs."

"Well—you are there and I am here . . ." she murmured, running her hands over her thighs and upward to cup her breasts. "And you are hard and I am not."

"Your nipples are hard for me, Messalina, aroused by the thought of my mouth on them."

She stroked one nipple to torment him, her body going wild with wet, hot need for him. "Yet you are there and I am here."

"I am hard and hot and waiting for you."

"And I am naked and willing and ready for you. And you're nowhere to be found," she said coyly, rubbing the underside of her breasts and lifting them up, as if she were offering them to him.

"Messalina to your soul," he muttered, jacking himself out of his chair. "Spread your legs." His voice was rough, and his hands. There was just enough light in the room for her to see everything he was doing—everything.

He lifted her so that she was braced against the beveled edge of the desk and centered himself and pushed, and she watched, and he pushed, and she watched, and he pushed and he pushed until every naked inch of him was inserted deep between her legs.

And she watched every movement, loving that he was clothed but for his one pleasure part, and that her moist, velvet sheath could contain the hot, throbbing length of him.

And the sensation of their joining was so breathtaking that she couldn't move.

His mouth slanted over hers, his words spoken just above a breath. "Messalina is just where she wants to be."

"Where is that, Sinclair?" She arched herself against him, her hips writhing against the coarse material of his suit.

"With my hot hardness between your legs."

"You think it feels so good?"

He shifted again. "I know it does. You're all filled up with *me,* Messalina. No one else could fill you up like this."

"You think so . . . ?" She pushed, seeking to pull him into her more tightly.

"I know it. I don't want to move. You're so hot and wet, I can't get enough of it. . . ."

She writhed and bore down on his quiescent root, making sharp little hisses of pleasure. "I want to see you do it again."

"Do what, Messalina?"

"I want to watch you embed yourself inside me again."

"I'm not moving."

"I need to see it. I need to see how long and strong you are, and how you just . . . just—" She felt him withdrawing. ". . . just—" She could hardly breathe for the excitement of it and the pure sense of loss when he finally removed himself and stood poised before her, his manhood glistening with the wet of her sex.

She leaned back, bracing her arms on the desk and her legs splayed against his hips, and she watched as he slowly pushed himself into her . . . slowly, slowly, huge and hard and pushing into her, disappearing into her velvet cleft inch by inch until she totally enveloped him.

"And now, Messalina . . ."

"You are just where *you* want to be," she whispered, shimmying her hips. She could not keep still and just feel him there. She wanted more of him and more. She was born to be naked for him, to take him completely and fully; her body was made for him.

"I live between your legs—" He shifted and she felt a pure silver slide of pleasure and gasped. "You need me between your legs." Another shift, another cascade of sensation. "You want only me between your legs." Another shift, another wave of molten feeling. "My hardness. My root. My pleasure . . ."

His hands were all over her, feeling her bare skin, caressing her breasts, fondling her nipples, resting on her nipples, rolling them between his fingers, squeezing, gently squeezing and pushing and squeezing and his words, his throaty, possessive words—"Tell me, Messalina—no other man, no one hard, hot man—promise me . . ." as he caressed the very tip of one taut, pointed nipple.

She writhed at the pure molten pleasure of it—his hot, hard penetration, his knowing, stroking fingers on the pleasure points of her nipples, one, both, compressing gently, holding the nipple tip as he rammed himself into her tighter and tighter and she wrapped her legs around him to keep him from moving because she wanted only to feel his hardness and his fingers stroking and squeezing and thumbing the hard, pointed tips of her nipples.

"Messalina—" he growled.

"I'm coming . . ." She was coming—she couldn't believe she was coming, or that his playing with her nipples and cramming himself into her would give her such creamy, insatiable pleasure.

She gave herself to him, arching her nipples into his hands as she wriggled and shimmied against his ramrod male root.

There was never such pleasure—as if all the pleasure points were connected, from his fine erotic stroking of her nipples to the lush nub between her legs that demanded the hard, hot presence of him to exploit its possibilities—it was all connected in one long, opulent avalanche of sensation, centered just there—and just there—and just . . . *there,* as the feeling skyrocketed and burst into a thousand hot lights that danced all over her body.

She pumped him, she crammed his hands on her breasts, she rode his heat and his hardness; it didn't stop, it didn't stop—the feeling kept skeining through her body and she didn't want him to move. He was all hers, all of him, and the pleasure was as torrid as anything she had experienced with him and all she wanted was more and more and more.

"Messalina—" his voice in her ear, raw and rough, and then the telling strokes of his body, withdrawing and thrusting, withdrawing and thrusting, once, twice, three times—and he climaxed in a ferocious ejaculation, spasming a half-dozen times, holding her nipples, feeling her heat, taking her soul.

They lay naked in bed. She was asleep, curved against him, her buttocks nestled against his quiescent member.

It could not have been more than an hour later when he awakened, utterly aroused by her once again.

He braced himself on one elbow and began gently stroking her body. Her lush, willing body. Her sensitive nipples. Her pillowy buttocks. Her voracious mouth. Her hot, wet, feminine fold . . . He cupped her mound, feeling the faint fuzz of her feminine hair starting to grow back.

Her movement as she sensed his hands feeling her naked body.

"Messalina . . ." he whispered in her ear as he inserted his fingers into her hot, tight sheath.

"Ummm," she sighed, angling her legs so that he could go deeper, and then clamping them together to hold him there.

"You're wet for me now."

"Ummmmmm . . ."

"You want me there now . . ."

"You are there now—" she whispered as he played with her between her legs.

"Messalina . . ."

"What *now?*" she murmured in an aggrieved voice.

"Let me shave you . . ."

*"What?"*

"Let me . . . there growth is coming—and I want you naked to me in all ways—*all* ways, Messalina . . ."

She caught her breath. *All ways, every way naked to him, ready—willing . . . nothing impeding—*

*Let him beg for it . . .*

"Messalina—"

She said nothing.

"Let me shave you. Trust me to shave you . . ."

*Ah, trust . . .*

*"Let me . . ."*

She heard the undercurrent of raw excitement in his whisper.

"I want to shave you. Only me."

*Let him beg me . . .*

"Messalina . . . totally naked for your lover . . . your lover must see everything, your lover must feel everything, your lover wants to shave you . . . let me . . . let me . . ." His words were hypnotic, sensual, his fingers a voluptuous counterpoint, his thumb grazing her mound where her feminine hair was a faint fuzz like baby's hair.

"This is how I'll do it—I'll cover you with lather—thick, creamy wet lather between your legs—and then I'll get very close; very, very close; I have this cunning little folding razor, so small, made to shave the most intimate of places, and gently, gently I'll shave away the lather and anything else that impedes a lover's view. Gently. Touching you. Feeling you. Preparing you for your lover . . . Say yes, Messalina—say yes to your lover who wants to shave you . . ."

*How did he make her want it, how? She wanted it. She wanted—*

"Say yes, Messalina. Let me do it . . . let me shave you now . . ."

*. . . between her legs . . . he lived—she wanted . . . anything—*

"Messalina . . ."

She couldn't resist the sensually ragged note in his hoarse importuning whisper.

She twisted her body so she could see him, and she reveled in his tight, harsh expression, as if he was restraining himself beyond reason.

And he should. He was like granite, his muscles corded tightly under her fingers, his manhood naked and straining for her.

Just the way she wanted him. With his fingers between her legs, his throbbing root reaching for her, his explosive desire a minute away from detonation.

"Yes," she whispered, running her hand all over his hot erection, "when a man is bursting for a woman the way you are for me, she cannot deny him what he wants. I'll let you . . . I'll let you shave me."

She didn't know what to expect. All she had to do was lie back in the bed with the pillows under her buttocks, her legs angled outward, her body canted toward him, her restless hands skimming her heated naked skin as she lay breathless and waiting . . .

The waiting was a compelling pleasure in itself, her own excitement escalating as she remembered his imploring words and his rock-hard sex, and imagined his erotic preparations.

*Naked . . . soaking the shaver in hot water, watching himself in the mirror with the shaving cup and brush, mixing the lather, mixing it thick and creamy and moist—*

*As he is—thick, and creamy and—*

She caught her breath as his shadowy figure blotted out the light and approached the bed.

And then the creak of the bed as he climbed onto it.

And the ineffable moment of erotic suspense . . . her awareness of him, her nakedness, his excitement, his heat, her breathless vulnerability as she sensed him looking at her body . . .

She couldn't quite see him, and she shuddered with a voluptuous expectation of the moment he would touch her.

Touch her how . . . ? Her body was still streaming with the luscious feeling of his invasive fingers. She wanted them there again . . . there and everywhere . . .

Breathless with anticipation, she waited, knowing he couldn't take his eyes from her, knowing he wanted her, knowing he was ram-hard for her . . .

She heard his gratifying growl of pure male need.

And then . . . and then his one hand cupping her buttocks and lifting her, and the other . . . oh, the other applying something hot and thick and creamy all over her mound and between her legs . . . she was imagining it, seeing it thick and white all over her, like cream he could lick . . . rubbing it gently and erotically into her most intimate skin and then applying more, and more, heaping the creamy foam onto her body, softening her for him.

And then he shifted her legs onto his shoulders, spread her legs wide, and he knelt down low and very softly began to shave her.

She closed her eyes at the first gentle scrape.

What did it feel like? Like rough and cream, like his face when he hadn't shaved; a faint rasping sensation and the feeling of mounds of cream pulling away from her tender skin.

And he was right where he said he would be—so close, right there, his fingers softly pulling and probing and easing the way. He touched her, just as he promised, in all the furling places of her pleasure. Carefully, he shaved her, trustfully, every delicate edge, feeling his way, caressing her with cream and then shaving it off lightly, meticulously, slowly, mounding the cream on her inch by inch so that she felt the sensations even more intensely as he progressed further and further between her legs.

All that warm, wet, thick cream clotted between her legs, with meticulous attention to massaging it in and then him slathering on still more. And then the faint licking sensation of him shaving her, probing her, stroking her.

And then he repeated the procedure all over again, all the way, all the way—every tender part massaged and creamed and shaved and then lathered with creamy soap once again.

She could hear his breathing, heavy, thick, shuddery with excitement; he was almost done and she didn't want him to finish. Not yet, not yet.

He applied another lob of creamy foam deep between her legs and began massaging it in.

She felt the rasp of the shaver, the tenuous pull of his fingers at her feminine fold; she felt something invasive, something wet, something delicious licking her and sucking at her. She felt him lifting her so he could bury his face between her legs and take her for a wild ride on his tongue.

She came to him, shaved and naked and willing, and he gorged himself on her until she was bucking and screaming for mercy, and then he withdrew from her, and he mounded the remainder of the thick, creamy soap between her legs and he rammed his rutting, aching manhood into her, and he pounded them both to a thrashing, spewing, heavenly oblivion.

"Messalina . . ."A breath in her ear.

"*What?*"

"I'm hard for you."

"That's just how I want you."

"Let me feel you."

"Feel how naked and smooth I am."

"I want to look at you. I'm hot for you. I want to see how your lover shaved you."

"There is nothing to impede my lover now."

"Let me see."

"Turn on the light."

He flicked on the gaslight; it shed a soft glow on the bed and shadows in the corners.

She swung her legs over the bed, feeling her nakedness, reveling in his raw, hot desire.

"I know just what you want," she whispered, eyeing his throbbing stone-hard erection.

"Messalina always does."

She knew—and she wanted to entice him beyond all endurance. She was breathless with excitement as she posed for him like the Position Girl she was.

She knew just how to angle her legs, spreading them wide, then closing them to hide herself from him. She knew just when to conceal her hard, pointed nipples and how to strut herself before him, revealing just a little of that coveted part of her he wanted to see.

She knew how to climb on the bed and pose with her legs splayed to reveal everything. She knew how to writhe onto her stomach and then shift to her knees so he could see her from behind.

And she knew just how to undulate her hips invitingly to compel him to fondle the bare shaved part of her that wanted his hot penetration.

"Messalina . . ." His voice was constricted with excitement.

"Now you can see everything. . . . Messalina is utterly naked for you . . ."

"Promise me . . ."

She shimmied her hips. "Messalina makes no promises."

He fingered her lush feminine fold. "I need your promise."

"Messalina promises nothing." She gyrated her hips, pushing against his fingers. "That isn't what I want to feel there."

"Your promise . . ."

She sent him a withering look over her shoulder and wriggled her hips again.

"Promise you *what?*" she demanded testily.

"Let me shave you again." His fingers stroked her nakedness. "Messalina loved it."

"Did she?" *She did, she did . . .*

He inserted his fingers just where she wanted to feel them. "She did. And she's so smooth for me now. So naked. So hot . . . promise—"

He was all there, stroking her hot velvet with his fingers.

"I might promise," she said thoughtfully as she writhed against his invading fingers. "If you do something for me."

"Messalina always has conditions."

She ignored him. "You know what I want."

"I have what I want." He cupped her there, feeling her satiny flesh. "Promise."

She groaned. "This . . . this I will promise you. My lover will shave me when the next time comes."

"Then it is up to me to continue to be your lover," he growled.

"*Something* is up to you, Sinclair . . ."

"I named you well, Messalina. Insatiable Messalina . . ."

She whipped away from him and rolled onto her back, onto the pillows, folding her legs so that he could see all of her.

"Look your fill, Sinclair. I'm tired of waiting."

"Don't think I won't." He took up a position on the edge of

the bed where he could lean comfortably against the footboard, and she could see every rampaging inch of him lusting for her.

The air between them thickened perceptibly. It got hot, hotter. Her naked body moved sinuously, tormentingly. Her hands brushed her taut, hard nipples and tantalized her velvety flesh. Her eyes were defiant, challenging; her mouth lush, pouting.

He watched her, his hand cupping his erection, stroking it, shifting his body occasionally so she could see it silhouetted in all its potent, thrusting power.

The power of *her,* the mystery of her waiting to claim him; he wanted to fathom it. He wanted to immerse himself in it. He wanted to know it forever.

She combed her fingers through her hair and lifted it from her neck. She was hot, so hot, and she wanted him in the most primitive way. All of him. The impenetrable nakedness of him. Unfathomable. Virile. Forceful. Enfolded and contained by her.

*Now . . .*

She swung her legs off the bed and stood up, aware of her every movement, and his eyes following her as she paced over to the desk.

*Ah, yes, the desk . . . with the soft edges . . . like him—*

She braced her arms at each end of the desk and leaned over it, looking back over her shoulder.

"Take me now, Sinclair."

He came toward her slowly, appreciating the arch of her back, the curve of her buttocks, splay of her legs that revealed everything.

"Messalina . . ."

"I want it—*now,*" she growled.

He gave it to her, driving himself ferociously into her ripe, wet heat, over and over and over and over, pumping at her in short, fertile strokes, covering her, his arms surrounding her, caressing the shaven part of her between her thighs.

Her body flailed around under him; she could feel everything—the hot, hard length of him, the pistonlike strokes, his fingers penetrating, fondling, feeling her intimate flesh . . . her taut-tipped breasts pressed against the desktop, her hands grasping to hold on to something, anything, as he inexorably pounded her willing body to surrender.

His potent manhood was the center of the world, all she could feel, all the intensity of his possession, different than before, more powerful still, his fingers probing, spreading, knowing her; his strokes quick and sharp and violent with his raging need to possess her.

He knew what she wanted and he gave it to her. He poured himself into her, compelling her to follow him to a simultaneous, tempestuous, bone-crackling culmination.

He did not withdraw from her for a long time. She was asleep by then, her head pillowed in her arm, her body limp with exhaustion.

*Just how I want you to be, Messalina. Exhausted and unwilling to take any other lover but me . . .*

He carried her easily to the bed and laid her down gently.

*Beautiful, delicious Messalina—passion slave and courtesan—and mine . . . completely and only . . . mine—*

Such passion—such all-consuming, undreamt-of passion—she stretched luxuriously in her sleep, inhaling the fragrance of sex and satisfaction.

She felt ripe, fertile, suffused with a kind of ecstatic well-being that was on a plane above all mortal concerns.

The bed was warm, her boneless body awash in the cream of his passion. She loved the feeling; she loved the scent. She loved it that she made him so hard, so lustful, so possessive. She loved being naked for him, and curling her body next to his and absorbing his heat and his violent need.

A woman could not want more than this—a naked, virile man in her bed who desired her beyond reason.

She waited, holding her breath in delicious anticipation. She wanted him already. She knew he had gotten up, and then had come back to bed. She knew he was watching her, lying on his side, propped up on one elbow.

She felt him radiating sensual heat, and his lusty manhood flexing with impatience.

"Messalina—" just a breath.

"Yes . . ."

"It's time for breakfast—"

"Oh, yes." She didn't bother opening her eyes. "Just what is breakfast?"

"Strawberries and cream . . ."

She felt him brush it against her lips and opened her mouth and took a bite of the strawberry and a lick of the cream.

He dipped the strawberry again and pushed it against her lips, and she bit into it and a mouthful of cream.

His tongue followed, sucking on her lips, lapping up the cream from her tongue, delving into her mouth ferociously in a lush good-morning kiss.

"Messalina and cream," he whispered against her lips, and she felt the heat of his teeth nipping her, and then, suddenly, the cool wet of the cream on one taut nipple.

He moved from her lips to that distended pleasure point, covering it with the heat of his mouth, encircling it, sucking it, tonguing it, pulling at it, squeezing the hard tip between his lips, all the while feeling her writhing surrender to his hot, wet lapping of it.

"God . . . Messalina . . ."

She moaned, arching herself upward, demanding that he keep on with his erotic sucking of her nipple.

She bucked as she felt the cool, thick cream clotting between her legs. And his free hand holding her there, in the wet, in the cream, feeling the intensity of her response to his greedy tugging, goaded by the powerful undulation of her body to keep sucking, to keep swamping her with the cool, wet, thick cream between her legs, rubbing her with it, smooth cream mixing with her feminine cream and the spasms of her body as she came and came and came to his rhythmic sucking of her lush cream-coated nipple.

But he wasn't done. He rolled over her shuddering body, flattened himself out as if he were worshipping her, and began licking the thick sweet cream from between her legs.

The sensations following hard on her climax were almost too much to bear; his desire to do this was formidable. He rained kisses all over her, every inch of her; he tasted the cream and he tasted her; he probed her satiety and he made her want him all over again with the thrusting strength of his tongue, and he never slaked off as he took her there and energetically brought her to another hot, writhing, shattering climax.

And no more; she could take no more. It was too much, too much, and yet it was not enough. She wanted his hardness—it would never be enough unless he mounted her and plunged himself deep inside her.

Instead, he straddled her so that all she could see was his hard throbbing length. "Do this . . ." he canted his body so that his shaft lay between her breasts and he squeezed them together. "Like that. That's what I want. I want it like that. . . ."

She moved her hands and pressed her breasts together, and as he drove himself between them, she lifted her head and caught the thick tip of him in her mouth, once, twice, another time, sucking at its lush head and then releasing it.

She adored it; there was nothing like it. Nothing like him lunging into the narrow space between her breasts and into her hot mouth for yet another long, engorging sucking of his head, and then back out again to pump relentlessly against the pillow of her breasts.

"You . . . you are—" he could barely speak; the sight of her hot, pointed nipples and her billowing breasts enfolding him and her moist mouth open to take him, was almost more than he could stand. He wanted to spend his lust all over her breasts.

He wanted . . . the friction of his thrusts caught him by surprise—he wanted—he came in a violent wash of sensation that racked his body with a volcanic ejaculation. He spewed the cream of his desire all over her breasts, her nipples, her shoulders, chin and mouth. . . .

In the heat of his spuming pleasure he saw her lick her lips to taste his passion, and in that sublime and wracking moment he knew he wanted her forever.

There were things that could not be forgotten about in the heat of passion; she slept, he lay awake, his hand possessively cupping her shaven mound.

She felt him; even in her sleep, she must have done, because her hips surged sensually toward the warmth of his palm. Her nipples hardened. Her body arched luxuriously. Her lips parted, as if to invite his kiss.

His burgeoning manhood shot to attention, and gently he

kissed her, all honey warm from sleep, her lips so soft, her mouth welcoming his hot invasive tongue.

And he wanted her.

It took nothing, just the moist taste of her tongue and the feel of her shaven mound against his palm.

He wanted her.

Without breaking the kiss, he straddled her, he spread her legs, he nudged her and slowly he pressed himself against her and into her. Deep, deep, deep, the kiss, the possession; slowly, slowly, so slowly enfolded by that hot wet part of her so that the root of him was tightly wedged against her smoothly shaven cleft, rocking gently, riding her heat.

So slow . . . so luscious—the feel of her honey sweet, sleeping, unfurling for him, knowing that he was hard for her and he couldn't wait for her; taking him into her sweet heat and letting him, letting him fill her and find surcease for his hunger and his need.

His strokes were so soft, so gentle—his mouth was sweet like cream; he rode her smooth as cream, his thick strokes long and leisurely, his tongue in her mouth long and leisurely, his body covering her, surrounding her, utterly possessing her.

He climaxed on the end of one forceful thrust; his body convulsed and ejaculated in a violent geyser of male cream, on and on and on, a torrent of sensation that finally eddied away in short, spurting spasms that left him breathless and totally spent.

*There were things that could not be forgotten,* he thought as he lay with his head buried against her shoulder. He could barely move. In a moment or two he would move. He had things to do.

Things to do: when he was able he withdrew from her, still hard as rock and covered with his cream, which was flowing copiously from her body.

*I want that . . .* He was still erect and wanting and there were things—and he still wanted her . . .

He rooted around for her drawers and ripped off a narrow strip of material and gently blotted her between her legs, letting it soak up their mingled essence. Then he took the strip of cotton and wiped himself carefully and thoroughly, and then he lifted it to his face and inhaled the scent of their sex.

*He would never get anything accomplished with this as his talisman—*

He knew just where he wanted to keep it. He tied it gently around his spent member, and then he began to dress.

So when she awakened, taut as a bowstring and with a quickening urgency to couple with him, she was immediately aware he was not in bed with her. She sat up instantly, looking for him.

*Damn him, damn him—I want him now—*

"Sinclair . . . ?"

"In here."

He was in the dressing room, just finishing with his tie. He could see her behind him in the mirror, her swelling lips, her flushed face and tousled hair. Her aroused nipples. Her knowing eyes.

He turned slowly, his gaze sweeping her body, his reaction instantaneous.

"Are you hard for me, Sinclair?"

"You know I am."

"You look like you're ready to take care of other business when I need you to take care of *my* business. I want to feel it."

"You can feel me anytime, Messalina."

His muscles tensed as she reached out and slid her hand against his rocked, ridged erection, and then began pulling apart his trousers.

"Messalina . . . I can't . . . now—"

"But you will." She reached in and grasped him and released him. "Ohh, aren't you a rock today. And what's this?" She pulled at the cotton.

"That's you, Messalina, to take with me wherever I go."

She lifted it to her face. The scent of them.

Holding his eyes, she slipped the cotton between her legs. "The scent of me, Sinclair, and perhaps all you will ever get if you walk out the door now."

She rubbed it gently against her wet, covering her nakedness with it, letting him watch her for a long, explosive moment, and then turning away from him to go back into the bedroom.

He grasped her arm and pulled her back to him.

"Don't you ever hide your nakedness from me again."

"Don't you ever leave me without servicing me when I'm hot for you," she spat, throwing the cotton strip at him.

He caught it and inhaled it, and then tied it around his neck. "Spread your legs, Messalina. I'll give you what you want."

"Maybe I don't want it . . . now—"

"Oh, you want it. You are so wet for me . . . I'd be a fool not to service you when I'm hard for you and you're so hot for it. . . ."

"I'd be a fool to waste such a massive erection. Come and get me, Sinclair."

He walked toward her, backing her against the dressing-room wall, his jutting length stiff as a poker and ready to ram itself home.

He had cornered her against the armoire.

"There it is, Messalina, all yours—and I'll give it to you just the way you want it." He pushed himself onto her, and he mounted her, cramming his mouth and his body deeply against hers.

He felt her body give way against his savage possession of her. The scent of her surrounded him. He ripped apart his trousers and let them fall to the floor. He raised her left leg and hooked it around him, and lifted her more tightly onto his ramrod erection so that only his hands on her buttocks and his towering sex supported her.

"Now, Messalina . . . now you get what you want. . . ." he growled against her lips.

"I'm waiting . . ." she hissed, feeling the awesome power and potency of him deep, deep, within her. This was it, this was what she wanted; she needed to feel. All of him rammed inside her, filling her, pleasuring her. "What do you think I want, Sinclair?"

His muscles contracted and he thrust himself into her. "This." Again. "And this . . ." He backed her up against the armoire to give him purchase to drive himself into her. "And this . . ."

"And . . ." His mouth covered hers in a violent kiss.

And then there was nothing else, no words, no taunts, no time—just the flagrant sensuality of his body and his mouth forcefully and inexorably taking hers.

Nor could she move; this was possession—total, utter, complete—and she reveled in it. She wanted it. She fought him for it, thrashing against the burnished wooden door of the armoire, trying to climb away from his relentless drive to pleasure her.

She felt him intensely in all his hard, male dominance of her. She loved it; she couldn't get enough of it. She made him work for it; she wanted to exhaust him, dry him up, tap out his power, make him beg, she wanted . . .

She was a queen and he was her slave; the whole of his focused force centered on her volatile ride to culmination.

When it came she was helpless before his power. It was his drive, his force, his strength that took her over the edge and into the white-hot fury of her stunning surrender.

It consumed her like nothing she had ever felt before, all incandescent and rushing toward her like a flood, pulling her with it, a torrent of torrid sensation between her legs, rushing on and on and on and on until he broke with it, drenching her with a ferocious climax that shook him to his very core.

He eased her down slowly, between kisses, and her incoherent murmuring—*don't go, don't go . . .*

He dressed himself and then carried her to the bed and, untying the oblong of cotton, he wiped away the residue of his come and tucked the strip away.

She was still shuddering with the aftershocks of pleasure. He leaned over her and kissed one stiffened nipple—and immediately felt a stirring in himself.

"Sayra . . . I have to go out."

"I know."

"Stay in bed. I want you naked for me when I return. I want you willing and ready for me. I could take you again, right now, I'm so hot for you."

"Why don't you?" she murmured, her body twinging with a sensual quickening.

"Because sometimes, insatiable Messalina, waiting enhances the pleasure."

"I hate waiting." Her voice was suffused with drowsiness.

"Don't we all . . ." His voice was a distance away, and she knew he was at the door and he had turned once again to look at her.

She stretched luxuriously for him, turning over and crawling onto her stomach and settling herself with much wriggling and writhing into a comfortable position against the pillows.

But she couldn't seduce him. She heard the door close emphatically behind him and she smiled knowingly to herself. An hour, no more, and he would be back between her legs again, and just where she wanted him.

# Chapter 19

She had been going to do exactly as he wanted: just lie in bed and wait for him. So easy to do, to spend a morning in complete repose, thinking about his hard, hot body possessing her; so arousing, as if her body had its own separate memory and need for him.

She felt lush and buoyant; she loved lounging in bed, her legs splayed, in this state of heightened anticipation. She was ready for him, naked for him. Her skin felt like rich silk, her nipples like rock candy, her lips swollen from his hard, greedy kisses.

She was utterly open for him, waiting for him, hating it and loving it at the same time. She was so wet for him; her excitement escalated with the waiting.

The silence grew thick with her sensual need.

She tossed restlessly as the time passed and he did not return. How could he not come back to her and claim her naked, willing body?

She got up and paced the room restlessly. He had said he was hard for her, that he wanted her willing and waiting for him. Well, she was more than ready for him and he was nowhere, and she didn't like that one bit.

*Messalina might wait—but only for a little while. Messalina would find another man and make him hard for her. And that would teach him to make promises to her and not keep them.*

There was a discreet knock on the door and she whirled around, startled.

*I could invite whoever is outside my door into this room and let him find us naked and coupling together so he would know exactly what he gave up with his false promises. . . .*

"Who's there?"

"A visitor, mum. Mr. Tristan awaits you in the lobby. May I send him up?"

*Tristan! Perfect!*

"Yes—no . . . tell him I will be down in five minutes."

*Five minutes . . . five minutes to dress and make myself seductive to him, how?*

*Easy—what man can't tell when a woman is both satisfied and restless. Tristan . . . it couldn't be better—*

*Sinclair will be livid. . . .*

He was so tall, so handsome, so beautifully dressed, so impeccably mannered—he took her hands and drew her down next to him onto the sofa and murmured, "Ah, the beautiful and obviously well-loved Wrentham bride."

She felt herself flushing under his intense scrutiny, she was cursing the fact that she only had the plain seersucker dress to wear.

"Sayra—forgive me, I couldn't keep away."

"Why would I want you to?" she asked, knowing she sounded coy and aware of his shimmering light eyes that were just devouring her.

"I was hoping you would say that. Declan is so secretive. And last night—well, a lovely dinner, and Ismail got to pry a little, but that's not family. I thought we might have lunch together."

*Perfect, perfect, perfect, and just the thing to teach a lesson to the arrogant and possessive Sinclair . . .*

"I think that's a lovely idea."

"That is, if Declan isn't—he won't . . . ?" He paused delicately.

"Declan . . ." *She would never get used to calling him that . . .* "Declan is taking care of business today. So I'm sure he would be very happy to know his brother is taking care of me."

"Well—that's decided, then. I know exactly the place. Come . . ."

She gave him her hand. His was cool to the touch, pale-skinned, long-fingered like Sinclair. He wore a long cape and a broad-brimmed hat that he put on as they went out the door.

It was a beautiful day, crisp, the sun so bright she wished she had thought to buy a hat, the streets swarming with carriages, hacks, drays, buses and humanity.

She felt herself recoiling. Such a crowded place; so many people . . .

But he had a hansom cab waiting, and he helped her into its cool, dark interior and climbed in next to her, then tucked her hand into the crook of his elbow. "Here we go, Sayra. Our destination, which is Plimptons-on-Strand, is just a few blocks from here, but it's always so much easier to let someone else negotiate the streets. You might pull down the shade so we can be cozy in here and not have to witness any of the cabman's close calls."

She felt grateful for that. She pulled the shade, as he had done on his side, and immediately they were enveloped in a snug opaque darkness.

"I feel like I've known you forever," Tristan said.

"What a nice compliment."

"But I'm sure there's so much more to know about you."

"I would like to think so."

"Tell me, are you happy?"

"I'm not happy about . . . Declan's going off and leaving me this morning."

"Dear girl, who would be?" Tristan patted her hand. "But take heart; you can always call on me if Declan mistreats you so badly."

"I'm counting on it," she murmured, and she knew it sounded coy but she just didn't care.

"Are you comfortable?"

"Very."

"Then let me suggest something. We're so delightfully alone here, so deliciously intimate; I wonder if you would mind us picking up a picnic basket at Plimpton's, and just driving around the city. That way we can talk as long as we want to with no interruptions. Would you like that?"

*Do I like that? Do I like that? It couldn't be more excellent. . . .*

"It sounds lovely."

"And would you be angry to know I had anticipated your answer and ordered the basket?"

"I think it's charming."

"It should be waiting for us. Ah, the cab stops. We're there. The cabman has instructions to procure it for us."

Several minutes later there was a rap at the door, and Sayra opened it.

"Guvnor . . ." The cabman passed a huge wicker basket over her lap and onto the opposite seat.

"That's fine. Now—give us about an hour."

"That I will." The cabman shut the door, and they felt the carriage depress with his weight as he climbed back onto his perch.

Tristan was already rummaging in the basket and removing the fine linen napkins and a tray of sandwiches cut into bite-sized pieces. "Oh, lovely." He took one and popped it into her mouth. "There you go—creamed chicken, I believe?"

It was just light enough in the carriage to see him; he watched her intently as she licked the residue from her lips and then fed her another.

"Delicious, isn't it? Here's another . . ."

He took one himself and fed her another, then one of chopped cucumber and another of ham and mustard; there were also cold asparagus spears, potato balls, oyster sausages, all of which he fed to her while she laughed at the absurdity of it all.

There was fruit, cheese, gingerbread to round the meal and a split of champagne, already chilled, wrapped and corked, and two flutes.

"We need to toast your marriage, Sayra dear. Hold your flute steady now. There we go." He lifted his glass and touched hers. "To the first Wrentham bride. May she be kissed with long life."

They sipped and a companionable silence ensued, broken by the sound of wheels on cobbles and the occasional shout and curse.

"Sayra—"

She turned to him. "Yes, Tristan?"

"I wish I had met you first. You're so beautiful, so tender, so young and yet so knowledgeable. I'm sitting here and imagining you with *him* and it is monstrous to think about. Is he good to you?"

*Is he? Is he? He wasn't good this morning almost leaving her like that, and then going and not coming back. That wasn't what Messalina called "good."*

But she didn't really need to answer.

"One has only to look at you and *know,* Sayra. You have such a carnal aura. I'm sitting beside you envisioning you naked and in my brother's arms, and I'm insane with disappointment that you will never be mine."

"Tristan . . ."

"No, let me say it. A man can see those things. Can tell what a woman is like under all that whalebone and crinoline. This is how I imagine you—all prim and proper on the outside and voraciously sexual in private. What a body you must have. What breasts. What nipples. A man's perfect fantasy. And my brother has you. What a travesty. My brother—when I could give you everything he could, and more.

"Listen to me, Sayra, and don't be offended. A man can tell. I wanted you the minute I saw you. You know that. It was in your eyes, all that carnal awareness. A woman should be immortalized for being a wanton. A woman who knows the fecund power of her naked body should be deified. And that's what you are, Sayra. A goddess."

His words were so hypnotic. She felt like a goddess. She felt the potency of her sex in his soft, insinuating words.

"A goddess belongs to all men. All men desire her. So you could . . . give yourself to any man you wanted . . . any man who had the stamina to pleasure your insatiable, voluptuous body . . ."

Her breathing grew constricted as she visualized it. *All men, at her feet, hard for her, begging to possess her nakedness . . .*

The words hung between them. He wanted her. Her body twinged with pleasure. *Any man . . . the goddess queen could spread her legs for any man . . .*

"Me, Sayra," he whispered. "Me."

She caught her breath. Her heart pounded wildly. The air in the cab was close and thick. He was close, close enough to kiss her. To take what he wanted. If she didn't move, she could experience another man, this other man, who thought she was a goddess, and a wanton.

*She was . . .*

"Would you . . ." His words a breath in her ear. "Don't say anything. Just nod. You love what I'm telling you." She nodded. "You love when men notice you." She couldn't say yes.

"You want all men to notice you." *No—just one . . .*

"You move your body to make sure they notice your breasts." No movement.

"You love the hard part of a man inside you." Barely a nod.

"You want it all the time." She didn't react.

"If you could have ten men a day between your legs, you would." *I do.* She didn't move.

"You love being naked." Still.

"You wish you were naked right now." No reaction.

"You love being naked in bed with a man." She couldn't breathe.

"You love it when a man sucks your nipples." She didn't move.

"A bitch-goddess. Holding back. Just like they all do. Sayra . . . hear me—I know you. I just proved I know you. I want you.

"But I'm not going to say anything else like that to you again, except—I *am* your friend, and if you need anything, *anything*, you must call me. Promise you'll do that."

"Tristan—"

"Forgive me, Sayra. A man gets carried away when he's alone in the dark with a beautiful, sensual woman he can never have. Say you forgive me; promise you'll call on me."

His tone of voice now was winsome, rueful. As if he hadn't said those carnally exciting words.

*A goddess—to him—immortal . . . how could she not forgive him for worshipping her?*

"You're forgiven." The smile was in her voice. "And I will call you, but I'm certain I'll never have to keep that promise."

"Dear girl." He lifted her hand to his lips just as the cab jolted to a stop. "And look—we're back at the hotel." He raised his shade. "Oh, no, Declan is waiting, and he doesn't look at all happy. Ah, well. Come—" as the cabman opened her door and held out his hand to help her out.

He was there all right, glowering and just as angry as a bull.

Tristan slid over to her side of the carriage and poked his head out the door. "Good afternoon, Declan. Sayra and I have just had a charming picnic lunch. Don't be too hard on her. She had no idea where to reach you."

Sinclair pointedly slammed the door shut and took Sayra's arm and propelled her in the front door and through the lobby to the elevator.

"Don't be hard on you. The bastard . . . I'm going to be so hard on you, you're going to beg for mercy."

He closed the gate and punched the button, and the elevator moved.

There was no one else in the car; his fury was like a palpable third presence. She backed away from him into a corner and held on to the brass railing.

He jammed his fist into a button and the car shuddered to a stop between the third and fourth floors.

"So—Messalina comes to London and already she becomes bitch of the world, going after any man in sight."

"Not any man—that man," she shot back, in a rage at his high-handedness. *A man who thinks I'm a goddess. A man who wants whatever I choose to give him . . . what an enchanting thought—a man who would beg for what he wanted . . .*

"You're damned right—that man. The last man you should be chasing after. Any man but him. Obviously one man isn't enough for you. No man is enough for you. Lift your skirt."

"What for? Where were you when I wanted you?"

"I told you, dammit. Lift your skirt or I'll rip it off."

She felt reckless. After all, another man had just begged for her carnal favors. "Make me."

She knew he would. He was a lot stronger than she, and a lot angrier. He reached for her; he grasped the skirt and he gave it one mighty yank—and everything tore apart in his hands.

"Well, well, well—look at this. Messalina goes out in a carriage with another man with not a stitch of underclothing on. Naked under her dress, so a man can get to her body whenever, wherever he wants. How clever of you. Why didn't you just strip off all your clothes for him? Maybe you did. Or maybe he copulated with you in the carriage as you bent over the seat and presented your enticing bottom to him . . . maybe he fondled that private shaven place that is mine and only mine to possess—did he? Did he, Messalina?"

She swallowed. "He didn't touch me."

"How can one believe that when it was a simple thing for you to unbutton your bodice so he could massage your nipples."

"He didn't." *He wanted to . . .* "I was waiting for you. I wanted you. And you were nowhere around."

"I was coming."

"You didn't come and he did, and I went with him even though I wanted you. We talked. He did nothing." *He made me a goddess . . .* "And all I wanted was you."

"How interesting. As angry as I am, I am hard for you. I want to see how much Messalina wants me." He released his throbbing, bone-hard erection to her avid gaze. "It's time for atonement. Show me how much you want me . . . get down on your knees to me. Convince me he didn't couple with you."

There was no one like him. She knelt before him as if he were a god and rained kisses all over him, squeezing and caressing the muscular length of him, licking him and pumping him, and holding him tightly at his powerful root so she could take him in her mouth and suck the pliant ridged tip of him.

And then there was more of him there, and more, and he was thrusting in short, erotic little bursts, and she took him, all he could give her, and she ran her tongue all over him and sucked at him and sucked at him until the urgency was on him, and she tasted the first creamy drop of him, and then she used her avid mouth to pull it from him, all the cream, all over her, until she had sucked him bone dry.

All his strength, she had sapped him; he sagged against the brass rails, gripping them tightly, his eyes flaming with desire even in the aftermath of his release.

His one hand groped for the button to release the mechanism to start the elevator car; it jerked and moved upward as she slowly and triumphantly got to her feet.

"Don't trust him."

"But he's so charming. And he's so much like you." *You love being naked . . .*

"He's nothing like me."

"It was perfectly innocent, honestly . . ." *If you could have ten men a day between your legs, you would. . . .*

"Don't go near him." *You love the hard part of a man inside you. . . .*

"Really, he wants to be a friend—he's family. . . ." *You could give yourself to any man who has the stamina to pleasure your insatiable body. . . .*

"I don't want to talk about him."

*Me, Sayra . . . Me—*

"We won't talk about him." *You want it all the time. . . .*

"You were alone with him—for over an hour you were alone with him."

"Let's not talk about him." She flounced away from him to the opposite side of the room. She was naked except for her stockings, garters and kid boots. And he was all tucked away and still dressed.

And his animosity toward Tristan, and his jealousy, made no sense to her. *No, it makes every sense, because he knows Tristan wants me. He just doesn't know how much, or what he said and how close I came to thinking about . . . exploring it—*

*. . . you want it all the time . . . you love the hard part of a man inside you. . . .*

*He knew her not and he knew her too well, and why Sinclair didn't know her at all was beyond her.*

*. . . ten men a day . . .*

*. . . one man, ten times a day, naked in bed . . .*

*. . . now—*

"I want to know what you did with him."

"Nothing happened. We talked. We had lunch."

"I don't believe it; damn the bastard, I don't believe it—get dressed. Get on some clothes right now. The skirt and jacket—that's it—that's all you need."

He was in a frenzy of anger, practically dressing her himself, and then taking her arm and propelling her to the elevator, down to the lobby and out the door.

"What are you doing?"

He signaled for a cab. "Get in." He pushed her inside and barked at the cabman, "Drive until I tell you to stop. Here—" He shoved some money in his hand, and then he climbed in next to her.

The cab lurched forward.

"Now tell me . . ."

"But there's not much room to do anything in here, Sinclair."

His tone was obdurate. "Go on . . ."

"The shades were down." *Oh, she shouldn't have said that.*

"You pulled the shades." His tone was neutral and seething with rage. "Then what?"

"We drove to Plimpton's and picked up a basket of food."

"And then?"

"He had the cabman drive us around while we ate and talked."

"And just what did he feast on, Messalina?"

"Sandwiches, Sinclair. And fruit and cheese and—" She stopped short of mentioning the champagne, and just in time, too.

"I see. And he didn't try to kiss you?"

"No," she said emphatically.

"He was this close to you and he didn't even *try . . . ?*"

*. . . watching her mouth move as he fed her—as close as a kiss . . . ?*

She felt him grasp her chin and turn her face to his.

"This close . . ." He slanted his mouth over hers, poised, a breath away from her lips. "This close . . . ?"

But it was *his* mouth and *his* tongue and she wanted them, she wanted *him;* she reached for his kiss, devoured his kiss. That close and he conquered her. *Him.*

"So easy to kiss Messalina," he murmured, breaking the kiss. "So easy to slide up her skirt and feel for the moist, delicious part of her—and how accustomed she is to spreading her legs. . . ."

"*Your* hand," she whispered as it closed over her smooth-shaven mound. "*Your* hand feels so good there. . . ."

"So easy when Messalina is naked under her clothes."

"Naked for *you.*" She writhed against him, pulling up her skirt to ease his way until it was around her waist and nothing impeded him.

His fingers delved into her and she moaned at the feel of them between her legs; she pulled her thighs together to imprison him there.

"Do that," she whispered. "Do . . . just that. Don't move them. Just keep them there. I want to feel them there. . . ."

"Is that what he did? He got you in the dark so he could burrow under your skirt and feel you up between your legs?"

"He didn't know I was naked. . . ." *Maybe he did—You love being naked. . . .*

"You let him feel you—"

"He never touched me."

"He tried—I know he tried. . . ."

She drew in a sharp breath as he pressed his fingers tighter.

"More . . . harder—" . . . *a goddess belongs to all men . . . any man who has the stamina to pleasure her insatiable body . . .*

"I could kill him for trying to touch you. . . ."

"He didn't . . . I swear he didn't. . . ." *He spoke words, words that touched me. . . .*

"How could Messalina help it? You always want it. . . ."

. . . *all the time . . .*

"I want you . . ." . . . *all men . . .*

He crammed his fingers tighter.

. . . *all the time . . .*

"Did you feel him fingering your nakedness?"

"I swear . . ." . . . *all men, hard for her . . . bursting to possess her . . . ten a day . . .* ". . . he didn't—"

"He fondled your mound. . . ."

"Oh, oh . . . more . . . tighter—"

"There was room and time for him to have done this much and more with the naked Messalina."

"I'm only naked for you . . ." she breathed, "waiting for you, wet for you . . . that's what Messalina needs—the hardness of you . . . right there, right where your fingers are embedded. . . ."

"It was too easy for him to slide up your skirt and feel you."

"Ahhh . . . he didn't know I was naked; I was naked for you, hot for you . . ."

"Ready for anyone's fingers to fondle you . . ." he growled savagely as he pushed still deeper between her legs.

. . . *give yourself to any man . . .*

"Kiss me . . ."

He splayed his fingers deep inside her. "I'm kissing you now. Or can't you feel it . . ."

"It feels so goooood . . ." she sighed. "Ahhh . . ."

"Hard enough for you . . . ?"

"Not as hard as you . . ." she whispered. "Oh, don't move. Oh, that's perfect, perfect . . ."

"Not as hard as *him,* you mean."

"I don't know . . . about that . . ."

"Messalina knows all men . . ."

*. . . all men want her . . . all men know it, see it in your eyes . . .*

*. . . a wanton . . .*

*. . . a goddess . . .*

She hissed with pleasure as he twisted his fingers within her, and she bore down on him in rhythm with the sway of the carriage, feeding on his distrust and jealousy, and on Tristan's seductive words.

She reveled in her nakedness and her potent power to bring him to this raging need to imprint her with his possession.

She needed it, she wanted it. She was all-woman, all powerful, and he controlled nothing except as the instrument of her pleasure.

She gyrated her body against his fingers; she spread her legs wide to give him the utmost purchase to penetrate her.

"I know . . . only this . . . man . . ." she panted . . . *the goddess knows all men—*

She gasped as he thrust deeper, and she felt the first spiraling spasms of pleasure. *"Harder . . ."*

He pushed harder and her body responded, in a paroxysm of sensation that exploded all over his probing fingers.

He didn't release her after the pleasure eddied away. He rested there, claiming her, and she felt him there, adored him there, wanted him to remain there . . . felt her body responding to him there not three minutes after her climax.

He wasn't moved.

He gave the cabman instructions to return to the hotel and he deliberately didn't remove his fingers until the moment the cab drove up to the door.

"Take off your clothes."

They were one step over the threshold of their room, and he was ripping off his jacket with that suppressed fury that hadn't diminished.

She held his eyes as she slowly stripped off her suit and walked to the bed.

She lay down and waited with a faintly mocking expression in her eyes.

He saw it, he ignored it; he swooped down on her and into her with one long, strong, forceful thrust.

He took her—a bull rutting in a willing body, pumping for all he was worth, wringing himself out, driving himself to exhaustion because he was never going to surrender to her—and his bastard brother . . .

He felt invincible. His was the power and she was the vessel; it was all she had ever been, and he was a fool to have expected more from a woman who personified the mystery of Eve, Aphrodite and Messalina all rolled into one. . . .

*She's mine . . .*

His body seized up at the thought. He tried desperately to push it away. He didn't want her. She had betrayed him.

*She is mine. . . .*

One more thrust—*mine . . .*

*Goddamn it—shit . . .*

And then he was hers, spending his seed in her convulsing, throbbing center as she rode his spurting member to frenzied oblivion.

He couldn't keep his hands off her naked body.

She lay on her belly, half asleep. He was sprawled beside her, his right hand idly stroking the crease between her buttocks while he watched with detached curiousity as his manhood slowly came to life.

He was amused at how easily his hand could slip down and finger her feminine fold, and stroke the smooth, luscious flesh surrounding it.

And by how much she wanted it; instantly she canted her bottom toward him and shimmied invitingly. He couldn't resist that—he crowded his fingers against the smooth, enticing flesh between her legs, perfectly willing to feel and fondle her the way she wanted.

And he lay there, perfectly content to cup and rub the supple, shaven flesh of her mound as she wriggled with carnal enjoyment.

She splayed her legs so he could reach her more easily; she undulated voluptuously against his stroking fingers, tempting them, tantalizing them with her erotic movements.

She was so soft there, so wet, so yielding, as he played with her; he was stone hard with wanting her and he didn't want to stop rubbing and fondling her sweet feminine fold.

He heard her seductive sighs and moans deep in her throat; he felt the urgency of her need as he kept massaging her pliant flesh. She spread her legs wider, enticing him to penetrate her.

His manhood was bursting to possess her. And he didn't want to move. He wanted to fondle that lush, submissive part of her body all day, all night, forever.

He held himself back; the waiting escalated his ferocious lust to drive himself into her naked heat. The waiting was a statement to her that her hot, naked body belonged to him, and only he could bring her to this explosive point of pure carnal need.

For him. Only for him and what he could give her. For his hard part and no one else's.

She was shuddering with excitement, aching for his forceful possession of her. She loved how he was feeling her, his fingers sliding all over her mound and teasing her slick, swollen womanhood that only wanted his hot, hard penetration.

She could see him, hard as a rock, lying there, towering with his lusty need for her, his fingers endlessly exploring the supple fold between her legs as if he were fondling her for the first time and he had all the time in the world.

"Beg me, Messalina." His voice was ragged with his need for her.

"My body is telling you . . ." she whispered.

"Your body could be naked and wet for any man. Beg me."

She writhed with excitement. "I'm naked and wet for you, Sinclair."

"You're so hot any man would do. Beg me."

"You're so hard for me, you can't wait to possess me."

"You think so, Messalina? I can walk away from it."

She was shaking with erotic tension. "You can't walk away from *me,* Sinclair. You're naked and hard for *me.* So why don't *you* beg *me?"*

His fingers stopped moving, poised on her throbbing feminine fold.

"Who begs who, Messalina?"

"You want it."

"You want *this*—" he stroked his pulsating length with his free hand. "*—there*—" He stroked her there. "So beg for it. Beg me because I'm the only one who can give it to you as hard and hot as you want it."

*It was true; any naked willing woman could slake his lust. But any man could not diminish her erotic need for his* hard penetration.

But she would never let him know it.

"Not the only one, Sinclair," she murmured insinuatingly.

He understood perfectly. "Bitch."

"Take me then and show me how hot you are for me . . . let me feel how hard I make you. . . ."

"Bitch . . ."

"I'm so wet for you, Sinclair. I'm aching to feel something naked and hard between my legs."

"Slut . . ."

She undulated her bottom. "Now, Sinclair—I need it now. . . ."

"Whore . . ."

And she knew, suddenly, she had the power.

She put one hand on her buttocks and began rubbing herself to entice him. "I'm so hot for you, Sinclair. I want it as hard as you can give it to me."

"You wanton bitch . . ."

"You want it, too. You want it hard and hot with a naked, willing body. . . ."

"Whorebitch—" He was straddling her from behind. "That's exactly what you are—a naked, willing bitch who spreads her legs when she's told to. . . ."

"Oh, no, Sinclair. I'm Messalina the courtesan queen who chooses the penis she'll copulate with. And I only want a naked man I can watch get bursting hard for me so I can measure how much he really wants me. I watched you when you felt me up between my legs. I saw how deliciously long and thick and stiff you got when you fondled me. You love fondling my naked body. And you get granite hard every time. You can't stop yourself . . . you can't help yourself . . . your fingers are spreading me to prepare me and still you *have* to fondle me there—yessss—before you ram that hot, luscious poker of yours . . . *hard* . . . ah!—right

. . . ohhh! . . . where . . . ummmh . . . oh, yes—oh, yes—oh, yes—right . . . *there* . . ."

*There* . . .

She swooned with pleasure as he embedded himself there in total, complete, hips-to-buttocks penetration, so that his throbbing hardness was their only fleshy connection.

"Only Messalina loves bending over for a man . . ."

. . . *ten men a day* . . . She shimmied against his inflexible hips.

"Messalina loves what she's feeling now between her legs . . ."

"And I love seeing your bitchy naked body submitting to me."

"Oh, no, Sinclair. I chose to let you dominate. Now you have to *make* me submit."

"You're so hot for what's between your legs, you'll come in a minute."

"You can just stay rooted there; I love a hot, throbbing bone inside me. . . ."

"Oh, no, Messalina-slut, I'm going to make you feel it like you've never felt it before."

"I can't wait. . . ." she hissed.

He pulled back and jammed himself into her. "Feel that, you hot bitch. . . ." And again. "And that, you naked slut . . ." And again, hard and forceful, potent and powerful, just the way she was begging for it.

"And that . . ." As he crammed himself tightly inside her melting, yielding nakedness with every inch of his juicy hot manhood. "And that's just a taste of what I've got for you, bitch. I've got you down on your knees and you have to beg me for it."

"I don't have to beg you for it; I've got it—all hot and hard and just where I want it." She undulated her buttocks erotically against his flat hips, and he growled.

"Beg me," she whispered.

"I don't beg naked sluts. I give them what they're aching for. . . ."

"What are you waiting for? You named me for a naked slut and that's what I am . . . a naked slut who can't wait to feel every hard, naked inch of you giving it to me. . . . I want it—I need it . . . I never stop wanting it—aahh . . . yesss—"

He pounded himself into her. "Whenever we're alone I want you naked for me. . . ."

"Oh, yes . . ."

"When you're dressed I want you naked under your clothes for me—"

"Oh . . . oh . . . oh . . . yes—"

"Whenever you sit I want your legs spread for me—"

". . . yesss . . . oh, yes—"

"Even when you have clothes on, I want to know your legs are spread for me. . . ."

"Oh . . . oh . . . oh . . . yes . . . yes—"

"Whenever I'm hard for you . . ."

"Y—essss . . ."

"I want to know my naked slut wants it from me. . . ."

". . . y . . . es, yes . . . oh, yes . . . ssssss—"

Her body contracted, goaded by his salacious need for her nakedness. She wanted to be naked for him forever, servicing him, feeling the lusty, carnal pleasure of his hard, hot penetration taking her . . . naked for him . . . always—

"I'm coming . . . oh, yes oh, yes—I feel it . . . oh . . ." as she tumbled headlong into a fierce, spasmic climax that kept coming and coming and coming, riding him, riding his pleasure until he reached completion.

He drove into her again and again . . . *take that and that and that and that—mine mine mine mine mine*—until his body seized up and in one mighty heave he spent himself inside her in a potent, churning gush of cream.

In the aftermath she reclined on the bed, pillows propped up behind her back so that her body arched and her breasts were prominent. Her legs were angled and splayed so that all of her enticing femininity was visible, and he lounged against the footboard just looking at her nakedness, as she idly rubbed her hands all over her body.

He was already hard for her again.

"You love it," he growled, grasping his unruly male root.

"I love how you look at my naked body and get hard as a rock." Her fingers grazed her taut, pointed nipples, and she gave him a knowing smile.

"I was hard before I left you."

"I know; I felt it. I hated when you took it out."

"I wanted to see you with your legs spread for me."

"Do you like what you see?"

"I like looking at it and knowing it's naked and ready for me. I like shaving it. I especially like feeling it up. I want to feel it up right now. . . ."

"I want you to . . ."

He pushed her legs apart still farther and lay down between them. "I want to see everything."

He used all his fingers in his sensual probing of her feminine fold. All she had to do was lean back and let him worship her there, her body reacting to every little push and pull and insistent revelation of his fingers. And wherever she responded he went back and fondled and probed some more, spreading her gently, feeling up her wet, hot center, learning her secrets and coming back for more.

"I can't get enough of you. . . ."

"I love how you're fingering me—"

"You're so wet for me. . . ."

She writhed with pleasure against his exploring fingers. "I'm so hot for you. . . ."

"You think you can handle a hot, hard man . . . ?"

"I can handle you—"

"Let's see if you can. . . ."

He was on his knees and between her legs in an instant, and pushing himself into her, grinding himself into her, in slow, incremental inches as they both watched—and a minute later he was gone, in a rhythmic explosion of lust and mystical insight.

*. . . Jesus Christ . . .*

He sat back on his heels, still embedded in her, still hard and long enough to pump her through to her bouncing, hectic, unquenchable surrender.

"Sayra . . ."

*Messalina no more, when real life intruded.*

She roused herself. "*What?*"

"I just thought of something."

"What?" *Now real life was intruding. Why they were there, what they had come for, and it wasn't for an orgy of the senses.*

"Tell me . . . Jesus, it just occurred to me—"

"What?"

"How did Tristan know we were here?" They stared at each other. "I registered under a false name. How did he know where to find us?"

# Chapter 20

*When you don't know what to do, when things are caving in all around you,* she thought, *there is only one thing you can do.*

*Order food.*

It came in two huge trays from the hotel restaurant: covered salvers of poached eggs on anchovy toast, baked potatoes, larded sweetbreads, broiled tomatoes, fried oysters, fruit, tea and a fat pot of chocolate—too much food, almost as if he was trying to distract them both from their ravenous desire for each other, and from the intrusion of preternatural reality.

They sat across from each other at the desk; he had donned his trousers and she was draped in a sheet that emanated the faint scent of their sex.

She wasn't hungry. She picked at the eggs, tomatoes and oysters, and drank the chocolate. The chocolate made her think of other things—she loved its rich, thick, clotted taste.

"You were saying . . ." she whispered, wriggling her hips just to call attention to herself. She knew it. It was crazy. She was so aroused, she was shuddering with her urgent need.

"Damn it . . . shit—God, I want you—"

"Let me feel how much . . ."

He stood before her and dropped his trousers. He was all there, rigid and tight and throbbing, and tied around the base of his root, the cotton oblong with which he had blotted away their commingled juices.

"Messalina is always with me. . . ."

She couldn't speak—she was so excited; she just wanted to massage that delectable bone-hard part of him; she wanted to rub him against her nipples; she wanted to devour him.

She took him between her hands and rolled her palms all up and down his iron shaft. He was so huge, so gorgeous, so mouth-wateringly luscious; she squeezed the pliant tip of him and brought it to her mouth and kissed it all over, licked it, nibbled on it and delicately sucked on it until she tasted a pearly drop of his cream.

"Messalina . . ."

She looked up at him, her mouth still full of his lust.

"I can't take much more."

"What more could you possibly want?" she murmured coyly as she licked him as if he were rock candy. He was so delicious. She was so open for him. She felt the wet streaming between her legs where she wanted him. And she wanted to keep on rolling her hot, wet tongue all over his massive maleness.

And he wanted . . .

Her eyes met his as she wiped a drop of it from her lips with the tip of her tongue.

*. . . for me . . .*

*She was; even in the midst of the turmoil, he knew she had positioned her legs under the sheet exactly the way he had dictated.*

*Passion slave to the center of her being. Thinking only of that—wanting only that . . .*

*She was aroused already, between the scent of the sheet, the taste of the chocolate and the feeling of being utterly open for him . . .*

*She had to stop this . . . she had to—*

"It is time to make a plan." His ragged voice broke into her thoughts.

It gave her something to jump on, something to rail about so she wouldn't think about other things.

*. . . other things . . .*

"A plan? A plan? How do you make a plan when nothing makes sense, you have no idea who or what or even where the enemy is . . . or how to fight it—"

The look in his eyes deepened. "*One* thing makes sense . . ."

Her head dropped back and her eyes closed. "I know . . ." she whispered. "I know . . ."

He shook himself and rubbed his hand across his forehead.

"I can't stand this. I'm so hard for you, I could explode. Take off the damned sheet. Move the chair over here. I need to see you naked."

She threw off the sheet and shifted the chair with shaking hands to where the light filtered into the room, and she sat, positioning herself with her legs splayed and her hardened nipples thrust out.

It was obvious what he wanted as he thrust himself against her willing tongue and moved closer to her, and closer, until he was straddling her. His hands were perfect, just easing her body toward his as he maneuvered himself downward.

She wrapped her legs around his hips and pulled him still closer so he could slowly plunge himself deeply into her.

This was for him, everything for him. His hands devoured her, his eyes devoured her—every reaction, every nuance of her response to him. Everything. She felt it. She felt it intensely, and in some stirring and different way she could not define.

She was utterly his, complete in her surrender, and yet he belonged to *her.* She had never felt it more insistently . . . he was *hers,* and she shuddered at the power of it, the all encompassing feeling of it.

All of his strength, all of his spirit, his body and soul, hers, hers, hers . . . to claim, to possess, to . . . no . . . *no!*—this was enough, this tumultuous magic they made together . . . this was—

. . . enough . . . as his body contracted and he gave one mighty push against the luxurious quickening of her body . . . he knew, oh—he knew . . . and he came, just toppled over into the bottomless chasm of his explosive release, while he massaged the unfurling bud of her climax to culminate with his.

He carried her to the bed, after, and they lay side by side for a long, quiet while.

She felt boneless, weightless, buoyant. Nothing could touch her. Nothing could seize the power. In that moment there had been no games, no tests, no distance, no him, no her. Just them.

*Them . . . whatever that meant—whatever would come of . . . them.*

She didn't want to move, didn't want to break the tenuous connection she was feeling.

And he? She couldn't tell at all what he was feeling; he had gone away already, she sensed it. He was staring at the ceiling and she could almost see his focus shifting and his thoughts jumping from one point to another.

*The monsters just wouldn't go away. Nor could she forget—ever—that she was the daughter of a monster, and that they had chased across two continents to find no proof of anything.*

*Proof of the power of their sensual need only.*

*She wanted more.*

*Dear God, the moment she had feared had come when she least expected it.*

*She wanted more.*

*And he wanted to talk about monsters.*

*What was between them was a monster, seductive and devouring, feeding on its need for itself . . .*

She closed her eyes and willed her illicit thoughts out of her mind. There was no time for that.

They had come back to London to find a monster. To chop off its medusa head so that no other monsters would exist ever again.

Lying next to him, hip to hip, with the smooth feel of his skin melting against hers and the sun streaming in the hotel window and pooling in the tray of leftovers on the desk, she just could not believe in monsters, and the rational truth was, Luddington was a sot, and she had dreamed all the rest.

Even Sinclair.

Sinclair was the embodiment of the dream of the doxy in the pub who removed her clothes for money, the knight who would fall so deeply in desire for her that he only wanted to take her away and would defy every convention to have her.

She had the ring to prove it, if not her marriage lines.

She had *him*.

And she knew that he was going to bring her crashing down to earth and talk about monsters.

"We have to have some kind of plan," he said finally.

"A plan," she interpolated. "Against something so amorphous, you have no idea who or what it is or where to begin looking. I liked your intervening plan a lot better."

"Nevertheless . . . I went to the Foreign Office today to make my report. Luddington's back on the job—just as if nothing happened. And now we have Tristan, honing in straight to where we're staying, in spite of no one knowing and my using an assumed name. Or don't you find that odd?

"And my father, protecting Luddington. The excuses they made that he's a drunkard. There's nothing on record about that anywhere. And surely the Privy Council or Ismail would have done something about it, if not Her Majesty. How do they explain the absences? By my count—five or six. And I'm not the first to be sent after him. I discovered that three different agents have disappeared in the course of tracking him down. Or is that not odd either?

"I spoke to the one other agent who was also involved. A wild goose chase, he said, because Luddington always wound up back in Cabinet chambers within two weeks, hale and hearty and mystified about the fuss.

"So why did Ismail need to send *me* when there was another agent who had dealt with this before? An oddity.

"Secondly: Why is my father protecting Luddington?

"Thirdly: Who killed your father? He survived all those years with no one knowing his secret, not even you. Why him, why now?

"And then why would my father suggest we come live with him? This is extraordinary. We have no relationship, he and I; I left Wrentham House a long time back, and I had not gone there for four years prior to our visit the other night, even to see him. He's all wrapped up in Tristan. He always has been: Tristan is the anointed heir and my father has never seen anything else. Although he certainly saw *you,* Sayra."

*. . . oh, yes . . . the first Wrentham bride, his father said—*

"And let us not forget Tristan . . ." The timbre of his voice changed. He hated Tristan; perceptive, handsome, laughing Tristan.

*Sinclair never laughs . . . but who was to say he wasn't right—*

"And none of it explains the fortress or Brother Giurgiu," he went on.

"Maybe we don't need to explain them," she said tentatively.

*Maybe we don't want to explain them, because if we could, it would mean the monsters really existed. . . .*

He sent her a skeptical look. "We need to explain them. And I think we need to accept my father's invitation to Wrentham House. That means we have to get you outfitted as befits my wife . . . and to my specifications," he added meaningfully. "That's first. Oxford Street for your dresses, and Barron's store for the rest. That should take the better part of the day, and we'll just pretend there are no monsters."

"I thought that was what we had been doing," she murmured.

He swung his legs over the bed and turned to her. He was elongating already, just looking at her.

"And sometimes, insatiable Messalina, we even succeed."

Oxford Street was a long, winding avenue in the heart of London, crowded cheek by jowl with shops catering to every conceivable want and need.

She wasn't in the least shocked that Sinclair knew all the best dressmakers and everything about purchasing a wardrobe for a lady. And she was a little amused that no one dared look askance at her rumpled blue crepe as she undressed in the back room in the shop of Fontaine, a well known and exclusive dressmaker who easily consented to put together some fashionable outfits *quickly* for madame when she saw the amount of money Sinclair was prepared to spend.

*That* even shocked her, as he flashed banknotes and negotiated in flawless French to have something ready for her this very afternoon, and the rest by the end of the week and sent to the hotel.

Fontaine's assistants turned her every which way, measured every inch of her, brought to her bulging books of fabric samples and patterns to choose from, paid close heed to Sinclair's adamant instructions that he would not have her wearing a *tourneur,* and therefore they must be careful how they designed the skirt of each dress and suit, and when they were done she calculated he had bought for her three walking suits, four afternoon dresses and two elaborate evening dresses. In addition, Fontaine had a selection of ready-made shirtwaists, skirts and jerseys that could be altered to her size quickly, so that the benighted blue crepe could be left to be sent with the rest of the order when it was completed.

And Sinclair had very strong ideas about how he wanted her to dress. The colors—strong colors, cobalt and black, wine and ivory. The dresses, close fitting, with the suggestion of a fashionable bustle made by poufing the material of the overskirt just at her waist. Ribbons, yes. Frilly lace, no. For her, flounces and pleats, braiding and ruchings, with velvet and silk, nainsook and linen for daywear and brocade and nun's veiling for night. Illusion net and satin, with matching beaded slippers—she felt like Cinderella on her way to the ball.

And with it, a French corset, sateen and lace disguising the constricting whalebone, twenty hooks at least, all in aid of supporting her breasts. A corset cover of cambric and embroidered lace over a matching pair of drawers and the softest lisle stockings.

No steel cage around her waist to support the shape of her skirt: Sinclair would have none of it. The skirt must be altered to fit her without a petticoat.

Monsieur's wishes were paramount, he was so emphatic about it; if madame were not wearing a ring, such a showy ring, on her left hand, they would have assumed she was his mistress, because men were just not that particular about their wives.

They made the alterations and she donned the poplin skirt in a pattern of variegated stripes; the shirtwaist of fine lawn with little pintucks down the front, and a plain jacket of black jersey.

Four hours later they were ready to go, with Fontaine's promises that all would be completed and delivered by the weekend, and Sinclair's promise that the balance of the amount due would be paid in hand at that time.

It was teatime by then. Oxford Street was swarming with people taking advantage of several sales; the street was crowded and a little frightening, as patrons pushed their way past them into the shops.

They walked a little, his hand protectively at her elbow, and she felt fashionable and cared for and that nothing could touch her.

He paused a moment, and then turned down Duke Street and

paused again on the corner of Grosvenor Square, an area of beautiful pedimented limestone buildings.

One of them caught his eye, and he propelled her slowly toward it.

"The Union Lyceum," he said, his voice pitched at an odd inflection. "It was a guildhall hundreds of years ago, and it now houses a museum and a library . . . and a crypt."

She shivered. Noticeably. Something about his tone of voice. And the way he mounted the steps, as if he was walking into the unknown.

He grasped her hand and pulled her with him, up the steep steps and past the columned entrance.

And into the library.

It was huge. Flooded with light from windows at the north and south ends. The ceiling was forty feet high, overarched by wooden spines with Gothic motifs. Each nave was filled with shelves of books and decorated with stone arches and sculpted figures of prominent men whose works were represented on the shelves.

Two dozen small oak desks were aligned next to the sections of books, down the center aisle.

It was hushed in here; there was a feeling of reverence.

At least ten of the desks were occupied by someone reading or doing some kind of research.

They kept walking down the center aisle and into a reading room, where there were comfortable chairs set around a large open fireplace, and in a far corner, a stone staircase leading downward.

He kept walking, as if something was drawing him there.

Down the stone steps from which the smooth edges were worn away. The walls were cold, stone cold, the air denser as they made their way past the second level, which housed the museum, and went farther down.

It was darker here, musty.

As they came to the landing, they found a niche with a lamp, a wick and some matches.

He lit the lamp, and they stepped through the stone archway and into the anteroom of the crypt.

Everything was stone here, from the floors to the ceiling. There was a darkness, an emptiness, as if no one ever came.

In the middle of the wall there was a massive arched oak door, and hanging beside it, the key.

She held the lamp as he inserted the key and opened the door.

She didn't know what they expected to find—but surely not this: a long rectangular room, with stone casement windows and lustrous oak ribs arching downward from the ceiling and ending in thick columns set into the stone floor.

There was nothing else—just four symmetrical rows of columns across the room and down, supporting the arched ceiling spandrels—no furniture, no paintings, no tombs.

"Wait a minute. . . ." Sinclair held up the light for a closer look. "Look. Coats of arms carved into the wood. We would have seen them if we had approached from the opposite end of the room. There's another door, so there's probably another staircase there."

"How odd," she murmured. "What could these represent? A cross and a sword. Treble swords. A field of hawks surmounted by leaves. Gryphons rampant. A lion and a sword . . ." her voice trailed off. "Sinclair!"

He was beside her in a moment, holding up the light.

She was staring at the carved image of a face, peering out from a curtain of draperies, its eyes cut in such a way that she felt as if it was looking directly at her, following her, its gaping mouth revealing feral pointed teeth, and blood dripping from its lips.

"Oh, that." They had routed out the museum director and asked him about the carved face. "Strange, isn't it, among the heraldic arms plates. Said to be a folklore figure—a one who feeds on the blood of the living. Some odd name. Moodie can tell you more about it. Librarian. I think he's in till nine."

They raced up the steps to the library.

Moodie was at tea. Sinclair impatiently prowled the shelves of books, looking for treatises on folklore.

"Remember what Brother Giurgiu said? He said I know what I need to know. He said he had given me what I couldn't find in a book. But what did I find? Only the legends, the superstitions.

And now we find he was here four . . . hundred years ago he was here . . . and he's here now, damn it, and we have to find him. We *have* to . . ."

He wheeled as he heard footsteps coming toward them down the center aisle and someone came into view. A tall, slight, ascetic-looking man with pale skin and rimmed glasses, elegantly dressed and mannered.

"I am Moodie. What can I do for you?"

Sayra immediately felt he would do anything. There was something about him, a courtliness, an intellectualism. A keen and absorbing curiosity. He loved books. And he loved life.

"I'm Sinclair; this is . . . my wife, Sayra. We were just down in the crypt. That face . . . among the heraldic arms . . ."

"Ah, yes, Ferenc. The bloodsucking vulture. Come with me, won't you?" He led them down the aisle and into his office. "Did you know that England does not have a vampire tradition? That the telling of it only took root here during the Middle Ages, fostered by translations of legends, folklore and stories of other countries. Fascinating, really, where in the world you find vampires. Everywhere, except here, and perhaps America. One really is forced to ask: Were they invented or do they exist?

"You know, of course, they are thought to be immortal. And yet, you must be aware, they can be destroyed. I see you know some of this. What *is* your question, Mr. Sinclair?"

"The carving of the face. How long has it been here?"

"It has been documented as being there for several hundred years."

"Why among the coats of arms?"

Moodie leaned back in his chair. "The crypt is a crypt, you know. Under each of those columns are the tombs of the families represented by their emblems. He killed them. And that is why his face is represented too—"

"He's . . . buried there?" Sayra whispered.

"Quite. They destroyed him in the 1500s. He's been there ever since."

They didn't exist. They were stories in books, and one festering legend of a madman who had murdered five families and had been, in turn, slaughtered himself.

It didn't make him a vampire. Legend had done that, feeding on his bloodlust to annihilate five families for reasons that were now lost in time.

And thus was a vampire born.

Named Ferenc.

If the name hadn't been Ferenc . . .

"How did they destroy him?"

"The usual way, of course. Stake through the heart; cut off his head. Stuffed him with garlic and seed; burned the coffin right into the ground and then covered it with twenty feet of dirt. And then they built the crypt over it. And later the guildhall and the museum. No one's sighted him since, I'm happy to report."

*Don't be so happy . . .*

"The thing is really a memorial to a mass murderer, nothing more, nothing less," Moodie went on. "People just don't go down there. There's relatively little to see except those exceptional arches, which are really only of interest to architecture students. Most people don't even notice the emblems or the face."

"Someone noticed," Sinclair said.

"Yes, and everything I've told you does seem to have meaning to you. How more may I enlighten you?"

"I'm not sure. I need to know . . . how you can destroy them."

"Each folklore has its own ritual, Mr. Sinclair. It's commonly accepted in Rumania, for example, that corpses are routinely dug up shortly after burial to see if the deceased has become one of the undead. If the body hasn't decomposed, if there's a plumpness to the skin, if the limbs can be easily moved . . . well, you get the idea. Even if there is some medically feasible reason for all of this, it is assumed that the deceased has become one of the living dead.

"There are a host of reasons why in every culture, from an unavenged murder to a person committing suicide. Unnatural acts seem to open a decedent's soul to be taken over by the forces of evil.

"And since they become in effect supernatural, their reflections can't be seen; some of them, by superstition, can't abide bright light; they can transmogrify themselves into animals or the elements.

"They are strong; they are said to be able to alter their size and shape; they can fly. But most importantly, they can transform any living being into one of their own by hypnotizing and sapping all of the victim's psychic energy so that he won't resist.

"So it may seem as though he is indestructible. If we are not seduced by the romance of the bloodsucking villain, we can assume that Ferenc was really just a man out to get rid of his enemies. He just happened to have a lot of them. However, there are records as to how they killed him. And those methods are the traditional means of eliminating a vampire. That is, staking him through the heart, beheading him, stuffing the body with garlic and burning the corpse.

"In some cultures it is enough to stake him and bury him with his head at his feet. Or you might stake him, cut out his heart and burn it and then bury the body with religious icons and crocks of holy water, and seal the coffin, which must be made of lead, with tar and screws.

"Have I answered your questions, Mr. Sinclair?"

"Yes," he said briefly.

"Is it presumptuous of me to inquire why you and your wife are so interested in this subject?"

Sinclair hesitated for a moment. "We were traveling in Rumania and came across an odd priest in a monastery. His name was Brother Giurgiu. He claimed to have lived in that place for many, many years, and that one of the noviates in times past was called Ferenc. This Ferenc came to the brotherhood solely to feed unchecked on the holy body of the monks. This he did, until the war in the Crimea; he left only one of them living—Brother Giurgiu, who told us this story—in a netherworld of immortality and living death. And that is where we heard the name. And what we know of the story."

"Fascinating. A monk, of all people. A monastery. Subject to no rules, no laws other than its governing body. He ate the Host. Marvelous—if true. More than likely some kind of tourist hoax, don't you think? There are no vampires, Mr. Sinclair, plain and simple. But the folklore is an astonishing study."

Moodie rose and held out his hand. "Please let me know if there's anything more I can do for you. Truth be told, I really enjoyed showing off my knowledge of the subject. Let me escort you out."

He preceded them out of his office and down the long aisle through the library.

"There you are. You're headed where?"

"I know exactly where I am, Mr. Moodie. But thank you. I deeply appreciate your taking all this time with us."

"My pleasure." Moodie opened the doors and they emerged into an early evening mist that was damp and promised rain.

Sinclair waited until the doors swung shut behind them. He looked at her and said, "There are monsters and something—*something*—prompted me to come in this direction and go into the library. And I don't know what it was. Unless . . . unless it was *him*."

And then he took her hand and they raced down the steps toward Bond Street, almost as if he wanted to outrun the monsters.

But at Bond Street he paused again, as his sense of objectivity returned. There were still more people here, filing in and out of the clubs and shops. Traffic, diverted from Oxford Street, turning the corner and heading toward the square. People going about their business in their usual harried and hurried way.

"We'll go to my flat," he said finally, and he didn't know why he felt the urge to go there.

They took a hansom cab to St. James Square, where Sinclair maintained his apartments. By then everything was obscured by a deep, drifting fog, and only the shadowy bulk of the Foreign Office building was visible over the trees. The gaslights in front of the townhouses lining the park pierced the fog with an unearthly glow.

Everything seemed otherworldly and preternaturally quiet.

There was no one around. The cabman was unnaturally silent. The horse's hooves sounded hollow on the cobbled street as the cab rolled away.

A dog howled somewhere across the park as Sinclair opened the door to his building.

Sayra scurried inside, chilled by the sound and the feel of the damp fog against her face. This was too much on top of their visit to the library, and she was trying as hard as a child not to think about the consequences of that.

A dim banister lamp lit the carpeted staircase. All the doors on this floor were closed; locked, probably. There was not a sound. It was as if they were the only ones in the world.

At the top of the stairs there was only darkness.

Sinclair led the way, his expression set.

Up she went, into the darkness, wanting to grasp hold of his frock coat to anchor herself.

There was a light on the second floor: a sconce in the wall, shedding a flickering glow on the passage from one flight of steps to the next.

And up again.

They heard the dog howl once again, its keening wail penetrating even the thick walls of the townhouse.

The third floor.

Sinclair paused here, rooted for his key, and then led her to a door just by the opposite staircase.

There was a sliver of light showing under the door.

Her heart started pounding.

"The landlady, no doubt," Sinclair said, utterly undisturbed by this mystery. "She cleans and freshens the linens twice a week."

He pushed open the door.

"Welcome home, Declan. I was wondering when you'd finally get here." The voice was Tristan's, but he was nowhere to be seen.

Sinclair slowly closed the door behind them as they stepped into the large front room that was his parlor.

There was no one there.

There was one lamp lit on a table by the fireplace, and everything emanating from it was cast in long, eerie shadows that pooled in every dark corner.

There was no other sound but the click of the latch, Sayra's labored breathing and the insistent howling of the dog in the park.

"Tristan?" Sinclair, sounding angrier than a parlor trick warranted.

There was no answer.

He moved into the room and turned up the lamp. Tristan was not in the room.

"Tristan?" He knocked on one of the doors leading from the parlor.

There was dead silence.

He stared at Sayra over the glowing lamp. The air thickened with a pulse of its own.

"This is ridiculous. Tristan is either here or he isn't. Tristan!"

His voice echoed back to him in the silence.

And then, suddenly, the lamplight flickered and went out, and they were left in a throbbing darkness that only intensified their fears.

# Chapter 21

Terror. Pure illogical terror gripped her as she groped her way toward the table.

Sinclair sensed her movement. "Stay put—"

"I can't see anything. . . ." They were whispering and she didn't know why.

The dog howled again.

Sinclair was moving, master of his surroundings.

A moment later the lamp flickered into life.

And a booming knock sounded at the door.

Sinclair wheeled around as the door slowly opened.

"Tristan!" That was *her* voice, suffused with relief.

"I called to you," Tristan said as he marched into the room, his arms full of packages. "From downstairs. You must not have heard me."

"We heard you," Sinclair said shortly as he went around the room, turning up the gaslights in the wall sconces. "What the devil are you doing here?"

"Oh, I've been in the way of looking after the place after you went off on your last assignment. And here, I've brought some viands for you—"

"How did you know we'd be here?" Sinclair interrupted roughly.

"I didn't. I come by now and again to make sure everything is in order. I just happened to see you come up in the cab. Truly, I hoped you wouldn't mind. Well, Sayra doesn't mind. I must say, this place is a mess. No wonder you didn't want to bring her here. You really should consider taking up residence at Wrentham House."

He was unpacking as he spoke—trays of salads, cold meats, shrimp—almost as if he had planned an impromptu picnic. . . .

*A man who likes spur-of-the-moment picnics—a charming trait—and yet Sinclair looks thunderous. He hates this man.*

"And what would that profit me?" Sinclair asked.

"Do come sit and have a bite to eat, Declan. You're always so formidable when you frown that way. Why not? We haven't been close as a family for years, and now we have a bride, and she ought to be surrounded by the support of family and live graciously, not in this catch-as-catch-can flat of yours."

He handed around plates of ham and au gratin potatoes. "You need a cook and servants, and a butler and valet, maids and who knows what all that you can't have here. And I expect you aren't quite ready to set up a household yourself, so what could be more convenient than Wrentham when there is so much room, you wouldn't even be noticed if you didn't want to be."

"And what would Sayra do with herself there?"

"Oh, I would undertake to keep her entertained while you're out chasing enemies of the government. No problem there. Or you could think about the country house. You know—Father ought to get together a party at the country house one weekend. Would you come?"

He looked at Sayra with his light eyes that were warm like the sun and not frosty like Sinclair's, and she just about melted from the heat of them.

"Sayra would come. I think Sayra would love to come. She might not be expert in the society we move in, Declan. This would give her a good chance to meet all the people important to us—have some shrimp, Sayra—and see just how we get on in our lives. The Wrentham seat is quite something. A big old hulk of a house, dating from Tudor times. Huge. Historic and quite beautiful. Scholars study it. The family rarely uses it—the last time we were there, Declan?—the summer that Mother died?"

"That sounds right," Sinclair said briefly.

He wasn't eating either, Sayra observed, and he was just on the cusp of outright rudeness. But this was the first mention she had ever heard of their mother.

"When did your mother pass away?" she asked curiously.

"The autumn of 1860," Sinclair answered in that same clipped tone. "I was ten, Tristan was fourteen."

"That's right," Tristan amplified. "Father had come home in

'56 from Sebastapol very ill, and it was only that summer that he had recuperated enough to go up to Flamborough. And so he recovered and Mother fell ill, and there was nothing to be done for her. She died before the school quarter started.

"It was so awful. You can't imagine. She just wasted away. The doctors didn't know what to do for her. She was out of her mind at the end."

"Maybe she wasn't," Sinclair said, and there was a challenge in his tone, as if this was an old argument.

"You were so young," Tristan said. "And it's neither here nor there. The point is, the doctors couldn't help her. It was an awful tragedy. But Father got well. We had Father."

"*You* had Father."

Tristan made a little *tching* sound. "You have to forgive us, Sayra. These are old wounds, and all it takes is a heartbeat to open them up again. Fine, Declan. I had Father. You had freedom. Which would a man choose, I wonder."

"Nonsense. He sent me up to Exeter and Oxford and never even cared to ask after my health from one term to the next and grudgingly allowed me home at Christmas. Oh, it was a fine, idealized childhood. Cold rooms. Awful food. Wretches for roommates. A barbaric system of bullying you couldn't replicate in a prison. Freedom . . . while you sat at Father's knee in warm rooms, basking in his favor. I haven't forgotten."

"Please. Father is a tyrant, as you well know. No bullies, no cold rooms. Only golden chains, Declan, and everything must be done his way or no way. Nothing is ever good enough for him. And anything you try is never enough. And now I'm tied to him forever—the oldest son and all the expectations devolving on me when he dies."

"The bastard will live forever," Sinclair said grittily.

"Fathers always seem immortal," Tristan said. "Well, there you go, Sayra. Airing the dirty laundry when this was supposed to be a surprise get-together. I don't think we've talked this much in years. I don't even think we've mentioned Mother in years. So perhaps—perhaps it was a good thing. Let me clean up now and I'll be on my way. Come on, Declan. Forget the past. You can't change anything."

"I heard what I heard," Sinclair said.

"You were ten years old. You heard what you needed to hear."

"And you're denying it only because it's in your best interests."

"We'll never agree," Tristan said, his voice frosty. "Believe me, I didn't mean for this to happen. I wish we could just leave it, Declan."

"You heard it, too."

"I did not hear what you heard."

"You chose not to have heard it," Sinclair said. "The lines are still drawn."

"Well, I think I have everything tucked away now."

"Yes, you do," Sinclair said. "Everything."

"Perhaps Sayra's wiser head will prevail. Let him tell you the whole sometime, my dear. Let's see if an objective person—albeit one who loves you—perceives the thing the same way. Good night, Declan. A pleasure, in spite of the bickering. Dear Sayra, come visit us soon."

He drifted out the door, the basket of leftover food on his arm.

Sinclair stared after him for several long, fraught moments, his expression hard and unforgiving, and then he slammed the door.

"Goddamnit . . . Goddamn him—"

His words sliced through the silence like knives.

"Son of a bitch—" He stormed through the parlor like a rampaging lion. "Goddamn hell." His arm swooped out and a piece of glass went flying.

"Do you know why he came here? Can you even guess?"

"Sinclair . . ."

"Shit . . . the bastard; the pair of them. Never leave a thing alone. Flexing their damned power. You want to know how it was after my mother died? Do you really want to know? Let me tell you. She was like a ghost—emaciated, white, lethargic; she had no energy, no will. She had been like that for weeks, and every morning we came to see her, she seemed worse and weaker, straining even to speak. She couldn't sleep. Or she didn't sleep; I never knew which.

"And she knew when the end was coming. She wanted it by then. Even I could tell that. We called for the priest. She asked to see Father, and Tristan told her he wasn't available. She lifted her head, as if she was listening, as if she could hear something we couldn't. And then she said it, and she died. I heard it; Tristan heard it and he's denied it ever since."

Sayra felt it, the matte moment of this unknown woman's death. She felt it deep inside her, like a spell she didn't want to break. But she had to know, just the way Sinclair had always known.

"What . . . what did she say?"

He looked at her as if he expected that she already knew.

"She said . . . *I am the resurrection and the life . . . and he that eats of my body and drinks of my blood shall have . . . life everlasting . . .*"

"And what did Tristan hear?"

"He didn't hear the liturgy. He heard *'Oh, God, please restore me to life at last . . .'* and he was certain I imagined the rest."

"What do you think she meant?" she whispered.

"I don't know . . . I don't know—damnit, I goddamn don't know. But I had the insane thought that she was trying to tell me that my father had something to do with her death."

Tristan had been right—he had been a child, and what did a child know? A child took on all burdens, including death.

She could see it in her mind's eye—a ten-year-old boy, close to his mother, watching her waste away, helpless, frantic, needing to blame someone, and who more likely than his father, who could not render her impervious to death.

How frightening for him. How abandoned he must have felt.

She understood so completely. She had lost her mother in a similar way as well. She had been older, perhaps as old as Tristan had been then. It was a horror a child did not forget, and in her case, only the exigency of having to earn money and care for her father had pushed every feeling into a subterranean place that she had chosen not to explore.

She was stunned to find the memories creeping up on her as they traveled back to the hotel.

*What memories? Awful memories. Her mother was a drab who knew only one way to earn a living . . . oh, yes . . . she had always known it, too, and she had pushed that deep into that buried place as well. Her father could do nothing after he re-*

*turned from the war ill and seized with a burning thirst that needed to be constantly cauterized with drink. And then he lay in a stupor while her mother did . . . what her mother did . . . and she was off at the village school learning what little they could pound into her frenzied mind.*

*And those were the good times.*

*The bad . . . oh, the bad—she had truly chosen never to remember the bad times; her father howling, her mother hysterical, throwing things, running from the house with her, staying away for days and then returning to find her father passed out in his bed of rags, and the hovel a mess from marauding rats and other vermin.*

*So when Sayra had been able to get out, to earn her own money, she did. Her mother had not been young even then, and when Sayra started working her mother stopped walking the streets and only took an occasional customer for old times' sake.*

*Until she got ill.*

*The illness. The life-draining wasting illness.*

*Two mothers.*

*From two different worlds.*

*The doctors could do nothing, he said.*

*One doctor looked at her mother and just gave up. Nothing to do, he had said. Save your money. Save your da. She's dying. Let her go. Give her peace . . .*

*How did one let go of a mother?*

*Sinclair hadn't, not after all these years. His voice was ravaged as he spoke of her; he was ten years old again as he spoke of her. He would never understand, never give up trying to understand.*

*And she had given up the moment she decided to let her mother go.*

*She felt the tears crowding the corners of her eyes.*

*Nonsense. She had mourned her mother. Until her father needed his next bottle. That night it was . . .*

*The wonder was, he hadn't forced her into the streets.*

*No, she had taken the easy way out—removing her clothes for paying parties who got to look but not touch.*

*Except that one time.*

*What would her mother have thought of that?*

*What would Sinclair's mother have thought?*

*She wouldn't have had to think about it: In that life, Sayra Mansour, the Position Girl, would never have met Declan Sinclair, diplomat and second son of the earl of Wrentham.*

*Fate was laughing.*

*Fate had given them each a father who had returned from a war corrupted by all the death and killing, ill and dependent. And their mothers dead of similar circumstances.*

*So who was to say that in that other life they might have found each other, having those corresponding experiences.*

*She had the fleeting thought that something about that was important, but she couldn't define what or why.*

*And then—the monsters.*

*A monster tomb in the heart of London, and five families decimated in his bloodbath, all buried together and united for eternity . . . while the monster . . .*

*The monster . . . what?*

*. . . still lived . . . ?*

*. . . exiled in a fortress . . . survived in a monastery . . . lived in a hovel in an impoverished seaside town . . . rode on a train to London like any other ordinary citizen . . .*

Her blood ran cold.

*Never forget the monster who lives in your skin . . . who gave you your life . . .*

*Dear God . . .*

*But then . . . why had he never . . . ?*

*He drank—he drank to burn away the aching hunger of his bloodlust . . . he lay in dirt and rags and filth and would not move and lived for the feel of the bottle against his lips . . .*

*Her father, who had put a name to the monster—*

*A name that was memorialized on an emblem in a crypt where he had been buried four hundred years before.*

Nothing made sense.

No, the bright lights of the hotel made sense. Even Sinclair's hard silence made sense.

Monsters did not exist in the busy world of central London, even on such a muggy, foggy evening. People went about their business, knowing nothing of monsters: beautifully dressed men and women swarmed in and out of the hotel restaurant, having come to dine before proceeding to the theater; tourists, arriving late from some steamship line, made their way briskly into the hotel to engage rooms. Passersby on their way somewhere important went by the hotel without giving it a second glance.

No monsters. She didn't see a one anywhere as they alighted from the cab.

*Except a monster could be anyone—even her father.*

*Even a tosspot like Luddington . . .*

Her fears crowded in on her again.

*. . . anyone . . .*

They made their way through the lobby and into the lift, which was already crowded with hotel guests jostling one another to fit in, everyone in a hurry, with places to go and things to do.

*But they had done everything they needed to do—today.*

*She wondered what would be the next part of this nebulous plan of Sinclair's. The one that started out with the purchase of that delicious wardrobe and led to subterranean crypts and monsters . . .*

Sinclair was so quiet, it was almost frightening. It was as if he had gone deep into himself and was seeing something he didn't want to share.

She shrugged out of her jersey jacket almost the minute he opened the door, while he turned up every light in the room.

"I have had enough of my brother, damn him to hell," he said, his voice jagged with suppressed emotion. "The son of a bitch. Spying on me. Watching my rooms. Courting my wife . . ."

She sent him a startled look that he did not see as he paced the room and ranted on.

"Taking over everything. Trying to coerce me into doing what I most don't want to do, *and* trying to enlist your sympathy in the matter of my mother's death. The bastard. Greeks bearing gifts. Disseminating the poison and making sure they don't ingest it themselves. He didn't eat a thing, goddamn him. Did you notice? It was all a plot and a ploy, and he's after something, but I'm damned if I know what."

He stopped in front of her. "Maybe brother mine wants—*you.*"

"Sinclair—" she said warningly, but she knew he could see the warmth of her feelings in her eyes. She just couldn't believe him about Tristan. Not after he had delved into her soul.

"Ah—Messalina will defend him to the death. Any man who takes an interest in her."

That made her snap. "Oh, truly? I'm so pleased to know I will have a hundred protectors once you give me my *congee*. I'm not so sure about it, but I count for naught here. You may do as you wish, Sinclair. You can give me a ring, call me your wife, dress me like a queen, insinuate me into your family, call me your passion slave, your courtesan—but at the end of it, whenever you and I find what truths we seek, you will still have your life; but I will never be able to go back to mine. Tell me about all the men who will have me after you take back your ring. Tell me which men will want Sinclair's cast-off doxy."

She stood toe-to-toe with him, her body shaking. She knew—she had always known—it would come to this someday; she just hadn't envisioned it would happen so soon.

*Too soon . . .*

"Tell me what I am, Sinclair. A whore or a wife? What *is* a wanton named Messalina in the world of Wrentham's son?"

He reached for her in one explosive movement and grasped her arms, pushing her backward toward the bed.

"She is whatever *I* want her to be. Who else could she be? Who else, Messalina? You . . . are . . . *mine*—" He felt it, he wanted it, he couldn't go beyond it.

"And after? *After?*" she whispered as the back of her knees caught the bed and she sank onto it under the pressure of his hands.

"You will have a much better life than the one you could have gone back to," he said brutally. "I'll make sure of it."

He turned and stalked out of the room.

*He didn't mean it; he could not have meant it. He was upset about Tristan, his mother, everything. . . .*

*Oh, dear God, to have it end like this . . .*

*Who was the monster after all?*

*Only a man who took what he wanted and was already preparing to cast it aside.*

*The blame should lie with her for letting him so thoroughly seduce her.*

*And how she would live without his touch, she didn't know.*

*Perhaps it was time to work her wiles on Tristan. Whatever wiles she possessed.*

*Tristan, who knew her deepest, darkest secret already.*

*. . . you love the hard part of a man inside you . . .*

*. . . if you could have ten men a day between your legs . . .*

*. . . a goddess . . . who could give herself to any man who had the stamina to pleasure her—*

*. . . me, Sayra—me . . .*

*So like Sinclair, but without the darkness. And with just the right words to entice her. And those light eyes glowing for her. Seeing into her soul.*

*Yes . . . Tristan—had he not been trying to seduce her after all?*

Her body felt warm as she slowly removed her clothes.

*He had trained her well. Naked and waiting, even for a phantom lover.*

*She had done what she needed to do to escape the fortress and return to England.*

*The pleasure . . . was mine—*

She lay down on the bed.

No matter what Sinclair said in the aftermath of this, and even if she chose to ignore what had happened or just put it aside, she would from now on be open to all of Tristan's compliments and cajoling.

And she would make sure she would not be so easy to get—this time. The Messalinas of the world learned their lessons the hard way. But they learned them. She would make Tristan wait—and then wait some more. Let him talk his sweet, erotic talk. Let him make all manner of promises.

When he was ripe, she would pluck him.

And in the meantime she would take all the pleasure she wanted from the reluctant Sinclair.

She didn't know what awakened her: the sense of some discovery she had made in her dreams or the urgency of a man's hands fondling her body.

She had been dreaming of Tristan worshipping her. Touching her reverently, not with Sinclair's suppressed violence that only wanted to open her up so he could pole himself into her.

"Messalina—" She knew that ragged, harsh whisper.

"I'm here . . ."

"I need you—" He rolled her over and lifted her legs up onto his chest. "Like this . . ." And pushed her over in the way of the harem slave.

"Whatever way you want me—" *That was what Messalina would say. . . .*

Master to slave, he drove into her, pinioning her so she could not move; only he could move, control, dictate.

She grasped the edges of the mattress and let him plow into her. He was in a frenzy of wanting her, huge, hot, bone hard, a piston, propelling himself dangerously close to the edge of surrender.

But not before he demonstrated every nuance of his power over her.

For the first time she examined it with clear eyes and from a distance, and she sensed he knew that she was not fully engaged.

It made him work harder; made him determined to master her and bend her to his strength and his pounding possession, even though she was slippery with acceptance of him, the petals of her pleasure unfurling slowly and luxuriously with each and every hard stroke.

She deliberately and clear-headedly withheld herself from him.

And watched him as he worked himself into a lather to bring her to her crowning point of climax, while she gave him everything he wanted and resisted succumbing to a tumultuous release.

*Who had the power now?*

*She reveled in the way he was pushing himself to oblivion; this night, she would not culminate for him, and damn the consequences. He could not have it all his own way.*

*Oh, she exulted in her potent ability to drive him to the edge.*

*He wanted it, he wanted all of it, and she would not not not give him what he wanted.*

*Men killed to possess a responsive body like hers. Let him learn. Let him get down on his knees to it, for it; let him beg for that she had always been willing to give.*

*This was the price every wanton must exact.*

*And she intended to get her money's worth . . .*

"Messalina—" his voice was harsh, just on the edge of control.

"I am here for you," she whispered.

"Come for me. . . ."

"Take your release in me."

"I won't."

"I can't . . ."

"Damn it . . . you've never—"

"Tonight is different . . ."

"I see." And he did; he saw it clearly in the dark. He saw the crossroads, the moment of decision and capitulation, and he wasn't going to take that road. Not yet. Not bloody yet . . .

She said nothing. It was better to say nothing, and better for him to play out his anger on her body.

Better so, as he rammed himself into her; he would not beg. And that was the difference between Sinclair and his brother. Now he would take, and make her regret what she had willingly given up.

Her body almost betrayed her; ecstasy was so near, so tight, so close. It was so hard, so hard not to let it sweep her away.

She kept it close; she lavished all her thoughts on Tristan. She let him pump her body until he capitulated and spent his lust in a violent spume of a climax that left him utterly exhausted and angrier still.

He eased her down slowly and withdrew from her.

And it was just like that—his body, his mind separated from her as if he had cleanly severed it with a knife.

She smiled to herself in the darkness, knowing she had the power as she delicately completed the last lingering act of pleasure.

# Chapter 22

The invitation came in the morning, and it was as if there had never been any acrimonious words between Sinclair and his brother, as if nothing out of the ordinary had happened during the night.

Only she felt the difference, and she was not about to make it known to him.

A bellboy delivered the thick, embossed envelope.

"Well, well, well, Tristan does work fast," Sinclair said. "Here is the invitation to spend a week at Flamborough, commencing from tomorrow; you and I, Father, Tristan, Ismail, Evelina and a dozen or so of our other close friends. Hunting, fishing, a maze, cards, concerts and other like entertainments. Tristan must really want you all to himself. I would take advantage of the opportunity if I were you, Messalina."

She shot him an insolent look. "I intend to."

His mouth tightened. "Bitch."

She got out of bed and wrapped herself in a sheet. "So, Sinclair. No more monsters—except the green-eyed one, is that it?"

He grasped the end of the sheet and yanked it from her body. "Your body is still mine, Messalina. Your body doesn't forget."

*No, my body remembers all too well; my body aches to be fulfilled by his strength and his will.*

*But I won't give in to it—I won't . . .*

"The timing is perfect. All my lovely clothes will be here by then. I would love to go to Flamborough."

"I wager you would, Messalina. Lots of high-flying saviors there. Perhaps Tristan will look puny by comparison." He eyed her naked body consideringly. "Yes—I think I would like to see you at work, selling yourself to the highest bidder."

She felt herself snapping again. "And just think—*you* didn't have to pay a farthing."

"Exactly; I only saved your life. What's that worth on the open market? And who would have done the like had he been in my place? Your gratitude is overwhelming."

"You've gotten full value, Sinclair. You've gotten everything. And more."

"There's always more, Messalina. With women like you—there's bound to be more."

"We'll see then, won't we? We'll see about more." She felt a savage victory; he was stiff as a poker and raring to pop, and she deliberately rested her gaze on him. "Or less. Or—nothing."

"Nothing, Messalina? *Nothing?* No, the passion slave does not get to choose *nothing*. Until another man claims you, and unless you want to walk the streets, there will be *something*."

"For you most certainly—"

"Messalina . . ."

"Oh, no, Sinclair. Oh, no. Messalina has learned her lesson. And this is it: that a man may claim a woman, may save her from certain death, may possess her with all his might, may chase after monsters with her across two continents, may even call her his wife, and yet still he has the power to reject her. Who would submit willingly to such treatment? Not I."

"Until yesterday—you did . . ."

"Yesterday I found wisdom. Today I have strength. A Messalina keeps her heart, her counsel, her desires to herself. She exists solely to provide pleasure for whoever claims her. And when you finally renounce me, you're right—I will find another. Make no mistake, Sinclair. I will find another and you will owe me nothing, and I will never demand anything from you. So let us go to Flamborough, and I will seek to relieve you of your burden."

A deadly silence fell between them.

He looked at her and through her, his eyes icy, his expression like stone. "Damn you, Messalina. Damn you to hell. . . ."

"Or I may find heaven, Sinclair," she said, with that same knowing insolence. "You never can tell."

* * *

She had no choice but to wear the same outfit she had worn the day before. She dressed in the bathroom. She could hear him slamming around the bedroom, angry as a bear.

*Well, why shouldn't he? Why should a man get to eat the honey and throw away the pot?*

She felt a wave of despair that was as intense as any culmination.

*I didn't want it to come to a head so soon.*

*After everything—*

*After such voluptuous pleasure . . .*

*After . . .*

As if her life had begun in the hellhole fortress. As if nothing existed before Sinclair.

*Nonsense.*

*Everything had existed before Sinclair. Including her.*

*But not this persona. Not this woman with the heady knowledge of her power who could wield it on any other man but the one she so desperately desired.*

She stared at her ring.

*. . . this is . . . my wife—*

*This is . . . my life—*

He didn't need to take her to Flamborough. She could stay right in London and probably do just as well. Maybe better. There were places a sophisticated woman could go where she might find a protector.

She would end the charade this morning. There was no more need to prolong things. He could seek out the truth about Luddington himself. And the rest was probably only just her overactive imagination.

*. . . but the fortress . . .*

*Was thousands of miles away. Nothing to do with her now. And she did not ever want to think of the fate of three other girls or even Zenaide. She hadn't thought about them in over a month. A dream. A fantastic, phantasmic dream . . . and all that vampire talk at the Lyceum yesterday—an academician taking advantage of two gullible people.*

*Explanations for everything.*

*Except why she had had to fall in love with Declan Sinclair . . .*

She jumped as she heard the door slam.

*Sinclair. On his way somewhere . . .*

*Not without me—*

She yanked open the bathroom door and raced out into the hallway. He was in the elevator already. She pulled the room door closed behind her and went for the stairs.

He was out the door by the time she reached the lobby and hailing a cab; in it and gone as she came out the front door of the hotel, so she flagged a cab of her own.

"Follow that carriage." She felt like a fictional sleuth as the cab lurched forward into the midmorning traffic after Sinclair.

*I have no money . . .*

*No matter; Sinclair will pay.*

*Oh, he will pay . . .*

In and out of the traffic they went, her cabman weaving a suicidal path through the oncoming vehicles in pursuit of Sinclair, until the cab rounded a corner and began to slow down.

She recognized the place they had come to: the Union Lyceum . . . again, but for what purpose she couldn't fathom.

"Sinclair!" She popped her head out the window and called to him as he stepped onto the pavement.

The expression on his face altered for just an instant as he turned toward her voice and then strolled over to her cab.

"Well, well, well, Messalina as undercover spy. It doesn't work. You just don't blend into the scenery."

"You have to pay the cab. I have no money."

"But you have other assets. Messalina. I'm sure you could make some kind of bargain. . . ."

"*Sinclair . . . !*" She felt like killing him.

"I'll be happy to pay him, Messalina. But what will I get in return?"

"What you always get, Sinclair. The best of the bargain."

She hated the snide little smile on his lips as he handed the cabman his money and then helped her out of the cab.

"What are you doing here, anyway?"

"I don't know. I had some more questions."

They walked up the steps and through the columns.

There was a printed notice pinned to the door.

CLOSED ON ACCOUNT OF DEATH.
TO REOPEN 9:00 A.M. MONDAY NEXT.

"Whose death?" Sayra whispered.

"I think we need to find out," Sinclair said. He lifted the door-knocker and banged it loud and long; no one came in response to the noise.

No one. It was as if the whole Lyceum were dead.

He tried again, the sound of the brass striking wood rattling the air like thunder.

No one answered the door, but a voice from below them shouted, " 'ey— 'ey . . . you on the steps—"

They turned to find a rag tag elderly man leaning on a cane. " 'oo you lookin' for, up there when the place is closed? Din'cha read the sign?"

They came down the steps slowly toward the old man. He was a decrepit old thing, stooped, dressed in rags, his face obscured by a wide-brimmed hat. They couldn't see his eyes; his face was covered by a long unkempt beard that flowed down his chest. His hands were gloved and pressing down on the cane for dear life.

"We were here yesterday," Sinclair said. "We were talking to a Mr. Moodie. The librarian."

"Ooh, the librarian. 'Im. That's the one. 'E's gone and 'ad an accident, 'e 'as. And another one, too . . ."

They looked at each other. "What kind of . . . accident?"

"They found 'em this mornin', the librarian on the floor in the stacks. Dead as a bug, 'e was. And down in the crypt—the other one—the museum man. Two gone, and Scotland Yard prowlin' the place and settin' up guards and all. They ain't gonna open up Monday, I can tell you. Two with one blow—no, they ain't gonna let no one near the place come Monday. . . ."

"What kind of accident?" Sinclair asked again, impatience coloring his voice this time.

"Din't I say? Oh, the kiss of death was on 'em; they was layin' there face up, white as my mother's Irish linen, arms wide like they was welcomin' whatever come for 'em. They say there wasn't a drop of blood around, just some pricking wounds on the bodies in a half-dozen places; and no one knows for sure what took 'em. But somethin' did. Somethin' for sure did."

Sinclair dug in his pocket for some coins and handed them to the old man.

"Many thanks and not necessary," he said in a token protest as he palmed the coins and shoved them into a pocket somewhere in the mess of clothing he wore. "I guess you shoulda finished your talkin' with 'im yesterday."

"Thanks for the information," Sinclair said. "Let's go." He took Sayra's elbow and steered her around the opposite way, so that they were walking toward Duke Street.

"Oh, my God," Sayra murmured. "Oh, my God."

"More than my God," Sinclair said grimly. "How about—Luddington?"

"Oh, no—no . . . you're not saying—"

"I don't know what I'm saying anymore," he muttered. "You know—I should have asked that old guy . . ." He wheeled around to call to him and there was no one there.

The old man had utterly disappeared.

"We're going to my father's house."

"No, we're not."

"Yes, we are, and you're going to use those lusty charms of yours on Tristan, and I'm going to find out where the hell Luddington is."

"Sinclair—you are over the top with this."

"Am I? Am I? You think this was all some bad dream, and it just stopped the minute we got off the train and there was Luddington? There's something going on here. Something. What murders have we not heard of where the victim died with *pricking wounds* on their bodies? And you think it's just a coincidence that Moodie died directly after talking to us about vampires? And that there's one buried under the Lyceum with the very same name of the one we seek? Oh, I think not, and I think Luddington had better have some answers for us, because I'm damned tired of only finding questions."

They found a cab on Oxford Street and he gave directions for Wrentham House. And they didn't talk. She thought he was crazy, chasing after the unknown. It had all been an illusion, and every incongruity seemed, in the light of day, a figment of both their imaginations.

A cloud drifted over the sun.

"If I were a superstitious man, I would say . . . I would say—someone is sending us a sign. But I'm not, and this is real, and you had best gird yourself to distract Tristan because I'm going to corner my father and find out the truth."

He sounded so determined, she wasn't going to argue with him, especially when she was now eager to see Tristan again.

"Whatever you say, Sinclair."

"Blast you, too," he growled. "The problem with Tristan is he has nothing to do with his time," and then he said nothing more until the carriage drew up in front of his father's house. He paid the cabman and rang the doorbell while she followed slowly up the steps.

Holm opened the door. "Mr. Declan."

"Tell Tristan and my father we're here."

"Oh now, Mr. Edmund has gone down to Flamborough. We'll be following in a day or two, after we finish the packing. But do come in. I believe Mr. Tristan is about."

He shuffled down the hallway, after pointing them into the library.

A moment later Tristan appeared. "You've come to apologize for your amazingly bad manners yesterday?"

"I don't think so," Sinclair said. "I need to talk to Luddington."

"Whatever for?"

"Not your business. I thought he might still be here."

"For heaven's sake—he's back to work. How much time do you think they allow him for these stupid peccadillos? He's a lucky man, I must say. I suppose you could go on over to the Privy Council offices and see if you could find him there."

"I suppose I could. Sayra . . . ?"

"No—leave Sayra with me for a while, won't you? I'll show her around the house and we'll have lunch, and then I'll bring her back to the hotel."

*Yes—I like that idea a lot. Let him do it, Sinclair, since you've very plainly declared your intentions.*

He looked at her questioningly, his face hardening once more into that formidable, unreadable expression.

"By all means. One happy family, now and forever."

"Perhaps I can convince her that you and she should come to live here."

"I have no doubt you will," Sinclair said, and left them.

Tristan sat there just shaking his head. "Never, ever had decent manners, my brother. Always angry about something. And yet somehow he managed to find sunshine. You, Sayra."

She felt his warmth, his concern. "Pretty words, Tristan. He is a complicated man. And I'm sure you are, too."

"Oh, infinitely. Trust me, he would not want all the nonsense that goes along with being my father's heir. Would you like to see the house? Cook is preparing something for us to eat. We were closing up the house for the week, actually, so there are covers over some of the furniture. But you certainly can get an idea . . . come—"

He led her from the library and down the hallway toward the back of the house, past the dining room, past the pantry and through a door that led to another hallway to a separate wing.

"I must say, Father always thought I would be the one to occupy this wing. No one had any idea that Declan would marry first. Of course, he and Evelina . . . but—water under the bridge there. He never declared and she never could manipulate events and force him to. A beautiful woman, but just as cold as snow. In through here now—"

He swung open another door to reveal a long corridor with built-in cupboards lining it, and a substantial staircase winding up one wall of what was a beautiful parlor with a bank of windows that overlooked yet another garden.

The furnishings were less sophisticated, more homey—walnut and mahagony instead of bleached wood and gilt. Glowing gilt- and oak-framed landscapes on the walls. Brass lamps. A pretty walnut desk by the window. Comfortable chairs. And, through a door by the staircase, the dining room, a small, intimate room with a large, many-leafed rope-turned table and chairs and a breakfront. Underfoot, lovely scrolling rugs in rich colors. The kitchen beyond that, smaller, nicely equipped.

Upstairs, two bedrooms—one for the master and his wife, the other meant to be a nursery. Again, massive walnut furniture, the bed like a throne in the center of the room, with its ornate head and footboard decorated with applied moldings. Matching wardrobes and dressers. A fireplace, over which a painting of flowers immediately drew the eye, and lent the pallette of colors for the room.

Draperies at every window, drawn so the sun would not bleach the carpets and the upholstery.

"Declan could have stayed here, lived here, and he chose not to. One just doesn't understand why. But that is his choice. There are two maid's rooms above, by the way, so it's possible to have adequate help, and of course Father's staff whenever you want.

"Now tell me truthfully, beautiful Sayra, would you not love to live here?"

"It's lovely," she murmured as she ran her hand over the glossy furniture and stared at the paintings and imagined herself in such surroundings. "Just lovely."

"And we'd be so close by."

"That would be lovely."

"Would it? Would it, Sayra? Would you like that?"

"Of course I would," she said lightly. "You are the best of all brothers-in-law. You think I'm a goddess."

"And I know all your secrets," he added playfully as he led her back downstairs to the parlor.

"Surely not all," she said. *Too coy by half. And yet—and yet . . . after Flamborough, there would be nothing, and she must fend for herself. So why not flirt with a possible interested suitor?*

"Perhaps not," he said. "A woman like you . . . you haven't forgotten a thing I said, have you, Sayra?"

She turned to look at him. He was so Sinclair, it pierced her heart. Better than Sinclair, because of how deeply he had seen into her soul. "No, I haven't," she said frankly.

"I'm looking forward to Flamborough," he said.

"Why is that?"

"Well, there is something about being away from where one is accustomed to. There's a feeling of liberation, of letting go. Of intimacy you can obtain only in a new place with new friends. The air is different there, somehow. Do you understand, Sayra?"

She understood perfectly. "I'm not sure I do, Tristan," she said, letting a faintly petulant tone creep into her voice. "This is all so new to me, of course. . . ."

"Of course."

They were walking back toward the main part of the house now.

"Would you like to see upstairs?"

"Surely."

They climbed the main staircase to the bedroom landing. There were four doors here, as Tristan pointed them out: "That was Declan's bedroom. Father uses it as his study now. Father's bedroom. My room. The guest room. Upstairs, the servants' quarters. Father's study first. We stored Declan's furniture. He rents the St. James flat furnished. He always was stubborn."

He opened the door.

It was a big square room, lined with bookshelves and lit by one lamp on a pedestal next to a well-worn leather chair. There was a huge table littered with papers in the center of the room, and chairs around that.

And that was all.

"Father tends to be spartan in his surroundings. You'll see in his bedroom." He opened that door to reveal a narrow bed, and the most minimal of furnishings. The windows were curtained and the floor was bare.

"Like a monk," Tristan said. "While my home—I call my room my home, you see—" He opened his bedroom door to a scene of sybaritic luxury: a huge bed, thick carpets, silk-hung walls and curtains, opulent, overstuffed furniture, a massive desk on one wall and an armoire on the other, all done in deep magenta and black and blue.

"You could just sink into that room, couldn't you, Sayra?"

"I love it."

"Yes, you do. You love things that appeal to the senses. You see—I *do* know you; I know you so well."

"Tell me what you meant about Flamborough, about the intimacy of it."

"It's interesting. You can be surrounded by people and still feel that things can be—oh, close, private, secret, just between you and me . . . more so than anywhere in the city. And we do have a secret, don't we, Sayra?"

"Do we?"

He came toward her softly and lifted her chin so that he could see deeply into her eyes.

"Don't we, delicious Sayra? Don't we know exactly how much you would love to experience—shall we say?—every man that you meet? I can't wait for the rest of them to see you. They'll adore you. They'll want you, and isn't that what you desire more than anything else? All those men at your feet, begging for your favors? I promise you, they will. And if that boor of a brother of mine ever—no, we won't talk of that. Because you already know which man's hard part desperately yearns to possess you. And I'll keep my promise not to say anything more. Not yet.

"But maybe . . ." He closed the door to his room. "Maybe at Flamborough. Maybe then you'll take pity . . . Come, lunch is ready . . . and we can talk of other things. . . ."

He was superb at directing conversation, too. His eyes never left her face. He was interested in everything that had to do with her, and she felt a certain small triumph that she had captivated him so. But even if he wanted her because Declan had her, and she had become a pawn in some vicious covert rivalry—so be it.

She had to be practical.

He took her back to the hotel in the Wrentham carriage, with its drawn curtains, lush tufted leather seats and air of intimacy.

"We could just tell the driver to pass the hotel and go on forever," Tristan murmured. "There is something about you. You are dressed like a suburban matron and yet you emanate such a sensuality that a man alone with you feels like a king."

"Oh, really—" she murmured.

"Only a king is a fit consort to a goddess," Tristan said, and his tone of voice told her he was dead serious.

"Tristan . . ." *Surely this was going too far . . .*

He heard the faint distress in her voice; his expression changed. "My dear, you have no idea how desirable you are. My brother is an ass to leave you alone for even one moment with another man. Especially his brother. But you do like me a little, don't you?"

"More than a little," she confessed, letting him have just that scrap of acknowledgment.

"And yet you must return to Declan. What a miscarriage of fate. Well—we will see you in Flamborough in a matter of days. Perhaps the country air will give you a different perspective."

She slanted a coquettish glance at him. "Perhaps."

The carriage skidded to a stop.

"And we're still friends?"

"Perhaps."

The coachman opened the door and offered his hand.

"And you're not at all sorry you spent the afternoon with me."

A statement, that.

She slipped out of the carriage and brushed her skirts. She could barely see him within, but she could feel his palpable presence.

She hesitated a moment. And then, "No."

The door closed as if he was eminently satisfied with that answer.

As she was. She had taken the first step; it felt as if it was the beginning of something.

She just didn't know what.

"Luddington is missing."

She stopped dead on the threshold. "What do you mean?"

He was lying in bed, naked, waiting, angry, about to explode as she opened the door and entered the room.

"I mean he's gone missing. No one's seem him. No one knows where he is. No one knows *what* he is. Maybe he was with you for the last three hours."

"Surely not three hours." She closed the door behind her. "And no one was with us for the last . . . if you say . . . three—hours." And then she realized what a mistake it was to tell him that much.

"Luddington missing, two men murdered, vampires at your feet practically, and you and my brother—alone at last—what the goddamn hell were you thinking?"

She inched her way out of her jacket to keep a rein on her temper. "I was thinking he would be a very nice successor to you."

"Bitch. You are not taking this seriously."

"I take what I just said to you very seriously, Sinclair. Your brother is very fond of me. And it isn't too much to assume he might like to take it further. At least from things that he has said."

"I wouldn't put it past the bastard—but it won't make me come to the point, Messalina. You have to go to Flamborough—

and then you can take your ring and put it through my brother's nose."

"Well—that's clear, isn't it . . . the daughter of a sot is good enough for your brother, but not for you." *And there was some other point about that—she almost grasped it, but it slipped away in her anger, her humiliation.*

"We've had this conversation."

"Yes, we have. I'm so looking forward to going to Flamborough. I assume some of my clothes will be ready?"

"We'll check first thing tomorrow. Although you would be perfectly comfortable without them, Messalina."

"Yes, but now I can see that was part of my problem. One learns these little secrets as one goes along. Never give a man what he wants."

"You did that very nicely last night."

"Yes, I did, didn't I? All part of the game, Sinclair, just like everything else. How else could I have escaped the fortress and gotten back to England?"

"Ah, the fortress. The place that exists or doesn't exist, according to your whim."

"Perhaps Luddington went back to the fortress," she suggested slyly, easing herself into a nearby chair.

His expression darkened. "I don't think so. He gorged himself enough. He doesn't need to go back to the fortress. I think he goes there when he can't feed his bloodlust here. Or when it's dangerous. Or someone gets close. And I think I'm close."

"Close to what?"

"I don't know, and you obviously don't care."

"But then it will be over—whatever it is."

"You tell me what *it* is, Messalina. You tell me who abducted you. Or how you would have escaped without me. Or how you could discount everything Brother Giurgiu told us. Tell me how it could be you didn't know your father's secret. Or how you can just ignore what has happened since we returned. Maybe *you* are *it,* Messalina. Maybe you're the link—the daughter of a monster—the seductress, the temptress, forever distracting a man with sex—Jesus God . . . with me every minute, every clue—"

*Oh, God—this is getting out of hand . . .*

"Sinclair—"

"Don't move." His voice was deadly. "Don't say a word. *You* found Luddington in the fortress. And now you're the one who keeps insisting maybe we imagined it all, and you want to pretend everything is nice and normal. Oh, you're a clever piece, Messalina. Who sent you there?"

He was over her now, his hands grasping her arms. "*Who sent you there?*"

She didn't answer, and he thrust her away from him in disgust.

"No wonder we got away so easily. Jesus, if this doesn't explain a hundred things. Not why. Not who. That's what I need to find out—*why* and *who.*" He jammed his arms into his shirt and plucked up his trousers. "God almighty. Shit. And I goddamn believed it—believed *you,* a piece of trash they hired to do their dirty work. Your father could have been the vampire king, for all I know. Jesus, I can't believe this. . . ."

He was dressed by then, and prowling the room; ready, she thought, to jump on her if she made any conciliatory move.

"All right. I'm about ready to throw you out the window. You've already had better than you deserve. But it's not over. So you're going to Flamborough, just as we planned. And we're going to find Luddington. And then we're going to find out everything, because you and he are going to finally tell me the truth."

# Chapter 23

She felt as if she had fallen down the rabbit hole. It was so unreal, she was shaking with the horror of it.

*He believes . . . he couldn't believe—*

He guarded her all night like she was a prisoner, and in the morning they went to Oxford Street and took what was finished of her dresses, and then went on to Barron's store and purchased the rest: suitcases, ready-made suits for him, underthings, sturdy shoes, jackets, day dresses, whatever she would need in the country to go hunting ghouls.

He bought their train tickets, he packed the suitcases, he didn't let her out of his sight for a moment, not even to wash and to change outfits.

She wore another of the skirts and jersey jackets from Fontaine's shop for the train trip. They left from Victoria Station at noon.

So different from the last train trip from Berlin to Calais.

So different from everything.

He bought them a compartment, this time for isolation, and a basket of food to go with them.

There was a horrible, forbidding look in his eye as he settled them in, with her seated directly opposite him on the tufted velvet banquette. There was a little fold-up table under the window that had matching curtains to draw at night, and brass lamps in four corners to light the interior.

For the first time she felt scared and uncertain. And he wouldn't answer any questions.

"But why Flamborough; why do you think Luddington's there?" she kept asking futilely. She couldn't think of one reason, but obviously he could. Or maybe he just wanted to foist her off on Tristan before he went after Luddington.

It would be a three-hour train trip, and another half hour from the station to the house.

All that time, with all that suspicion. As if he expected her to turn into something supernatural before his very eyes.

She had turned into a passion slave for him. She knew nothing else.

The train moved smoothly out of the station. She looked out the window at the crowded platform and all the people waving a final good-bye to departing friends or relatives.

*Good-bye for me, too—good-bye to everything . . . there will be nothing after we leave Flamborough. Nothing.*

She couldn't believe it, even now. He hadn't said those words; he hadn't meant them. To think she was part of it . . . some kind of ghoulish conspiracy—to what purpose, *what?*

*Her father—the vampire king . . . really . . . !*

*. . . maybe not* her *father . . .*

*Now where did that insidious thought come from? Was she so desperate for a turnabout?*

*No . . . it was just that he was adamant about going to Flamborough. And his father was already there.*

*Now wait . . . there was something—*

The train picked up speed as it came out into daylight.

*She couldn't quite catch it. Something to do with . . .*

She looked up at him. His face was set, his eyes icy. Like the first time she had seen him, as she strutted her naked body for the begoun's pleasure . . . *and what had the begoun really been looking for—the plumpest morsel who would gush the most blood . . . ?*

*God, I have to stop thinking like this—how could he think I could forget a moment of it . . .*

*The begoun was the vampire king . . . no, wait—*

*Something . . . what—?*

*She had been ruminating about it before . . . fathers—*

*. . . fathers—*

*Yes—wait . . .*

Not *her father—*

*No, not that.*

*Not* that.

*But she didn't know* what.

She stared out the window as the cityscape flew by and changed slowly and inexorably into suburban sprawl. Bigger houses. Little gardens. Dirt roads. Children playing along the track, and running after the trains, waving at them as if they were the best of friends.

Innocence.

Purity.

Unaware of monsters.

*Anyone can be a monster.*

*My father.*

*Me . . .*

*Even—he . . .*

It was a long, silent, harrowing trip.

They arrived in Flamborough at close to four o'clock, due to station holdups and track slowdowns.

There was a carriage waiting, provided by his father, a regular custom when he was in residence; whether guests were expected or not, a conveyance was always to be available.

That grace note did not improve Sinclair's temper. His father always did the proper thing—publicly. And Tristan would do the same.

He climbed grudgingly into the carriage beside Sayra. He hadn't been to Flamborough in all this time. The village had changed, grown. New homes and shops lined a main street that he remembered as having been sparsely populated.

Even as they left the village there were intermittent clusters of homes he had never seen before. And farmland enclosed by fences. Cows and horses grazing where once the forest was wild.

All of it, cut back and shaped to the needs of men.

And then, on the edge of what had been the forest, the homes of the wealthy, the *cottages* of respite from the ravages of town living.

The Wrentham seat was a huge pile of stone and half-timbering set low to the ground, and surrounded by manicured gardens in which his father had no interest whatsoever. A paid retainer cared for the terraced lawns and flower beds that were purely for public consumption.

Sinclair doubted his father ever walked in the garden.

His mother, however, had loved the flowers.

The carriage turned into a broad driveway overhung with trees that swept into a gentle curve toward the front door.

Before the carriage pulled to a stop, Holm appeared at the door.

"Ah, Mr. Declan. Mr. Tristan arrived this morning with Miss Evelina. And of course Mr. Ismail. Everyone else is due tomorrow. Dinner is in an hour, so you'll have time to freshen up. Baxter will take your bags."

Baxter. He didn't remember a Baxter; Baxter turned out to be young, farm-fresh and energetic. He could carry four suitcases at a time without duress. He knew already which room was theirs, and he led them up the wide staircase to the upper hallway and the third door on the left.

It was a generous-sized room, fully paneled, with built-in closets, a molded ceiling and a huge fireplace.

There was a massive bed facing that, several dressers, a washstand, a chair by the window and two in front of the fireplace.

The Oriental rug underfoot covered the entire floor.

"I'll send a maid to you," Baxter said as he withdrew.

"All the amenities," Sinclair murmured, pulling open the closets that were hidden in the panelling. "Amazing. I totally forgot. Don't move, Messalina. You'll change for dinner."

"Sinclair . . ."

"I know. Everything seems perfect, normal. Right. But we know differently now, don't we? *Nothing* is normal. And nothing is what it seems."

But how did that apply to Tristan. And Evelina. And Ismail who had come with his father.

The dinner was outstanding—mock turtle soup, shoulder of mutton *carbonnade,* vegetable salad, asparagus supreme, and a parfait of chocolate—and served in the vast dining room, with its stained-glass windows and built-in sideboards and its low, romantic lighting.

The servants swarmed around them, removing plates, offering a second serving, refilling wine glasses.

This time Sayra felt the equal of the pallid blond Evelina in her dramatic wine silk evening dress. Evelina was dressed in blue once again, satin this time, with a draped bustle and illusion net covering her shoulders and arms and dipping daringly down toward her bosom.

And she was eyeing Sayra across the table as if she was measuring Sayra's dress to see if it would fit *her.*

Tristan, thank heaven, was seated next to her, and he managed to divert her attention from Sayra just when it looked like she was going to say something sticky.

*Water under the bridge . . . Tristan had said so, but perhaps if she knew that Sinclair was ready to relinquish me, she would . . .*

*She didn't want to think what Evelina would . . .*

And then there was Ismail, so charming. A statesman even at the informal dining table of a country house. Here was a man who directed conversation, steered everyone toward topics of common interest, deflected all differences of opinion and still seemed like a man who kept his counsel.

He was quite charming to her, asking after all the details of her first days in London and where Sinclair had taken her shopping (which he very much approved and said he could tell her dress was indeed Fontaine), and if she had been able to see any of the sights.

She looked at Sinclair. His eyes flickered, and she could not read any kind of message there.

*. . . the vampire king . . .*

*Maybe not her father—*

"We did manage," she said in answer to Ismail's question, "to visit the Union Lyceum."

"Did you? Did you find it fascinating? All those books. And the museum. It dates from four hundred or so years ago and was originally a guildhall, if I recall my history correctly. Amazing, these old buildings. They hold up so well, and then the city courageously puts them to modern usage so that we keep our heritage intact. Yes, the Lyceum. I know it well."

He took a sip of water. "Of course you have to do the traditional sights—the Tower of London, St. George's (everyone gets married there, you know), Westminster Abbey, Madame Tussaud's—really,

Declan, I think you've been remiss. The Lyceum is dry bones compared to a wax museum."

"I'll undertake to remedy the situation," Sinclair said dryly.

"But you did do Fontaine's for her clothes, so that's something. She's lovely."

"Isn't she?" Again that dry tone of voice. She wanted to shake him.

"Excellent vintage, that shade of wine silk. Lovely. You are a credit to your husband, my dear. I can't conceive where he found you."

*In a fortress, sir, with two bloodthirsty ghouls . . .*

Nor did he expect a response to that.

Evelina, however, was looking slightly nauseated by the conversation; it was quite obvious that she was used to being the center of attention.

He went on, "You come to me if he makes you unhappy. I know how to handle Declan."

Sayra looked straight at Sinclair. "May I say, sir, so do I."

"Ho ho ho—Declan—a worthy opponent."

"Come, everybody—" Tristan, now, also looking a little out of sorts at the way Ismail was flattering her, "let's adjourn to the library."

This room was at the front of the houses, with a bay window that overlooked the drive.

Holm had lit a fire in the huge fireplace and drawn chairs up around it, and set a table with brandy and goblets.

Everyone took a goblet; Tristan poured and then made the toast: "To Declan and his bride . . ."

Sayra watched them over the rim of her glass. She took the merest sip. But so did Evelina, Tristan and his father. The only ones who downed any brandy were Sinclair and Ismail.

It struck her, too, that Sinclair's father had not said a word since they arrived.

She studied him as everyone sank into a chair by the fireplace.

He chose the seat in the farthest corner. He watched everyone with his gleaming, rheumy, icy eyes. He watched her—and Tristan—as Tristan pulled a chair over so he could sit next to her, while Evelina perched on the arm of Sinclair's chair.

And Sayra found she did not like that. *Not at all.*

*. . . he never declared . . . and she never could manipulate events and force him to—*

But she very much liked Tristan by her side as Ismail made a comment on national politics that immediately precipitated a discussion of his policy vis-à-vis the protocol. And on this topic Edmund Sinclair found his voice.

"You are so beautiful I can hardly stand it," Tristan whispered under the vehement argument.

"Tristan—"

"Are you naked under your dress, Sayra? I think you are. And not for *him.* You do look like a goddess tonight."

Sinclair was watching them, his brooding eyes resting on his brother, expressionless, with a killing intensity, and nothing Evelina did or said could distract him.

She looked around the room.

They were bathed in the soft glow of candlelight; shadows hovered in the corners of the room as genteel people made genteel after-dinner conversation, arguing politics and plays, exchanging malicious gossip that cut well-known people to ribbons.

Nothing threatening here; nothing to suppose that Luddington or any of his ilk were anywhere near. No reason at all for Sinclair to conclude that she was the dupe of her father's delusion.

*I'm going crazy . . . and if that woman doesn't stop stroking Sinclair's sleeve, I will* bite *her—*

"Let me take you for a walk tomorrow after breakfast," Tristan said.

She tore her eyes away from Sinclair to look up at him—adoringly, she hoped. Sinclair was a lost cause. And Tristan wanted her. When was she going to get that through her head?

Tomorrow morning might just do.

"I would like that," she murmured.

"You see what I mean about the intimacy of the place."

"Oh, I do."

"I hate the idea of your going back upstairs with *him.*"

"Ah, Tristan . . ."

"You'll come with me because—because . . ."

"We're friends," she said. "You know my secrets."

"Does he?"

"Someday you might know."

"I'll live for that day," he whispered, taking her hand and kissing it.

His lips were cool, and his touch. But his eyes weren't. His eyes glowed with heat every time he looked at her. In his eyes she was perfect. What else could a goddess be? And she did like being a goddess—to him.

"When tomorrow?" she asked hesitantly.

"After breakfast?"

"Which is when?"

"Whenever a goddess wishes to have it."

"Tristan . . ." She knew her protest sounded coy. And she loved the fact that Sinclair was helpless to stop her. And that he kept swatting away Evelina's hand as if it were a fly.

"If you could have any man in this room now, who would it be?"

*Oh—a loaded question. Dear Lord, just how did Tristan expect her to answer it? She knew—and she couldn't—and she wanted to choose Ismail as the seat of power, and she couldn't even fairly do that.*

*What she had to do was play his game.*

"Must a goddess choose? Did you not say yourself I could have any man who had the stamina? I remember everything you said, Tristan. What does that tell you?"

"It tells me—you want *me* . . ."

She smiled. "Perhaps we can talk more about that tomorrow."

"I want you, beautiful Sayra."

She smiled again but chose not to answer. It was better not to answer such blandishments—not yet. Monsters were lurking. And Sinclair, with his cannonball eyes. If he could have killed Tristan on the spot, he would have.

"I do think we are tired from the journey up," he said at last, and she, if no one else, could hear the thread of fury coloring his voice.

"Oh, he's ready to pop," Tristan whispered. "Mollify him if you must."

"I am tired," she said as Tristan helped her up. "Good night, all."

Sinclair let her precede him out of the room. She could feel his heat and his anger pulsating behind her as they climbed the stairs. She could hear the conversation resuming below. She felt a kind of regret that she had to forgo Tristan's balming words to accompany Sinclair upstairs.

And she felt a heady triumph that Tristan had admitted he wanted her.

Only, she was such a novice at this kind of thing. How did a woman leave one man for another? One brother for another?

*Oh, if Sinclair had any inkling of my thoughts . . .*

She jumped as he slammed the door behind them.

"Oh, you are something, Messalina. It's a treat to watch you work your wiles on another poor besotted fool."

She shrugged. "Well, it's obvious you're impervious to these things. Evelina couldn't even get a rise out of you, let alone a decent word of conversation."

"Evelina is a dead issue."

"She seems to think not."

"You seem to have watched very closely."

"But not as closely as you, Sinclair. Work my wiles—honestly!"

"You're right. A passion slave doesn't have to do a thing but be there for the man who wants her."

"Exactly. And there is a man who wants me. So I don't understand what all this discussion is about."

"You're as blatant as a five-pound trollop."

"Perhaps that's just what I am. Along with all the other guises you've invented for me. A passion slave. A courtesan. A wife. A dupe in collusion with bloodthirsty murderers. And I gulled you into the bargain."

"I've always known what you were," he said brutally.

"Well, I missed the cues about you. And then this last piece of insanity . . . oh! I can't talk about it anymore. It makes no sense. Nothing makes sense."

"No—everything is starting to make sense."

"Then tell me how."

He stared at her for a long uncompromising moment. "No. No. Tristan is your meal ticket now. Believe me, those arrangements will be very easy to make. Just be aware—I will get to the truth, no matter where it leads."

"And where *could* it lead, Sinclair?"

"Right back to you, Messalina. Right back to you."

He didn't sleep with her that night, though he was in the room. She awakened the next morning thoroughly disgusted with him and his secrets and his nonsense, and raring to take that walk with Tristan so he could declare himself.

What to wear . . . what to wear?

One of the neat walking suits from Fontaine, perhaps. The sturdy shoes. Her hair piled on her head to reveal her profile . . . men did love to take down a woman's hair—The suit, of black-and-brown striped poplin, had a gored skirt that had two tiers of flounces at the hem, and a jacket that fit snugly over her hips. It was light, fresh, summery in spite of its dark coloring, and it fit her body closely, sensuously.

She felt sensual for the first time in days. She felt Sinclair watching her as she got dressed. She felt his heat. His enmity. The split between what he knew and what he wanted.

And she knew in spite of what he had said that he still wanted her.

*And she still wanted him . . .*

*Oh, no—not that trap; she would just set all those wants and needs aside and let Tristan seduce her.*

*Into a kiss.*

*Perhaps . . .*

The day was overcast. They could see the gray sky through the windows as they came downstairs for breakfast, which was set out on one of the two built-in sideboards in the dining room.

There was so much food, it looked as if no one had yet been down to eat.

She took some eggs, toast, fruit and tea.

He served himself eggs, steak and a glass of milk.

"Tristan has invited me to go for a walk this morning."

"How cozy."

"You're not advocating I should be rude to him?"

"Why not? On the other hand, maybe you'll bite him and he'll die."

"Sinclair . . . "

"Bitch." He sliced into the steak as if he wished it were her.

"You can't have it all ways."

"And what does Mistress bitch know about which way I'd like to have it?"

"Who knows better?" she retorted, setting down her knife and fork. She had lost her appetite. And Tristan was nowhere in sight.

"Impossible bitch. Tristan is welcome to you."

"Ah!" Tristan, at the door. "I'm so happy to have the husband's permission. It makes life so much easier."

"Go to hell," Sinclair said, jacking himself up abruptly so that everything in front of him went flying.

"We make our own hell," Tristan said gently. "Come, Sayra. Declan is being his usual boorish self. And we don't have to stand for that."

"No," she said, "we don't."

She took one last sip of tea, rose from the table and brushed by the tense and simmering Sinclair to take Tristan's arm.

And she didn't look back as she left the room.

He was dressed in a dark suit and wore a broad-brimmed hat in spite of the fact that there was no sun.

"An affectation, perhaps," he admitted. "I like the look of it. It's become habit now and I feel odd without it."

She was willing to accept anything. This was Tristan, after all, with his warm eyes and clear understanding of her.

"You look beautiful in the morning, too," Tristan said, with the faintest catch in his voice. "Or is it because he pleasured you so well last night?"

She didn't let herself feel shock at that question. "It's because I'm with you," she murmured.

"I pictured you naked and moaning in his arms last night."

"Tristan . . ."

"And calling out *my* name—"

"Why are you doing this?" *Only she didn't mind it—not really . . .*

"I can't bear to think of him making love to you. You ought to have met me first."

"But I didn't."

"A goddess shouldn't have to accept less than her due."

"I like the sound of that," she said lightly.

"You like everything I say to you. You know it's the truth. And that I know all your secrets—" His voice dropped to a whisper. "Remember what I said? Remember? You belong to all men, and you can give yourself to any man who desires you—any man, Sayra. Any man who is hard and strong enough to pleasure you. A goddess always wants so much more than mortal women. I can see it in your eyes. You want it all the time. And where is there a man hard enough to give it to you all the time?"

She drew in a hissing breath.

"That day in the carriage . . . you wanted to be naked for me, didn't you? You wanted it then—me, between your legs, giving it to you as long and as hard as you could take it . . . you insatiable goddess. I'll wager you're never satisfied. I'll wager you push a man to his limits and then beyond, and that there hasn't been a man yet who can stay hard enough to pleasure you."

She made a vibrant, protesting sound.

He let the words hang between them as they walked farther into the gardens.

"Sayra . . ." His voice was raspy with his need. "Be naked for me. Give yourself to me. Be my immortal goddess. Take my hardness for your pleasure. Let me work, let me strain every muscle of my being to worship your naked body. I will be every man you could ever want. Let me, Sayra . . . let me—"

She was breathing so hard at the images his words evoked. She wanted to say yes; she wanted to tell him that Sinclair was going to abandon her. She wanted . . .

"Sayra . . ." He backed her up against a tree. "Sayra . . . just your name—Sayra . . . oh I want you, Sayra, wholly and nakedly mine . . . say yes, Sayra. Say yes, yes, you want me; yes, you want my hardness. Yes, you want my worship . . . yes, you want me to be every man for you . . . yes, say yes—"

She didn't need explanations after all. She had only to say it. And she whispered, "Yes."

Bless Tristan; after his impassioned plea, he had the tact, the discretion not to implore her further.

They spent a pleasant hour strolling the grounds of the house, and only by indirect inference did he refer to his proposal.

But as they came back to the house, he murmured, "You will have to tell my brother that your luscious naked body will now be mine. I don't envy your task, darling Sayra; be haughty and righteous with him, as a goddess should be. He doesn't deserve you, but we won't do anything to dishonor him."

"I'll tell him."

He caught her hand. "I want you to move to my room tonight. I want to savor your naked body next to mine. . . . No one has to know, insatiable one, that you have deigned to bestow the gift of your nakedness on me."

She hesitated a moment. A hot, beseeching man to worship her femininity . . . she looked at her ring. How fast ought she move to grasp the chance? No—better to make Tristan wait; arouse his hunger to the swooning point. Let him cajole her with his hot sensual words. Let him worship in his mind the *idea* of her.

And *then* let him experience the reality.

*. . . a five-pound trollop . . .*

*Surely both Tristan and Sinclair had demonstrated she was worth more than that . . .*

"*He* will know. And I do still have some obligation to him. Perhaps it wouldn't be seemly in your father's house . . ."

"Dear heaven, how do you expect me to restrain myself when I know you will be mine?"

"As I will," she said gently.

"And how do I know *he* won't be visiting himself on your naked body at night?"

"You will just have to trust me that he isn't. And he won't."

"But he has . . ."

"He . . ." she almost tripped over the word, the lie ". . . married me. With all that entails."

"And sometime you will tell me the truth about why. Because no man in his sane mind would give up such a naked treasure."

She slanted what she hoped was an enigmatic smile at him.

"And when we are naked and exchanging carnal secrets I want you to tell me the intimate details of his sex . . . because I need to understand how he could possess such a voluptuous goddess and then let her go. I hate it that he knows your naked body. That you have enfolded his hardness in you. That he might—*might*—have given you *some* degree of pleasure. I hate it, Sayra, and nothing less will suffice than you tell me everything."

"But not here," she temporized. "This is not the place to tell you my most erotic secrets."

"When, then?"

"If I come to you after we return to London? I will let you undress me and we can sink into that opulent bed of yours, and I promise I will be yours, and I will tell you everything you want to hear."

*Good trollop, telling the customer exactly what he wants . . .*

The warmth in his eyes turned burning bright. "The moment you return to London? Naked in my bed with me?"

"I can't wait, Tristan." *Anything to seal the bargain and keep his interest at a fever pitch.*

"Naked, and I can do anything I want with your luscious body—?"

"Anything," she whispered fervently.

"A man could die for such a promise. A goddess in his bed, naked and waiting to be worshipped . . ."

"In just a few days. Can you wait?"

"Can you, insatiable one?"

"I can try . . ."

"And I will wait, because I want to sink myself into you so badly. And because I know the reality can only exceed anything I could ever imagine."

"Tristan . . ." she sighed, melting into his embrace.

"My naked goddess."

"I adore the words you say to me."

"You love being worshipped. You love being naked with a man. All you desire is a man's hardness driving your insatiable need. And I promise I will keep you naked and sated from the moment I take you into my bed."

"I can't wait . . ." she breathed.

"Insatiable one. You will learn who has the stamina to pleasure your naked sex. You will know who worships your wanton nature. Who deifies your carnal desires. Who knew what you were the moment he saw you: a naked goddess who needed a god to satiate her."

"Are you a god?" she murmured.

"I feel like one, now your insatiable body will be mine to pleasure."

"You make me feel like a goddess."

"Women like you should be worshipped. Women who withhold themselves . . . how can they know such carnal ecstasy? Your body was born to be possessed by any man who can tame you."

"Tristan, you have to stop. Your words are making me so hot."

"Ahhh, what a tribute to the insatiable goddess; how easily she is aroused. How delectable her protest. What man wouldn't succumb to such an entreaty? I can't wait to possess you, my naked one."

"We're almost at the house, Tristan."

"My insatiable one is modest as well. What a combination of contradictions you are. You can't imagine how much I want you. And how much waiting will enhance the pleasure."

*Someone else had said that—*

"Yes . . ."

"And now anytime I look at you across the room, across the table, my goddess, I will be seeing you naked in my bed."

"I hope so," she murmured. "I have to go—I must change for lunch. Dear Tristan, have I told you how our second meeting—the picnic in the carriage—affected me? No? When we are naked in bed together I'll tell you."

And she left him with that, whirling away from him and darting into the doorway and into the house.

She looked back only when she was at the staircase.

He was still standing in front of the house, a statue. A man besotted by a woman who had just given her ultimate carnal promise.

She hated it that she had lied—just a little.

But Tristan did not have to know that, and neither did Sinclair, who was in a towering rage when she entered their room.

"He didn't eat you for lunch, I see. He looked like he was going to."

"You were spying."

"Look out the window, Messalina. The poor fool is still standing there. Your parting words turned him to stone."

"You're the one made of stone, Sinclair. I have to change for lunch."

"So—has he committed to taking you?"

"I won't answer that. This is so painful, Sinclair, after everything we've been through. You're the one who insisted we come here. You're the one who is still seeing monsters. They are just *not* here. Maybe back in London. Maybe *you* should go back to London."

"My son-of-a-bitch brother is a monster."

"He wants me."

"Goddamn everyone wants you."

"Except you." She pulled a fresh dress out of the built-in closet. The words hung in the air between them, and she refused to take them back or soften them with anything remotely conciliating. "We can end this farce by just leaving tomorrow."

"I would be perfectly happy to put *you* on a train tomorrow, Messalina."

"I'll suggest it to Tristan. Perhaps he would like to go back with me and we can start our new life together."

She turned her back on him as she said that, and began divesting herself of her jacket and skirt. And anyway, it was a delicious thought, Tristan by her side, uttering those erotically charged words in her ear, arousing them both for the three hours of the journey until they both couldn't stand it anymore.

And then—and then . . . she would let him—

She would let him worship her.

She slipped on one of her ready-made dresses with shaking hands. *Let Tristan's cool hands touch her, feel her, caress her naked body. Let his carnal words heat her up so that she wouldn't care who it was bringing her to ecstasy.*

*No, she wasn't going to think that way. She wasn't. She could want Tristan just as easily as Sinclair. And Tristan adored her, wanted to idolize her, called her his goddess . . .*

*What more could a woman want?*

She eased the dress over her hips and turned herself this way and that in the mirror that was attached to the closet door. The dress was a cobalt blue silk crepe, with ribbon trim at the neck, wrists and hem, and the bodice fit her tightly, and the skirt rustled with her every move.

"Perfect," she murmured, taking a brush to work on her hair. "Are you coming to lunch, Sinclair?"

"We will put on a show, together."

"How boring." She twisted her thick tresses into a chignon and fastened it at her neck. "I'm ready."

"I haven't forgotten you're always ready."

"But that's for someone else's pleasure now," she said tightly, and preceded him out the door.

There were no monsters in the dining room. Just platters of food laid out to be eaten *en buffet:* a compote of fruit, fried oysters, sweetbreads in cream with mushrooms and peas, fillets of steak, lamb cutlets, saffron rice, *petits pains,* autumn salad, strawberries and cream, tea, coffee, *cafe au lait* and chocolate.

She ate sparingly; it was only the two of them after all, seated apart at the table, he at one end and she at the other.

And she hated the brooding look in those cold, light eyes.

And then Tristan entered the room, and what Sinclair thought was of no moment.

He took a plate full of food, his burning gaze on her all the time, until he finally came to sit next to her.

"My greedy goddess," he whispered, bending toward her so that Sinclair could not hear. "When you were upstairs, changing your clothes, did you think of me?"

"I thought of all the erotic words you spoke to me," she whispered back.

"After lunch let me take you someplace where I can tell you more."

"That would be perfect."

She ate. She didn't know how she ate. Or what she ate. The fruit. The sweetbreads. Some of the oysters. The salad. A sip of chocolate.

Tristan hardly ate at all. "Come," he whispered. "Come."

She didn't think twice.

And she didn't look back.

They were on the bedroom floor, at the far end of the house from the bedrooms, at the back staircase beside which there was a wide window that overlooked the gardens of Wrentham, which were now all in bloom.

"Like you," Tristan murmured hoarsely. He was standing behind her, his hands on her shoulders as she enjoyed the view.

"You're all furled like a flower bud, waiting for the heat of a man's hard body to bring you to full bloom."

"Tell me more," she whispered.

"When we're naked and alone, my insatiable goddess, you will unfurl every delicate petal for my eyes only. You will open your unappeasable nakedness to me and only me, and I will sate you. And when I'm done, and you're greedy for more, it will be my hard part that will bring you to ecstasy all over again. *My* hard part, my goddess."

His hands caressed her shoulders. "And you love hearing everything I want to do to you, don't you, insatiable one? You're probably dreaming up ways to bring me to my knees, even now. My voracious goddess who can never get enough of a man. Isn't it true? All you desire is the hardness of a man to give you pleasure. That's what a goddess does: She demands a man's hot, hard part all the time."

She made a sound.

"My carnal goddess wants to hear more. Nothing else matters but a man's hardness. And the pleasure. You can't get enough of the pleasure. So true, my voluptuous one—you feel the pleasure even when there isn't a man between your legs."

"Ah, Tristan—"

"I will treasure your nakedness, my goddess. I promise to worship it, to pleasure it, to be within it when you want it . . . let me—let me kiss your beautiful neck, your swan neck—"

She tilted her head and felt his cool lips brushing the curling hair at the nape of her neck.

She felt nothing.

He moved his lips, planting soft kisses and cool little bites all along the edge of her collar, his words muffled, his excitement escalating.

"A goddess neck, such silky skin—let me leave a kiss here, a nip there—let me suck your luscious skin—" as he pulled at a tender place near her ear. "I feel you responding to me. The goddess is pleased. Her supplicant is in ecstasy . . ." as he sucked again, this time behind her ear. "My naked treasure, my erotic mistress, my immortal one . . ."

She swooned at the words, at the feel of his lips rooting at her ear. *Yes, yes—I can do this—I can . . .*

Her eyes closed, her body swayed against his.

"Let's not wait, my insatiable darling; I want you now. . . ."

Her eyes popped open, and out the window and beyond the gardens she caught a glimpse of a rider galloping recklessly toward the far fields.

*Riding . . .*

*. . . me—*

*Make him wait . . .*

"Dear Tristan—"

"You protest too much, when your body is aching for satiation."

"We promised. And anyone . . . anyone could come upon us here. But in London, in your room, with soft low candlelight, and that luscious thick bed—we'll be naked under the covers and you can do everything you ever dreamed of to your goddess's willing, naked body. And it will be so much the sweeter for the waiting. . . ."

"If we left tomorrow . . ." he growled.

"And on the train you could whisper all those enticing erotic words to me. Three hours of this arousing, carnal conversation—could you restrain yourself, Tristan? Could you give me such pleasure with only words?"

"We will go to London together tomorrow," he said, his voice tinged with a kind of violence. "I'll wait if I must. But no longer than tomorrow. And I will arouse you like you've never been aroused before, and then when we're alone in my house, in my room, in my bed, I will take your naked, willing body as many times as you can stand it. And you will find such ecstasy that you will beg for my hard part to take you over and over again. If that is what you want, darling Sayra, you will leave my brother and come back to London with me tomorrow and be my naked goddess and I will give it to you just the way you want it."

*The words she wanted to hear: the commitment from him to take her, with his lips on her neck, on her cheek, near her mouth . . . leaving Sinclair forever . . .*

*Why not? What else was there for her but a complete immersion in the senses? A goddess she was not—but a passion slave . . . yes, forever.*

And so it was easy—easier—to say, "I will—I will leave Sinclair and go back with you, Tristan. With all that means to both of us."

He turned her around so that he could look at her. He touched her face with his cool finger. "Immortal goddess—you will never regret it."

# Chapter 24

He rode like the wind across the fields of his childhood. He couldn't outrun her. Not the feel of her, the scent of her, his need for her.

His fury with her.

A wanton who couldn't wait. Was there ever one who could?

And so there was Tristan, picking up the pieces.

He couldn't stand it anymore.

It was a stupid idea, coming to Flamborough on the heels of this divisiveness between them. He still didn't know what he had hoped to find.

And instead he had lost everything.

And Tristan had won, again.

He had never understood quite how that had all worked. Tristan, the oldest son and heir, the charming, golden boy, a twin to his brooding persona, and a liar in his teeth to boot.

That had always been so: Tristan would always have his way. His father had trained him to expect it, no matter what he had to do to get it.

There had never been any recourse for an ethical younger son but to leave.

And now here he was, home again—for this had been home while his mother lived—and he couldn't begin to sort out his feelings.

Sayra was right; there was nothing here. Just a house party to celebrate a marriage that did not exist. And so he had discovered he had no qualms about telling lies either.

For Sayra. Only for Sayra.

Who now, damn her soul, was willing to take Tristan as her lover.

He spurred the horse again at the unbearable thought of it.

*Sayra—Sayra in his soul—too much a part of him now to ever let go—and yet . . . and yet—she would relinquish him as calmly and coolly as any mistress who knows her time is past.*

*He had rewarded her already, and Tristan was wealthy enough to do the rest. He need not think about her ever again.*

*But all he could think about was her and the indelible first time he had seen her in the fortress . . .*

*Ah, the fortress.*

*The fortress was real. The fortress* was *real. And everything that had happened since.*

*And Luddington was the clue, but he didn't know to what.*

*Bloodthirsty monsters everywhere, hiding under a facade of normalcy—and only he and Sayra holding the key because they knew the monsters existed.*

*. . . kill the one and you kill them all . . .*

*And now two more were dead, with prick wounds all over their bodies. When he got back to London he would go to the Yard and find out how many more had died that way.*

*He was wasting time in Flamborough.*

*Sayra would be fine. Tristan would keep her for as long as she interested him, and then he would make sure to buy her off for a fair amount of money.*

*That was all a passion slave could hope for.*

*And better than her lot in Wixoe.*

He reined in his mount at the top of a rise that overlooked all of the Wrentham land and the house.

It was so far away, it looked like an oversized doll's house. And in it, people were going about their business, having lunch, setting up cards, whatever it was they did on a country weekend.

While Tristan was mouthing pretty words in Sayra's receptive ear, and she had forgotten everything else and everyone else already.

No monsters.

*But in Wixoe there had been a monster.*

*So who was to say there wasn't one here?*

He shook himself.

*Why was the feeling so insistent?*

*He was missing something and he didn't know what the hell it was.*

*Or he didn't want to know—*
*Sayra . . .*
He spurred on his horse.
*Sayra . . . damn her—*
*Sayra—*

In the library Ismail had organized a card game consisting of himself, Evelina, Sayra and a friend who had arrived barely an hour before.

"Tristan, of course, must make himself available to his guests," Ismail said as he dealt the cards. "And Edmund tires easily these days; I believe he is resting. So now there's us, all cozy in the corner. I think we decided Marchand and the lovely Sayra will pair. Who leads?"

And the game began.

The time flew by; Sayra noticed intermittently that other guests had arrived, marching by the library door on their way to their rooms and then coming down again to the library, where Holm had laid out tea an hour early.

He brought refreshments to the library as well. They heard voices discussing what to do and the decision made to shoot skeets, and Baxter summoned to take the guests to the shooting range.

A woman sauntered into the library with a book and snuggled into a chair by the window.

A portly man entered with a portfolio and settled himself at a table to do some work, after a perfunctory nod at Ismail.

Two more gentlemen settled themselves at the chess table. Two women brought with them a box with a puzzle.

The conversation was low, lulling, soothing.

Holm drew the curtain over the window so that the sun would not interfere with the guests' activities.

Sayra and Marchand went down to Ismail and Evelina in a trice, and immediately demanded a rematch.

Sinclair stamped into the house and paused at the library door to survey the scene.

*No monsters.*

*No Tristan.*

*And, Ismail had better check his charm at the door.*

He studied Evelina for a moment.

She was glacially beautiful, with flushed, pale skin and eyes that glowed with a brilliant light. She always wore blue. Her perfect blond hair was always coiled and pinned up. She was the epitome of the society belle his father would have wanted him to marry.

For a time he had considered it. But she was too insubstantial for him. And too spiteful. When she had shown up at Wrentham House with Tristan he had assumed that his brother was attached to her.

So, instead, Tristan was courting Sayra, almost from the moment he saw her, damn his eyes.

And there she was, all aglow and dealing cards as if she had been playing for years. Ismail was absolutely taken with her, the old roué. And Marchand—couldn't keep his eyes off her.

And neither could he.

He wrenched himself away from the library and retreated to the dining room, helping himself to some tea and cakes.

*No monsters here.*

*He had misjudged the situation entirely.*

*There was only the happy sound of guests arriving and clumping up the steps and down, light conversation and the door slamming as people made their way to the various activities that had been planned.*

*The way things should always have been.*

*Laughter, conversation, surrounded by friends and family—*

He felt a sudden bone-deep yearning for that kind of life. He had no strictures on him as to whom he could marry. And his father had accepted Sayra readily enough.

*Too readily . . .*

*Wait a minute—*

He set down his cup.

*The Wrentham bride, he had called her, almost as if she was married to the lot of them.*

"There you are." His father bearing down on him. "You have no idea what joy it gives me to have my sons and my first daughter-in-law and all my friends attendant here. This is the start of a new era, my boy. We'll put the past behind us. You'll come to Wrentham House. We'll be a family again."

He stared down into his father's pale, rheumy eyes, and it seemed to him that his father's face was as fragile as a mummy's wrappings. He looked so old suddenly, with his eyes the only living, burning part of him.

*His father could die . . .*

"Your darling wife—what a joy . . . everyone loves her. Ismail is head over heels, a man of his age. I've never seen him like this. Playing cards for hours, for heaven's sake. Making everyone laugh. Her Majesty would turn top over tail if she saw him. But of course she won't. And tomorrow or the next day, when he goes down to London, he'll be the perfect statesman once again. Say yes, dear boy."

*My wife is going to abscond with your beloved heir, Father dear. . . .*

He couldn't bear to break the spell. "I'll think about it."

"I can't ask for more. Ah! Here comes Lauderback. You remember James, don't you? Come . . ." And he was off, pulling Sinclair with him and reintroducing him to friends that Sinclair vaguely remembered from his youth.

He ducked away from that as soon as he could and hunted up something stronger to drink.

Tristan had come down and was now milling among the newly arrived guests, and it seemed to Sinclair that he sought him out in the hallway.

"I think this is the last. There might be two or three others. Father is so enjoying this, have you noticed?"

"And you aren't?" Sinclair said pointedly.

"Listen to me, brother mine. You are married to a goddess, and if you don't know it, or can't appreciate her the way she should be appreciated, then you can only blame yourself if you lose her."

And with that cryptic remark he turned into the library and deliberately sought out Sayra, knowing full well that Sinclair was watching.

*Goddamn hell . . .*

He slammed out of the house and strode across to the stable.

No action here. The stableboys were sitting around with nothing to do.

"Ain't no one ridin' today," one of them volunteered. "All's in the house, guv'nor. You lookin' for a good horse . . . ?"

"No." He flipped the boy a coin. "I just had a ride."

*And it took me right back where I started from.*

He climbed up onto a paddock fence and stared broodingly at the house. From somewhere in the distance he heard the hollow echo of a gun blast. He heard the birds, the whickering of the horses, he felt the sun hot on his face, he felt a kind of fractious peace.

*His father could die . . .*

*Fathers always seemed immortal.*

*And all this would devolve on Tristan.*

*This would be Sayra's world.*

*Damn it damn it damn it, all to hell, damn it—*

It was a perfect weekend in the country.

All his father's friends.

No monsters.

The woman he wanted about to decamp with his brother.

Perfect.

A doll's house, even from the angle of the stables. There was something about the way it was built so low to the ground that made it seem smaller than it was.

It looked manageable, comfortable. Just the place for a country weekend.

*And not a place you buried monsters.*

Dinner was a noisy affair. There were at least twenty people around the dining table, all of them acquainted with each other, so conversation ebbed and flowed at a comfortable level.

Tristan sat next to Sayra. Sinclair was across the table next to Evelina. Ismail and Edmund anchored either end. And Ismail directed the conversation as if he was conducting a symphony.

"Inspired seating," Tristan whispered in her ear as she took some creamed onions.

"Your father looks frail to me," she said. "I didn't notice when I came, but tonight—or perhaps it's the lighting." She passed the vegetable bowl to her right.

"He's perfectly fine. I'm not. You're not paying attention to me."

"I'm paying an exorbitant amount of attention to you, and everyone has noticed. I truly don't want to embarrass your father or Ismail."

"You couldn't. Ismail's an old warhorse who takes everything in stride, and I'm certain my father sees the lay of the land. He misses nothing."

"He doesn't look well to me."

"Dear goose, eat your goose and be certain that Father will take care of himself. It's probably the old war wounds. They kick up every once in a while. Come—pass the potatoes, darling Sayra, and let the adults tend to themselves."

Later he cornered her again as the guests got up a game of Forfeits in the library.

"Don't stay with him. Come to my room tonight."

"You know I can't."

"I've been thinking about it all afternoon. I don't know why you can't—unless you're a tease, and all you really want to do is provoke me."

"Did it sound like that was what I wanted to do?"

"If you were so eager, you would come to me."

"We'll be in London tomorrow, Tristan. The waiting whets the appetite. If we give in tonight, we diminish what awaits us tomorrow."

"If I find out that he has spent himself on you this night, I don't know what I'll do."

"It won't happen, Tristan. I promise. I'm excited just thinking about our train trip and all those hours we'll have to whisper voluptuous things to each other."

He touched her face with his cool fingers. "What a wise goddess you are to remind me of all the sensual delights that await me."

"Oh, no, Tristan. You are the wise one, and I am only the fortuitous recipient of the erotic bounty of your arousing words. I can't wait for tomorrow, and all that it will bring."

She looked into his glowing light eyes as she said the words, and she wasn't at all sure that she meant them.

He took her hand. "You are the most beautiful, the most perceptive goddess there ever was."

"Let us mingle with the guests rather than calling attention to ourselves. It can only be hurtful to your father."

"I'm overjoyed you have such concern for my father."

She turned to look at him. He was talking to Ismail and he seemed stooped and frail to her. Different even than when Sinclair had brought her for the first time to Wrentham House.

"I lost my own father not long ago," she murmured before she thought, and then she could have bitten her tongue.

"My poor darling. How?"

*How? How did one lose a monster?*

"He died in a fire," she said finally, her eyes still resting on his father. "It was a tragic loss."

"Then you must let me console you."

"I have come to terms with it. Tristan. There is no need to cast a shadow over our rendezvous. We have so much to look forward to."

"I'll take that as a promise, my darling Sayra. And now I will mingle with the guests. You, too. You are a jewel in this setting, and every man here is consumed with envy."

He moved away from her then, and Sinclair took his place without missing a beat.

"You have him lapping at your feet, Messalina. It's a treat to watch."

"But I've landed on my feet, Sinclair. And I think you will be groveling on your knees." She smiled at a guest who was easing his Bay past her with a drink in hand. "It's lovely party; just what I would have imagined."

"Store up the memories, Messalina. This is about as high as your ambition will take you. And Tristan is sure to bring you low sooner or later."

*Well, she knew that—look at what his brother had done. . . .*

"Your father looks ill to me."

Sinclair slanted a look at Edmund, who was now conversing with Evelina and Marchand. "Probably the war wounds; I wouldn't worry about him, Messalina. I would worry about how you're going to explain the fact that you've suddenly become Tristan's mistress and you were never my wife."

"I'll leave you to explain that," she said tartly. "I'd love to be a fly on the wall and hear your version."

"No one would believe the bloody truth."

"Sometimes I think I don't believe it either."

She left him then and did a quick turn around the room, talking to people, eyeing Edmund Sinclair from various angles, wondering why the state of his health niggled at her.

Finally she settled herself in a chair by the library fireplace and watched the guests do their conversational quadrille, and Edmund, who always seemed to be in the thick of things.

*... probably the old war wounds ...*

*... war wounds—*

*He didn't look good at all, Edmund.*

*... .war—*

She closed her eyes for a moment. There was something about that; she remembered it almost being in her grasp. And here it was again, some thought, dangling tantalizingly out of reach. Something important.

*About war wounds?*

*About ... fathers?*

*Both wounded in the war ...*

*No—in the Crimea ...*

She chewed on that fact for a moment or two.

*Both in the Crimea.*

*... not my father ...*

*She had said that. Not her father.*

*Or maybe she meant—*

*What had she meant?*

*Two fathers on the same battlefield that a monster had prowled, seeking victims to slake his bloodthirst.*

*One father rescued and transmogrified into a ghoul ...*

*... not my father ...*

*... why not—*

*—why not ...*

*... the other ... ?*

She shuddered as a chill coursed through her body.

*Ohmygod—oh my God ...*

*No ... she had it all wrong; this wasn't the elusive thought she couldn't grasp. She had made this up so that she wouldn't have to deal with—*

*With what?*

*With what?*

*Monsters ...*

*No, there was something else—*

*Back to the thought; forget the monsters . . .*

*The two fathers. War wounds. The same battlefield. Home and ill, to recuperate. Different families. Different lives.*

*. . . two dead wives . . .*

She felt her heartbeat accelerate. This was it—this was the thing that had slid by her that she had meant to think about.

Two dead wives.

*Two women . . . of different worlds, dead of similar circumstances . . . wasted away, doctors couldn't treat them, couldn't hold them—emaciated, bloodless, the very life sapped from their bodies—*

*. . . what had Sinclair's mother said?*

. . . he that . . . drinks of my blood shall have . . . life. . . . everlasting—

*. . . oh no . . . oh no—no . . . no—*

*—not my father—*

*Maybe . . .*

*His—*

She felt her very skin contract at the thought.

*No . . . no—she wouldn't do that to herself . . . not even Sinclair would go that far . . .*

She got up from her chair abruptly, as if it contained the secrets that were insinuating themselves into her mind.

"Hello dear girl." It was Ismail, and she had to hide her distress and smile at him. How could anyone help smiling at him? "Lovely party. Edmund knows just how to put the right people together, doesn't he? You're enjoying yourself, I trust?"

"Enormously."

"That's wonderful. Excuse me, won't you?"

She couldn't excuse him fast enough. She made her way through the crowd and up the steps to their bedroom without even half realizing where she was going.

She had to think.

There was some other explanation than the convoluted nonsense her mind had dreamed up.

*Oh, really? Then how do you explain the war wounds, the battlefield, the mothers, the fortress, Brother Giurgiu, Luddington . . .*

*I don't explain them. They just are.*

*Edmund protecting Luddington, lying for Luddington—*

*And two mothers who just wasted . . .*

*Or did they die from bloodlust?*

She buried her face in her hands. She refused to think of what it meant.

It just couldn't mean that.

She ought to just go prove it didn't mean that.

Because otherwise she might never be able to let it rest.

. . . *not my father* . . .

Her head felt like it was going to explode.

Because even if it was true, it still didn't explain so many things . . .

She had to know if it was true.

*How could she find out if it was true?*

. . . *search his room* . . .

*Everyone is downstairs. Tell one of the maids to inform Tristan you've just come upstairs to freshen up.*

*And then . . . and then be quick . . .*

. . . *because there are monsters everywhere* . . .

Edmund's bedroom was the last door on the right side of the hallway.

She crept down toward it shivering with trepidation. The maid had been told and promised to tell Mr. Tristan, and she prayed that her lie would deflect anyone from coming to look for her.

But she wasn't sure about Tristan; he might see it as an opportunity to make love to her in spite of his pretty promises to abstain while they were here.

She couldn't think about that now.

The hallway was empty, hushed; the long Oriental runner muffled her footsteps. She felt her heart pounding right out of her chest, and her blood rushing so thick and fast, she was sure Edmund could hear it one floor below.

She held her breath as she reached for the doorknob, fully expecting it to be locked.

But no—every appearance of normalcy was observed; the door swung open noiselessly and she slipped into the room.

She had brought with her a candle and some matches, and she lit the candle and surveyed the room.

Here, Edmund's room was a little less spartan than in the city. There was carpeting on the floor and satin curtains at the windows. The room was paneled, as were all the bedrooms, and with, she surmised, the same kind of closets built into the woodwork.

The narrow bed was in the center of the room and there was nothing else. Not a painting. Not a mirror. Not a chair. Not a washstand.

*Monsters wouldn't wash their hands . . .*

She tiptoed over to the bed. It had a squared headboard and a low footboard. It was covered in a plain cotton cloth and there was no pillow.

She girded herself and pulled back the cover—

And she choked down a scream. Scattered all over the sheet were dead insects in various stages of desiccation.

She dropped the cover and backed away from the bed.

A nightmare. Proof . . .

Of what . . . ?

She bumped against the wall.

*The closet . . .*

She ran her hands over the woodwork, looking for the closet.

She thought her heart was going to stop as the closet door swung open under her touch. But there was nothing to hide here. It contained three black suits, all hung neatly in line. No mirror on the door. No shoes on the floor. Just the suits.

She walked into the closet and pushed at the back wall.

Nothing.

Stupid.

Bad housekeeping was all. The bed probably hadn't been changed in days.

There was nothing, nothing about monsters in Edmund's room.

She pushed aside Edmund's suits with an impatient hand.

And stopped in terror as she heard something creaking behind her.

Slowly, she turned, slowly . . . to find a gaping dark hole where the wall had been.

*Oh, my God . . .*

She held up the candle. Black as the night.

*Oh, God, did she dare?*

*How different was it from the fortress? How different?*

She stepped over the threshold slowly, putting one foot after the other in a deliberate pace so that all she would think about was maintaining her balance rather than what was in this secret room.

The darkness was unnerving. But there were no steps downward. Just straight, blinding blackness, lit only by the puny flame from her candle.

Twenty-five feet in—and then suddenly there was a step.

She almost tripped over it and fell on her face; she caught herself, scraping her delicate palm against the rough stone walls.

*So like the fortress . . . it's eerie.*

She stepped down and held up the light.

And now she could see the truth and the horror—

The monsters were everywhere . . . and they carried with them cages of rats and vermin, and boxes of gloves smeared with dirt; and a casket filled with soil in which Luddington lay, his body bloated with blood and stiff as death.

# Chapter 25

She ran. She dropped the candle and ran. Out of the darkness. Into the room, slamming the closet door behind her. Yanking open the bedroom door, into the hallway, running as fast as she could, stifling her screams of terror, bursting into her room and throwing herself on the bed and muffling her hysteria in a pillow.

She was still running, in her mind, her heart thumping, so loud, the monsters could hear it and would come after her at any moment.

She didn't have one coherent thought. She just screamed into the pillow, and screamed and screamed and screamed because she didn't know what else to do.

*Luddington lived . . . in death—*

*Sinclair was right. . . .*

*I was right. . . .*

*Oh God, oh God, oh God, oh God—*

There was a knock on the door and she froze.

"Sayra darling . . ."

Tristan, just as she expected.

"I'm fine, Tristan." *Her voice wasn't shaky? A miracle . . .*

"Do let me in . . ."

*Had she locked the door? She didn't think so . . .*

"Tristan dear, I just need a few minutes."

"But we could take advantage . . ."

*So predictable . . .*

"You promised."

"He isn't in there with you—is he?"

"No, he's not. I'll be downstairs in a few moments, Tristan, I promise."

"He'd better not be with you."

"You'll see—he's downstairs, probably talking to Ismail or having a drink."

She heard the soft fall of his footsteps down the stairs, and she sat up.

*Oh, my God . . .*

She didn't know what to do first. Or last.

*Ferenc lives . . .*

*Ferenc comes—*

*Oh, God, oh, God . . . she had to get calm, she had to think . . .*

*There was nothing in this house to fight the monsters.*

*She couldn't even remember anything that had been said . . . no, wait—their driver in Berenjevic—all the symbols he had insisted on. Bells and crosses and . . . oh—the seed and . . . what had Moodie said about killing them . . . killing them . . . garlic . . . there was something about garlic—*

Reaction was setting in; she was shaking as if she was about to erupt.

She had to calm down. She had to *think*.

There were things she could do. She could tell Sinclair, for one.

And surely one of the maids would have a cross she could borrow. Garlic from the kitchen. Good, good. Seed from . . . where? The gardener—maybe Baxter would know, *if* she could find him. And a stake—the stables for that.

*Did she really think she could sneak around the house and compile an arsenal to fight the monsters?*

She didn't know, but she planned to try.

She stood up. Her legs were wobbly. She felt dizzy. She wanted to lie down and finish sleeping off the nightmare.

*The nightmare is real. Real is the nightmare. All those lovely people down there utterly unaware of what lies sleeping a floor above.*

*End of a dream.*

*She had to expose Edmund for what he was so the nightmares would end.*

*How could she do that to Tristan, Sinclair—Ismail?*

*But how could she get up from this bed and go downstairs and pretend that monsters didn't exist?*

She was so scared, she didn't know what to do.

She smoothed down her dress, touched her hair, took a step. She almost couldn't think to do anything more.

*I have to find Sinclair. . . .*

*Oh, that was good—that gave her a purpose, a goal. Find Sinclair, dump the whole on him and let him take control—*

*Control of what?*

*They were in control of nothing.*

She took another step, and another. There was nothing else to do.

She was calm, she could do this; she would figure out the rest once she got downstairs.

It was a lively party.

Holm had had the fires lit in the library and the parlor. In one, a group was playing a roaring game of rattle and snap. In the library they were at cards with a seriousness that verged on combativeness.

Sinclair lounged in one of the chairs, a bottle at his elbow and a goblet in his hand.

And Tristan—was waiting right by the staircase as she made her way down.

"Well—here I am. I didn't take too long."

"It seemed like ages to me."

"Nevertheless, don't make a scene just because I had to repair my hem. And, as you see, your brother is keeping company with a bottle and not much else."

He patted her hand. "You're right. I'll be in the parlor. Father and Ismail are engaged in a bloody war over the cards. We've learned not to interrupt them at play."

"Let me get something to drink and I'll join you."

She drifted away from him and into the dining room, where even more food was set out for a midnight snack.

One of the maids came scurrying by.

"Excuse me—"

The maid stopped in her tracks, her eyes wide.

*Now, how did one ask if a maid were wearing a religious symbol?*

"We're playing a game in there. Each of us has a list of items we need to find. I wonder . . . I know this sounds strange, but I have on my list a cross. You don't happen to be wearing a cross, do you?"

"No, mum. But Janet might well have one. Did you want me to be askin' her?"

"Please. And I'll stay right here. Oh—and another thing"—*In for a penny, in for a farthing*—"a string of garlic . . . ? from the kitchen? It would look so odd if I . . ."

"Yes, mum . . ." The maid scuttled away.

*I sounded like a lunatic.*

*I think I am a lunatic. . . .*

Her heart was pounding so hard, she could barely breathe.

The maid poked her head into the dining room.

"Janet says what she's got is her rosary, and she'd be wantin' some recompense if she was to loan it to you, bein' as how it could get lost or somethin'."

"How much?"

"Up to you, mum . . ."

"Stay there. . . ."

*Now this was dicey. To ask Sinclair for money. And not explain.*

He was standing by the fireplace.

She slipped over next to him and pretended to watch his father and Ismail.

*. . . engaged in a bloody war . . .*

"I need five pounds." Her voice was barely above a whisper.

"Are you crazy?"

"Please."

He heard the note in her voice. She moved away. A moment later he followed her into the hallway and surreptitiously slipped a banknote into her hand.

She didn't even look at him. A moment later she handed it to the maid in exchange for the rosary and a quarter of a rotting braid of garlic.

She plucked off the bulbs and stuffed them and the rosary into her dress, and she was just tossing the braid under the tablecloth when she heard Evelina's censuring voice.

"What on earth are you doing?"

"I came to see what Holm was laying out for midnight supper. I'm hungry, aren't you?"

"One tries not to think about eating," Evelina said condescendingly. "Tristan is looking everywhere for you."

"Imagine—and I'm right here."

She went back to the parlor to be greeted by his petulant look of disappointment, which was getting more wearing by the moment.

"Tristan, you're being far too possessive of your brother's wife."

"Well, I am."

"You must wait until tomorrow. I promise everything will be just as you want. Now you must let me mingle."

"Go ahead then. I treasure every promise."

Out in the hallway again, and feeling frantic to find a way to unmask Edmund somehow in private.

And there came Baxter with an armload of wood to feed the fires.

Chopped wood . . .

*They chopped off his head and stuffed it with . . .*

*Oh, God . . .*

She stopped him as he came back through the hallway.

"Baxter, isn't it?"

"Mum?"

"I'm Mr. Declan's . . . wife."

"Yes, mum."

"I'm thinking we need . . . um—an ax nearby, in case we have to cut the wood down to fit the fireplace."

"Oh, I done that already, mum."

"Well, perhaps you can humor me, and provide me with an ax to keep at the ready? I'm Lord Edmund's daughter-in-law, you know, and I'm sure he wants you to treat me as if I was his own."

"Whatever you say, mum. Where do you want it?"

She hadn't thought about that. She hadn't expected him to capitulate so fast, so easily. "Uh—bring it to the dining room."

*She couldn't think, she couldn't, and she was beginning to believe she had imagined what she had seen.*

He returned almost instantly with the implement wrapped in a square of burlap. "There you are, mum."

She was astonished at his shrewdness, his subtlety in getting it into the house, his awareness that it had to be done covertly.

She took the thing from him gingerly. It was at least two feet long and heavy as a body. "You can go now."

Now where, where in the dining room?

*Under the table . . . everything under the table—cards, secrets, axes . . .*

It was done before she had finished the thought.

Now. She swallowed hard. Now.

She paused at the doorway just in time to hear Holm announce that midnight supper was being served, and a moment later twenty-five hungry guests converged on the dining room.

Tristan filled her plate. Sinclair looked right through her. His father and Ismail were still at play, totally ignoring the rush to the dinner table.

She couldn't eat. She could barely be civil. She had to get to Sinclair. And Tristan was keeping an eagle eye on her.

She felt absolutely no comfort in her symbols; she felt like a fool.

She looked around her.

It was a perfectly normal scene, a clutch of well-entertained guests milling around and having conversation over a midnight snack.

*But wait—when you looked closer—no one was eating. They were waving food around, and then putting it back on the table. They were talking, but they were saying nothing.*

*And then, one by one or two, they left the room.*

*What was going on here?*

Sinclair stepped into the room.

"What the hell was that about?" he hissed.

"Listen . . . I found Luddington."

"*Where?*"

She dreaded telling him. "In your father's room."

"Shit." *He wasn't shocked. He wasn't anything.*

The doorbell rang. Everyone froze and then, as if they responded to a signal, they continued on their way to the library or parlor.

"Guests at this time of night?" Tristan from the parlor, hurrying to the front door.

"Show me," Sinclair whispered, and then he went out into the hallway. She followed him and they moved toward the staircase.

Holm swung open the door. They heard his voice: "Welcome, gentlemen."

He stood aside to admit the new guests. The director of the Lyceum Museum, Moodie and Luddington stepped over the threshold.

*"Don't move."*

They were talking to her—and Sinclair, and she understood that, but she was in such shock, she couldn't have moved if they had hitched her to a wagon and pulled her.

*Whose voice? Tristan's?*

"Bring them to the library."

She felt very substantial hands pushing her along the hallway, her and Sinclair. She couldn't bear to look at him.

This was insanity, and she was teetering on the brink, and she did not want to fall over and take him with her.

Edmund looked up as they entered the room and set aside his cards.

*He knows—but what does he know?*

"Sit down." Edmund's voice now, directing them and then turning to the newcomers. "Mr. Moodie, Mr. Lydecker. Welcome. Ronald—careless again, and look what has happened."

"I'll go back to the fortress then."

"Yes, I believe you will. And this time—this time you stay. . . ."

He swung back to her and Sinclair.

"How resourceful you two are. You were not supposed to have survived."

"Good of you to say so, sir," Sinclair said bitingly.

"You—" his father pointed a gloved finger at him, "have been a thorn in my side for years. But tonight—tonight we will have a feeding frenzy. Tonight you will be converted—or you will die."

"Why?" Sinclair again. "When, how?"

"Your beautiful passion slave knows the answer to that, don't you, my dear?"

*Ohhhh—he knew everything . . . everything—*

She lifted her chin. "War wounds, from the Crimea . . . Ferenc chose him, too. I thought it was only my father. But our mothers—they died in similar circumstances. Our fathers were feeding on them until they totally sapped the life from them. And then, I think, *your* father went on to bigger things. His friends, perhaps? His political cronies?" *Oh, no—not that . . . not him . . .* "Ismail?"

She looked across the room at him, and he nodded regretfully. She couldn't bear it. "Tristan?"

"Tomorrow I would have offered you immortality—or death."

*His immortal goddess . . .* "Oh, my God . . ." She sucked in a deep, harrowing breath. "Sinclair?"

"No," he said shortly. "For some reason my father chose to keep me pure."

"But you suspected," Edmund said. "I know you suspected."

"So you sent me after Luddington."

"You found my box of gloves, boy. Saturated with the soil of the Crimea, Sayra. Soil of the country of origin. Your father slept in it, too."

"No . . . !" *But he had, on the floor of the hovel, in dirt and rags and shame . . .*

"The soil when rubbed on the skin permits us to go about our business in daylight if we are well covered up. In my case, it's to hide my hands as well. A giveaway, to say the least. I was forced to retire and manipulate events from Wrentham House.

"And you never knew: We were the masters of your fate—we were the Voice who taunted you in the fortress, and the cold, creeping fog that seeped into your bones. We followed you everywhere, *everywhere* . . . we derailed a train for you; we killed for you, Declan—the child in the village, and Sayra's father . . ."

He stiffened with rage. *The masters sent me . . . the masters who slaked their bloodlust on the innocent and from whom no man was safe, not even the consort of a queen.*

"Oh, yes, Prince Albert as well—the attempt on his life in '60, the death of his mother-in-law; the turning of the public against him, his untimely demise; all the war-mongering . . . who do you think, my son? Who could have engineered all those events? Who was named prime minister in '74, and who does Her Majesty dote upon? Who has access to her night and day? Who, Declan?"

He watched the skull face of the man he called father, who would goad him, push him, prod him to lose control. But what did his father know of him? The man, the ghoul, was less than nothing to him now, and he would not be distracted or deterred from his mission.

There was only one truth, only one question to be answered, and he was prepared for the consequences as he snapped it out one more time.

"Who is Ferenc?"

"Ferenc is buried in the crypt. Mr. Moodie explained that all to you."

"Ferenc lives, and he's not in the fortress. Where is he? Who is he?"

"I am he," his father said.

"No," Sinclair said. "No. There is a logic to this that I don't understand yet . . . but you—you are not he. . . ."

"Ferenc lives in all of us. We have thirsted for fresh blood, and it has come to us in the form of our greatest enemy. I should have taken you when I could, Declan."

"You'll never take me now—Father. . . ."

"Oh, you will be taken, Declan, and I don't think you will be offered a choice."

They were crowding in on him and Sayra. Ever so slowly, one step at a time. They could feel the collective hunger pulsating around them.

"You have to be taken, my boy. You know the secrets." Ismail speaking now, his voice tinged with that same regret.

"What secrets?"

"You are looking at them, my boy. Our brethren have overtaken the government, and the next step will be to infect the queen. And then we will rule the world."

"Who is Ferenc?"

"Ferenc is a legend, our soul, the father of us all."

"Ferenc lives."

"Ferenc is buried in a crypt in the middle of London."

"I don't believe you."

"Believe this, Declan, whom I have loved as a son. You will die tonight; my brethren have been instructed to show no mercy."

He laid a cold hand on Sayra's cheek. "A pity about you, my dear. You could have ruled the world, if you had made the right choice."

She felt her body shriveling against his touch.

She didn't expect what happened next: Sinclair jacked himself out of his seat and rammed into the crowd of them surrounding him.

She screamed, "Run—Sinclair—run!" as Tristan grabbed hold of her arm and five of the others took off after Sinclair.

She reached into her dress and yanked out the rosary beads. Tristan recoiled and dropped her arm.

"You think you're so smart."

"Maybe I am." She slipped the beads around her neck and held out the cross.

Slowly they moved away from her, as she stepped among them, forming a circle around her.

She could hear the frenzy in the other room—furniture smashing, snarling, shouts . . . She whirled so that she was facing the circle, and in her other hand she held the garlic bulbs.

She backed away from them warily, her breath coming in deep, panting heaves.

They were killing Sinclair. She had to get to them. She had to get help.

Edmund and Ismail looked unconcerned, as if they knew their prey could never escape.

She slammed the library door in their faces, knowing it wouldn't help at all, and raced to the back door and screamed into the night, "Baxter! *Baxter!*"

He came running. "Mum?"

"Vampires. Get the ax." She was back in the house, down the hallway to the parlor. And there was Sinclair, brandishing the leg of a table in one hand and holding them all at bay with the top.

She tossed the garlic to him and held out the cross.

Such puny objects to stave off death.

Yet even monsters respected icons.

The three of them—she, Sinclair and Baxter—backed them into the library.

"Oh admirable," Ismail said, applauding. "Edmund—get rid of young Baxter."

Edmund moved forward, salivating at the thought of fresh meat, and put his hand on Baxter's shoulder.

Baxter reacted, pulling a vial from his pocket and tossing it at Edmund.

Who opened his mouth in an unholy scream of terror. "Get him away from me—get him away! It's holy water. . . . I'm burning up, burning up—"

He dropped to the floor, moaning and writhing.

"Who is Ferenc?"

Ismail shook his head. "Dear boy—you can't possibly win. Give over. Let's have done—"

"*Who* is Ferenc?" Sinclair demanded, shoving the table leg in his face.

"I smell smoke," Sayra whispered, her voice shaky, her arm trembling from the force of holding out the cross.

"Who is Ferenc?"

The others were circling around them, muttering ominously.

"Ferenc is a figment of your imagination, my boy. Mr, Moodie—grab him!"

Moodie lunged; Baxter tripped him and he fell right at Sinclair's feet. Baxter sprinkled the holy water on him.

"You're so clever, Declan. But you can't win."

"I can destroy Ferenc."

"Nonsense. Ferenc was destroyed four hundred years ago."

"Yet he lives, and infects, and transforms . . . and kills—"

*Kill him, you kill them all—*

She heard the words—Brother Giurgiu, aching for rest . . .

*One of them is the incarnation of Ferenc . . .*

*But Sinclair knew that already—*

She watched in horror as the coven pulled away the writhing bodies of Edmund and Moodie and formed a circle around them.

One tiny cross.

A vial of holy water.

A bulb of garlic.

And a table.

"Say your prayers, Baxter," she muttered.

"Hail Mary, full of grace—" He didn't miss a beat. He held the vial of water in one hand, the ax in the other, and looked like the avenging angel of sin as he recited the prayer over and over.

The power of good over evil.

It would come to a head in minutes, and Sinclair had to make the right choice.

His father . . . Tristan . . . Moodie . . . Luddington . . . Ismail . . . Marchand? Or one of the two dozen others who surrounded them?

"Who is Ferenc?"

"Ferenc is the modern god, my boy, who has come to save the world."

"Who is Ferenc?"

"He is the god of immortality, his disciples worship him."

"Who is Ferenc?"

"Ferenc is every dream you have ever had, my boy, of owning the world."

They were coming closer and closer. The power of her cross seemed to diminish by the minute in counterpoint to the power of Baxter's voice reciting the prayer.

"Who is Ferenc?"

"He takes your blood for his sins—"

And Sinclair lunged, ramming the tabletop against Ismail, so that he tumbled backward and onto the floor. He tossed the table, cracked the table leg in two with his foot to get a ragged, pointed edge and, without mercy, thrust it with all his might into Ismail's heart.

She screamed—"The ax—the ax—" and she covered her eyes so she didn't see who wielded it; she heard the whacking sound as it struck Ismail's neck and felt tears streaming down her face. She heard the moans and howls of the ghouls and the sound of their bodies hitting the floor as if they had all been cut down as one man and then a horrible fizzling sound, as if the life was being sucked out of every shriveling, disintegrating body.

*When you destroy him, you destroy them all . . .*

*All of them; Tristan, Ismail—even Evelina—*

She couldn't look, she couldn't look. She hid her eyes, holding the cross before her. She felt Baxter's hand on her, guiding her. She heard Sinclair somewhere in the library heaving heavy objects. She smelled smoke, stronger now, in the hallway and coming from the library.

Then she was out in the fresh air and still couldn't look, and then she heard a huge explosive sound from inside the house and wheeled around to see it totally engulfed in flame.

And then, before she could move, before she could cry out, there was a second explosion, the roof caved in, the flames shot a hundred feet in the air and she heard the keening wail of the fiends from hell reverberating through the ages, across the continents and up to the sky, as though God was finally delivering the devil to his just reward.

And in the horrific heat and blaring flames, and the echoing death throes of the monsters, Sinclair was nowhere to be seen.

They called her the Position Girl.

She sat on a platform in the center of the cavernous room, surrounded by a crowd of men who had started drinking hours before she appeared from behind the curtain.

They knew what they wanted: They wanted *her,* and they had their money at the ready to entice her in this nightly mating dance for which everyone played by certain rules.

For them, she was a different woman every night.

Only her smile was the same—the mocking goading *make-me-do-it* smile, at once knowing and elusive.

They wanted to possess that smile, and possess as much of her as their money could buy, and her goal was to make them spend as much for her as any trollop they could take to one of the bedrooms upstairs.

She knew all about possession now.

All about the driving male need that spurred men to lay money on the stage with the hope that she would, this one day, take off her clothes and choose one of them to come and take her.

And yet she had run as fast and as far as she could from the man she ached for, and in consequence there wasn't a man among them to whom she could consider giving herself.

She was smarter now; she knew exactly how to handle herself and how to escape their hands, their words, their curses.

It would have been so easy; nothing to think about. She had been *that* close to surrendering to Tristan. She couldn't blame herself for grasping the opportunity, but she could not forgive Sinclair for letting her.

She didn't even know if he had survived the conflagration.

She just wanted to get away, away from him, away from the monsters, the nightmares, the memories.

For if Sinclair lived he was now the earl of Wrentham.

And she was still a passion slave.

And there was just too much in between.

"Gentlemen . . ." Her voice was soft and throaty. She had perfected the pitch of her voice; experience was such a wonderful teacher. She sounded as if she was eager, ready, desperate for a man.

She felt the tension in the room escalate as she began rubbing her satin-gloved hands over her beautifully gowned body.

*Lovely, lovely money. All for doing the thing I most like doing in the world: taking off my clothes for a man . . .*

*Jaded she was, her senses drowning in memories every time she looked into the audience, and looked into their eyes.*

*Not one of them wanted her the way Sinclair had wanted her.*

*The earl.*

*Unavailable.*

*Unobtainable.*

*She thought about him every night as she kept them all waiting. So easy to keep them waiting. Nothing like Sinclair and his explosive passion.*

*She would never experience the like of that again.*

She lowered herself to the platform and swept the room with her glimmering, goading gaze.

It was coming—it was coming.

She felt the restiveness in the crowd; she inhaled the unmistakable scent of ale, smoke, sweat—and sex.

"Gentlemen," she chided them. *Gentle men . . . nothing gentle about them. Nothing at all. She was back where she belonged, doing what she did best—taunting and teasing a man to bring him to the breaking point.*

"Gentlemen . . ." She rubbed herself gently between her breasts and then delicately removed one glove and tossed it into the crowd.

And the bidding began.

"One shilling for the other glove . . ."

"Two—"

"Three . . ."

"Five thousand pounds to keep your clothes *on.*"

Everything in the room stopped dead.

He stood framed in the doorway, obscuring the light. Had he always been so tall, so broad, so formidable?

"Everyone out of here." And so commanding?

She couldn't move.

"You—barkeep—close the pub."

"Ah, but—"

"And get *out*—all of you—this is a private performance for my eyes only." He tossed a roll of banknotes in the barkeep's direction.

*Not Harry,* she thought irrelevantly. *Harry was gone—mysteriously disappeared . . .* She couldn't get past the shock of seeing him. She didn't want to think about what it meant, his being here.

"Out—*now . . .*"

They couldn't disobey; he was a man who was accustomed to issuing orders and having people do his bidding.

They moved out slowly, reluctantly, annoyed that this stranger was interfering with their sport.

The barkeep ran to lock the doors behind them, put up a sign and draw the curtain.

"You—"

"Me?" The barkeep was quaking.

"I've paid you for your time. Leave me the key and get out. You can retrieve it at Mrs. Allnut's in the morning."

"Yessir . . . yessir—" The barkeep picked up the bills from the counter and clutched them against his chest. "Yessir . . ."

And then they were alone in the simmering silence.

"Messalina has returned to the hellholes of her past, I see."

"She has come back where she belongs."

"No, she has come seeking that which she most needs: men to admire her body. Men to tantalize and manipulate. Messalina learned many new tricks in her travels."

"There is one thing I never learned, Sinclair." She couldn't keep the bitterness out of her voice. Even though it was impossible. Even though they were too far apart. Even though. . . .

He ignored that. "Take off your clothes for me."

"I don't think so."

"I paid for you, Messalina. You can do nothing less." He leaned closer to her. "And you want to. You've been performing for these provincial swills, hoping to find among them a man. And yet you've always known where to find him. You just chose not to. And now he has chosen to find *you*. Take off your clothes."

"No. I don't perform for bullies."

"I paid five thousand pounds for the privilege, Messalina. And I am not a tyrant. You would withhold yourself from *me*—and reveal yourself to those louts? Oh, no."

"We've gotten high and mighty since we came into a title, haven't we?"

"It makes things infinitely easier," he agreed. "Take off your clothes. I believe you get a very nice percentage of that five thousand pounds, Messalina. Enough to keep you for a couple of years, hmmm?"

"Charity, Sinclair. I'd rather earn it, hour by hour, night by night."

*"Take off your clothes."*

"Beneficent Sinclair, dispensing alms in a pub. How mighty you are; how generous. How far down you have come for your voyeuristic pleasure."

*"Take off your goddamn clothes."*

There was no arguing with that tone. She would do it or he would tear them off for her.

She curled her legs under her and rose to her knees and then to her feet. "Very well, Sinclair. There's no reason why you can't have for five thousand pounds what everyone pays a shilling for."

She ripped off her glove and threw it in his face.

He caught it and rubbed it against his cheek. "Go on, Messalina."

It was nothing different than performing for the locals every night, except there was no feral excitement for her to feed from.

There was only the tense, pulsating memory of him and her, naked, coupling, goading, wanting, and the throbbing presence of him sitting in the shadows, waiting.

She kicked off her pumps, slid off her stockings, strutted all over the stage undulating her body every which way she could think of.

She was going to make him pay. She was going to show him everything and ask for nothing. Because after, she knew he was going to go out of her life forever.

She removed the dress next. Slowly, lingeringly, letting it slide over her breasts, down to her hips—a wriggle here, a shimmy there—and it fell, whisper soft, to her bare feet.

The corset . . . was there ever a device more tormenting than the corset? The way it both contained and lifted her breasts into lush swells of sweet flesh that threatened to spill into a man's hands . . . yes—oh, yes—

And the drawers—of transparent lawn and made a size smaller, so that they clung to her thighs and buttocks and made the daring split between her legs that much more prominent.

He was right—she knew all the tricks and she was as aroused by them as any man in her audience.

The corset next, cleverly contrived so that there were only three hooks to unfasten, and the long, torturous moment before she chose to reveal her taut hard nipples.

She tossed the corset into the air and turned her back on him as she began to wriggle out of her drawers.

Her excitement escalated to a pitch she had not felt in months.

Because of him. Because of him.

And he had known when he walked in the door and demanded her body that she would do whatever he wanted . . .

Because of him.

She stepped out of the drawers and bent over to pick them up, pausing a moment so that the line of her body and buttocks were prominent.

She turned, holding the undergarment in front of her, and then slowly and deliberately slipped it down between her legs, rubbed herself there and flung it at him.

*Because of him . . . she would never be the same again because of him. . . .*

He caught the flimsy bit of cotton and buried his face in it as she sank to her knees at the edge of the platform.

"I'm yours to command." Her voice was shaky with excitement as she watched him inhale her scent. Her breasts swinging gently, her nipples tight with arousal. Her whole body was shaking with a need she thought she had buried with everything else to do with him.

*No, nothing ever died. What did she have to lose? She would do what he wanted, and in the end she would take home enough money to keep her for a long while. He might even give her more if she didn't keep taking an adversarial stance. She was more than a five-pound trollop . . . she had truly found her calling here.*

"I'm hard for you. I want you. Now."

Harsh words. She didn't care.

"Come and take me. . . . I want you to take me, here, on the platform."

"Messalina . . ."

"Do it . . ."

He ripped off his clothes and she drew in a tight, short breath. He was hard as a rock, and tied at the root with the oblong of cotton she remembered so well.

"Messalina is with me, wherever I go. . . . Turn around."

He climbed onto the platform behind her, grasped her hips and plunged himself into her, fast, hard, elemental as his male sex.

She almost swooned at the sensation. She was so ready; she had been ready for days, months, all her life. He was in her, the life force of her, the hard, hot point from which everything emanated, and she could never escape her keening need for him and his naked, lusty possession of her.

Did it matter how it began?

Or how it ended?

She felt every long, hot stroke; she felt the rough grazing evidence of his desire for her . . . *Messalina is with me, wherever I go . . .* she felt herself teetering on the edge of capitulation.

She was easy, so easy. The culmination came, soft, soft, radiating out from the hot, jutting center of him and enfolding her in pure, rippling gold, pooling gently at her core and all over him. And when her heat and her wet poured all over him, when he felt it, felt her body wholly and completely give over to his power, he let himself go in a hard, hot shot of a climax that left him gasping for air. He collapsed on top of her, overwhelmed by the sweet, sensual scent of her sex that permeated the air.

*But this—this feels wrong. This feels . . .*

"Sayra . . ."

She roused herself, girding herself for a quick, abrupt goodbye.

"Come—sit up." He removed himself from her and pulled her to a sitting position.

How incongruous: two naked people who had just violently coupled sitting on a stage as if nothing had happened.

And him, untying the oblong and gently blotting her with it.

She watched him as if she were in the audience and he was onstage. And then he retied it around his still-flexing member.

She couldn't keep still; she had never known how to be quiet.

"How did you find me?"

"I always knew where you were. Where else could you go, besides coming to me? But you would never do that, would you, Sayra? So proud you are. Daughter of a ghoul, surviving by wit and guile—everything. And what did you ever think I was? So far above your touch that there was nothing left after all that has happened?

"Consider, Sayra—I'm the son of a fiend who wanted to use his vampiric powers to control men, events, a country and the world. There's the truth—we're a pair, you and I, spawns of evil. And here is a further truth—I am a killer. Without compunction I destroyed the host, I burned the bodies and I stole his head and buried it with the water, the garlic and a cross, where no one will ever find it.

"The monsters are gone, and in their place another has been created: a peer of the realm who could kill again in light of such an all-consuming, ungodly wickedness.

"So tell me, Sayra Messalina, tell me if a passion slave could consent to be the consort of a man like that . . ."

She made a sound as if her heart was breaking.

"You can't . . ."

"I can. I will. I want you. I need you. I need your sex; I need your heart. I have been without you far too long. Nothing else matters. Will you, Sayra Messalina? Will you, the passion slave, take a man who is a murderer and a peer of the realm?"

She held out her hand on which she still wore his ring.

"I would have worn it forever."

"And now you will wear *me* forever. Let's get out of here."

They scrambled into their clothes quickly, with him pulling her close to drop light kisses on her disbelieving mouth.

A fly buzzed overhead and alighted on the stage, right in the glare of the light.

"They say a vampire can transform himself into all manner of small animals," Sinclair said rather abstractedly as he watched the insect daintily pace across the pool of light. "Or insects. Wouldn't it be an irony if this little fly was in reality a new generation of vampires? Let's make sure he doesn't reproduce others of his kind." He slammed his boot down on the fly and brushed the carcass off the platform, and then turned to look deeply into Sayra's eyes.

She said not a word; the all-consuming wickedness could be anywhere around them, and who was she to say who was a murderer and who was a savior?

He was her savior, and that was all she needed or wanted to know.

He reached out his hand and took hers, and together they walked out into the cool, dark night and the future unknown.